EMMY'S EQUAL
Marcia Gruver

BARBOUR
PUBLISHING

OTHER BOOKS BY MARCIA GRUVER

TEXAS FORTUNES SERIES:

Diamond Duo
Chasing Charity

© 2009 by Marcia Gruver

ISBN 978-1-60260-207-6

All scripture quotations are taken from the King James Version of the Bible.

For more information about Marcia Gruver, please access the author's Web site at the following Internet address: www.marciagruver.com

Cover Design: The DesignWorks Group, Inc.; Clouds: Rebecca Frasier

Published by Barbour Publishing, Inc., P.O. Box 719, Uhrichsville, OH 44683, www.barbourbooks.com

Our mission is to publish and distribute inspirational products offering exceptional value and biblical encouragement to the masses.

ECPA Member of the
Evangelical Christian
Publishers Association

Printed in the United States of America.

DEDICATION

To my grandfather, Thomas A. Cooper—
May my efforts to carry on in your footsteps bring honor to your memory.

ACKNOWLEDGMENTS

To Rebecca Germany and Barbour Publishing for the chance to write
the books of my heart and for your continued care and support.
I'll be forever grateful.

To my dear friend Elizabeth Ludwig, word maestro extraordinaire.
Thanks for rounding out my rough edges. You helped make this book sing.

To Tracy Jones, my collaborator and plot consultant.

To Nina Gracia and Robert Gonzalez, my Spanish language consultants.

To Bert Lee Bell, for his kind assistance and for providing the wonderful
historical resource entitled Memories of Peter Tumlinson Bell,
compiled by Verner Lee Bell.

To Nelta Coggins and Jim Marmion for providing
invaluable reference material.

To Pete Wilson, my cattle consultant.

They shall not hunger nor thirst;
neither shall the heat nor sun smite them:
for he that hath mercy on them shall lead them,
even by the springs of water shall he guide them.

ISAIAH 49:10

CHAPTER 1

The stagnant well appeared bottomless, as dank and murky as a grave. Emmy rested her arms on the cold, jagged stones and leaned to peer into the abyss. Mama's embroidered lace hankie, shimmering in the meager light, hung from an outcropping of rock about six feet down. Narrowing her eyes, she peered at the spot of white that stood out from the surrounding darkness and heaved a sigh, stirring the fetid air below and raising a noxious odor that took her breath.

She pushed up her sleeves and blasted a droopy blond ringlet from her eyes with a frustrated puff of air. There was no help for it—at the risk of certain death, she had to retrieve that handkerchief.

A figure loomed, drawing alongside her with a grunt.

She jumped, and her heart shot past her throat. Chest pounding, she wasted a glare on the dark profile, noticing for the first time a scatter of lines around his eyes and tiny gray curlicues in his sideburns.

"Nash! I nearly leaped over the side." She swatted his arm. "I've asked you to stop sneaking up on me. I've a good mind to fit you with a cowbell."

A chuckle rumbled from his chest, as deep as the chasm. "I didn't go to scare you, Miss Emmy." He bent his lanky body so far she feared

5

he'd tumble headfirst into the never-ending shaft. "Say, what we looking for inside this hole?"

"We're not looking for anything. I've already found it." Emmy clutched his shirtsleeve and pulled him away. "Go fetch me a lantern, and be quick about it." She tucked her chin in the direction of the palomino pony lounging under a nearby oak, nibbling at the circle of high grass around the trunk. "Take Trouble. He'll be quicker than walking."

Nash frowned and rubbed the knuckles of one hand along his temple, as if an ache had sprung up there. "What you need a lantern for, with the sun up and shining the past five hours? There's plenty of light to see."

She braced herself and pointed. "Not down there."

Nash's sleepy eyes flew open. His startled gaze bounced along her finger to the circular wall of weathered stones. "Down there?" He took a cautious step back. "What's in this sour old pit that might concern you?"

Emmy swallowed hard. She could trust Nash with anything but dreaded his reaction all the same. "It's. . .one of Mama's hankies." She squeezed her eyes shut and ducked her head.

His shoulders eased, and he ambled over to gaze inside. "Is that all?"

If only it were. Emmy risked a peek at him. "You don't understand."

He winced as if she'd spoken a bad omen. "Uh, uh. Not from her good batch? Them she's always cackling about?"

Emmy cringed and nodded.

The delicate, lacy linens held an uncommon depth of meaning for Emmy's mama. Hand embroidered in Germany by her grandmother then brought to the Americas and placed in Mama's hope chest, they represented heart, hearth, and homeland to Magdalena Dane. In equal measure, they represented distress, discontent, and discord to her only daughter, because the bothersome bits of cloth seemed determined to cause Emmy grief.

Nash's stunned expression hardened into an accusing glare. "Why, Miss Emmy? Why you done brought about such misery? You ain't s'posed to touch 'em, and you know it." His graying brows fluttered like two moths bent on escape. "There's scarce few left, and your mama blames you for them what's missing."

She moaned and flapped her hands. "I didn't mean to take the silly thing. It was warm when I rode out this morning. I knew I'd likely sweat, so I snagged a hankie from the clothesline. I never looked at it until a few minutes ago. That's how this terrible mishap came about. I held it up as I rode, staring in disbelief. Trouble was galloping across the yard when the wind caught it and. . ." She motioned behind her. "The willful rag drifted down the well before I could stop the horse and chase after it."

Emmy lowered her eyes then peered up at him through her lashes. "None of this is my fault, Nash. Papa should've covered this smelly cistern months ago, and those wretched handkerchiefs have a mind of their own."

The hint of a smile played around Nash's lips. "If so, they harbor a mighty poor opinion of you."

She wrinkled her nose at him.

Wagging his head, he rested the back of his hand on his side. "In all my years of working for your family, of all the fits I've seen your mama pitch, the worst have been over the loss of them fancy scraps of cloth." He shuddered. "Miss Emmy, I'd be mighty grateful if you'd wait and break the news to her after I leave for the day. She gon' be powerful upset."

Emmy held up and wiggled a finger. "On the contrary. I won't be upsetting Mama."

"How you figure that?"

"Because there's no need to tell her."

Nash propped his elbow in one hand and rubbed his chin with the other. "Missy, I thought you was done telling lies and scheming. Don't forget you're a saint of God now."

A saint of God. Yes, she was, through no fault of her own. Like Elijah's fiery chariot, God had swirled into Emmy's life in a weak moment and delivered her from herself. Not that she minded His day-to-day presence. In fact, she rather enjoyed the peace He brought. It was during times of temptation when she found the constant stirring in her heart to do the right thing a bit of a bother. Yet no wonder, really. In the past, she'd had precious little practice in doing the right thing.

She blinked up at Nash. "I have no plans to lie, and I won't need to scheme. We're simply going to return Great-grandmother's hankie to Mama's clothesline, washed, rinsed, and fresh as a newborn calf."

7

Nash stared then shook his head. "No, ma'am. You jus' forget about what *we* gon' do. Question is how are *you* gon' pull it off?"

"I'll show you." She shooed him with her hands. "Run fetch that lantern like I asked and leave the rest to me."

Still shaking his head, Nash mounted Trouble and laid in his heels. The horse bolted across the yard to the well-kept shed tucked behind Emmy's two-story house. With a furtive glance toward the porch, Nash eased the door open and slipped inside.

While she waited, Emmy watched a rowdy band of crows swarm Nash's cornfield. The black bandits bickered and pecked for position before settling in for a meal, oblivious to the mop-headed stick Nash had dressed in a ragged shirt and floppy hat and then shoved in the ground. She dared not call his attention to the culprits or he'd bluster after them, shouting and waving his arms like a demented windmill, leaving her to cope alone with her pressing dilemma.

She jerked her gaze from the birds when Nash rode up and slid off Trouble to the ground, a lighted lantern in his hand.

Handing over the light with a flourish, he lowered one brow and pinned her with a squinty look. "Here's what you asked for. Jus' be sure to leave me plumb out of the story when you go explaining yourself to your mama."

He turned to go, but Emmy caught hold of his shirttail. "Not so fast. I'm not done with you."

Nash covered his ears and reeled away. "Don't tell me no mo'. I ain't seen nothing, and I ain't heard nothing. If anybody needs me, I'll be feeding the chickens."

Emmy aimed a haughty laugh at his back. "It's too late for that. You're in up to your hat, and it's no less punishment than you deserve for sneaking about all the time."

Nash dug in his heels and stood facing the grove of loblolly pine at the edge of the yard, his body stiff as a post.

Repentant, she softened her voice to a plea. "I'm sorry, Nash. I had no call to utter such a thing. It's just. . .I can't do this without you."

Arms dangling at his sides, he tipped his head toward the sky and whispered something, a prayer no doubt, before turning to face her. "What you want me to do?"

She peppered him with grateful kisses then grabbed his hand. "Come over here." Hauling him to the gaping cavity, she lowered the lamp. "See? There it is."

They gazed at the only bright spot in the oppressive gloom, their ability to see inside the shaft made no better by the frail circle of yellow light.

Nash shrugged and drew back from the side. "Too far down. May as well wave it good-bye then go 'fess up to what you done."

Emmy gripped his arm. "Nonsense. We can get it out of there."

"How, short of fishing it out with a cane pole? And I got no hooks." He scratched his head. "I reckon I could take my hammer and pound a bend in a nail."

She shook her head. "Too risky. If the hankie slips off it'll settle to the bottom, and that'll be the end of it." She drew a determined breath. "I have a better idea."

Nash's eyebrows rose on his forehead, reaching new heights, even for him. "What sort of idea? Harebrained or foolhardy? Them's the only two kinds you have."

She swallowed hard and fingered the wooden bucket sitting on the wall. "I'm going to straddle this, and you'll lower me down to fetch it."

The shaggy brows bested their last mark. "You cain't mean it, Miss Emmy."

"I do so."

"Then your idea is both harebrained and foolhardy. You must be plain tetched up under them pretty white locks. S'pose that rope snaps in two?"

"Oh, pooh." She patted the heavy hemp coiled around the crank. "This rope is thick and sound." She pointed over her shoulder at the horse. "You could lower Trouble down that well."

He nodded. "Yes'm. That's exactly what I'd be doing." He jerked off his weathered hat and dashed it against his leg. "Don't ask me to put you in that kind of danger. No, missy. I won't do it. Not for nothing in this wide world."

Touched, Emmy smiled at the man who'd been like a father to her over the years, far more of a parent than her own papa, who didn't stay home often enough to have much practice at the role. She took Nash's hand and squeezed it. "I won't be in any danger. As long as you're holding the handle, I know I'll be safe." She peered up into his sulky brown eyes. "You know if you don't help me I'll just find a way to do it myself. I have to get that hankie."

He gaped at her. "The silly thing ain't worth dying for, is it? Your mama has fussed at you before, and you lived to tell the tale. Why is this time so all-fired special?"

She squared around to face him. "I can't have her angry about anything just now. I'm planning to ask permission to go to St. Louis when Mama travels with Aunt Bertha to South Texas. It'll be hard enough to convince her as it is. If she gets in a snit, my plan is doomed."

"Why they going off so far?"

"It's Aunt Bertha's idea. Now that she has money, she's determined to go into the cattle business. She's bent on learning all she can. Papa knows a very successful rancher down south who's willing to teach her everything he knows."

"Cain't you jus' stay home?"

"They'll be gone for a month or better. Mama refuses to leave me here alone for that long, and I'd much prefer going to see Charity."

Nash smiled and nodded. " 'Specially with her jus' done birthing the little one."

Emmy beamed. "Exactly. I can help Charity bring him home."

A thrill coursed through her at the thought of seeing Charity and Buddy's new baby boy. Emmy and Charity were as close as twin sisters, best friends like their mamas had always been. Emmy's mama and Aunt Bertha had grown up together in Jefferson before moving to Humble.

Last year, a handsome young oilman came to town and found oil on Aunt Bertha's land. Charity wound up married to him and soon left for St. Louis to meet his parents. When Buddy found out she was expecting, he kept her in the city so she'd be close to good medical care.

Not a day had passed that Emmy didn't think of Charity and long to see her. She was coming home next month, bringing little Thad to meet the family.

Nash narrowed his eyes. "You ain't jus' trying to sneak off to St. Louis to see that oilman friend of Mistah Buddy's, are you? Don't think I didn't see you making eyes at him the whole time that preacher was trying to marry off Miss Charity."

Emmy whirled. "Who? Mr. Ritter?" She dismissed the thought with a wave of her hand. "Jerry Ritter was just a passing fancy."

Nash raised a cynical brow.

"Oh, pooh, Nash! You stop that!" She fiddled with the row of tiny buttons on her sleeve. "Besides. . .Aunt Bertha claims Mr. Ritter was recently betrothed to a childhood sweetheart." She flicked off an insect from the cuff of her blouse and dashed away her humiliation with the same resolve. "Therefore, my desire to be in St. Louis has nothing to do with him. I just need to see Charity. If I get into any more trouble, Mama's bound to haul me with them to that dreadful desert town instead. If she does, I'll just dry up along with it and perish. I mean it!"

Grinding the toe of his oversized boot in the dirt, Nash sighed and shifted his weight. "I don't know, Miss Emmy. . ."

Emmy stifled a grin. She had him. "I'll be just fine. I promise. Now help me climb up."

Still mumbling his objections, he offered an elbow to Emmy so she could pull up and sit on the uneven stones. Unfastening the buttoned flap on her split skirt, she swung her legs over and settled on the side, trying hard not to look past her boots. "Turn your head while I sit astride the pail. It won't look so dainty in this outfit."

Nash gazed toward the field, obviously too distracted to notice the raiding crows.

Still clinging to his arm, Emmy held her breath and pulled the dangling rope closer, guiding it between her legs. "All right, I'm ready. Lean your weight into the handle. I'm about to push off."

Nash shifted his gaze to the sky. "Oh, sweet Jesus. Please protect this chil'."

Holding her breath, she scooted from the edge, squealing when her body spun and dipped about a foot. "Nash! Have you got it?"

"I've got it. Stop squirming now. You heavier than you look."

Emmy forced herself to still, more afraid than she'd expected to be. She felt more than saw the yawning gulf, a great gaping mouth poised to swallow her whole. "Hand me the lantern and then you can lower me. But go slowly, for heaven's sake."

She breathed a prayer as she spiraled past the opening and descended. Glancing up, she bit her lip and watched the rope unwind from the wobbly reel, outlined by a circle of light. Misguided but determined white roots that had pushed through cracks in the mortar groped at her, snagging her hem and sleeves. Crisscrossed nets of taut, silky threads offered whispers of resistance before giving way and sticking to the exposed parts of her legs. Emmy held the soft glow of the lamp closer to the side, shuddering when eight-legged bodies skittered in every direction. She gritted her teeth, suppressing a shriek and the urge to order Nash to haul her out of the wide-awake nightmare.

You can do this. Just a little more and you'll be there. Three more turns and you'll have Mama's hankie in your hands. This will all be worth it then.

Exhaling her relief, she drew even with the jutting rock that had caught the precious heirloom. Holding the lantern out of the way, she swayed her body until the motion brought her closer to the wall.

She snatched at the white spot. Instead of soft linen, she felt thick, sticky padding. In place of the crush of a napkin gathered in her palm, there was the unmistakable writhing of something alive.

CHAPTER 2

Carrizo Springs, Texas

Y ou will find what you seek in the fire, Isi."

Diego Isi Marcelo ducked his head and cast a dour look at his walking companion. "Please, Mother. I've asked you never to call me that in town. Around here I'm known as Diego."

A rolling tumble of weeds skipped across the windblown street and bounced through the heart of Carrizo Springs, dodging pedestrians, horses' hooves, and ox-drawn carts headed for the fields. Diego sidestepped a laughing boy rolling a barrel hoop with a stick, his face the color of buttonwood leaves in the fall. A skinny dog and three other sun-baked children chased behind him.

Diego's mother clutched his arm and pinned him with endless brown eyes. "Diego is the name your father bestowed to appease your grandmamma. Still, *Señora* Marcelo never forgave him for marrying a Choctaw." She nudged him and smiled. "There's nothing wrong with Little Deer, Isi. It's a fine Indian name. Besides"—her wounded expression erased the smile, and she swept her upturned palm toward the crowd of men in wide sombreros, short jackets, and ruffled shirts— "which of these prancing *charros* delivered you under his skirts beneath a desert moon?" She jutted her chin. "I would think my opinion should concern you more."

Laughing, Diego raised both hands in the air. "I surrender. Call me what you will." Wrapping his arm around her shoulders, he snuggled

13

his tiny mother close. "Now then, what's this about finding what I seek? In the fire, you said? Sounds like more tribal superstition."

She shot him a warning glance. "You'd do well to heed my visions, son. And even better not to scorn them. They come to me from *Chihowa Palami*."

Diego sighed. "I would think the Almighty had more pressing matters to concern Him." He tucked his thumb inside his belt and affected a saucy strut. "Actually, I don't need anything your fire might bring. I like my life just fine the way it is."

Her short, dark lashes fluttered, the motion almost hidden by high cheekbones and deep-set eyelids. "Your posing may work on John Rawson and his *vaqueros*. Some days you manage to conceal your disquieted soul even from me. Just don't think you can fool the Great Spirit."

He grinned. "Now, Mother, I know for a fact God's Spirit is too busy to worry about Diego Marcelo's disquieted soul. He has His hands full hiding Pancho Villa from the *Rurales*." He leaned close to her face. "Oh, and keeping Theodore Roosevelt from shooting off his toes."

Her lips tightened into a determined line, and her fingers brushed his hand. "I don't wish to astonish you, Isi, but God is more concerned about your future than I am."

Diego feigned shock. His mother waved off his teasing then raised her strong chin and stared into the distance. "Chihowa Palami sees you on the inside. He's in every beat of your lonely heart. God's love for you is great. Many times He has whispered of you in my dreams. Your future will appear in a whirlwind of smoke and rise to meet you in flames brighter than the beard of my Irish father."

He leaned closer and whispered next to her ear. "That future wouldn't happen to have blond hair and blue eyes, now would it?"

She elbowed his ribs. "If so, she wouldn't be the one you speak of."

His brows lifted. "Not the lovely *Señorita* Rawson? Are you certain? I find myself disappointed."

There was a slight pause in her stride before she recovered. "You fancy Greta Rawson?"

Diego guided her up the steps of the boardwalk. "So there's something about me you don't know? *That* astonishes me, Mother." He winked and caressed her head between her dark braids. "As a matter of fact, I'm having serious thoughts about asking Mr. Rawson's permission to court his fair daughter."

She tilted her head to look at him, her eyes guarded. "Careful, son. Once outside the gate, you must ride the horse you're sitting."

He chuckled. "What sort of Choctaw proverb is that?"

"Only the wisdom of a concerned mother. Good sense speaks every language, except in matters of the heart. If you shame Greta Rawson, you shame her people. You'll wind up the foreman of a different ranch." She shot him a weighty glance. "In a different state."

"Shame Greta? You know me better. My intentions are honorable."

"Because you are honorable, Isi. I only meant that when you discover she's not the right woman for you, you'll have to end the relationship or live in misery for the rest of your life."

He gave her a piercing look. "*When* I find out? You talk like you know something you're not telling me."

She tightened her grip on his arm and focused on something in the distance. Diego smiled and shook his head. Watching her noble, determined profile, he wondered what secrets she kept and what mischief lay ahead for him.

A curse rang out from inside the grocer's shop as they passed. Hurried footsteps brought the man who'd uttered the vulgar words onto the walkway behind them. "Whoo-ee! I thought my eyes was playing tricks, but sure enough, that's a real red-skinned Injun squaw."

Diego stopped walking so fast he nearly tripped his mother. He spun, his arm tightening around her shoulders.

Smiling widely, the jovial-looking, raw-faced fellow stood ten feet away, both hands on his hips. "Look at her, prancing down the street like she belongs there. If that don't take the biscuit."

Cuddy Rawson, the son of Diego's boss, ducked out of the store behind the man. He shoved his hat on his blond head, his eyes round pools of disbelief.

Several others, with expressions similar to Cuddy's, followed him outside.

The senseless dolt on the boardwalk cupped his hands around his mouth. "Hey, Pocahontas. . ." Laughing now, he pointed north, presumably toward the Indian territories. "Your tribe went that way."

Diego left his mother and approached the grinning *bufón*. "I'm feeling generous today, mister. I'll give you one chance to apologize to my mother, but make it quick."

The stranger furrowed his brow. "You mean that little buffalo muncher is your mama? Sorry, Cochise. I figured you fer a local."

Cuddy rushed him at the same time as Diego, but Cuddy got there first. Catching the man by the scruff of his neck, he whirled him into the waiting crowd, who surrounded him and hustled him down the street.

"Hey," he cried to his captors. "What the devil do you think you're doing?"

"A *muy* big favor, *señor*," one of them answered. "We're saving your life."

Cuddy gripped Diego's arms, holding him until the gang of men rounded the corner behind the livery. When his fists uncurled and his breathing slowed, Cuddy released him then shrugged and grinned. "Sorry, Diego. I had to step in and help him out. He's new in town. Poor man had no idea what kind of trouble he was in."

Diego drew a trembling hand through his brown curls and gave a shaky laugh. "It's for the best, my friend." He worked tense kinks from his neck then tugged his leather vest into place. "I suppose God watches out for fools."

Cuddy glanced toward the spot where the crowd had disappeared. "He sure enough rescued that one."

Diego winked and patted Cuddy on the back. "I was referring to myself."

Cuddy tipped his Stetson at Diego's mother. "Melatha. Good to see you're feeling better."

Diego's mother smiled and nodded. Diego rejoined her and she slipped beneath his arm, her face void of expression. "I appreciate what you meant to do, but there was no need."

"No need? He insulted you."

"With empty words? No, Little Deer, he insulted himself and his people. If not for Cuddy, you would have done the same." She patted his hand. "I do wish you'd learn to control your temper, son. A public brawl is no fit way to settle a quarrel. Remember, your ancestors were tranquil people."

He drew back. "Tranquil? You're forgetting a few ancestors, Mother. The Spaniards on my father's side had lively dispositions, as did your father's Irish relations, whose tempers boiled the blood in their veins. Both of those men would've avoided a public brawl, too. They'd have shot him where he stood."

"I'd prefer you sought the way of the Choctaw. The way of peace."

He wagged his finger in her face. "There, you see? If my soul is disquieted, there's your reason. How could I know the proper way to conduct myself? I'm a mixed breed. A mongrel. A man without a past."

Her brows bunched in disapproval. "Nonsense. Your past is rich in culture."

"Which culture would that be? The blood is so mixed in my veins, I've lost all notion of who I am."

"Tradition is stronger than blood, Isi. You learned this at your mother's knee, and I've strived to teach you well. More to the point, only one bloodline really matters—that of Chihowa Ushi, the blessed Son of God."

⁂

Melatha sat alone at her roughhewn kitchen table, gazing through the window at the rear entrance of the bunkhouse. Isi had disappeared through the door the minute they returned from town, his mood brooding and restless. His state of unease would add many prayers to her lips come nightfall.

Her gaze shifted past the vaqueros' quarters to the field where wind-ripples danced through the tall grass like spirits playing tag. Scattered cactus stood with upraised arms, offering dark purple pears as sweet, juicy sacrifices. The fluffy white vine that young Cuddy called "old man's beard" grew along the barbed wire fence in mounded clumps like the piled-up snowdrifts back home.

The Bible spread open on the table pulled Melatha's attention to the present. She finished the passage in chapter 8 of Solomon's Song.

"Love is strong as death; jealousy is cruel as the grave: the coals thereof are coals of fire, which hath a most vehement flame."

She shuddered. The ancient words struck her heart with another confirmation of her fiery vision.

Chihowa Palami, bow my son to Your will. A bent reed turns to iron in the Father's hand.

As she always did before closing the worn leather book, she read the words inscribed in bold script in the center of the first page: *Melatha Rhona Flynn, daughter of Kelly Mícheál and Hatabushik Loosa Flynn. May you ever heed the truth revealed within these pages.*

"Ah, Isi," she whispered, her fingers tracing the letters, "your grandfather's words are your heritage, the connection to the past you seek. Though you can't see it yet, they're the path to your future as well."

His restless soul filled with longing, Isi had run so fast from himself he'd landed them both in Carrizo Springs near the border of Texas and Mexico. But no matter how far he'd run, his destiny perched on the horizon, determined to overtake him.

As for Melatha, she didn't mind where her son's desperate flight had driven them. She loved South Texas, the land Isi called "God's country," and had plans to settle in for good.

When they first arrived, the Rawsons had welcomed her into a room in their home but soon realized she needed her own space. Mr. Rawson graciously offered the northeast corner of the yard where Isi built her a spacious *jacal* out of mud and sticks. He'd seen to it that the walls were sturdy and sound, and Melatha blessed the day she'd first set foot beneath its humble thatched roof.

There was a spare corner in the house for Isi's bed, but he insisted on sleeping in the drafty bunkhouse with his men. He claimed he needed their respect more than his own comfort, and he'd never ask them to do anything he hadn't first done himself.

The strength of her son's character and his willingness to take a stand in such matters was the reason Mr. Rawson promoted him from a greenhorn to foreman in only three short years.

Strength of character failed her son when the odor of griddlecakes drifted from her hearth in the mornings, or roasted ears of corn at night. For meals he left his charges to eat Cook's grub in the bunkhouse and joined his mother at her table—a fact that warmed her heart as hot as her coals and kept her skillet sizzling.

Melatha had no knowledge of the life Isi had lived during their five years apart, and she had never asked him. Her interest lay in his future, not his past.

God's Spirit had shown her this future while she prayed. Not a clear image—only hair as white as the vine tangled along the fence and eyes like a fair summer sky.

EMMY'S EQUAL

A lively young filly would come to her brooding son from the north. Their hearts would meld in a whirlwind of fire, and their passion would restore Isi to life.

CHAPTER 3

Emmy couldn't open her hand fast enough. . .or sling the hideous spider far enough. Chest aching, she realized it had been a matted web she'd seen all along. Mama's hankie likely floated atop the foul pool below—forever lost.

"Nash!" a shrill voice called from above her head.

Emmy grew rigid. *Mama!*

She heard a muffled gasp from Nash then the rattle and whir of the crack as she plummeted wildly. Before she could think, scream, or pray—before she stood facing her Maker—she came to a jarring halt with a jerk and twang of the rope.

The ancient bucket collapsed beneath her, parts of it scraping and pinging off the rocks before landing with a splash. She gasped and tightened her legs on the remaining slats, gripping the rope so tightly the rough hemp burned her palms. Bile rose in her throat, made worse by the rancid smell of the water, much closer now. Even more disturbing, the plunge had snuffed her light.

Something cold sailed out of the darkness, landing on her bare skin then slithering up her leg. Not a snake, the thing had tiny grasping feet.

Frantic, Emmy brushed it off before clinging to her lifeline with trembling fingers. She opened her mouth to cry out to Nash, but Mama got to him first.

"Here you are. For corn's sake, where've you been all morning?

I've scoured the place for you."

The fact that Mama stood somewhere above, her deep, strident voice echoing in Emmy's ears, scared her nearly as much as the fall.

Get shed of her, Nash! And hurry!

"You been huntin' me, Miz Dane?" Nash's strained words tumbled down the hole. "Why, I been right here all along."

"I've called and called. Why didn't you answer?" Mama's tone meant her hands had gone to her hips.

" 'Cause I ain't heard nary a one of them calls until now. I 'spose you might've yelled louder."

"Oh, never mind. Have you seen Emmy?"

After a tense silence, Nash began to sputter. "H–Have I seen Miss Emmy? Now, that's a good question. I did see her right after breakfast, sure 'nough. 'Course I saw her yesterday, too, and–"

"Just tell her this when you see her–Willem is on his way home. He'll arrive by train tomorrow. He's decided it ain't safe for me and Bertha to go south alone, so he's coming with us."

Emmy's heart lurched. Papa going with Mama to South Texas? The new development made it infinitely more important that she avoid the trip. Emmy's relationship with her papa wouldn't exactly inspire sentimental sonnets. On the rare occasions when he happened to be home, he spent all of his time correcting her, perhaps to make up for lost time, or ignoring her completely as if she made him uneasy. If given a choice, she preferred the lectures to his silence.

"Yes'm, I'll tell Miss Emmy jus' what you said. When I see her, that is."

Emmy prayed with renewed vigor for the strength to wait Mama out. Busting her skull or drowning in stinky water might definitely impede her plans to visit St. Louis. Dying in a well or emerging from it a raving lunatic covered in newts and spiders meant she'd never have the chance to see Charity's baby. However, all of these possibilities were more enticing than an extended trip with her papa or facing her mama's wrath. She tightened her grip and held on for all she was worth.

"What are you doing out here anyway?" Mama said to Nash. "There's no time today for lollygagging. You have work to do."

"Yes, ma'am, I sho' do."

"Get on with it, then. What are you waiting for? The stalls won't sweep themselves."

"Um. . .yes'm, Miz Dane. Jus' as soon as I finish drawing a bucket for Miss Emmy's horse."

"Emmy's horse? Well, I'll be switched and tickled, there he is. What's Trouble doing out here?"

"I. . .brung him out to get a drink."

Emmy could almost hear the gears churning in Mama's head. "So, you're telling me instead of taking water to the horse you brought the horse to water? To a hole full of putrid water, in fact?"

"W–What I meant to say was," Nash stammered, "I didn't remember this well being bad till I got out here."

The hush meant more whirling parts in Mama's head. Emmy thought she could smell the smoke.

"I see. So, why's he saddled?"

"Hmm. Yes, ma'am, he's saddled all right. I can see why you'd ask that question, too. I reckon it's because Miss Emmy wants him ready to ride when I'm done watering him."

Mama blew out her breath in a whoosh that rattled all the way down the well to Emmy. "That's enough out of you. I don't know what you and that girl are up to, and I don't have time to ponder. Go on and get to those chores. Take Trouble with you. He can drink from the trough the way a critter's meant to."

"But I ain't done hauling up the bucket." With each word, Nash's voice climbed the scale toward a soprano.

"Move aside. I'll take care of it."

"I cain't let you do that, Miz Dane. It be too heavy for a lady."

"Nash, give me the crank."

"No!"

Heavy, cloying silence oozed down the shaft. Emmy hung surrounded in it until Mama recovered enough to speak.

"What did you say to me?"

"I said no. I mean, no, ma'am."

"Jonas Nash. . ."

Emmy cringed. She'd gotten Nash into terrible trouble. Mama had used his Christian name.

"I reckon I pay you fair enough wages to get a 'yes, ma'am' to most anything I ask you to do around here. Especially something as trifling as this. Now give me that handle."

Taller than most men and as solid as a boulder, Emmy's bossy, controlling mama was a formidable opponent. The tumble of russet curls pinned up on her head made her appear even larger, like the ruffled feathers of a bird facing down a rival. Grown men cowered before her no-nonsense voice, and few of them in Humble, least of all Nash, had the pluck to stand up to her when she got angry.

Even so, surely he'd never relinquish his hold and scurry off to do her bidding, leaving Emmy to plunge to her death in the gloomy deep. She held her breath and wondered at the depth of the lapping water, hoping she'd break her neck and die on the way down rather than drown in the nasty stuff.

A scuffle ensued—Nash desperately pleading, Mama as mad as a whole nest of hornets.

Emmy felt the exchange of hands on the crank when she dropped a foot lower. She started to cry softly and pray with all of her might.

"Don't let go, Miz Dane. Please, ma'am. Don't you dare let go."

"For pity's sake! What have you got at the end of this rope?"

Her mama cranked the handle and Emmy eased up a few turns. With a grunt, Mama laid her weight into it, and Emmy shot toward the circle of light in jerky bursts. She cleared the top in time to see the backside of Nash scurrying toward the barn.

Mama yelped and let go of the handle briefly before latching onto it with both hands. "Emily Bertha Dane!" she screeched. "If this ain't the last place I expected to find you." She glared toward Nash, who broke into a trot after one last anxious glance over his shoulder. "I'll deal with him later. As for you, climb out of there and explain yourself."

Emmy held out her hand.

Mama grasped it and pulled her to the side.

Emmy longed to kneel and kiss the ground, but the look on her mama's face told her she'd best save her knees for prayer.

Mama glared at her. "Do you realize you could've been killed?"

Trembling from head to toe, Emmy could only nod.

Still scowling, Mama pulled the busted bucket over the wall and rested it on the opposite side of the well. A puzzled look crossed her face before she leaned to pick something up from the ground. Holding her hand-embroidered handkerchief aloft, she gaped at Emmy in surprise. "Would you look at this? It's one of my hankies." She cocked her head and stared at it dumbly. "How do you suppose this wound up way out here?"

CHAPTER 4

*E*mmy's heart sped up as Daniel Clark's arms slid around her waist, his grasping hands cruelly biting into her flesh.

"Stop," she whimpered. "You're holding me too tight."

Instead of loosening, his eager fingers curled, digging deeper in her back. Emmy cringed and started to cry.

Lightning crashed overhead. "Forget about Charity," Daniel whispered. "She doesn't matter."

Emmy lifted her gaze and stared into the haunted hollows of Daniel's eyes. "She matters to me."

He stepped away from her and raised a pistol to his head.

Panic struck and sobs wracked her body. "No, Daniel!"

Anger, hatred, and blame burned in his eyes. "Time to get up, Emmy," he called, his voice shrill and distant.

"Don't do it, Daniel. Please. I said I'm sorry."

He tilted his head to the swirling black clouds and closed his eyes, his finger tightening on the trigger.

Charity stepped from the shadows and wrenched the gun from Daniel's hand. Pushing past him, she raised the barrel of the gun and aimed it straight at Emmy's chest.

Emmy's heartbreak turned to terror. "Charity, what are you doing? It's me."

Charity smiled. "I said get up right now. You hear me?" The pistol exploded with a crash that rattled the house.

Emmy opened her mouth to scream and. . .

"Emily Bertha Dane!"

Emmy's eyes flew open.

The bedroom door that had hit the wall with a resounding bang swung back toward Mama. She stood on the threshold, her plump arms folded across her buxom chest. "You'd best shake that floor, little miss. I've been shouting for ten minutes."

The bright, cheery room enveloped Emmy in a rush of yellow wallpaper and lace curtains. The shock of normalcy and light crashed against the darkness of her dream in a collision that hurt her head. She squeezed her eyelids together to block out the sun.

"Oh, honey." Mama crossed the room and sank onto the side of the bed, pulling the mattress down and rolling Emmy against her thigh. "You had the dream again, didn't you?"

Struggling to sit upright, Emmy shuddered. "How did you know?"

Mama tilted her head and sighed. "If the fright on your face hadn't told me, your tears would've given you away." She smoothed back Emmy's hair. "Did Daniel kill himself again?"

Halfway through a nod, Emmy stopped and shook her head. "No. He started to, but it was different this time." She frowned. "Charity appeared and turned the gun on me."

"Charity?" Mama crowed. "Why, she'd kiss you before she'd shoot you. You saved that girl's life. Well, from an unhappy life with that horrible Daniel, anyway." Her eyes softened. "Why can't you turn these memories loose, honey?"

Shame drew Emmy's shoulders down. "Maybe because I stole my best friend's fiancé. What sort of person does that?"

Mama nodded. "It was a plain awful thing to do, Emmy. But if you hadn't, Charity wouldn't be happily married to the man she really loves."

Emmy scrubbed her face with her hands, trying to erase the last trace of the nightmare. "Still, I actually prefer the way this dream ended. The bullet finally found the true culprit."

Mama patted her hands. "Hush that kind of talk. First off, you needn't worry about Daniel Clark's empty threat to take his own life. He holds too dear the image in his mirror. God and Charity forgave you a long time ago. You need to forgive yourself and get on with it."

"Forgiving myself is hard to do in this town, with Eunice Clark waiting around every corner to pounce."

"Daniel's mama took it hard when he up and left Humble for good. I don't suppose she'll draw in her claws any time soon." Mama's bosom heaved in a sigh. "Don't let her pin the blame on you, sugar. I suspect Daniel had leaving on his mind all along."

Emmy sat up in bed and swung her legs over the side. "Tell that to Eunice, if you don't mind."

Mama swatted Emmy's bare leg so hard it stung. "I just might do that the next time I see her. Which may be today. You and me need to take a run into town."

The forced brightness in Mama's voice set off a warning in Emmy's head. Rubbing the pink-tinged mark on her leg, she peered up past one lowered brow. "What for?"

"We got us a mess of shopping to do. Won't that be grand?" Her tone was far too cheerful, and her gaze waltzed around Emmy's, never once making contact with her eyes. "Your papa wants to buy us a brand new wardrobe."

"New clothes? Our closets are full."

Mama cleared her throat. "He insists we'll need things cut from lightweight fabric. . .since the summer months are so hot in South Texas."

"No!" Emmy shrieked and leaped to her feet. "You said he was thinking of letting me go to St. Louis."

Mama held up both hands. "Calm down, child. He did think about it and decided to say no. It's too far for you to travel without an escort, and we don't have time to arrange a proper chaperone."

"Then let me stay here," Emmy begged.

"Absolutely not. Papa forbids you staying here alone. After the incident in the well, I quite agree. You've been so moody lately. Some time away from Humble will do you good."

"St. Louis is away from Humble."

"Let it go, Emmy. St. Louis is out of the question."

Emmy's hands balled into fists. "Did you tell him about the well?"

"I said I wouldn't, didn't I?"

"Then why!"

"For your own sake. Those dreams you've been having are part of the reason. Besides, your papa would like to spend a few days with

26

you this summer." Mama's eyes turned sorrowful. "Is that so much to ask?"

Emmy groaned inside. Far too much, coming from him. She dropped her gaze. "Can Nash come along?"

"Of course not."

"Oh, please? I need him there. Who will I talk to when I'm bored out of my mind?"

"Someone besides Nash. You know he has to stay here and run things while we're gone. You're not his only concern, Emmy. Nash has a family of his own."

She closed her eyes and let her head fall back. "Oh, bother! When do we leave?"

"Next Monday."

"So soon? That's only a week from today."

"Exactly the reason we'd best get a move on. Chances are we won't find enough suitable clothes for the heat. If we need to hire some things made to fit, a week's not very long." She leaned to kiss the top of Emmy's head. "Hurry down for breakfast, sugar. Bertha made her special biscuits."

"Why does Aunt Bert still make breakfast for us? She has enough money to hire ten cooks."

Mama smiled. "I reckon long-standing habits are hard to break. For both of us. Get a move on, sugar. It's getting late." She started to go then turned. "Don't fret over the trip. You're going to have fun."

Fun?

Emmy frowned as her mama closed the door. Living a week under the same roof as Papa would be less than fun. The word for surviving him while serving a prison sentence in a smoldering wasteland wasn't even in Emmy's dictionary.

❧

Diego rode up even with the porch of the *casa mayor*, the big main house where Cuddy Rawson reclined in a bentwood rocker, his boots crossed high on the whitewashed rail. A tall, sweaty glass garnished with lemon slivers dangled in his hand. His vacant stare and the slight upturn of his mouth meant his thoughts had drifted elsewhere.

Diego cleared his throat.

Cuddy's stricken look and even quicker duck and shift of his eyes confirmed what Diego already suspected. He bumped his hat off his forehead with the leather handle of his quirt. "I'm happy to see you're making a speedy recovery, *amigo*."

Cuddy bit back a grin, pulling his feet to the porch and sitting upright in the chair. He held up his glass. "I owe it to Greta's tender care. She's bent on nursing me back to health."

Diego glanced at the front door. "Would your lovely sister offer a cup of comfort if she knew the reason for your pain?" He nodded at the icy drink. "Lemonade's the latest cure for a hangover, then?"

Cuddy winced then affected an injured look. "Your judgment is harsh, my friend." He cocked back in the rocker again. "How could you suggest such a thing about your most faithful companion?"

"Save your recitals for Greta. This is me you're talking to." Diego dismounted and leaned his back against the handrail while toying with the braided band on his hat. He cleared his throat. "Cuddy, I thought you decided to go easy on the liquor."

A cloud moved across Cuddy's eyes, and he forcefully lifted one hand.

Diego nodded. "Very well, friend. I'll change the subject. For instance, can you explain what you were considering with such intensity when I arrived?"

The shadow passed from Cuddy's face, replaced by a wily twinkle. "You mean before you interrupted my lofty thoughts?"

"I doubt they were very noble."

Cuddy's huge grin brought his countenance to life, restoring some of the color behind his freckles. "We got company coming."

The Rawsons seldom hosted visitors, but when they did, it was cause for celebration—South Texas–style. The prospect of roasting beef on the spit, dancing in the courtyard, singing, laughing, and talking to new faces brought a smile to Diego's face, too. "Bravo! Who are we expecting?"

"Father's old friend, Willem Dane. His wife and her lady friend are traveling with him."

Diego narrowed his eyes. "And. . . ?"

"Isn't that enough for you?"

"Plenty for me, but don't forget, I'm well acquainted with your tricks. A visit from a gentleman accompanied by two old ladies wouldn't set off the look I saw on your face."

Cuddy slapped his leg and laughed. "My, but you're intent on insulting me today."

"Who else is coming, Cuddy?"

He leaned forward and winked. "None other than the fair Miss Emily Dane."

Diego's brow rose.

"Willem's daughter," Cuddy clarified. "Papa claims she's the prettiest little thing he's ever set two eyes on."

"Ah! Now it makes sense. As a devoted son, you'll be standing close by to offer your heartfelt welcome."

"Of course! Only a rank scoundrel would think to do otherwise."

Hinges squealed behind them, stifling Cuddy's bawdy laughter. Greta swept out in a rush of blue skirts and matching hair bows, her hands laden with a silver tray.

Diego took the steps in two leaps. "Let me take that, Miss Greta. I'd hate to see you trip and poor Cuddy here wind up wearing these fine-looking sandwiches."

A flush crept past Greta's high-buttoned collar, staining her porcelain skin a pale pink. "You say such naughty things, Diego, but they're spoken with a certain flair. I can't keep from laughing." She offered the tray with a dimpled smile and the lingering gaze she'd perfected on him lately—the one that had him thinking about her in a completely different way. "Thank you."

He returned her searching look until he felt himself blushing as well. "Of course."

Greta smoothed Cuddy's yellow hair. "Feeling better, big brother?"

Cuddy rubbed his stomach and leaned to gaze hungrily at the tray. "I will as soon as I force down a few bites."

He went for a sandwich, but Diego jerked the tray out of his reach. "Whoa, amigo! None for you." He placed the food on a table out of Cuddy's reach. "Your sister means well, but you know what they say, 'If you stuff a cold, then you're going to have to feed a fever later.' " He aimed his brightest smile at Greta. "We don't want old Cuddy coming down with a fever, do we? I think he needs to rest his frail constitution so he'll fully recover."

Greta clutched the sash at her waist. "Gracious, you may be right. I never once thought. . ."

Diego patted her hand. "Your intentions were admirable, and I applaud them. Besides, just because Cuddy can't enjoy the fruit of your efforts is no reason they should go to waste." Ignoring Cuddy's glare, his fingers hovered above a plump, meat-stuffed triangle. "May I?"

"By all means, Diego. Help yourself."

Cuddy spun around and snatched the roast beef sandwich before it reached Diego's mouth. "I'll take that off your hands, thank you."

Greta scowled. "Cuddy!"

"I'm feeling better, sis. Honest. Diego's company perked me right up."

"Well, if you're sure. . ."

"Positive," he said, with a smirk in Diego's direction.

Before Diego could react, John Rawson rounded the house on horseback with two rugged ranch hands on his heels. The aging *ranchero* sat his horse like a much younger man, with the vigor and authority befitting the owner of a spread like the Twisted-R Ranch. Diego held much respect for the big man and his principles. He'd taken Diego to his heart as a beloved son. In return, Diego loved him like a father.

"Ho! What good fortune to have caught you here together. Now I won't need to waste half the day tracking Cuddy."

Smiling, Diego crossed to the rail. "How may we be of service, sir?"

Still seated, Cuddy snorted. "Speak for yourself, I'm not well, remember."

Mr. Rawson frowned slightly at Cuddy then addressed Diego. "I suppose you've heard we have guests on the way?"

Diego nodded.

"We have a week to spruce the place up. I'll need you boys to help." He leaned to see around Diego. "That means you, too, mister."

Cuddy groaned, but his father ignored him.

"We've gone long enough giving this ranch a lick and a promise. I won't have it going to seed. Just a little effort on our parts and we'll have the place looking natty again. Inside and out."

Diego bit back a smile. Under Mr. Rawson's command, the staff of the Twisted-R kept the house and grounds in immaculate condition.

The gentleman's wife slipped out of the door behind Greta and slid one arm around her daughter's waist. "Focus your energy on the outside, John. Greta and I will take care of the inside."

"Fine, fine," he blustered. "Greta, help Mother and Rosita make preparations in the house. You'll need to wash and air out the bed linens and tablecloths and pull out the best silverware."

"I'll see to it, dear. Did they say how long they'll be staying?"

"No, but I expect it will be several weeks. We'll prepare for an extended visit. Have Rosita bring in her sisters to help with the cooking."

Mrs. Rawson stepped over and leaned on the rail. "Relax, John. I have everything under control."

"Forgive my exuberance, family, but Willem Dane is a very old friend. The last time we broke bread together was around my father's table in Ripponden. You remember, Katherine, the year before we left England."

She nodded. "I remember Willem well. He seemed like a wonderful man."

"Of course, I've seen him a few times since, and we've exchanged letters. Now I'd like to give him a hearty South Texas welcome."

Mrs. Rawson smiled sweetly. "And so we shall. I'm anxious to meet his family." She addressed Greta over her shoulder. "We'll put Mr. and Mrs. Dane in the north corner, Mrs. Bloom directly across the hall. Air out the room that faces east for young Emily. She can withstand the morning heat better than her elders."

Cuddy perked up from where he lounged in the rocker, interested in the conversation for the first time. "Good plan! That room's balcony connects with mine."

His mother's blush brightened her rouge. "Yes, Cuthbert, it does. That's exactly why you'll be bunking with Diego while they're here."

He shot to his feet. "What?"

"It's the only proper thing to do. I won't have Emily uncomfortable."

"That's a ludicrous suggestion."

"Watch your tone, Cuddy," Mr. Rawson warned. "You're speaking to your mother."

"Sorry, Father, but the bunkhouse? Why can't I just switch rooms with Greta?"

Greta spun. "Excuse me? Banish me to that awful hog wallow? I think not! The walls reek of sweat, sour whiskey, and dung-crusted boots."

Diego's brows lifted. *So she does know.*

Cuddy pressed close to Greta's face. "I would expect you to feel right at home in a hog wallow, precious."

She blustered. "How dare you! After I nursed your booze-sodden behind all morning long, waiting on you hand and foot."

"I never asked you—"

"That's enough!"

All eyes jerked toward the bellowed roar and the blotchy-faced Mr. Rawson seated on his horse.

"I'll have no more, understand? Greta Rawson, follow your mother into the house and start the errands I've charged to you."

With a sheepish glance at Diego, Greta hustled inside on her mother's heels.

Mr. Rawson leaned forward in the saddle. "Cuddy. . .in the future, son, you'll conduct yourself like a Rawson under every circumstance. Like a gentleman." He jutted his chin. "Like Diego here. You'd do well to follow his lead."

Cuddy smirked. "I guess that's where I got confused, Father. I didn't realize Diego was a Rawson now."

Anger flashed in Mr. Rawson's eyes. "Not another word, Cuthbert."

Cuddy slumped in the chair, his sullen gaze directed between his knees.

Stern eyes locked on his son, Mr. Rawson turned his horse. "Diego, I'll leave it in your hands to see that everything gets tended. I know I can count on you, son."

Wincing inside, Diego nodded. "Yes, sir."

Mr. Rawson rode off a few yards then left his companions and closed the distance to the porch.

Trepidation in his eyes, Cuddy studied his father's brooding face. "Yes, sir?"

"Do I need to remind you of the proper manner for conducting yourself in the company of a young lady?"

Cuddy stiffened in his chair. "Absolutely not, sir."

Mr. Rawson gave a curt nod. "I didn't think so." He pulled his horse around and cantered away.

Cuddy sat quietly, clasping and unclasping his fingers, his curling knuckles going white. When Diego could stand no more silence, he gripped his friend's shoulder. "I suppose there's a lot to be done, amigo. You ready to get going?"

Cuddy released a long, weary breath. "Sure thing, big brother. I was just waiting to follow your lead."

CHAPTER 5

"You're going on a holiday, Emily, not to a wake."

Mama held up Emmy's least favorite dress, a gray gabardine with puffed sleeves gathered below the shoulders and banded with black appliquéd flowers. Four large, round buttons fastened the long-sleeved jacket in front. Mama gaped at the dress then dropped it on the bed beside Emmy's suitcase and went fishing for more. "This fur-trimmed collar won't do either, sugar. What were you thinking?"

"Do forgive me." Emmy took the garment from Mama's hand and tossed it on the growing pile of rejects. "I'm not up-to-date on the proper attire for a visit to Hades."

Mama slumped on the side of the bed, Emmy's faded flannel nightgown clutched in her hands. "I know your heart's not in this trip, honey, but you're not even trying to be cheerful."

Emmy gave her a glum look. "Cheerfulness wasn't in the bargain, was it? I don't recall that clause when I signed my name in blood."

Mama pointed at her. "Now you're being a pill. Tell me why you're packing these wretched rags and not the new things we got."

"I won't wear my good things to frolic among cockleburs and cactus. I hope to return to civilization one day, and I'd like something decent left to wear when I get here."

Mama scooped up a double handful from the bag. "You'll roast in all of this."

"I don't care. Regardless of what I wear, I'm sure to be thoroughly

34

miserable." Emmy flounced to the mirror. Quite pleased with her image on most days, she leaned nose-to-nose with her reflection and sighed. Her usually pert white ringlets sagged, and dark circles ringed her shaded blue eyes. Scowl lines etched the flawless forehead, and the corners of her pouting mouth turned down.

Snow White dared not inquire of the looking glass today. The dejected toad gazing back wasn't the fairest of any land. She sagged against the dressing table. "I suppose I'm destined to be unhappy until this awful trip is behind me and Papa is back on the road."

An ominous stirring in the looking glass quickened her heartbeat. A distorted image loomed from behind, swirling in a dark cloud of fury like Snow White's evil queen. Emmy should've seen it coming. One could push Mama only so far.

A biting grip on Emmy's arm spun her, inches from Mama's mottled face and blazing eyes. "I've a good mind to give you your stubborn way and let you ride into Carrizo Springs with nothing to wear but tweed and fur collars, though the temperature soars to one hundred degrees in the shade. As your parent and protector, I'll save you from yourself. March your behind downstairs. *I* will see to your packing."

"But, Mama—"

"I said go!"

"You can't pack my—"

"Now!"

Stinging from the rebuke, Emmy fought tears as she bunched her skirt in trembling fingers and dashed from the room, wincing when the door slammed shut behind her. She had seen that much anger displayed by Mama before but never directed at her. Standing behind a barrier wider than oak and hinges, she burned with outrage and guilt—anger because Mama had never understood the rift between her and Papa, guilt because she'd crossed a forbidden line.

"Honour thy father and thy mother: that thy days may be long upon the land which the LORD *thy God giveth thee."*

Pondering the scripture, Emmy touched the doorknob with her fingertips. She supposed it meant her days on earth would be shortened. For all of Mama's vexing ways, she was infinitely easier to honor than the stern stranger in the parlor.

At the landing, she eased down three steps then paused to spy out the landscape. No rustling newspaper spread open in front of the chair, no stocking-covered feet crossed on the arm of the sofa, no odor of pipe tobacco or haze of smoke in the room. She was safe.

Still wary, she took the rest of the stairs slowly, watching for movement by the kitchen door. Near the bottom step, she bent at the waist to peer out the front window.

"What in blazes are you up to, Emily?"

Blood surged to Emmy's head, ringing her ears like a gong. She released her skirt and clutched her chest, at the same time attempting to flee the gruff voice at her back. Tripping on her hem, she fell from the third step and landed in a heap of tangled legs and twisted cloth. Rolling to her back, she propped up on her elbows and stared dumbly at her flush-faced papa.

"Daughter, I've repeatedly asked you not to play games on the staircase."

"I wasn't. . ."

"Don't dispute my words, Emily. I just came down behind you and witnessed your antics." He frowned. "All that creeping about, the stopping and starting. . . What were you doing? I nearly blundered into you."

Feeling foolish, her gaze dropped to his stockinged feet. Well, pooh! No wonder she hadn't heard him. "Sorry, Papa."

He descended with decidedly more grace than she had and offered his hand. "I expect you'll heed my warnings in the future?"

As Emmy latched on and he hauled her to her feet, the warmth of his touch flashed a memory through her mind in a muddled haze. As a child, she'd fallen asleep in the carriage on the way home from an outing and awakened nestled against Papa's shoulder as he carried her inside. The tender way he held her, the warmth of his fingers beneath her hair had so overwhelmed her with feelings of comfort and love she hadn't wanted it to end, so she pretended to stay asleep.

As fast as it came the memory disappeared, leaving behind an ache that swelled her throat. She pulled her hand free and Papa brushed past her to the parlor. "I heard your mother shouting. Are you the cause?"

Cringing, she lowered her head. "I suppose I am."

He settled in his easy chair, as unyielding as the high, straight back of the furniture. "What sort of answer is that? You either are the cause or you're not."

She glanced up and opened her mouth to speak then looked down again as the words stuck in her throat.

He heaved an exaggerated sigh. "Come over here, please."

She complied, standing in front of him with her arms behind her back like a naughty child awaiting punishment. How did he make her feel so diminished?

"Emily, I've tried to be patient with you, but I understand you've been up to one thing or the other the whole time I've been gone, and a couple more escapades since I've arrived home."

Mama told! Emmy's heart plunged and the oft-repeated words sprang to her lips. "I'm sorry, Papa." She sucked in air, her mind scrambling for a good explanation. "I guess I just didn't think it through. I know the well is dangerous, and—"

"The well?" He sat forward. "I was referring to an incident involving your mama's best linens. It seems one of them wound up tossed in the yard. She suspects you are somehow implicated."

Emmy's chin sank to her chest.

Papa snorted. "Just as we thought, and after your mama has asked you numerous times to leave them be."

"I took one by mistake. I thought—"

His hand shot up. "No excuses. You should pay closer attention." He frowned, his brows nearly touching over the bridge of his nose. "Now then, let's return to this confession concerning the well, shall we?"

Dread tensed Emmy's shoulders. "Yes, sir. I, um. . ."

"I meant to tell you, Willem. . ." Her mama's unruffled voice resounded from the top landing.

Emmy breathed a sigh of relief, her grateful gaze following Mama down the stairs.

"Your daughter put something down the shaft that doesn't belong there." She shifted her attention to Emmy and her eyes softened. "Something quite precious." She swept across the room, skirts rustling, and headed off Papa's next question with a pass of her hand. "Never mind, dear. There was no harm done. We got it out in one piece."

"Even so, wife, it sounds like a foolhardy thing to do and the act of an irresponsible child. One would think the girl had just turned twelve, not twenty-one."

Mama dismissed his insult with a flick of her ruffle-cluttered wrist. "Careful, or we'll turn your game of reversing numbers against you, dear. You're so grumpy of late, one might mistake you for ninety-four."

Thankfully, her teasing tone softened the blow. Papa's face twitched, as if torn between a smile at her clever twist or a frown at her rebuke. The smile won out, of course. As firm as he was with Emmy, he seldom disputed his wife. Unlike most men in town, his tiptoed waltzing around her feelings stemmed from his great fondness for her rather than fear. Emmy's parents had always held each other in the highest regard.

Pausing in the front hall, Mama pulled on her gloves, her vacant gaze fixed on a spot above the doorpost. "Let's see. . .we're all packed and the house is buttoned down. I've prepared a basket of food to sustain us on the train tomorrow. I hope the blasted thing is on schedule. We waited better than an hour for our trip to the state fair last summer." Frowning, she fanned herself. "Positively gruesome in this heat."

She raised her brows at Papa. "I'm assuming you gave Nash the list of his added responsibilities?"

Papa nodded.

"Good. He's a capable man but downright forgetful these days. Must be his age."

Emmy frowned. "He's not that old. You make him sound fit for the grave."

Ignoring her, Mama opened the door. "All that's left to do is wake up and make our way to the station. With the luggage, there won't be room for much else, so Nash will drive us down first then go after Bertha." She regarded Emmy at last. "I expect you to put on the carriage dress I laid out for you and be downstairs and ready for breakfast by six. Understood?"

"Yes, ma'am." She took in her mama's gloves, hat, and the parasol she lifted from the hallway stand. "But, Mama, where are you going?"

"To see about Aunt Bert. If I don't help her pack, she'll do as good a job of it as you did. With Charity in St. Louis, I have to keep an eye on Bertha's shenanigans, or no telling what she'll get up to."

"May I go?"

Mama wagged her head. "No, you may not. What you may do,

however, is sit with your papa and keep him company until I return."

Emmy stole a glance at Papa's face to confirm he was no more thrilled than she at the prospect of an afternoon together. "Oh, please, Mama."

She gave Emmy a pointed look. "Do like I say, Emily. I mean business."

The door closed in Emmy's face. She grasped the knob, her slender fingers clutching with the desperation of a drowning cat. Leaning her head briefly against the cool wood panel, she prayed for rescue. When none came, she turned to find the man she was duty-bound to honor hiding behind his paper. With the sensation of a guillotine falling overhead, she crossed the room and took a seat in the chair farthest from her papa.

~∾~

Wheeling around the barn with a bucket of whitewash in one hand and a long-handled brush in the other, Diego bumped into Cuddy coming the other way with a pitchfork. "Whoa, my friend!" he cried, sidestepping the sloshing limewater and righting the pail. "You came close to turning a lighter complexion than how you were born."

Cuddy grimaced and held up the tool. "And you nearly wound up dangling from the end of these tines."

Diego set aside the brush and paint and draped one arm around Cuddy's neck. "I've had the feeling all morning that you'd be pleased to see me skewered."

Cuddy ducked his head. "Dreadful sorry, Diego. It ain't about you, really."

His arm still looped around Cuddy, Diego patted him on the chest, laughing when it thudded like a thumped muskmelon. "Forget it, partner. I know what's hung in your craw. I'd feel the same in your boots." He gripped Cuddy's shoulder. "Just don't take it so much to heart. Your father is very proud of you."

Cuddy held up his free hand. "Hold it right there. You're supposed to be whitewashing this barn, not the facts." He sighed and eased gently away. "Don't cry for me, Diego. I'm a big boy. I reckon I can handle the truth when it's dumped in my lap." He flashed a somber smile, shouldered the pitchfork, and rounded the corner of the barn.

Intent on Cuddy's hasty retreat, the *whoosh* of leather on sandy soil startled him. He spun around with balled fists.

Greta had managed to slip up from behind and stood inches away with a wide grin on her face. "I spooked you, didn't I?" She giggled. "I didn't think it possible to sneak up on an Indian, Diego. Melatha will be scandalized."

His hands relaxed at his sides. "Not as scandalized as your mama would be if I had sent you home with a shiner." He grinned. "I almost slugged you, Greta. What were you thinking?"

Her lashes swept down to cover her eyes, as if the truth about what she'd been thinking embarrassed her. "I brought food." She held up a plate covered with a red-checkered dishcloth then leaned to peer around him. "For Cuddy, too. Where'd he rush off to so fast?"

Diego raised the corner of the cloth to find fat rolls of shredded beef wrapped in corn tortillas. He whistled appreciatively. "These could easily spoil my appetite for lunch, Miss Rawson. But they will be well worth it."

She angled her head. "This is your lunch, Mr. Marcelo. I prepared it myself. You and Cuddy missed the noon meal by a half hour."

"We did?" He chuckled and nudged his hat aside. "No wonder these smell so good." He took the plate from her hands and sat on a nearby hay bale, balancing the feast on his knees. "I suppose we got so busy we lost track of time."

Greta perched beside him and offered him a napkin from the stack in her lap. "We figured as much, with everyone so set on getting the place in shape."

He folded the cloth back from the mounded dish and breathed in the aroma of seared beef, spices, and diced chilies. "Yes, ma'am, these look mighty fine." He widened his eyes and lifted his brows, as innocent as a fresh thrown calf. "But where's the rest?"

She blinked twice. "The rest?"

Diego elbowed her and winked. "I thought you made some for Cuddy, too."

Clearly pleased by his appreciation of her cooking, Greta tittered with glee and returned his jab in the ribs. "Oh, Diego. You're such a tease. I bless the day you came to this ranch."

Mid-bite, he twisted to look at her.

Blushing brighter than the red squares in the cloth, she busied herself refolding Cuddy's napkin. "What I meant to say is there was never any fun on the Twisted-R until you showed up." She stole a peek from under her lashes. "Now, we just laugh all the time."

Grinning, he gave an exaggerated tip of his hat. "Glad to be of service, Señorita Rawson. I will happily play the clown for you whenever you wish."

Greta tilted her still-rosy face, nearly blinding him with a smile that revealed tiny dimples he'd never noticed before.

Charmed, Diego stared, forgetting the savory lunch in his lap.

No doubt about it. The time had come for a discussion with John Rawson about his lovely daughter.

CHAPTER 6

Magda stood on her tiptoes to search past the bustling platform for any sign of Bertha then quickly regretted her impulse. The bunion on her left big toe and the bursitis in both knees throbbed a painful reminder that a woman her size ought not to try resisting gravity.

Shading her eyes, she peered along the tracks to the crossroad where Bertha Bloom had best show her irksome behind. . .and soon. The train to take them south was long overdue. Snarling in frustration, she snatched her skirt with both hands, hefted it up, and whirled on the platform. "Where is she, Willem? I sent Nash with the wagon most of an hour ago. They've had enough time to beat us to the station."

Willem arched one brow. "Sending Nash was your first mistake. No one can draw out a simple chore longer."

Magda sniffed. "You've got that right. Still, you'd think Bertha would hurry him along. This was her harebrained scheme. I don't know how she managed to drag me along on this excursion and then persuade you to boot." She curled her top lip. "Cattle of all things. Why can't she learn cattle-raising in Humble? We've got ranchers closer to home than Carrizo Springs, and that's for sure."

Willem latched onto his suspenders and puffed out his chest. "Not ranchers like John Rawson. There's no better man to teach Bertha what she needs to know." A smile plumped his ruddy face.

42

"Besides, this will give John and me a chance to catch up. It's been quite a spell since I saw him last."

Magda gripped his hand. "I do look forward to seeing John again and meeting his family." She shot a careful glance over her shoulder.

Emmy stood behind them, fiddling with a lock of her hair, a vision in her pale rose carriage dress and matching hat.

Most of the men standing nearby stared openly, eyes wide as if reluctant to blink and miss something.

Catching sight of her mama gazing at her, Emmy flashed a tight smile.

Magda returned it before turning her back to her daughter and lowering her voice. "None of this has made Emily easy to live with, I can tell you that."

One corner of Willem's mouth twitched. "What do you mean?"

"I haven't mentioned it, but she doesn't want to go. I've argued this trip with your daughter until I'm ready to yank out my hair."

"Better your hair than mine, Mama."

Magda's heart leaped and she spun. "Emily! How many times have I asked you not to skulk about?"

Emmy flashed her limitless dimples. "Skulking? I merely walked over to join you. Can I help it if I'm quiet?"

Willem frowned. "Don't sass your mama, girl."

Emmy flinched and bit her lip, suddenly interested in the wide bow stretched across one shoe. "Sorry, Papa. Never meant to sass."

The defeated look on Emmy's pale face fired lead at Magda's heart. She patted her daughter's hand. "Of course you didn't mean to sass, sugar."

"Don't take up for her, wife," Willem growled. "I heard what she said." He scowled at Emmy again. "There will be no more willful resistance to this trip. Understood?"

Emmy sighed. "Yes, sir."

Magda winced, watching her radiant daughter's confidence puddle at her feet. She was still beautiful even with the frown lines that sprang up between her brows. The girl came out of the womb the loveliest creature Magda had ever set eyes on. Tiny tufts of down had caressed her melon-round head, so white it disappeared except in sunlight, with darker lashes so long they rested on her chubby cheeks while she slept. A deep red blush colored her tiny puckered mouth, a mouth still plump and protruding, as if frozen in place from so much time pouting. Except when she smiled.

Emmy's smile was so glorious a transformation, it had the power to stop grown men in their tracks and halt the words on their tongues. When she turned up the full power of it, complete with the crinkle and flash of blue eyes, she mesmerized every man in the room.

Magda's gaze swept to Willem, the only exception. He stared at Emmy, red-faced and sulking, his bottom lip mottled and swollen like an ugly growth.

Squeezing his hand, Magda drew him closer. "Never mind, dear. Let's not spoil our holiday. Emmy's in much better spirits today."

Magda marveled at Willem's change toward their daughter in recent years. From the day she'd come into the world, no one had a greater hand in spoiling Emmy than Willem. He'd encouraged her precocious spirit, pulling her onto his lap and roaring with laughter at her outrageous antics.

When had it changed?

Magda lowered her gaze, pushing aside the disturbing notion that wriggled into her mind whenever she asked herself that question. The answering finger of guilt pointed firmly in her direction. She should learn to keep her trap shut about Emmy's escapades.

Her chin jerked up. "Oh, look. There's Nash with Bertha, and just in the nick of time. Here comes our train."

Nash turned the two-seater at the crossroad and rumbled along the narrow lane beside the tracks. He pulled to a stop next to the platform, then leaped to the ground and helped Bertha down.

Emmy hurried over to hug him good-bye.

The two stood whispering together, until Nash's cautious glance caught sight of Willem's scowl. He patted Emmy's hand and stepped away from her, an uncomfortable smile on his face.

Magda surveyed Bertha. "What on earth kept you?"

"Couldn't find a thing to wear. All my new clothes come six inches too long. Didn't know until after I slipped them on."

At the age of twelve, a sudden growth spurt took Bertha Maye Biddie from the height of four foot eight to four foot ten. After that, she simply stopped growing. Lucky for Bertha, Magda grew tall enough to hand most things down to her. Then Thaddeus Bloom wandered into Bertha's life, marrying her and replacing Magda. After he passed to his eternal reward, washed from Bertha's arms by a raging Texas river, Bertha found herself back where she started. . .in a world filled with out-of-reach places.

In other words, all of her dresses came six inches too long. She should be used to it by now.

Stringy strands had escaped Bertha's hairpins as usual, and the hem of her new frock was crooked.

Magda prayed she'd remembered her shoes. "I see you've been doing your own needlework again."

Bertha glanced down at her dress. "Had to."

Magda took her by the shoulders and turned her in a circle, tracking the erratic path of the fat stitches. "You've made a right mess of it, you know."

Bertha bristled and pointed at the rig. "You try sewing a straight line while riding in that contraption."

Arching her brows at Emmy and Willem to be certain she'd heard right—by the stunned looks on their faces, she had—Magda turned to gape at Bertha. "You hemmed your dress without taking it off?"

Bertha blinked up at her. "Couldn't sit there next to Nash in my corset and knickers, could I?"

Emmy hurriedly covered her smile with one hand, and Willem shook his head.

Magda pinched the fabric of Bertha's dress and raised it slightly to see her feet. Bertha slapped away her hand. "Stop that. I'm wearing them."

"Just checking."

The train pulled up beside them in a rush of blustery wind, smoke, and the loud squeal of brakes, ending the conversation. Magda shouted last-minute instructions to Nash then lifted two of the bulging bags, handing one off to her husband. "Come along, Emily. It's time to go."

With a last hurried kiss for Nash's cheek, Emmy gathered her things and swept onto the train, followed by Bertha, who tripped on the bottom step before righting herself and disappearing inside the car, her luggage thumping up the steps behind her.

Taking Willem's arm, Magda recoiled at the bright red circles staining his fleshy face. She groped for his hand and found his fists clenched. His stormy gaze still locked on Nash, Willem helped Magda on board, handing their bags to the white-coated porter who had appeared behind her.

Watching her husband struggle with his anger, the finger of guilt concerning the rift between Emmy and Willem shifted, lifting the load of blame from Magda's shoulders and replacing it with sudden clarity and a fresh new crop of trouble.

∽◈∾

The porter stopped next to a pair of empty seats, motioning with a smile and a nod for Emmy to sit. She groaned. The two wide benches faced each other across a narrow space that barely provided legroom, which meant that for looming endless miles there'd be no escaping Papa's stern glances and constant reprimands. However would she bear it? No doubt she'd arrive at their destination bunched tighter inside than her fists, which were clenched so tightly the tips of her nails stung her palms through the soft leather gloves.

She stole a peek over her shoulder and swallowed hard. Her parents, their mouths drawn like they'd shared a lemon, lumbered through the passenger car behind Aunt Bertha, who chattered wildly to no one in particular.

Wondering what had happened to put the sour looks on their faces, hoping it had nothing whatever to do with her, Emmy settled into a tense wad by the window, leaving plenty of room for Aunt Bertha to spread out beside her.

Mama plodded up and took her place opposite Aunt Bert, storing her parasol and an oversized basket of food beneath the seat.

Unreasonable panic crowded Emmy's throat as Papa settled across from her, a nameless storm brewing on his face. With no forethought, she sprang to her feet and pushed past them into the aisle, her head spinning.

Mama gaped up at her. "What are you doing, Emily? Sit yourself down."

She gripped the back of Aunt Bert's seat for balance. "I won't be a moment. I forgot something." Whirling, she traversed the narrow car, ignoring Papa's bellow—a reckless act of rebellion for which she'd pay dearly.

Praying with all of her might, she brushed past the wide-eyed conductor before he could speak the warning his upraised finger foretold. Nash would be outside waiting for the train to leave. He just had to be.

Eyes sweeping the outer rim of the crowd, she lifted the hem of her garment and helped herself down to the platform. Miraculously, Nash sat atop the wagon right where she'd left him, his expressive brows drawn to the middle of his forehead. Her heart in her throat, Emmy dashed over and clambered up beside him.

He blinked in surprise. "Miss Emmy, what you doing out here? You gon' miss your train."

She clenched her fists under her chin, wincing from the pain of pierced palms against the crush of leather. "I can't go with them, Nash. I simply can't. Please go ask Mama if I can stay here with you."

He slumped on the seat, his voice pitched to a whine. "You know I cain't do no such thing. Your mama's mind is set, not to mention Mr. Willem's. For all your pleadin', you ain't managed to sway 'em none. How you reckon they gon' listen to the likes of me?" He jabbed his finger behind her as if Papa stood there. "Mr. Willem had just as soon fire me on the spot—or worse—if I was to pull off a fool stunt like that." His head swung side to side. "No, chil'. You got to stop asking me for what ain't in my power to give."

Quivering inside, Emmy twined her fingers behind her neck and leaned her head back. "I'm desperate, Nash. I can't see how I'm going to survive a whole month under Papa's thumb."

Nash tugged on her arm until she let go and straightened to face him. His eyes softened to brown puddles of compassion, and he patted her hand. "The good Lord gon' see you through, that's how."

She groaned and fell against the seat. "Very comforting, Nash. Yet another crushing thumb I can't seem to avoid."

The tender pools in his eyes dried up and hardened to flint. "Why you want to say something like that for? Jus' cause you grew up with a stern papa don't mean you got to see God in the same light."

She opened her mouth to defend herself, but Mama's shrill voice turned the words to ash in the back of her throat. "Emily! Get down this instant and come with me."

Emmy was off the rig and standing beside her mama without remembering how she came to be there.

None too gently, Mama took her by the arm. "I don't know what you two are playing at, but just be glad you haven't missed that train.

While you're at it, count your blessings I was able to talk your father into letting me come for you instead of him."

Truth dawned, churning Emmy's insides. Her impulsive act did nothing toward improving the situation. Instead, the threat of a difficult trip had become an impending nightmare. With a last desperate glance at Nash, and with the conductor's final call to board ringing in her ears, Emmy allowed Mama to herd her onto the platform.

There was no hiding. She would step onto the train, face her papa, and reap what she'd sown in her haste.

CHAPTER 7

Isi pushed back his plate and stood. "Thank you, Mother. Muy *bueno*, as usual."

Heart swelling, Melatha beamed. "I'm happy you liked it." She left her own eggs and *frijoles* and rushed to the woodstove where tortillas warmed in a plate. Lifting two of the steaming rounds of corn, she spread mashed beans in a circle. With a square of braided rags, she hoisted the lid from her cast iron roasting pan and tore off chunks of crisp, golden hen, rolling them up in the slathered bread.

"Wait, son. You have a long day ahead. Let me wrap these for you to take with you."

Frowning, he hooked his thumbs in the top of his trousers. "You really think I need that?" He chuckled and tugged on his waistband. "I've just eaten enough for two grown men. Thanks to your good cooking, I'm about out of notches in my belt."

She tucked the cloth-wrapped bundle into his rabbit-skin knapsack and slung it over his shoulder. "A woman likes a sturdy man, Isi."

He lifted his brow. "Oh? And which woman are you fattening me up for?"

Melatha chose not to answer. Instead, she took his arm and walked him outside to the porch. Best to let him wait and see for himself.

With disgruntled squawks and a flurry of beating wings, her chickens announced an approaching visitor. John Rawson rounded

49

the bunkhouse and rode straight for them, scattering the frantic fowl in ten directions. He came so close to the steps before reining his horse, Melatha feared the big Appaloosa might stumble and throw him, obliging her to catch the overgrown man in her apron.

His urgent arrival stirred no fear in her heart. The man always scurried about in a frenzy. Though she feared for his health, she greatly admired his vigor.

Isi crossed to lay his hand on the animal's trembling shoulder. "Morning, sir. Care for a bite of breakfast?"

Mr. Rawson patted his bulging middle. "Thank you kindly, but Rosita and the girls fixed me up real good this morning." He nodded at Melatha. "Don't reckon it compares in flavor to your spread, ma'am, but it got the job done."

Isi winked at her. "See? I told you. Your cooking is legendary."

Melatha's face warmed. "Oh, you. . ." Uncomfortable with the attention, she nodded at his boss. "I'm certain Mr. Rawson didn't ride out here to listen to fables."

Mr. Rawson nodded. "Your mother's half right, son. While I'm certain your boasts about her skillet are true, I've come to entrust you with an errand. A very important task."

Isi bowed slightly. "I'm at your disposal. Whatever you need, sir."

A few more straggling chickens scurried past, running from Cuddy, who trotted toward them from the side yard. Stopping at the rail, he rested the sole of one dusty boot on the edge of the porch and brushed the soil and stickers from his bull-hide chaps.

Isi nodded and smiled at him.

Cuddy returned the gestures then tipped his hat at Melatha. "Mornin', ma'am."

"Morning, Cuddy. Would you like some eggs and tortillas? Isi finished the frijoles, but I have a roasted hen warming."

He grimaced. "Sounds right nice, but I believe I'll pass." He swiped his forehead with the sleeve of his white cotton shirt. "Working in this heat takes a man's appetite."

Melatha couldn't help wondering if his recent hankering for hard liquor was the real reason. Concerned, Isi had mentioned it and asked her to pray.

"Not every man." She laughed and pointed at Isi and Mr. Rawson. "Those two pushed away from the table with full bellies."

Cuddy cut around the porch and came to stand beside Isi. Watching Mr. Rawson pay no heed to his son's presence, Melatha's insides squirmed. She released her breath when at last he dipped his head at young Cuddy.

"Our guests are arriving tomorrow. I want you boys to meet them at the station in Uvalde and bring them here. Cuddy, rig up the two-seater. Diego will follow with your horses. After they join you, Mr. Dane can take over the reins and drive his family to the ranch. You'll be their escorts."

He leaned to rest his arm on the saddle horn then regarded them each in turn, his heavy brows flattened over squinty eyes. "You two make sure that family has a safe, uneventful trip. I'll expect to see them pull up in good spirits and in good condition."

Isi squared his shoulders. "You can count on us, sir."

If the warning on Mr. Rawson's face rattled Isi, he hid it well. Melatha's chest swelled with pride.

Casting a pointed look in her direction, the big man lowered his voice, though she heard every word. "Take your rifles. I don't expect any trouble from *banditos*, but Pancho Villa yet rides free. If you ran across him, I doubt he'd wait to hear where your loyalties lie."

Always mindful of her feelings, Isi shot a worried glance over his shoulder before speaking, his voice overly bright. "I doubt we'll have the pleasure of such an encounter. They say he stays mostly to the mountain regions, busy running from the law."

Mr. Rawson straightened in the saddle. "Nevertheless, be cautious. Villa has his share of admirers, young copycats eager to prove their manhood by acting the fool." He shoved his broad-brimmed hat to the back of his head. "It's been some years since I've seen Willem Dane. I don't want an unfortunate mishap cheating us out of a reunion."

An eager smile on his face, Cuddy gave his father a soldier's salute. "Like Diego said, you can count on us."

Mr. Rawson pulled back on the Appaloosa, tapping its sides with his heels. "That's the problem. I am counting on you, Cuddy." He nudged the horse around and scowled at his son. "Don't let me down."

Cuddy's gaze followed his father's broad back until the horse cantered out of sight. A mix of emotions played across his face, from an angry scowl to heavy lids lowered in shame. As he raised his eyes, they burned with a longing so deep Melatha's heart ached for him.

Isi closed the distance between them and wrapped his long arm around his friend's neck. "Wake up, amigo. We got us a ride to make."

Visibly shaking off his father's disappointment, Cuddy grinned. "You bet, brother. I'll go hitch the wagon." He wriggled loose from Isi and bounded down the steps toward the barn.

Isi moaned and dashed his hat on the rail. "Blast it, Mother! How can a man as kind as John Rawson be so cruel when it counts the most?"

Melatha squeezed his rigid shoulder. "There are many ways to be blind, my son. Mr. Rawson suffers the most crippling loss of vision." She turned Isi to face her, using his rumpled collar for an excuse to gather all the comfort she could muster into her nimble fingers and press it into his neck. "Just pray he regains his sight where our Cuddy is concerned, before one of them stumbles and falls."

∽∾

Emmy lowered her book a smidgen and stole a peek at her papa.

It had taken miles of clattering track for the last bit of color in his cheeks to subside. After sputtering threats and frightening promises, using admirable restraint to hold his volume in check, he'd settled against the seat in a grown man's version of a pout.

Emmy had taken refuge behind her copy of *Little Women*. At first, the story proved a convenient place to hide, but she soon became lost in the characters' lives, due in part to a revelation about her own nature revealed within the pages.

Emmy's temperament too closely matched that of headstrong, outspoken Jo. Like Jo, Emmy's problems sprang from a tongue that was often too quick and too sharp and a mind that seldom engaged before she took action. Jo's sister, the gentle, eager-to-please Beth, behaved more like kindhearted, forgiving Charity Bloom. It was as if Charity and Emmy were Louisa May Alcott's characters in the flesh.

Emmy's heart sank as Charity's pretty face swam in her head. How different she would feel if the southbound railcar on which she traveled was headed north instead, carrying her to St. Louis to spend time with Charity and her new baby.

Sighing, she laid the novel in her lap and leaned toward the window to peer out at the rushing countryside. The rolling hills to the west had given way to flatland as far as the eye could see.

They'd left the station in San Antonio some time ago. The stretch of her legs she'd enjoyed there hadn't been enough to ease the kinks from her bones. When she first heard of it, Emmy had dreaded the upcoming fifty-mile trek by wagon the most. Now, after hours spent sitting on the train, she couldn't wait to get it started. The distance from Houston to San Antonio wasn't the reason the train had trapped them for so long. Rather, it was the lingering stops at countless dingy, uninteresting depots along the route.

Emmy's back ached, not to mention an unmentionable part of her anatomy that had fallen soundly asleep. A mite jealous of the serene expression on her mama's face, Emmy longed for a little extra padding on her posterior region.

Sporting far less cushion than Emmy, tiny Aunt Bertha squirmed on the seat and moaned then pressed her nose to the glass. "Ain't we there yet, Willem?"

Before Papa had time to answer, the conductor appeared at the back of the car to announce Uvalde as the next stop.

Mama grinned at Aunt Bert from across the way. "Ask and ye shall receive, sugar."

"Well, it's a blessing my sore bottom's grateful for," Aunt Bertha announced, and none too discreetly.

Emmy stifled a laugh when Papa's mouth flew open. His head jerked around to nod and grimace at nearby passengers, most looking as scandalized as he did.

Evidently mentioning unmentionable parts in public didn't bother Aunt Bertha one bit. Considering his wife had been friends with the feisty, outspoken woman for going on forty years, one would think Papa would be used to her by now.

The train lurched to a stop with a squeal of brakes. The excited travelers, likely as stiff and sore as Emmy, shuffled into the aisle muttering their relief. Unaware of the stir she'd caused, Aunt Bert squatted to gather her luggage from beneath the seat. Standing, she hoisted the heavy bags and motioned with her head. "Let's go. Ain't none of these folks waiting for us."

Papa followed her with Mama close on his heels.

Grateful to escape the rolling prison, Emmy filed into the slow-moving line, clutching Mama's sleeve to maintain her balance. After so much time spent wobbling and rocking along the tracks, she felt a little dizzy now that the train was still. The crush of people around her made her breathless, and the odor of unwashed bodies in such close quarters pitched her queasy stomach.

Mama glanced over her shoulder. "You all right, baby?"

She nodded, but sweat beaded her top lip and her hands felt clammy.

When had it gotten so hot?

Unconvinced by her answer, Mama stepped aside and pulled Emmy between her and Papa. "We'll be off this contraption in a minute, sugar. You'll feel better after you get a breath of fresh air."

❧

"Do you see 'em, old pal?" Cuddy lumbered to his feet, dipping and swaying as he fought to stay upright.

Diego reached a steadying hand and braced Cuddy against the wagon bed. "Not yet, but I reckon when people actually start coming off the train, it'll be easier to catch sight of them."

His heart aching, Diego studied Cuddy's glassy eyes and unsteady stance, realizing there was no way under heaven to hide his drunkenness from Mr. Rawson's guests. If they complained to their host about Cuddy's sloppy state, it would seal his fate.

Diego had first smelled the liquor on his breath when they were saddling up at their campsite that morning and warned Cuddy to lay off the booze. Nearly to town, Diego caught him turning up a silver flask. Furious, he climbed aboard the rig and forcibly removed it, but by then the damage was done. When Cuddy wasn't looking, he stashed the troublesome container inside the jockey box under the driver's seat.

Cuddy pointed. "Eyes front. There they are."

Diego's gaze followed his wobbly finger. "How do you know it's the Danes?"

"Look at 'em. Three old geezers and a little gal." Cuddy released a whiskey-scented breath in a long, slow whistle, staring with eyes as hungry as a stray dog at the kitchen door.

A jolt shocked Diego's middle. As the party drew closer, the first muddled impression of perfection sharpened to rows of corn-silk curls beneath a jaunty hat, a blush-colored dress that couldn't begin to hide a lithe, perfect figure, and lips the same rosy color, stuck out like a petulant child's.

Lips that begged to be kissed.

"Ain't she something?" whispered Cuddy.

Diego tried to answer, but a lack of saliva had glued his tongue to the roof of his mouth—unlike Cuddy, who swiped drool from his face with his sleeve.

No doubt, she was the prettiest woman Diego had ever seen, but it wasn't just her beauty. Greta was pretty. This girl carried herself like a stallion, fierce and proud, yet her eyes were wide and cautious, like a doe protecting her young.

She followed her three companions across the platform, heading his direction. As she neared, Diego's chest tightened. When they came to a stop in front of the wagon, her roaming blue eyes locked on his, and he sucked air like a drowning man—a condition very difficult to hide. The effort rendered him speechless.

Luckily, Cuddy, who now seemed as sober as a preacher, stepped forward and offered his hand. "You folks must be the Danes."

The older gentleman latched onto his palm and gave it a hearty shake. "That we are. I'm Willem. You must be John Rawson's son."

"Guilty as charged, sir." Nodding at the women, Cuddy lifted his Stetson and pressed it to his chest, using the other hand to run his fingers through his hair. "Welcome to South Texas, ladies."

He tugged on Diego's sleeve, pulling him closer. "This here is Diego Marcelo, our foreman. We've come to escort you out to the Twisted-R Ranch."

A sizable woman with hair the color of coffee beans returned his nod. "Thank you kindly, son. I'm Magdalena Dane." She motioned to the slip of a woman at her side. "Allow me to present Mrs. Bertha Maye Bloom of Humble."

The smaller woman, spry as a barn swallow, bobbed her head like one, and then Mrs. Dane turned to the vision in pink. "This is our daughter, Miss Emily Dane."

The girl offered Cuddy her hand.

He bowed slightly and kissed it.

Diego's hat came off fast when she turned his way. He wet his lips and opened his mouth to speak, not certain any sound would come out. "Miss Dane. I'm honored to make your acquaintance."

"Thank you, Mr. Marcelo. I. . .I'm. . ." The glow of color drained from her face.

Mrs. Dane clutched her daughter's arm. "Emmy, are you all right?"

She nodded. "Fine. I just. . ."

She didn't look fine. She looked green.

Diego stepped forward. "Perhaps the lady could use a glass of cool water? This part of Texas can be hard on a person unaccustomed to the heat."

Swaying toward him, she blinked once before bending over and depositing her lunch in his hat.

CHAPTER 8

Once they left the depot in Uvalde, the scenery shifted and changed like the slow turns of a kaleidoscope. Instead of the miles of desert sand Emmy had expected, acres of waist-high grass covered the landscape, set off by an occasional grove of trees.

Farther along, after crossing the Nueces River, it changed even more. The grass alongside the road grew as high as the rider's stirrups in some places then disappeared in others, choked out by rocks, sand, and brush. Live oak trees lined up next to sapling elms along the riverbank. Wide vistas of patchy grass mixed with scattered scrub brush and squatty trees that sported a tangle of wiry branches. Cacti dotted the landscape, lone sentinels, their fat green arms laden with purple fruit.

This piqued Emmy's interest so much she couldn't sit quietly another second. Scooting to the edge of her seat, she waved her hankie at them. "Look, Mama. What are those lovely bulbs on that cactus? I've never seen anything like them."

Beside her, Aunt Bertha laughed. "That's because you ain't never seen any cactuses, child. Maybe the little ones in pots, but nothing like these beauties."

Papa, who seemed in much better spirits, leaned around Mama for a better look. "Those are cactus pears. Very juicy and sweet on the palate, once you get past the spines, which I understand is very hard to do."

"You mean you can eat them things?" Aunt Bertha's voice was shrill with wonder.

"Yes, you can, Bertha." Papa actually smiled. "According to John, they're regular fare on the Rawsons' table in season."

Mama twisted on the seat, her lips pinched. "No more questions, Emily. You need to sit back and rest."

Emmy's face warmed. "I'm feeling much better."

Mama smiled grimly. "I'm relieved to hear it." She turned to the front, muttering that it wouldn't be much help to Mr. Marcelo's hat.

The heat increased in Emmy's cheeks. The handsome young man rode a short distance in front of the wagon, squinting against the sun. He had pulled the red bandanna from around his neck and twisted it into a rope that he tied around his head. Still, the wind whipped his long curly hair in his face. Guilt squeezed her heart that he battled with the elements while she sat sheltered beneath the canopy of the two-seater.

They made camp at dusk, their two hosts graciously tending their every need, and were up and back on the trail as the sun peeked over the horizon. Emmy could hardly believe it when Papa grunted then nodded at the acres of plowed rows along the road. "We're getting closer now."

Mama shot him a quizzical glance. "How can you tell?"

"We're beginning to see tilled ground. Carrizo Springs is rich in farmland."

Frowning, Emmy voiced her confusion. "How can that be? I thought the south would be barren and desolate."

He shook his head. "Not these parts. The fields are watered by spring-fed creeks."

Aunt Bertha stretched closer to Papa. "What kind of creeks did you say, Willem?"

"Spring-fed. The area sits atop underground fountains called artesian wells. They bubble to the surface and create ready sources of fresh water." He shrugged. "That's not to say it's all lush and green. The ground is still dry in most places."

As if to vouch for his word, the wind bore down and snatched up a puff of sand. Invisible fingers fashioned a whirligig that danced across the open plain.

"Look!" Emmy cried. "Have you ever seen a dust devil so big?"

Grinning, Aunt Bert watched it wend its way toward them until it collapsed ten feet shy of the wagon in a shower of sand. "Will you look at that?" she hooted.

Emmy smiled. "I've never seen anything like this country. Lush here, desolate there. I guess it can't decide what sort of terrain it ought to be."

Mama and Papa laughed, and to her surprise, Emmy joined them. She had determined to despise South Texas, expected to have a miserable ride to the ranch, yet against her will the rugged charm of the land had worked its way under her skin and softened her resolve. Instead of enduring the long journey, the miles and hours swept by unnoticed.

She pointed at a staggered line of brush. "What are those curious spiny bushes?"

Her papa shook his head. "I can't answer that one. Perhaps one of our escorts can shed some light."

To her dismay, he put two fingers in his mouth and whistled. Both men's heads whipped around.

"My daughter has a question, gentlemen."

Since the dark-skinned fellow was closer, the one named Cuddy grinned and waved him over.

Emmy couldn't recall his name from their introduction because her head had started to whirl. She only remembered hair the color of raw sugar on his forehead and matching brown eyes—knowing, thoughtful eyes that must have witnessed things Emmy would never see. Yet the last expression she'd seen in their depths as she bowed her head to be sick was one of startled amazement. Luckily, she got a good glimpse because she didn't dare look at them again.

He angled his horse up beside them. "What can I do for you, miss?"

His voice, as rich as Christmas pudding, drew Emmy's attention to his mouth against her will. When he made an unconscious move to take off his hat—which wasn't there, thanks to her—the gesture broke the spell. Emmy dropped her gaze to her clenched fists.

Thankfully, Papa came to her rescue. "She's asking the name of that scrub brush yonder."

"Those old, straggly trees? Miss Emily, those are mesquite."

So he remembered her name. But then he would. After ruining

his hat, he'd likely never forget.

"Mesquite grows like a house afire and provides a nice habitat for the wildlife," he continued. "Cattle eat the beans when grass is scarce. Many people use them for food, too, as well as medicine."

Aunt Bertha flipped up the brim of her bonnet and gawked at Diego in disbelief. Slapping her leg, she laughed. "Young man, I swallowed that part about picking fruit off a cactus, but don't try to tell me folks around these parts eat trees."

He laughed softly. "Only the beans, Mrs. Bloom. Wood from the larger trees makes good shelter and beautiful furniture. But most mesquite that size grows across the Rio Grande." He shaded his eyes and stared, as if he could see the river. "It also fuels a fine cooking fire. Gives smoked meat a wonderful flavor."

Diego directed the last part to Emmy, so she raised her head and nodded to be polite. His warm smile flashed teeth so white against his bronzed skin it took her breath and delivered absolution to her repentant heart. She couldn't remember ever seeing so handsome a face. Even the no-account scoundrel from her past couldn't compare to this man, and she'd always thought Daniel Clark the best-looking man she'd ever met. . .until now.

Up ahead, lanky, towheaded Cuddy reined in his horse and turned in the saddle. "Hey, Diego!" He pointed toward a distant cloud of dust. The tension in his voice drew Emmy's attention. "Riders. Heading our way."

Diego. So that's his name.

Papa sat forward on the seat as Cuddy wheeled his horse and rode to meet them. "Can you tell who it is, young man?"

Cuddy shook his head. "Not from this distance, but they're closing fast."

"Maybe it's your father coming to greet us? Or someone sent by him?"

"No, sir, that's not Father's mount," he said grimly. "Besides, he sent us to greet you."

Mama gasped when Cuddy unsheathed his rifle and Diego slid a handgun from his boot.

Looking helpless, Papa frowned up at them. "So you expect trouble then? Banditos?"

Cuddy chewed his bottom lip before he answered. "Could be. I guess we're about to find out."

Papa spun toward Diego. "Do you have extra firepower? I'm a fair shot."

Aunt Bert stood up in the wagon. "I can blast a buzzard off a carcass from a hundred yards."

Diego sat straighter on his horse, his pleasing mouth a firm line. "We appreciate the offer, Mr. Dane." He nodded at Aunt Bert. "You, too, ma'am." His watchful eyes remained pinned on the horizon. "But you can be most helpful by sitting down and staying low."

Pulling his attention from the intruders, his comforting gaze settled on Emmy. "Don't you fret, miss. We're prepared to defend you with our lives."

His assurance made her feel better, but she prayed it wouldn't come to that.

Diego tipped his chin at Cuddy. "Let's ride out to meet them, draw them away from the wagon. No need to advertise all the luggage."

He pulled a shotgun from his scabbard and handed it down to Papa. "Keep the rig moving south toward the ranch while we stall them. You're almost there. If anything goes wrong, push this wagon as if the devil were chasing you." He gathered the reins, jutting his chin toward the horizon. "Don't worry about us. We'll catch up." Pausing, he nodded at the gun. "And don't be afraid to use that."

Papa patted the barrel. "If necessary, I'll find a use for it."

Diego tapped his horse's side with his heel and trotted toward the band of four men, closer now than Aunt Bertha's buzzard.

Cuddy followed, his rifle braced across his saddle.

Papa shook the leads and the wagon jerked into motion.

No one made a sound, save that of heavy breathing. Their rapid, shuddering pants reached Emmy's ears despite the creak of the wheels and the pounding of her heart. She had no desire to die that day but, oddly, didn't fear for herself. Her muddled thoughts centered on the safety of the winsome young escort who vowed his life to protect her.

Tension crackled in the air. Papa sat so stiffly on the seat Emmy feared his spine would snap. Mama mopped beads of sweat from her top lip with one hand and worried a tear in the brown leather seat with the other. Beside her, Aunt Bertha's jaw worked in circles, emitting the sound of grinding teeth.

"Watch them, ladies," Papa said. "If they so much as flinch, I'll lay the whip to the horse's back." Even as he issued the command, his head swiveled around three times to look for himself.

All eyes were fixed on the huddle of swarthy men in the distance. Emmy felt fixed in place, as if fear had melded the joints and sinews of her body into stone.

A sudden shout echoed across the plain. Papa's head jerked around and Emmy's legs tensed. She didn't understand the strangely beautiful words, but the tone translated into anger. Papa reached for the whip, and a whispered prayer sprang from Aunt Bertha's lips.

Then Cuddy let out a peal of raucous laughter.

Emmy's gaze flitted to Papa, hoping the laughter meant they wouldn't be scrambling for their lives. He released his breath in a rush and his rigid body slumped with relief. Warmth flooded Emmy's chest, leaving her legs limp and her arms useless sticks in her lap.

"It's all right, sugar. Everything's going to be fine," Aunt Bertha said, though her hand trembled as she patted Emmy's leg.

Papa called, "Whoa," to the team when the horsemen turned their mounts and headed toward them with Diego in the lead. Behind him rode a squat, older man even browner than Diego, with a long, heavy mustache. He rode alongside a slightly younger version of himself in similar clothes. Two men, closer in age to Diego, followed, with Cuddy bringing up the rear.

One of the straggling riders appeared to be the object of a joke. He suffered much teasing from the rest, especially Cuddy. They were all laughing or smiling, except the old man. As he reached the wagon, ridges in his forehead resembled a washboard, and his mustache sagged. Flashing eyes, so dark they appeared black, crinkled into sunburst patterns at the corners.

All of them wore big, peculiar hats sporting wide brims and tall crowns. Cuddy's companion took his off and swiped at him. "Laugh hearty, foolish *gringo*. I know what I saw." Catching sight of Emmy, he clutched the hat to his chest. "But what is this I see?"

He bowed from atop his horse, first at Papa, though he had to force his dark eyes to switch, then at Mama and Aunt Bert. "*Buenos días*, señores. Señoras."

Bowing lower, his gaze swung to Emmy. "Good afternoon, señorita."

They dismounted as Papa climbed down and held out his hand.

"Willem Dane at your service. This is my good wife, Magdalena, her companion, Bertha Bloom, and my daughter, Emily," he said, pointing at each of them in turn. "Happy to make your acquaintances."

Diego, his accent thicker in the company of the men, made introductions all around. Señor Boteo, elder brother to Narcisso, the man who resembled him, father to Francisco, and uncle to Rico, proved to be the link connecting the family. With the old fellow still scowling and the others still snickering, it took no time for the yarn to surface.

"Please to pardon these simpering pups, Señor Dane. They seek to make sport of my son"—he regarded Cuddy over his shoulder, one expressive brow climbing toward his hatband—"when they would do well to sober and heed his warning."

Grinning, Cuddy gripped Francisco's shoulder. "Sober? I doubt you were any too sober when you chased that old bloodsucker off your goat."

The old man made the sign of the cross. "It is unwise to jest about it, son. The stories of *el chupa sangre* are quite real. He has wandered this land for generations, feeding on our livestock, and in rare cases, our people."

Papa stepped closer, his brows meeting in the middle. "Señor Boteo, just what is this creature?"

The old man raised his chin, regarding Papa with intelligent eyes. "An animal not of this earth, señor. A fiend that walks on four legs or two as the mood strikes him. The size of a small bear with spines from his neck to the end of a tail that drags the ground. He has the face and hands of a man, though his eyes are very large and his fingers heavy with thick claws. He doesn't kill with his hands, however, but with two long fangs. With them, he slits the throat of his victim and drains it of blood with his mouth, wasting not a drop. He attacks under cover of night, and his eyes glow like burning embers while he feeds. When the herders or wranglers awaken, they find their animals shriveled on the ground like empty wineskins."

Mama sucked in her breath and he swung her way.

"I beg your pardon, señora." He tipped his hat. "I don't wish to frighten you, but the bloodsucker is quite real as my son can now bear witness. It's rash and dangerous to believe otherwise."

He turned and twirled his leather quirt in the air as if rounding up the men. "Let us be off, and let no more be said about it. We've upset the women enough."

With a shake of his head, Señor Boteo passed the still grinning Cuddy. Stopping in front of Diego, he peered up at him. "Keep your eyes open, son. We'll set a night watch over our flock. I suggest you do the same with your cattle." He held up one finger. "Be vigilant. Never underestimate el chupa sangre. He is swift and smart, and he's avoided capture for centuries."

Diego nodded soberly. "Good advice, señor. If he comes on the Twisted-R, we'll be ready."

Cuddy snorted. "You'll be ready. I'll be snug in my bed. You won't catch me lurking in a pasture all night because a mangy coyote killed a goat."

Jerking his head at Diego, he climbed on his horse and reined it past the rig. "Let's get going, now. The old man will be worried about the Danes. I don't need to wind up on the bad side of a conniption."

As Cuddy rode away, Diego ducked his head and mumbled in Spanish to Señor Boteo. The old gentleman patted him on the back. "Don't trouble yourself, Diego. I overlook him now because he's young, though Cuddy's papa would do well to spend more time on that boy's manners." He led his stout mare around and swung into the saddle.

"*Adios*, amigo," he called cheerfully to Diego and then tipped his hat. "Ladies. . .Señor Dane. . .very honored to meet you." He whistled for his family to follow, and they rode off, leaving swirling clouds of dust in their wake.

Up ahead, Cuddy stood in his stirrups and motioned impatiently with his hat.

Diego mounted his horse and nodded at Papa. "Are we ready, sir?"

Papa unwound the reins from the brake. "As ready as we're going to get, son."

Diego and Cuddy traveled apart for the rest of the way, not side by side, laughing and exchanging good-natured teasing as they had before. For some reason it made Emmy sad.

"We're just about there," Papa announced.

Mama shaded her sensitive eyes and squinted up at him. "Are you certain, Willem? I've had my fill of this wagon."

Papa nodded. "This old horse has ceased his plodding and picked up the pace pretty good. That's a sure sign we're nearing his stall."

"Nice try, Willem," Aunt Bertha muttered, "but I reckon your insight has more to do with that great big house sitting yonder."

Emmy leaned to peer between her parents. Sure enough, a building loomed beyond the sprinkling of misshapen scrub trees Diego had called mesquite. They pulled past the gate under a large scrollwork sign that read Bienvenidos al Rancho R Torcido.

Mama attempted to pronounce the words, craning her neck as they passed beneath until she was nearly in Aunt Bertha's lap. She nudged Papa. "What's it mean, dear?"

He repeated the phrase under his breath then shook his head. "I don't read much Spanish, Magda."

Diego pulled his horse even with the wagon. "It says 'Welcome,' Mrs. Dane, 'to the Twisted-R Ranch.' "

"I sec." Mama chuckled. "Well, that makes perfect sense, now don't it?"

A large powder gray creature with big eyes stared from behind a barbed wire fence. He locked gazes with Aunt Bertha as they rode past as if he hadn't witnessed anything quite like her.

Aunt Bert stared back with the same expression. "Will you look at that critter? He looks like a cow that's had his parts took off and put back cockeyed." She lowered her voice to a whisper. "You don't reckon it's one of them bloodsuckers?"

Papa stifled a grin. "It's a bull, Bertha. A Brahman to be exact."

"That don't look like no bull I ever seen. Look at his sad face and droopy ears. Why, his skin hangs slack as a bloodhound's." She pointed wildly. "Land sakes! He's sportin' a hump on his back! You sure he ain't a camel, Willem?"

Papa laughed. "The Brahman's a rare breed from India. Not many exist here in the States. John bought a couple from the King Ranch to start up a breeding program. From the looks of that big fellow, he has succeeded."

The lane stretched for some distance in a line as straight as an arrow from the gate to the front of a large house. They came to a stop when the lane did, and Emmy stared toward the two-story structure fashioned from plastered stone blocks. Posts jutted at intervals from the top beneath a roof as flat as a fritter. Spacious balconies jutted from the upstairs windows where sheer white curtains billowed in the breeze. A covered patio larger than the living area of their home in Humble extended off the side, and a broad door cut from striking, red-streaked wood adorned the portico, opening onto a roomy porch. Two wide steps led down to the ground.

A tiny barking dog pulled Emmy's attention beyond a nearby fence to a field where he chased an orange cat of impressive size to the edge of a pecan orchard then up a tree. The little brown dog danced around the trunk before planting his paws on it, yapping as if to say he was far too busy to entertain such shenanigans. Emmy grinned and spun on the seat to show her mama. Startled, she drew back, clutching her collar.

One of the largest men she'd ever seen, besides Nash, beamed up at them from the ground. He took off his hat and bowed his head. "Welcome, folks! John Holdsworth Rawson at your service."

CHAPTER 9

Diego's chest swelled with pride as the big man approached the wagon to greet his guests. Barrel-chested and broad-shouldered, he cut a fine figure for a man his age.

Born in Europe, Mr. Rawson liked to say he got to Carrizo Springs as fast as he could. At the age of twenty, he'd stepped off the boat in New York Harbor without a backward glance at his mother country. He bragged about doffing his top hat at Lady Liberty then laying it aside along with his frock coat in exchange for a Stetson hat, suspenders, and chaps. In the winter, he added a fringed coat like those worn by his heroes, Teddy Roosevelt and his band of Rough Riders.

He'd laid aside his accent as well, for the most part. Unlike Mrs. Rawson, whose lilting voice flowed like the strains of a haunting melody.

Diego dismounted, his mind fixed on lending a hand to young Miss Dane, but Cuddy beat him to the draw. He stood smiling up at her, one arm held out for her to grip and the other hand hovering near her waist.

Distracted by them, he almost didn't catch Mrs. Bloom when she tripped. By the time he steadied her, the family had reached Mr. Rawson. After hearty handshakes between the men, Mr. Rawson took the Dane women's arms and escorted them to the porch.

A quick glance told Diego his boss had ordered more work done on the ranch in their absence. Someone had swept the ever-present sand from the brick-paved veranda and washed the gray dust from the house and outbuildings, allowing the adobe to gleam in the sun—nearly as bright as Mrs. Rawson's smile, but nowhere close to the spark of pride in her husband's eyes as his arm encircled her waist.

"May I present my dear wife, Katherine Eliza Colbeck Rawson, of the Halifax Colbecks?"

The mistress of the Twisted-R Ranch looked awfully pretty. She'd pinned most of her blond hair on the top of her head, except for one long braid pulled over the shoulder of her new blue dress. She'd done whatever women do to make their waistlines disappear, and the delicate leather shoes peeking from under her hem were definitely not work boots.

Mrs. Rawson smiled. "You'll have to forgive my husband. He hasn't yet embraced the relaxed charm of our adopted country. He behaves as if we're still on the banks of the Ryburn." She held out her hand. "Please, call me Kate."

The elder Dane woman accepted her handclasp. "Magdalena. But you can call me Magda. Willem's spoken quite highly of you, Kate." She took her daughter's arm and pulled her forward. "This is our Emily."

Mrs. Rawson took both the girl's hands. "Hello, Emily. Gracious, how lovely you are."

Emily bowed her head.

With a flourish, Mrs. Dane presented the small woman. "And this is my dearest friend, Bertha Bloom."

"Hello, Bertha. I'm honored to meet each of you. We're so happy you've come. During your stay you must promise to consider this your home."

Mr. Rawson motioned to Cuddy. "Of course you met our boy, Cuthbert."

Cuddy cleared his throat and tipped his hat at Mrs. Dane. "Let's stick with Cuddy, ma'am."

His father frowned. "I've told you before, don't be embarrassed by your name, son. It was good enough for my old papa."

If she was trying to ease his discomfort, Cuddy's mother only made things worse. "Cuthbert is a delightful Old English name." She preened and winked at Mrs. Dane. "It means bright champion, you know." She patted Cuddy's face. "The perfect moniker for you, dear."

A rush of color flooded Cuddy's cheeks. He shot a glance at Emily Dane and so did Diego. Cuddy could relax. The girl seemed oblivious to his humiliation, and in fact to the whole conversation.

She stood with her hands laced behind her back, her chin lifted. The glow of the setting sun had turned her hair and skin the color of crushed peaches. A look of wonder lit her face as she peered around at the grounds.

"And this is our daughter, Greta."

For the first time, Diego noticed Greta standing in the shadows of the portico. At her father's mention, she stepped into the light and curtsied. Having just pulled his gaze from Miss Dane's thick mound of white curls and full ruby lips, Greta's blond hair appeared wispy and dirty by comparison, her lips thin and pinched. Was it only the day before when he found her so attractive?

Feeling guilty but unable to stop, he cut his eyes back to Miss Dane for one more assessment. His breath caught as she lowered her gaze to a goosefoot plant at her feet. Her lowered lashes gave her big eyes a pleasing, drowsy appeal until she raised them and caught him staring. The sleepy look melted into a sweet smile.

The tiny dimples he'd discovered hiding near the outer corners of Greta's mouth were no match for the deep impressions in Miss Dane's cheeks, clearly visible from a distance. He remembered seeing a hint of them even when her expression was sober. Those dimples defied description, as did her smile. Held in its grip, Diego stood rooted to the spot until she lowered her gaze and released him.

Mr. Rawson loudly cleared his throat.

Diego glanced around to find all eyes fixed on him, including his mother's, who had appeared on the side of the house. Her eyes darted over to Miss Dane, wide and wary as if she'd seen a band of restless spirits.

His boss gave an uneasy laugh. "As I was saying, Diego here is our top hand. Couldn't run the place without this boy. . .when his head's not in the clouds, that is."

The rush of warmth to Diego's face surely put Cuddy's blush to shame. He wondered what sort of doe-eyed fool he'd looked gawking across the yard all slack-jawed with his tongue hanging out. Anger followed his embarrassment when no one seemed ready to find something else to look at. Especially Greta, who stood spellbound watching him. Diego's eyes sought hers, but she turned away.

Mr. Rawson's booming voice broke the silence. "Well, don't just stand there, son. You and Diego unload their bags." He spun on his heel and held out wide, welcoming arms to his guests. "So, who's hungry? Kate and the girls have been in that kitchen for days, stirring savory-smelling dishes. Let's go see what they've cooked up."

Mrs. Dane took Mrs. Rawson's offered arm. "I hope you haven't gone to too much trouble on our account."

Her hostess patted her hand. "Nonsense. We love to entertain. Lord knows, we don't often get the opportunity living so far out. Besides, John prepared most of the meat. There's a plump hog roasting on the spit as we speak."

Cuddy passed Diego, stopping just behind him to speak low in his ear. "Don't waste your time staring, big brother. I saw that little filly first, so she's burned with my brand." He shifted closer. "The old man deems me second place in running this ranch, but even he knows I'm good at what I do best."

Diego snorted. "Drunk again, I see."

Cuddy didn't answer, so Diego looked behind him. Shoulders shaking with laughter, the cantankerous boy strolled toward the rig to unload the Danes' luggage.

Diego drew in deeply of the dry, dusty air, picking up the scent of John Rawson's fire pit. Though he loved Cuddy like a brother, at the moment he wouldn't mind seeing him lashed to the spit, spinning alongside the roasting pig.

~~∞~~

"Not this one, Chihowa Palami! A lively spirit, yes, but not this un-broken spawn of a cougar. Not this cat with hungry, searching eyes."

Melatha watched as her vision-come-to-life stood apart from the others the way a buck kept his distance from the herd. The girl sized up her surroundings, especially Isi, like a panther before the kill. Her claws unsheathed each time she felt his eyes on her, and she felt them, no mistake about it. She fooled Isi with her slant-eyed glances—drinking him down in great gulps to quench her thirst—but she couldn't fool Melatha.

There was no denying the white curls or her cool, sky blue gaze. Yet how could a girl like this be God's will for her son? Impossible!

Melatha had witnessed disaster when forces of nature collided. Fire struck the ground, splitting trees and burning forests. Dark, swirling whirlwinds thundered from the clouds, uprooting oaks and boulders, leaving a wide path of destruction. This power would be a trifle compared to a clash between White Hair and Isi.

Her attention crossed the yard to Greta standing as straight as a lotebush thorn, her hands clenched by her sides as she watched Isi lean into the wagon bed to gather the Danes' luggage. Emotions warred on the poor girl's face. What first appeared to be seething anger and outrage became jaws slack with fear. For the first time since Melatha met Greta, the mantle of security entitled to her as John Rawson's daughter had slipped, as if she suddenly realized her father couldn't buy her everything.

Dragging her feet, Greta turned and followed her guests inside the house.

"Mother?"

She spun to face him. "You startled me, Isi."

"Who are you spying on? The Rawsons and their guests. . .or me?"

She tucked guilty hands behind her back. "I thought no one could see me."

"No one did, except for me. What are you doing here?"

"Mrs. Rawson asked me to help Rosita and her sisters in the kitchen."

He drew back. "Cooking or serving?"

"What difference does it make?"

He snorted. "A lot. Mr. Rawson asked me to join them tonight. I won't have my own mother serve me at that fancy table when she should be seated beside me. It would be hard enough knowing you're standing in front of the stove."

She grinned. "I stand in front of the stove for you every day, son. Serve you, too. Don't let such high-minded notions trouble your soul." She patted his arm. "I'll gladly lay my hand to whatever task Mrs. Rawson requires of me. It's the least I can do to repay her great kindness."

One of Isi's men barreled past behind them. His head jerked around as he caught sight of Diego, and he drew to a breathless halt.

"He's out again, Diego."

Isi stared over his shoulder. "Again? That's not possible."

The man's eyes shifted to the ground. "*Sí, es* muy *posible*. He's not in the corral or the pasture. Nowhere on the grounds. He's gone."

Isi closed his eyes and let his head fall back. "Saddle my horse. I'll be right there."

He turned and tapped Melatha's chin with his work-roughened finger. "I have to go track that stubborn horse again. Tell Mrs. Rawson I'll be back in time for dinner." He furrowed his brow. "Don't let me return and find you dishing beans."

"What shall I tell Greta?"

Just as she planned, her question caught him off guard. "Leave Greta to me, if you don't mind." He tweaked her nose. "It's none of your business." Winking, he sauntered away, pausing once to tip his hat before rounding the house.

"Humph! None of my business?" Skirting a blackbrush thicket, she made her way to the back of the house, grumbling as she took to the steps. "We will see, my little deer. As surely as the sun sleeps at dusk, we will see."

Not that she believed Greta to be the woman God had for Isi, but after seeing the latest contender for his affection, Greta would do to distract him until the right one arrived.

CHAPTER 10

Magda ran her hand over the multicolored quilt and sighed. Satin, silk, and velvet pieces in vivid jewel tones set against an inky black background offered her fingertips a feast of sensations. "Will you look at this quilt, Bertha? Without a doubt, it's the prettiest thing I've ever seen." She glanced back. Bertha still lingered at the window, staring over the yard. "The grandest thing I've ever felt, too. Come over here and touch it."

Bertha swatted the air behind her. "Leave me be, Magda. I'll feel that thing soon enough. I have to sleep under it tonight."

Magda exhaled dreamily. "I hope ours isn't this nice or I won't sleep a wink for worrying about mussing something so fine." She lowered her voice. "Willem and I have been known to drool." Shifting away from the bed, she slid one finger along the marbled top of the tall, mirrored chest then touched the gilded frame around the glass. "One thing's for sure, most of this furniture came straight over on the boat with Kate Rawson. Handed down from her folks, most likely. You can't find workmanship like this anymore."

A knock at the door caused Magda to jump. Feeling guilty for snooping, she opened it to the young man called Diego.

He grinned and cocked his head. "I have luggage belonging to one of you ladies. Cuddy's on the stairs with more. Can you tell me which bags belong where?"

"Those two are Bertha's, sugar." She pushed aside the shoes

Bertha had kicked off in the corner. "Put them down right there, if you don't mind."

He did as she asked then gave a slight bow and ducked out again.

The Rawson boy appeared behind him bearing Emmy's luggage, one under his arm and one in each hand. He grinned, too. "How about these, ma'am?"

"Those are my daughter's." She pointed. "I believe her room is that way."

He smirked and nodded at Diego before sauntering past.

"That means the two on the wagon belong to my husband and me. You can bring them up and leave them outside our door."

Diego's gaze trailed Cuddy down the hall. "Are you sure? They're pretty heavy."

"Don't worry, young man. Mr. Dane is downstairs with the Rawsons, but he'll carry them in the second he comes up."

Diego mumbled a senseless reply and didn't appear to have the first idea of what she'd said. Laughter between Emmy and Cuddy had drawn his attention to where they stood talking. Each time Emmy giggled, the scowl etched on his forehead grew deeper.

Magda eased the door shut and shrugged at Bertha. "I might as well have talked to his hat. Wonder what put a burr in his bonnet?"

Bertha snorted and nudged Magda with her elbow. "Where are your spectacles, honey? The burr's in his behind, not his bonnet. Put there by your little burr specialist."

Magda twisted to stare at the door. "You think so? That's fast, even for Emmy."

"It don't take that girl long to weave her spells."

Magda tilted her head in thought. "You may be wrong this time, Bert. After all, she threw up in the boy's hat!"

"Maybe so, but that don't change the facts. Did you look at him? He's moonstruck and so is that other one. From where I sit, this situation carries the potential for big trouble."

Chewing on her thumbnail, Magda nodded slowly. "You're right. I'd best talk to Emmy."

Bertha chuckled. "You'll have to wait in line behind them two fellers. I suspect they're making plans to tie up all her free talking time." She yawned and stretched. "I'm ready to touch that fancy quilt now. Reckon I could take a nap before we eat?"

Tossing Bertha's bulging satchel on the bed, Magda shook a finger in her face. "No time for rest, missy. Take advantage of my idle hands and let's get you unpacked. The sooner we settle in, the sooner we eat." She raised her nose and sniffed the air. "I can taste that pig from here."

Unfastening the latch on the bag, Magda upended it and gave it a shake. Currency of every denomination spilled onto the bed in a shower of faded green bills. Dumbstruck, she lifted a tied bundle with two fingers and held it up. "What in the name of everything decent have you done?"

Bertha calmly scooped an armful of the money and stuffed it back in the satchel. "Not this one, sugar. I figured to leave it packed until I need it."

Trying to work things out in her mind, Magda pressed her fingers to her temples. "Are you telling me you hauled all of these greenbacks clear across the state of Texas?"

Bertha snatched the hefty bundle from Magda's hand. "Yep."

"Shoved under the seat in the train?"

"Why do you think I wouldn't let that porter carry my luggage?"

"Over rivers and streams, rocks and cactus, through country crawling with bandits?"

"How else was I supposed to get it here?"

Magda stretched the mouth of the bag and peered inside. "There's enough loot in here to buy your own state! What do you need it for?"

Flustered, Bertha closed the satchel and refastened the latch. "Suppose I find some cattle I want to buy?"

Laying the back of her hand on her hip, Magda studied Bertha's pouting face. "You ever hear of bank checks? Promissory notes?"

Another knock on the door sent Bertha scrambling to shove the money under the bed. After pushing it deeper with her foot, she hopped on the end of the high mattress and tried to appear dignified and nonchalant—difficult to pull off with knees straddled and bare feet dangling.

Magda shook her head and turned the knob.

Willem stood smiling on the other side. "The table is set downstairs. Are you two ready to eat?"

Bertha leaped off the bed and padded to the threshold. "That's a wasted question, Willem. When have you seen your wife not ready to eat?"

Magda elbowed her. "There are worse things than an appetite, you know." She shot Bertha a meaningful glare. "Taking chances with large sums of money, for instance."

Bertha pinched her arm. "What you call taking chances, I call being prepared."

Unfazed by their banter, Willem nodded down the hall. "What about Emmy? Is she dressed for dinner?"

A bell clanged somewhere on the grounds.

Emmy's door jerked open and Cuddy stepped out grinning—until he glanced up at Willem's reddening face. He winced then shoved his hat on his head and offered a weak smile. "Folks, that sound means dinner's served. Around here, if you're late, there won't be nothing left."

He tipped his hat at Emmy, who stood gaping at her papa from the door, and swaggered to the head of the stairs without another glance in their direction.

❧

Emmy had never witnessed such a flurry of activity around a table. Three Mexican girls bearing trays wove in and out on countless trips to the kitchen. When Emmy didn't think another platter would fit between the mounds of stringy pork, tall stacks of tortillas, steaming bowls of beans, and crockery pots filled with spicy-smelling dishes, one of the chattering girls brought in a charger filled with brilliant red slices of yet another food she didn't recognize.

Mr. Rawson forked a piece and held it up for inspection. "Know what this is?" he asked no one in particular.

Papa wiped his mouth and smiled. "I believe I do, but let the womenfolk have a guess."

Aunt Bertha leaned in closer. "Don't reckon I've ever seen such a fancy-colored food before." She shot a look at Mr. Rawson. "Assuming that *is* food."

Mr. Rawson transferred the item in question to her plate. "Why don't you tell me?"

She picked around it cautiously with the tip of her fork then raised her eyes to his. "You sure about this?"

He smiled. "You've eaten a watermelon, haven't you?"

She nodded.

"Well, it tastes a bit like that, only watered down."

Talked into it, she cut a big piece and shoved it in her mouth. Her broad smile pleased Mr. Rawson, if his booming laugh was any indication. "That's cactus pear, Mrs. Bloom. Fresh cut this morning."

"Call me Bertha, and I'll call you John. Is that all right?"

"Why, sure it is." He pointed at a nearby platter. "Those vegetables there are cactus pads, Bertha. *Nopalitos*, we call them. We brush them with oil and toss them on the grill. I think you'll find them delicious."

Mrs. Rawson passed Emmy a crock filled to the brim with a savory-looking dish. "And this is pork stew with *nopales*, a wonderfully tasty addition." She turned to Mama. "Magda, the preserves you just spread on that tortilla?" She nodded for emphasis. "Cactus jelly."

Aunt Bertha reached for another bright-red piece of pear and chewed it thoughtfully. "Let me get this straight. The leaves are a vegetable but the pears are a fruit. All from the same plant? How can that be?"

Their hostess beamed. "It's a versatile commodity in the South, as adaptable as this region and its resourceful people."

Cuddy laughed. "And just as prickly as these people when they're crossed." He had ignored his mother's place cards and planted himself in Greta's chair beside Emmy, earning him a sharp glare from Papa.

Greta didn't seem to mind since it put her opposite them next to Diego.

Emmy had explained to her parents that the door to her room wasn't plumb, so it had swung shut by itself when Cuddy walked her onto the balcony to see the view. Grouchy old Papa hadn't believed a single word.

A hand reached between Emmy and Cuddy to place a dish of deep-green peppers on the table.

Emmy followed the shawl-wrapped arm to find a new face among the servers, this one slightly older. Something about her solemn expression intrigued Emmy. Her serenity and the way she held herself said she was out of place in the role of a servant.

Her presence sparked a peculiar reaction in Diego that Emmy could feel from where she sat. Already somber, when he saw who stood there he tensed and laid down his fork. One side of his jaw twitched, and his eyes darkened with irritation.

One of the serving girls whispered to the newcomer in Spanish. She answered quietly. Mr. Rawson added something to the conversation, and Greta laughed and made a comment, too. Soon, most everyone at the table, including Emmy's bilingual papa, chatted easily in the musical language that Emmy, Aunt Bertha, and Mama didn't understand.

However, Emmy did understand that the soft-spoken stranger seemed overtly interested in her. Each time she looked up, the brooding eyes met hers boldly, until Emmy began to feel uncomfortable. As for Diego, he watched the mysterious lady gather dirty dishes, a frown lining his forehead. Usually skilled at sorting the dynamics of a situation, the scowl on Diego's face and the server's careful appraisal threw Emmy quite off track.

Helping herself to one more glance at Emmy, she picked up an empty tray and turned to go.

Mrs. Rawson held up her hand. "Wait, Melatha. I'd like to introduce you." Standing, she walked around the table and slid her arm around the woman's waist. "Friends, this is Diego's little mother. She's not usually working in our kitchen but has graciously offered to lend a hand today for our special occasion. Melatha's the best cook in South Texas." She tightened her grip. "She's also a dear friend. The Rawsons consider her and Diego a part of our family."

Diego's mother. This time Emmy flashed an appraising glance.

Silent until now, Diego bowed slightly. "I'm honored by your words, Mrs. Rawson. I'm certain my mother feels the same."

The glowing smile on his handsome face flipped Emmy's stomach.

"But if you'll pardon one bold observation," he continued, "isn't it customary for the staff to serve the table while the members of a family dine together?"

"Isi!" his mother hissed.

The light of understanding dawned in Mrs. Rawson's eyes. Flustered, but only briefly, she faced her friend. "He's right, of course! Melatha, put down those things and join us. You've made your contribution for the day."

"I really couldn't, Miss Kate. Besides, I'm not hungry." She gave a tight smile. "All that tasting in the kitchen. . ."

Mrs. Rawson took the stack of dishes from her hands. "That's all right. We're nearly done. I know you're fond of our English tea. Sit and share a cup with us. Allow my guests to benefit from your company."

Diego's mother opened her mouth to protest again, but a short, middle-aged man in dust-covered pants appeared in the archway behind her son. "Excuse me, Señor Rawson." He wadded his hat in his hands. "I need to see Diego, if you please."

Mr. Rawson's moustache twitched. "What now, Pete? Can't you men run things for five minutes without him? The man's having his dinner."

The intruder cut pleading eyes to Diego. "Forgive me. It's important."

Irritation brought out Mr. Rawson's British accent. "What's so flaming important that it can't wait?"

Looking as if he'd sooner lose his tongue, the man swallowed hard then mumbled his answer. "Faron, he's loose again, señor. He's still on the ranch, but none of the men will tangle with him. They call for Diego."

Diego groaned and rolled his eyes. "Not again. That's twice in one day."

Mr. Rawson tossed his napkin on his plate. "Blast that son of perdition!"

Mrs. Rawson gasped. "John! Watch your language."

"Sorry, Kate, but isn't there any fence that will hold that horse?"

Diego patted his boss's shoulder. "Relax, sir. Enjoy your dessert. I'll take care of it."

Worry creased his mother's brow. "Will you return tonight, Isi?"

He flashed a teasing smile. "I suppose that depends on Faron."

"Be careful, son."

He gazed at her with affection. "Don't fret, Mother. I'll come home in one piece." He excused himself and pushed back his chair. "Before I go, sir, Señor Boteo suggested we post a night watch for a few days." His eyes twinkled. "It seems they've had a run-in with el chupa sangre. Francisco chased him off a goat last night."

Cuddy slapped the table. "Come on, Diego! I'm surprised at you for giving that fable enough credence to repeat it."

Greta wiped her mouth then placed her hands in her lap. "Something's killing all those calves and sheep, Cuddy."

He cocked his head to the side and mimicked her. "We do have a coyote or two in Dimmit County, Greta."

Biting back a grin, Diego stood. Folding his napkin beside his plate, he nodded at each of the guests and took his leave.

The warmth of his eyes, lingering on Emmy as he bid her good night, sent chills down her spine. Greta, obviously lost in thoughts she'd not likely share, stared longingly toward a spot past the archway where he had disappeared.

Mrs. Rawson signaled to one of the girls. She ducked into the kitchen and returned with a stack of small plates and a tray filled with sweets. Serving dessert to her husband, Mrs. Rawson raised one tapered brow. "If I may be honest, John, I'm glad Faron got out again. I hope he pulls up lame this time, and you have to shoot him." She passed the tray to Willem then demurely folded her napkin across her lap. "Better yet, perhaps the stubborn thing will bail off into the river and break his hateful neck."

John Rawson paused mid-bite then laid down his fork and stared. "Why, Kate. It's not like you to say so mean-spirited a thing."

She regarded him matter-of-factly. "That animal is the devil himself. I fear I'll live to see him kill you. If not Cuddy or Diego."

Her husband dropped his big hand over hers. "There's no danger of Faron killing anyone, honey. No one can ride him. He's strong-willed is all. I like that trait in an intelligent creature." He leaned to caress her chin. "The very thing that attracted me to you was your feisty nature."

Concern softened her features, and she swatted his arm. "Stop. I'm serious. It makes no sense to keep that stallion on the ranch. He's never been anything but a nuisance."

Papa settled his elbows on the table. "Tell me about this horse, John."

Eyes aglow, Mr. Rawson faced him. "Oh, he's a beauty, Willem. Purebred Spanish. Andalusian, you see. Black as thunder with a heart to match and shrewder than the two of us put together, not to mention the fastest thing on four legs. I admit he's the meanest bundle of horseflesh ever spawned, but"—he twisted around to wink at his wife—"he's worth every second of trouble."

Easing back in his chair, he reached for a small cake to nibble. "The thing is, Faron will only let me near him." He absently waved his hand. "Well, Diego, of course, and he tolerates Little Pete, the man you saw earlier." Leaning in, he nodded for emphasis. "But no man can ride the ornery beast. You should've been here the first time I tried." He chuckled. "The old boy put up a right rowdy kerfuffle."

Aunt Bertha blinked. "That's a good thing?"

The Rawsons laughed so heartily, Emmy's family had to join them, including Aunt Bert.

"Bertha, my dear, let's just say he won the skirmish and leave it at that."

For the first time, Emmy realized Diego's mother had slipped away unnoticed. Though she had gone, the memory of her probing eyes still warmed Emmy's flesh.

Mrs. Rawson placed her delicate hands on Papa's and Mr. Rawson's forearms. "Let's take our coffee on the veranda, shall we? It's a beautiful night."

CHAPTER 11

Diego ran his palm over Faron's trembling flank.

The horse sidestepped into the wall of the stall, snorting his disapproval.

"I know you don't like small spaces, señor, but that's too bad. Perhaps a few days without liberty to move will teach you to appreciate the freedom of your pasture."

Faron kicked at the boards behind him.

Diego laughed. "Spit and sputter all you like, young man. You won't be getting out of here." He brought his ear closer to Faron's nose. "What's that you say? Pretty señoritas throughout the county will be pining for you? I understand completely, for I suffer the same dilemma. Good looks are a curse, are they not?"

Pulling a wilted carrot from his pocket, Diego snapped off the root. "Perhaps this will soothe your battered ego, my friend."

Faron snuffled the offering, lifted it from Diego's palm with his soft lips, then nuzzled for more.

"Hungry, eh? I suppose so, after all your carousing. Tell you what, let's get you something more substantial, shall we?" He chuckled and jumped off the rail to the ground, giving Faron one last scratch between the ears. "Adios for now. Try to behave yourself, sí?" On the way out of the barn, he gave instructions for the horse to be fed and groomed.

As he neared the back door to report to Mr. Rawson, voices from the terrace led him through the hedges instead. A dozen lanterns set along the low-walled enclosure lit the patio while a healthy blaze in the fire pit flickered on the relaxed faces of the Rawsons and their guests. A coffee service rested on the table in front of the women. Deep in conversation, the men took their ease in comfortable padded chairs.

When Emily Dane came into sight, he paused in the shadows to watch her. She sat some distance from the others, balancing a cup of coffee on her knees while she gazed at the starlit sky. With her head thrown so far back, her neck looked impossibly long, and the moonlight turned her skin the same shade as the bone china she held. She sat up and sipped her coffee, the motion pursing the generous lips he couldn't stop thinking about to save his life.

"Diego?"

He leaped, warmth flooding his body. "Greta. I didn't see you there."

"Of course not. You weren't looking for me." She tried to smile, but suspicion crept into her eyes. "Have you taken to skulking in bushes and spying on my family?"

Burning with shame, he laughed to make light of her comment. "I was on my way to speak to your father. I found Faron. Courting a filly in Mr. Tumlinson's pasture."

A genuine smile back in place, she slid her arm through his. "I'm sure he'll be glad to hear. Let's go tell him."

John Rawson's deep rumble held court over his guests as they approached. "Both our families lived in Ripponden near Halifax, overlooking the River Ryburn. An overly impressive name for hardly more than a stream running through the village." He gazed around as if the night hadn't shrouded the scenery in darkness. "Nothing at all like this place."

Mr. Dane lowered his saucer to the table. "Tell us about the region, John."

"South Texas? You could say it's a country inhabited by bandits on both sides of the border. They're locked in a dispute over land rights—a battle as old as Genesis. Which is a whole other story, and I've talked long enough." He glanced up at Greta and Diego. "Here's the man who can fill you in on the landscape. He's chased my horse across it from east to west. Did you find him, son?"

"Yes, sir."

"I knew without asking, or else you wouldn't be standing here. I see you made it back in one piece, but has he?"

"Not a scratch, though that could change by morning. I've locked him in a stall."

Mr. Rawson shook his head. "I hate to hear that." He sighed. "Well, there's no remedy for it, is there?"

"None that I can see."

"Very well, then. Pull up a chair and enjoy the night air. You deserve a rest." He glanced around the terrace. "Where'd that Cuddy get off to? He was here a minute ago."

Emily leaned to look past her father. "Cuddy went into the house, sir. He said he'd be right back."

Diego nodded at the older folks and gave Emily a tight smile before settling into the empty chair next to her. Cuddy's vacated seat, no doubt.

Greta flounced over and dropped onto the chaise alongside her mother. Tight-lipped and sullen, she was obviously angry.

What did she expect? He could hardly stretch his six-foot-three body onto that silly reclining chair between Mrs. Dane and Mrs. Rawson. Peeved, he determined to ignore her.

"I've never seen so many stars." Emily's breathless voice suited the night. Serene yet refreshing, like the pleasant breeze blowing from the west.

Diego gazed at the canopy of pinpoint lights, thicker than lentil stew in places. "Are there no stars in Humble, Texas?"

"Of course, but not like these."

He chuckled. "They are the very same ones, I assure you. It's only the unobstructed view and the absence of light here that makes them seem to jump right out of the sky."

In the near distance, a lone coyote howled, followed by a series of short, high-pitched yips. Its quavering cry was soon answered, the mournful howl even closer than the first.

Emily shivered and glanced behind her.

"Are you cold, Miss Dane? I can fetch you a shawl. Despite the warmth of the days, nights in Carrizo can be quite cool. Especially when the wind blows."

She settled back again. "No, thank you. I'm fine."

He watched her from the corner of his eye. "Are you certain?"

"Yes. It's very kind of you, though, considering. . ."

He angled his chair toward her. "Considering?"

She placed her cup on the arm of the chair and laced her hands in her lap, staring at them. She hadn't yet looked at him straight on, and he found himself wishing she would. After a tense silence, her lashes swept up and she gazed into his eyes. "I never apologized for ruining your hat."

He held up his hand. "No apologies necessary, I assure you."

"I've never done anything so awful before. I won't rest until you say you forgive me."

He grinned. "Well, we can't have that, now, can we? Consider yourself officially forgiven."

Her dimples hit bottom as she giggled and pulled her gaze away. "Very good. Can we start over?"

Diego's heart danced a peculiar jig in his chest. "I'd like that." An uneasy silence passed before he leaned closer. "So. . .how do we go about starting over?"

She turned in her chair and offered her hand. "Let's begin with this, since I spoiled it last time. I'm Emily Dane. Happy to make your acquaintance."

"Diego Marcelo, ma'am." He held out his hand and Emily gave it a vigorous shake.

She laughed merrily and so did he.

"Do me a great favor, Mr. Marcelo, and call me Emmy. It's the name my friends use, and I much prefer it to Emily."

"Emmy. Very nice. I will, but only if you call me Diego."

"I've never heard that name before. I believe I like it." A curious light touched her eyes. "I noticed your mama calls you something different."

Flustered, he cleared his throat. "Yes, she—"

"¡Oye, amigo, I see you've kept my seat warm for me."

Cuddy's firm grip on Diego's shoulder startled him, but not as much as the cloying scent of his breath. It angered Diego that he would do so reckless a thing with his father seated a few feet away. He glared up into Cuddy's eyes. "I believe you forgot something in the house, my friend."

"Oh? And what was that?" Cuddy's answer was slurred.

"Your blanket and pillow. It's long past your bedtime, I see."

Cuddy's boisterous laugh was too loud. Diego waited for Mr. Rawson's head to spin around, but the man was engrossed in his friends. Diego swung his gaze to Emmy.

Watching Cuddy with understanding eyes, she held out her cup to Diego. "I could use more of that strong, hot coffee, please. Pour Cuddy some while you're there, why don't you?"

Diego nodded gratefully and took the saucer from her hand. Cuddy slipped into Diego's chair the second he found it free, but Diego didn't mind. Better to have him seated than staggering over the veranda.

As he bent to pour, Mr. Rawson touched his arm. "Here's the man to ask, Bertha. Son, the lady's interested in buying some cattle. Who do we know that may have some for sale?"

Diego returned the pot to the tray without pouring. "As a matter of fact, there's a rancher down Catarina way who's looking to thin his pastures. Started his herd from stock off the Taft Ranch. They're breeding quality cattle down there."

"You know him?"

"Somewhat. I'm acquainted with both of his sons."

"Catarina?" Mr. Dane asked. "I'm not familiar with that town."

"It's not a town, Willem," Mr. Rawson said. "Just a sizable ranch owned by a fellow named Charles Taft. Nowadays they call the whole region Catarina." He looked at Diego. "What's the man's name that's selling his stock?"

"Buck Campbell, sir. His sons are Lester and Joe."

Mrs. Bloom scooted closer. "Can you take me there?"

Diego studied her face. She wasn't joking. "It's a long ride, ma'am. Twenty miles or better over rough terrain. A wagon might bear up on that rugged trail, but it'll slow you down considerably. Can you ride a horse?"

"I reckon so." Looking insulted, she waved at the surroundings. "I may not live way out like this, but we ain't exactly from the city."

Diego bit back a grin. "Yes, ma'am."

Mr. Rawson shook his head. "I couldn't do without Diego around here, Mrs. Bloom, but there's no reason I couldn't take you folks to Catarina."

Emmy's mother frowned and leaned forward in her chair. "Bertha, this is taking a turn toward crazy. I thought you came here to learn about cattle, not carry half of them back to Humble."

"I want me some South Texas cows."

"We have cows back home."

"Not like these. Willem said they breed the finest stock here, and I won't settle for less."

Sighing with exasperation, Mrs. Dane attempted a final argument. "Just how do you propose to get them home? There's no more room in your satchel."

Mrs. Bloom winked. "Why do you reckon that satchel's so full? I already studied on ways to get them home. By rail, for one. They have special cars that carry cattle all over this country." She nudged Mr. Rawson. "Ain't that so?"

"Yes, it's so, and it'll be no problem to load yours at the station in Uvalde. As long as you have the money to pay for shipping."

She leveled him with a gaze. "I have the money."

He lifted his eyes to the Danes.

"She has the money," they said in unison.

"The Humble oil boom," Mr. Dane explained.

Mr. Rawson chuckled. "Very well, then. I suppose you do."

Mrs. Rawson touched her husband's arm. "How do you propose to get them from Catarina to Uvalde, John?"

He sat tall in his chair. "We'll drive them, Katie! By golly, this is still South Texas. The devil's rope be hanged!"

Mrs. Bloom gave an excited hoot. "The devil's rope? What's that?"

"Barbed wire, ma'am. The worst thing to ever happen to a drover." He patted her hand. "But don't you worry. We'll stick to the roads and trails and still get your stock to Uvalde in perfect health." He picked up the coffeepot and poured a cup for himself, then filled the two in Diego's hands. "So it's settled. We'll start planning our trip tomorrow." He wagged his big finger in Mrs. Bloom's face. "But there's no need to get in a hurry. I have plans to show you around Carrizo Springs before we traipse all over Catarina. So sit back and enjoy your coffee."

The swish of shoes on the sandy soil beyond the tile caught his attention. He swiveled in his chair to look. "And here's our Rosita, with *empanadas* fresh from the oven if my nose doesn't lie. Grab one, folks, and eat them while they're hot."

Diego waited until the ladies were served, then wrapped a pie in a napkin and tucked it under his arm. Hustling back to where

Emmy and Cuddy sat, he handed Emmy her coffee. "Forgive me. I was detained." He shoved the other cup and pie to Cuddy. "Eat this," he growled, "and no arguments. You need food on your stomach."

Cuddy reeled drunkenly and laughed. Leaning close to peer into Emmy's eyes, he pointed at Diego. "He thinks I've had one too many."

She drew away and held her napkin to her nose. "I'm afraid he may be right. Please eat something, Cuddy."

He waved his hand. "Nah! Not hungry." He swung to Diego. "I've just been telling Miss Emily about the river. She agreed to let me show it to her tomorrow." He took hold of Diego's shoulder and shook him. "What do you think about that, amigo?"

Diego looked over his shoulder. Mr. Rawson and Mrs. Bloom were huddled together, rambling about cattle no doubt. The others sat talking, not paying the least bit of attention. Except for Greta. She reclined on the chaise, twisting a napkin into a knot and casting doe-eyed glances their way. He sighed. If she would only turn away, he could somehow get Cuddy into the house.

"Diego?"

Emmy's urgent voice sent a jolt along his spine. "What's wrong?"

Her eyes wide with concern, she tipped her head at Cuddy, slumped in the chair and dead to the world. "I'm afraid you were too late with that coffee."

Diego handed off Cuddy's spilled cup to her and knelt to steady him in the chair. "I have to get him to his room without his father's notice."

Her eyes shifted to Mr. Rawson. "How will you manage with him so close?"

"I'll need a favor from you. Can you create a diversion?"

Emmy seemed eager to help. "I'll try." Standing, she smoothed her shirt and, with a grimace over her shoulder at Diego, sauntered toward the others.

"Emily," Mrs. Rawson called, "it's about time you decided to join us." She patted the end of Greta's chaise. "Have a seat right here. I'll serve you one of Rosita's sweet pies. She's renowned in Dimmit County for her empanadas."

Greta snatched her legs away as if in danger of losing them.

Emmy ignored her and delicately perched on the chaise. She

accepted Mrs. Rawson's offering then clutched her mother's arm. "Mama, tell our hosts how oil was discovered on Aunt Bertha's land." She turned a dazzling smile on John Rawson. "I believe you'll find this story quite entertaining."

Grateful for Cuddy's smaller size, Diego slid one arm beneath his shoulders and stood him up. He mumbled incoherently, and Diego shushed him, checking over his shoulder to see if anyone had heard. They seemed to be in the clear, so he hustled Cuddy over the low patio wall and across the yard as fast as he could manage.

Rosita met them in the hall. Without a word, she slipped beneath Cuddy's other arm and helped Diego wrestle him upstairs to his room.

After tucking Cuddy into bed, Diego hurried to rejoin Emmy and the others on the veranda, but when he exited the house, they were standing together bidding each other good night.

Not until he had crawled into his own cot did Diego remember that Cuddy had orders to bed down with the fellows in the bunkhouse. His heart in his throat, he considered going after him but knew it wouldn't be possible. The Danes, Bertha Bloom, and Emmy were settling into rooms off the same hall where he'd have to drag Cuddy's lifeless body.

Pondering the facts, Diego took a measure of comfort from Cuddy's condition. Mr. Rawson needn't fear him slipping across the hall to endanger Miss Dane's virtue or his father's reputation. Tucked beneath his covers, snoring the rafters down, Cuddy Rawson was as mischief-proof as they came. Diego would deal with the rest come morning.

CHAPTER 12

"Well, for heaven's sake! Is that Bertha I hear outside? It's barely daylight."

Willem looked up from slipping on his boot and grimaced. "Who else would be cackling? It's too early for the chickens."

Magda pushed open the patio door and searched the dimly lit grounds below. She followed another loud burst of laugher to where Bertha jumped up and down in the middle of the backyard, holding her side.

Catching a touch of her mirth, Magda grinned. "What's so funny, Bertha?"

Bertha stood with Diego's mother. The drawn-up, somber little woman who served them supper the night before had gone, replaced by a woman with a gleeful expression and dancing eyes.

Bertha pointed. "Look up yonder. On that windmill."

Magda squinted and gazed across the yard. She could just make out the unmistakable shape of a saddle horn and stirrups outlined in the early dawn sky. "Why, that's a saddle! Come see this, Willem. Somebody saddled a windmill."

Emmy stepped onto the balcony from her room. "What's all the commotion out here? They can hear you in Humble."

Diego bounded off the porch beneath them and smiled up at her. "I'm afraid it's my fault." He pointed behind him. "That's a grievous act of retribution directed at me."

"It's his saddle," Bertha cried, obviously privy to the whole explanation. "His men did it to get him back for what he done to them."

Smiling, Willem snorted. "Whatever he did, it must've been bad."

A sheepish look crept over Diego's face. "I guess it all depends on how you look at it. All I did was sweeten their morning ritual."

Bertha winked up at Magda. "With a generous portion of molasses poured down each of their boots. They found out when they pulled them on."

"A sleepy cowboy with sticky boots?" Magda nodded at the windmill. "Son, I'd say justice is served."

A bell clanged, interrupting their fun and signaling breakfast.

Willem patted Magda's shoulder. "Round up Bertha and come to the table. I'm starved."

"You wait for me, Willem Dane. I'm hungry, too. Rounding up Bertha won't take but a minute." She placed two fingers in her mouth and blew.

Attuned to their signal, Bertha's head jerked up.

Magda motioned with her arm. "Come along. You're keeping me from breakfast."

Bertha started for the house. "You won't have to wait on me. I plan to beat you to the table."

Diego stood staring up at Emmy.

Blushing, she flashed him a dimpled smile. "Are you coming, too?"

Greta Rawson eased from behind a trellis and slipped her arm around Mrs. Marcelo. It dawned on Magda that Greta had been standing there in the shadows all along. "He takes his breakfast at his mother's table." She fluttered her lashes. "Don't you, Diego?"

Embarrassed, or maybe flushed with annoyance, Diego nodded then directed his answer at Emmy. "Yes, unless I dine at the bunkhouse. I don't usually eat meals in the house."

Emmy backed away from the rail. "Oh, I see."

Diego took off his hat. "Enjoy your breakfast, Miss Dane." He bowed toward Magda. "And you, Mrs. Dane." His eyes cut back to Emmy. "Perhaps I'll see you tonight."

John Rawson opened the door under Magda's balcony. She couldn't see him but his booming voice rattled the boards at her feet. "You bet you'll see her tonight. We're going to a *pachanga*! You're all invited."

Magda guessed by the wide grin on Diego's face that a pachanga was a good thing.

Bertha required an explanation. She caught Diego by the shirt and spun him around. "A what?"

"*Un partido mejicano*, Mrs. Bloom." He swept his mother into his arms and waltzed her around the yard as the first bursts of light announced the rising sun. "A rowdy Mexican party. We shall eat our fill and dance to a mariachi band."

"Stop, Isi!" his mother cried, giggling like a girl. "I'm getting dizzy!"

He turned her loose and faced the porch. "Whose house, sir? And what is the occasion?"

"Jose Bosques. His daughter's *quince años*."

Diego's face lit up even more. "A *Quinceañera*?" He snatched his unsuspecting mother from behind and whirled her again. "Then we shall dance all night!"

Willem tugged on Magda's sleeve. "There's a plate of ham and eggs downstairs with my name on it. You've kept me from my breakfast so long I won't mind eating yours, too."

She pushed away from the rail. "You won't get the chance." With one last whistle for Bertha, she followed Willem downstairs. At the bottom landing, she spoke her thoughts aloud. "Willem, what is a quince. . .a quincea. . .? What is that thing they said?"

He shrugged. "I don't know, but the mention of it sure stirred things up." They reached the table and he held out her chair, nodding a good morning to Rosita before she scurried back to the kitchen. "One thing's for certain, dear. We're about to find out."

❧

Emmy stood behind the wooden shutters, spying on Diego and Greta. Sneaking about and prying into people's affairs was a habit Mama had worked diligently with Emmy to break. Emmy had tried to mend her ways but found opportunities too frequent and temptations too irresistible. Especially the one taking place in the yard below.

Greta leaned against the adobe wall of a shed, hands behind her back, staring up at Diego. He rested against the wall, too, a respectable distance between them. Greta wore a cotton dress, pale yellow like the ribbon in her hair. Unless Emmy judged her too harshly, she'd spent some time in her mirror tugging the neckline down—not enough to be scandalous but enough to reveal a circle of milky white skin.

Diego's earlier irritation had vanished with the morning dew. He was at ease with Greta, laughing and talking freely, the latter punctuated by pointing, waving, and gesturing with his hands. He seemed in such high spirits, Emmy waited for him to pull Greta into his arms and dance her about the yard. She couldn't help wondering if it was the upcoming party or being with Greta that caused his mood.

His head jerked around to her window as if attracted by sudden motion.

Emmy eased out of sight, wondering what he had seen. Had she moved the shutter and given herself away? Blushing, she hurried to her dressing table, scolding herself for being caught at something she ought not to have been doing in the first place. Sighing, she realized a voice stronger than Mama's had cautioned her to mind her own business. Wishing she'd learn to obey, Emmy whispered a prayer of repentance and one for the strength to change.

After one last glance in the mirror, she stepped into the hall and closed the bedroom door. As she turned to go, a growl from behind nearly jolted her from her shoes. Visions of claws and fangs and goats shriveled to wineskins flashed through her mind as she spun toward the shadows. "Who's there?"

"If it's all the same to you, we can do without slamming doors."

Emmy took a step closer. "Cuddy? Is that you?"

Another moan. "There's no need to shout either."

She smiled. "I'm not shouting. Are you all right?"

He groaned again.

Emmy followed the sound to the dark corner and found him sitting on the floor hugging his knees, his head hanging down. She sat beside him, tucking her legs beneath her and covering them with her skirt. "Is there anything I can do?"

He groped for her hand and held it.

Surprised, she let him. "Why do you do this to yourself, Cuddy? If drinking causes this, why drink?"

He shrugged. "It's fun?"

She shook her head. "You weren't having fun last night, and you're certainly not now. This is more like punishment." Emmy could see him clearly, now that she'd adjusted to the light.

He cut his eyes to her. "You may be onto something there."

She pondered his confession then shook her head. "Why would you feel the need to punish yourself? You're a handsome young man with a wonderful family, a lovely home, and a thriving ranch."

He perked up and grinned. "Handsome?"

"In short, you have everything a man could want."

He snorted. "Miss Dane, 'everything' can be a pretty hefty burden at times. Especially when you're born into a situation you never asked for." He studied her with bleary eyes then hung his head again. "Or when there's someone reminding you at every step that you're not who you should be." He pulled his hand away and wrapped it around his knees again. "But how could someone like you be expected to understand?"

Stunned, Emmy sat quietly, Papa's scowling face looming in her mind. Her heart aching over their shared grief, she reached to caress his fingers. "I understand more than you know."

He raised his head and quirked his brows. She nodded. Smiling sweetly, he twined his fingers around hers and squeezed.

"Emily!"

Emmy pushed off the floor, the stern face she'd envisioned glaring at her from three feet away. She hadn't even heard his footsteps. "Sorry, Papa." Her heart pounded so hard, she knew Cuddy was bound to hear.

He stood, too, and came to her defense. "Emily was tending me, Mr. Dane. That's all. I'm feeling poorly this morning, and she was concerned."

Papa's bottom jaw stuck out, and his breath came in rapid gasps. He pointed behind him. "They're holding breakfast for you downstairs, Emily. See how fast you can get there. We'll deal with this shameless display after we eat."

Emmy stumbled away, casting a nervous glance at Cuddy.

He stared after her with renewed understanding.

Papa herded her to the stairwell, a firm hand at her back. He paused at the landing and turned, his finger aimed at Cuddy like a weapon. "Keep your distance from my daughter, Cuthbert Rawson, or I shall have to speak to John."

"Yes, sir," Cuddy barked, his voice steady and strong.

More sad than frightened, Emmy followed her fuming papa down the stairs. Near the bottom, a gaily hummed tune floated back to her from inside the house. As they rounded the landing, the back of a yellow dress disappeared into the dining room through the arched doorway.

Emmy cringed. She wondered how much Greta had heard and how fast she would tell Diego. It seemed Emmy wasn't the only snoop on the Twisted-R Ranch.

Jaunty footsteps on the stairs and a merry whistle announced Cuddy coming to join them at the table. He breezed through the door and took a seat, flapping his napkin with flair and placing it on his lap.

Astonished, Emmy stared. Evidently, his anger with Papa had shoved aside his misery.

His mother glanced up. "Good morning, Cuthbert."

He grimaced. "Careful with the name-calling, Mother. You'll spoil my good mood."

The creases in Papa's forehead grew impossibly deep. "I thought you were ill." To the casual listener, his tone might be mistaken for concern. Emmy clearly heard the accusation.

Passing Aunt Bertha the gravy bowl, Mrs. Rawson paused. "Oh? Are you all right, son?"

Cuddy flashed Papa a brilliant smile. "Feeling much better now, Mr. Dane. Thanks to your lovely daughter."

Papa blustered and took up his fork, going after his eggs as if they were Cuddy instead.

Emmy shrank five inches in her chair.

Stabbing his fork into a sizable slab of ham on the serving platter, Cuddy lifted his eyes to Mr. Rawson. "Miss Dane is interested in seeing the river, Father. I thought I might saddle a couple of horses and take her out there this morning." He raised his brows innocently toward Emmy's mama. "If it's all right with her parents, of course."

Papa tried to protest, but his mouth was full. He snatched up his coffee to take a drink, but he was too late.

"A splendid idea, son." Mr. Rawson beamed at Emmy and then smiled across the table at his daughter. "Greta will go along to chaperone."

This time Greta sputtered. "The river? Cuddy, there's nothing remotely interesting about that muddy old cesspool. Why, it's hardly worth the ride." He ignored her so she directed her objections to her mother. "You know I don't like the sun. It dries my skin."

Mrs. Rawson shot her a weighted look. "You'll be fine, Greta. Our guest would like to go."

"Can Diego come along?"

Her mother drew back. "Greta Rawson! For pity's sake."

Caught with her knickers inside out, Greta lowered her eyes. "Sorry, Mother. It's just that Diego's so clever and fun. I thought he might make the trip more tolerable."

"Greta!"

Her father held up his hand. "Hush, daughter. Diego is far too busy running this ranch to run off and play."

"But you can spare Cuddy?"

Mr. Rawson tossed a tortilla onto his plate. "Cuddy's a different story."

Emmy checked for Cuddy's reaction to his father's words. He had none.

Taking advantage of the silence, Emmy's papa cleared his throat. "John, I don't think—"

"They'll be fine, Willem. Don't worry. Cuddy knows his way around."

Papa cringed.

Emmy hid her grin behind her napkin. With the boldness of the falsely accused, Cuddy had called Papa's bluff and won most handily. She had to wonder how long Cuddy's victory would last. Willem Dane wasn't used to losing.

Cuddy folded his napkin over his plate. "So it's settled. We'd best get going while it's cool. The ride won't be tolerable in the heat of the day."

His mother swept her arm over the table. "What about all this food? You've hardly touched your plates."

"Have Rosita wrap it and we'll take it with us."

"A picnic?" She beamed. "How fun! You'll have us wanting to join you."

Cuddy stood. "I'm afraid old codgers aren't invited, Mother dear." Grinning, he kissed the top of her head. "Besides, you couldn't keep up with us youngsters."

CHAPTER 13

The Nueces River wound along the back of the Twisted-R Ranch, providing a source of fresh water and a natural boundary. Like an oasis in the desert, an assortment of trees grew along the banks, stretching in a line as far as the eye could see in either direction. As Emmy and the Rawsons drew closer, the sparse ground cover and mesquite gave way to lush green grass and live oak trees, a scene not unlike the banks of the San Jacinto River back home. It was hard to believe the two environments were part of the same landscape. Once Emmy thought about it, she realized the South Texas terrain had been as fickle as a female since she got off the train in Uvalde.

The horses picked up speed as they neared the slope, and Cuddy winked. "They smell the water."

Emmy didn't blame them. If she were on foot, she'd be trotting, too. If Cuddy considered the morning cool, she dreaded the ride home. The sun shone directly at them from above the eastern horizon, already so bright Emmy couldn't bear it in her eyes. Greta had grudgingly lent her a straw hat that Emmy pulled low on her forehead, grateful for the band of shade it provided.

At Mrs. Rawson's suggestion, Emmy had changed into riding britches and a light yellow top. Still, sweat pooled and rolled down her back, tickling her between the shoulder blades. She was relieved to reach the cover of the oaks.

They dismounted and Cuddy tied off the reins. He pulled a carefully wrapped bundle from his saddlebag and handed it to Emmy. "Give this to Greta. Tell her to pick a good spot and spread the blanket."

"I can spread a blanket, Cuddy. I'm capable."

He caught her wrist. "Let Greta, please. And don't wander off by yourself. It could be dangerous."

A chill touched her spine. "Dangerous?"

"Rattlers. They don't play nice around these parts. And the scorpions. . .they'll invite themselves to lunch. You won't know they're there until they sting you."

Her eyes must have conveyed her fear, because he laughed and patted her shoulder. "Stay close to Greta. For all her prissy ways, she's well adjusted to her environment." He took the bundle from Emmy and handed it off to Greta, who had joined them. "Eyes like a hawk. Right, sis?"

She took the pack from him none too gently and stalked toward the bank. "I'm not speaking to my brother, in case he hasn't noticed."

Cuddy widened his eyes at Emmy. "This outing holds promise."

Emmy stifled a laugh.

Though the river hardly lived up to the term *cesspool*, Greta was right in saying there was nothing spectacular about the Nueces. It offered low, murky water and muddy banks, exposed roots along the opposite wall, and stagnant pockets topped by green scum. Still, it was the wettest place Emmy had seen since she'd arrived in South Texas. When she threw in the grass tickling her legs beneath the cover, abundant restful shade, and the wind whistling through the overhead treetops, their little picnic became a refreshing retreat from the heat—and a respite from Papa's broad thumb. She untied the ribbon of her hat and took it off. Shaking her hair out behind her, she turned her face to catch the breeze.

Greta tossed her half-eaten sandwich aside and pushed to her knees. Staring toward the water, she stretched and yawned, then rose without a word and walked away. Spreading her shawl in a grassy spot near the bank, she pulled out a small green book and pen and sat down to write.

Cuddy chuckled. "She's writing scathing insults about me in her diary."

Emmy glanced at Greta hunched over the book balanced on her knees, biting the end of her pencil. "How do you know?"

He winked. "My ears are itching."

Emmy passed him a napkin. "Your ears deceive you. If she's writing scathing insults, they're directed at me." She wiped her mouth. "She doesn't care much for me, does she?"

Cuddy lay back on his folded arms, staring at the brilliant blue sky. "You may not believe it, but Greta couldn't wait for you to arrive."

Emmy gaped at him.

He gave her a fleeting look. "It's true. There aren't many unmarried women her age around Carrizo Springs. She's looked forward to your visit for weeks, made elaborate plans for you two." He rolled onto his side, propping up on one arm. "Truthfully, I got tired of her rattling. To hear her talk, you two should be practically sisters by now."

Emmy scooted around to face him. "So I made a horrid first impression? We haven't shared three words, yet she hates me."

He smirked like a naughty little boy. "It's not that she hates you, sweetheart." He stole a quick look to be sure Greta wasn't listening. "Little sister wasn't prepared for how much Diego would like you."

Heat flooded Emmy's neck. She stared hard at the red plaid blanket between them. "Diego doesn't. . ."

Cuddy pushed up and sat cross-legged, his knees touching hers. "Oh, yes, ma'am. He does." He pulled a long stalk of grass and tickled her hand with the seedy head. "Does that knowledge please you?" He ducked, trying to see her eyes. "I suppose it makes Greta's ill treatment worthwhile, doesn't it?"

Emmy changed her position and brushed off the weedy stalk. "You're the most vexing man I've ever met, Cuddy Rawson."

He flashed a grin. "And you're the prettiest woman I've ever seen, Emily Dane."

She laughed and shook her head.

"It's true, honey." He tapped her on the chin. "Don't try to act like you don't know."

Emmy shrugged. "Some days I know. Some days I'm not so sure." She peeked at him from under her lashes. "I wanted to thank you for this morning."

Cuddy sighed. "The old man is pretty tough on you, isn't he?"

She grimaced. "I wouldn't mind so much if I knew why. Not knowing keeps me off balance, keeps me guessing."

Compassion warmed his pale blue eyes. "That's part of their game, darlin'. To make you doubt yourself."

She studied his face. "I don't think so. Not in my case, at least. I know in my heart there's a reason Papa deals so harshly with me." Her throat swelled unexpectedly. She swallowed. "He wasn't always this way. When I was younger, he was quite affectionate, which makes it even harder." She paused. "You know?"

He scooted closer and pulled her head to his shoulder. "As it happens, I do know."

Emmy's chest ached with unshed tears. "If I could pinpoint the day everything changed, I'd be able to figure out what I did wrong."

She raised her head and they gazed into each other's eyes. Cuddy lifted two fingers and caressed her cheek. "Don't let him change who you are, Emily."

"Diego!" They sprang apart as Greta rushed by. "Look! Diego's here."

Emmy stretched to look past Cuddy's shoulder. Diego sat his horse at the top of the slope, staring down at them. As Greta rushed toward him, he dismounted and walked to meet her.

"You came after all," Greta cooed. "I'm so glad." The change in the girl was astounding. "Come sit with us and share our food. Have you eaten lunch?"

Sit with us? Under different circumstances, Emmy would find Greta's statement quite funny. At the moment, she was busy fretting over how her shared moment with Cuddy looked from atop the rise.

Cuddy whirled around, coming to rest with his arms propped on his knees. "They sent you out here to spy on us, didn't they?"

"Don't be a dolt," Diego growled, a rosy glow on his cheeks. "Your mother feared you might keep the women out in the heat too long. From the look of things, it appears she was right."

Cuddy stood and brushed off his hands. "It is getting late. Pack up, ladies, and we'll head on back."

"There's no need to rush, Cuddy." Greta plopped down and patted the spot beside her. "Sit for a spell, Diego, and have something to eat. We're just now starting to have fun."

Emmy shared a look with Cuddy. He rolled his eyes and she nearly bit her lip in two trying to stifle a laugh.

Diego smiled sweetly and patted his midsection. "Thank you, but I'm still working off Mother's sunflower seed cakes. Besides"—he drew closer to Greta's face—"unless I'm mistaken, the real reason she wants you home has something to do with the pachanga. When I left the yard, she was airing pretty dresses on the clothesline."

Greta spun toward her brother. "Let's go, then. She's bound to be freshening that horrid green gown for me. I don't know why she loves it so. The ruffles make me look like a dowdy schoolgirl."

The mischievous glint in Cuddy's eyes shouted the taunt he bit back. "If you're in such a hurry, pack up these things while Diego helps me water the horses."

Emmy began gathering utensils and tying up the cloth holding the leftover tortillas. To her surprise, Greta squared around to face her, a warm smile on her lips. "I hope you enjoyed yourself this morning, Emmy. I come here often just to think and write in my diary. It's quite a peaceful spot."

Emmy gave her a sideways glance. "I thought you didn't like to come here at all."

Greta blushed and ducked her head. "I suppose I did give that impression." She looked up, regret in her eyes. "I'm sorry, Emily. I've acted the shrew, haven't I? I don't know what came over me. I hope you'll forgive me." She picked up Emmy's hand. "Is it possible that we could start over?"

Shocked, Emmy stared wordlessly at their tangled fingers.

"If we're friends, tonight will be so much more fun. We can help each other dress. I'd love to pin your hair. You have such lovely blond curls."

Emmy's hand rose to her hair. "Why, thank you."

"Did you know I had a quince años party, too?" She dreamily rolled her eyes. "It was a grand affair! Quince años means fifteen years. Of course, it's not our custom, but when I turned fifteen, the locals insisted out of respect for my family."

Greta gazed over Emmy's shoulder with a dazed expression, as if she could see into the past. "I wore the sweetest little dress." She grinned and touched Emmy's arm. "No, not the one with green ruffles."

Emmy laughed to be polite.

"Mama piled my hair on my head," Greta continued, "and wove flowers into the curls like a crown." She sighed. "We danced until dawn. All of my friends attended." A wistful shadow stole over her eyes. She squeezed them shut and shook her head. "They're all married now, except for Mary English. She moved to New York last year to become a journalist. Nearly broke her mother's heart."

Emmy widened her eyes as Greta came up for air. The girl had uttered more words in thirty seconds than she had for two days. Still reeling from the sudden change of heart, Emmy sat speechless.

Smiling prettily, Greta touched her cheek. "I'm elated to see you and my brother are getting along so well."

Ah, Emmy thought, *the reason for the change in her attitude.*

"Cuddy needs someone," Greta said. "He has me to talk to, but a brother won't confide in a sister the way he would a. . .well, a special friend like you."

Greta beamed so brightly Emmy watched for cherubs with harps to alight on her shoulders. She groped for something to say. "We have a lot in common." It was the best she could do.

"We do!" Greta squealed. "I've noticed it, too. We're both fair-haired and about the same age." She nodded matter-of-factly. "You prefer tea to coffee in the mornings just as I do." She wiggled her hand wildly and sat up on her heels. "And look! We're wearing the same colored blouse."

Her cheeks warming, Emmy offered a tight smile.

"Oh." Greta drooped like wilted lettuce and withdrew her hand. "You meant Cuddy, didn't you?"

"Well, I. . ."

"Enough chitchat, ladies," Cuddy called from behind them. "Let's get you back to the ranch. I'd prefer not to incur the wrath of the fair Katie Rawson."

Diego bent to pick up Emmy's hat and gave it to her then offered his hand. She caught a glimpse of Greta's slight scowl as he pulled her to her feet first and took her arm to walk her to her mare. Holding her ground, she lifted her brows and tilted her head toward Greta.

Flustered, he back-stepped to the blanket. "Forgive me, dear girl. I thought Cuddy. . ."

It seemed a struggle for Greta to maintain her serene expression. The tiny creases on her forehead gave her away. "Never assume Cuddy will behave properly, Diego. The poor boy's ill equipped in situations requiring a show of manners." The creases deepened as she glared at her brother. "You see he has none."

Though Greta took out her frustration on her brother, Emmy guessed her irritation had little to do with him. Diego helped Greta onto her horse then turned to assist Emmy. Disappointment clouded his eyes when he found her already mounted.

"Let's ride," Cuddy said, still seeming oblivious. He turned his horse in a half circle and crowded between Emmy and Diego, in effect cutting them off from each other. One look at his satisfied face told Emmy he'd done it on purpose.

CHAPTER 14

Melatha's breath caught in her throat when Isi stepped over the threshold of the jacal. He wore his finest clothes, glossy black pants and a matching short jacket, adorned with shiny buttons in front and on the sleeves. A tanned snakeskin served for a hatband, fastened to the hat by a silver *concha* stamped with the Texas star. He had attached matching conchas to the strap of his best leather boots.

Standing in the shadows cast by the waning light, he looked like Reynaldo on their wedding day, and the sight brought tears to Melatha's eyes. "Oh, Isi. You will leave the Bosques home tonight with the hearts of all the women in your breast pocket."

Wearing a silly grin, he clicked his heels and bowed to kiss her hand. "There's only one heart I care about, Mother, and it's yours."

Snorting, she waved off his teasing. "It's not like you to lie, son. We both know there's another."

He colored and shoved past her. "She's a charming and beautiful girl, but she means nothing to me. Besides, she's already smitten with Cuddy."

Melatha pinned him with an innocent stare. "I was referring to Greta. Who do you mean?"

Caught, he glared over his shoulder. "Why can't you at least leave my thoughts to me? Why must you lay snares with twisted words until you expose my deepest feelings?" He stalked to her and spun her around, fumbling with her apron strings. "And why are you still wearing this? It's time to go."

Melatha turned and caught his hands. "If I have exposed what you feel for White Hair to the light then leave it there, so you might see it clearly." She shook her head. "I recognize her restless spirit, Isi. You have as much hope for breaking that devil, Faron."

He tossed her apron aside and lifted the basket of food she'd prepared for the party. With a haughty grin, he herded her toward the door. "That's encouraging, Mother. You see, I have Faron eating out of my hand."

❧

Diego loaded the vexing little woman and her sloshing crock of frijoles into the wagon and drove to the main house. He pulled in behind Cuddy's two-seater and set the brake. Mr. Rawson had parked his wagon in front of the line.

As the families filed onto the porch, the flurry of activity drew Diego's attention, but his eyes found and fixed on Emmy. She had on a gown of iridescent silk, the top rose-tinted beige, the bottom a shimmering deep purple. Black velvet ribbon crisscrossed the bodice and rimmed the billowing skirt. He feared she'd be too warm until the sun had set and the wind picked up. Frowning, he wondered why the women didn't tell her.

"She looks lovely."

He decided to turn his mother's game against her. "Greta? Yes, she does." Truthfully, he couldn't have named the color of Greta's dress, much less said how she looked. It shamed him that the same girl he'd finagled a chance to spend time with every chance he got now sparked as much interest in his heart as the backside of the barn. In truth, the last two days had opened his eyes to her true nature. Where was the teasing, smiling Greta hiding, and where had the scowling, pouting Greta come from?

"Do you like my new frock, Diego?"

He jerked his gaze to the ground. So Greta's dress was yellow. She wore an awful lot of yellow. "Yes, it's very nice."

Greta twirled. "Perfect for dancing. Wouldn't you say?"

Diego's grip tightened on the reins as Emmy started down the steps on Cuddy's arm. "Um, yes. I suppose so."

To Willem Dane's obvious displeasure, Cuddy escorted Emmy to his rig then climbed up beside her. Mrs. Bloom got into the rear.

Diego's mother nudged him with her elbow. Forcing his attention back to Greta, he smiled down at her. "It's a striking dress and perfect for dancing. I'm sure you'll get the chance to prove it tonight."

Mrs. Rawson paused to stare toward her daughter before climbing aboard the lead wagon with her husband and the Danes. Twisting on the seat, she waved her lace fan. "Greta? Come along. You're holding things up."

"Yes, Mother." She waited to catch Diego's eye one last time before dashing to join Mrs. Bloom on the back seat of Cuddy's wagon just as Mr. Rawson pulled away from the house.

Diego didn't look at his mother, tried not to feel her eyes watching him. They rode to the Bosques ranch in silence.

The sun had begun to slip toward the horizon as they pulled past the gate to the house. Mariachi music filled the evening air with the beat of a lively song. Señor Bosques had brought the band all the way from Cocula, in the Mexican state of Jalisco.

The wagons followed the singing and the laughter to the rear of the house and parked in the grass beside a large wooden dais. Before the party ended, the floor of the platform would be reduced to splinters by hard-driving heels pounding out the rhythm of the dance.

Diego helped his mother down. She stood swaying to the music while he lifted out her contribution to the night, her prized bean soup. Señora Bosques directed him to a line of tables laden with every sort of brightly colored food imaginable. So full was the table, his mother had to help him find a place for the huge pot of beans. She skillfully shifted a few platters and bowls, and he set her offering among them.

Following his mother across the yard, he got his first look at the band. They were dressed in white cotton trousers, loose flowing shirts, and big smiles. Leather sandals graced their feet. One played the five-stringed *vihuela*, blending with the haunting strains of two violins and the strum of the *guitarrón*. The tempo stirred Diego's blood and urged his feet to move.

The thought of dancing brought his mind instantly to Emmy. If he was to be honest with himself, he'd planned to dance with her since he first got wind of the pachanga—a plan he'd see fulfilled if he had to waltz across Cuddy in the process.

When it came to dancing, Cuddy couldn't compete. Having less rhythm than a bucking mule, he seldom tried, unless he'd had too much to drink, a trick he dare not pull around so many of his father's close friends. The penalty for so foolish an act would be grave.

Diego searched out Emmy, sitting between a chattering Greta and a wide-eyed Bertha Bloom. For all he knew, Emmy danced no better than Cuddy and had less inclination. He watched her for a sign that the music moved her and was rewarded by her swaying shoulders and furiously tapping toes.

He smiled. Just a bit longer to wait. In South Texas, feasting came before dancing.

Cuddy passed by grinning, weighed down with a heaping plate of food. He held it up and pointed. "I'm waiting on you like one hog waiting on another."

Diego smiled. "I see that." He glanced around to locate his mother. She stood out of earshot, chatting with one of the locals. "I hope there's a portion of bean soup on that plate. I don't look forward to the ride home unless that crock is empty. I'll never hear an end to her moaning."

Cuddy changed his route and came to thrust the deep plate under Diego's nose. "Is that enough to suit you?"

He chuckled. "I knew I could count on you."

With a jaunty salute, Cuddy went his way.

Diego was about to call him back and suggest he offer the plate to one of the women, but they had stood up and were making their way to the line. He met them there.

"I ain't never seen such a spread in my life," Mrs. Bloom announced to no one in particular.

Mrs. Dane nodded. "I don't see how they'll ever eat all this."

Diego handed her a plate. "Ma'am, you'd be surprised how much a hungry band of vaqueros can put away. Just ask Rosita. She feeds our men every day."

He stepped aside to allow her and Mrs. Bloom to go first. Smiling, he handed Emmy and Greta a plate each. "Hungry, ladies?"

Greta's fingers deliberately brushed Diego's when she took the dish. "We're starved, right, Emily?" Before Emmy could answer, Greta rushed ahead. "Be sure and take plenty of everything. Otherwise, you're certain to offend someone. They all worked so hard preparing the food."

Diego wondered how Greta would know the meaning of hard work. He also wondered why she didn't take her own advice. While Emmy was careful to spoon a little from each pot, Greta barely covered her plate.

He didn't have to wonder long. As soon as the first couples lined up on the floor, Greta pushed her meager portion aside and smiled at him. She had plied Emmy with food and the fear of offending the cooks so she'd be too busy eating, or worse, too full to dance.

Emmy bravely shoved another bite in her mouth.

Angry, Diego took away her fork and set her dish on a nearby table.

She flashed him a grateful look.

Greta flashed him one of a different sort when he led Emmy onto the dance floor.

Emmy felt just as he'd expected in his arms, only better. How could he have imagined the smell of her, a blend of lavender mixed with jasmine, stronger each time the wind blew her hair?

He saw right away that she loved to dance. She matched him step for step as they whirled about the edge of the platform, dodging the other couples and laughing. When the song ended and the slower tempo announced a waltz, he pulled her closer and tightened his arm around her waist.

Her scent enveloped him, and the warmth of her body through the silky fabric teased his fingertips. Fighting to control his rapid breathing, telling himself the dancing was the cause, he caught her eye and smiled. "Having fun?"

"Oh, yes. Very much."

"That's a beautiful dress."

She blushed. "Thank you. Until the sun went down, I feared I'd picked the wrong one. It's much cooler now, though."

He nodded. "Yes, it is."

He led her around the floor again, past a sea of men's faces, young and old watching her with admiring glances. "I never thanked you for last night."

She raised her tapered brows. "For?"

"Helping me with Cuddy." He winked. "You make a fine distraction, Miss Dane."

Her eyes twinkled. "I'll take that as a compliment."

"I assure you, it was most sincere."

She lifted her chin. "Then I thank you."

They giggled like children at their teasing formality, her laughter warming Diego's heart.

"So. . ." She cocked her head to one side. "Why doesn't your mama like me?"

Her question stunned him. Her boldness stunned him more.

He opened his mouth to protest, but Cuddy swaggered toward them, interrupting the lie. "I'm cutting in, brother."

Diego tightened his hold on Emmy's hand. "You'll only trample the poor girl's toes. Show some mercy, my friend."

Cuddy snorted and held his ground.

"Not now, Cuddy. Perhaps she'll save you a dance."

"No, now, Diego. Stop fooling around."

Frustrated, Diego searched Emmy's face. "Only if the lady agrees."

Blind to his pain, Emmy watched Cuddy with obvious amusement. Diego winced at the affection shining in her eyes. "I'd love to dance with you, Cuddy."

With a slight bow, Diego released her and stepped away. Cuddy glided into his place, catching Emmy's hand in his, sliding his arm around the warmth of her slender waist. Laughing, they whirled away from him and disappeared.

Churning inside and struggling to contain his passion, Diego strode across the floor to join Greta. Too late, he realized she seethed like a roiling kettle.

Hoping to calm her, he danced with her at last. By the second song, she began to relax until she caught him stealing a glance at Emmy and her brother. She grew rigid in his arms. "They make such a nice couple, don't they?"

He stiffened. "I hadn't noticed."

"But you must have. They're both blond and attractive. Cuddy's short like Emily. He doesn't tower over her the way you do."

"I meant I hadn't noticed they were a couple."

She drew away from him, tilted her head, and stared. "Of course they are! On the way to it at least." She glanced around then lowered her voice. "Yesterday morning they were caught sitting together in the hallway outside their rooms." She leaned closer for emphasis. "Holding hands."

Diego's stomach lurched. "Caught?"

She failed at hiding a smirk. "Willem Dane. Haven't you noticed how he watches them?"

Diego scanned the crowd for Emmy's father. Indeed, he scowled at her and Cuddy across the sea of swirling dancers.

"You caught them yourself at the river."

He vacantly studied Greta's face. What did he see at the river? They were sitting together on a blanket staring at him on the rise, though Emmy did wear a curious expression of guilt.

What took place right in front of him that he'd missed?

Diego stopped dancing mid-note. Catching Greta by the wrist, he hauled her back to her chair.

She squirmed away from his grip and whirled to face him. "What's wrong with you tonight? I've never seen you so restless."

"I'm tired of dancing, that's all." He took a deep breath to steady himself. "I need something cool to drink. Would you care for one?"

"I would."

He spun.

Emmy stood behind him, a plastered smile on her face. She clutched his arm. "In fact, I'll help you."

Ignoring the rage on Greta's face, he allowed Emmy to steer him toward the punch bowl. On the way, he decided to put himself out of his misery. He would ask her straight out if she had feelings for Cuddy. If she said yes, he would bow out of the picture. If she said no—

"Diego, we have a problem."

He blinked down at her. Had she read his mind?

"It's Cuddy."

His heart pounded. Even as she prepared to crush his hopes, he admired her strength. No woman he'd ever known got straight to the point. "It's all right, Emmy. I understand."

She took his sleeve and jerked him around. "No, you don't." Angling him toward the wooden platform, she pointed.

Cuddy wove drunkenly through the crowd—one hand splayed over his heart, the other arm stretched to the sky—singing along with the mariachis with all of his might. Some of the dancers laughed and shoved him away; others scowled when he bumped them from behind.

Diego swallowed. "I don't believe my eyes. He seemed fine before."

Emmy's gaze darted anxiously from him to Cuddy. "I smelled it on his breath as soon as you left us. There's a flask in his pocket, and he keeps taking long swigs." She met his eyes. "I believe he's getting worse every second."

"Some local brew, no doubt. They can be potent. I've warned Cuddy about that poison." Diego pressed his fists to his forehead. "Why would the foolish boy do this? He knows how his father—" His head came up, frantic eyes scouring the rim for Mr. Rawson.

He was seated with some other ranchers, his chair faced away from the dais, but it would be only a matter of time before he noticed the ruckus or someone pointed it out.

Diego gripped her shoulders. "Emmy?"

She swept past him. "I know what to do."

Diego caught her arm. "If my mother asks, tell her I'll be back."

She nodded.

Diego stood his ground until Emmy crossed the yard and pranced in front of the men, her lilting laughter and dimpled grin captivating John Rawson and every man at the table.

Avoiding Greta, he cut around to the rear of the dance floor and waited until Cuddy swept past. Reaching for the nape of his neck, he jerked him to the ground and hauled him spitting and sputtering to the front of the house and then circled back to the rig.

The fight had gone out of him by the time Diego loaded him none too gently into the bed of the wagon and climbed aboard. With Emmy's help, once again they'd saved Cuddy's ornery hide.

Diego turned the horse and pulled from behind Cuddy's wagon. Breathing a sigh of relief, he took one more look behind him, and his heart shot past his throat.

No matter how fast Emmy talked or how dazzling her smile, John Rawson, against a backdrop of flickering torchlight, stared over his shoulder at Diego, his face a frightening portrait of rage.

CHAPTER 15

Melatha handed the misshapen piece of chalk to Jose. "Your turn, *niño*. Draw the letters just as I've shown you." She adjusted his fingers. "Relax your hand. Choking the life from the chalk won't help."

He turned up a grimy, toothless grin. "Sí, Mama Melatha."

"Curl the tail of the J like the tail of a monkey. The tail of the P should be long and straight, like a puppy's."

This time his smile revealed a few teeth.

She pointed to a small plate mounded with scrambled eggs and tortillas. "When you're done, your breakfast will be waiting."

The boy took one look at the food then hunched over the writing board, his tongue stuck out of the side of his mouth and his forehead drawn to a knot.

Before long, she would be teaching him words then whole sentences. In no time at all, he would be reading halting passages to her from the Bible, learning about the Savior while he learned to read.

Melatha glanced at her father's Bible and sighed. How different life would have been had he lived to fulfill his vow to take her and her mother to Ireland. His family lived there, blood relations that Isi would never meet. When her happy, bright-eyed father died at the hands of a thieving vagabond, her mother returned to her people instead, so Melatha grew up among the Choctaw.

She cracked the rest of the eggs into a bowl and stirred them briskly with a fork. Pulling the skillet to a cooler spot on the cast-iron stove, she poured them into sizzling butter. They hissed and sputtered like her feverish mind. With the sun barely over the horizon, already her thoughts were restless. Against her will, they turned to her husband.

On a mission trip to the reservation, raven-haired Reynaldo Marcelo had noticed Melatha among the other maidens and asked to have her. Though she rejected him, her grandfather saw merit in the union, chiefly Reynaldo's prized Appaloosa, and made the trade. Yellow Tree claimed he approved the kindhearted Spaniard because he foresaw him in a vision.

Many moons had passed, and many visions of her own, before Melatha had come to believe him. She and Reynaldo fought with a fury at first, until he tamed her. Then they loved with great passion. She bore her tiny, squirming brave the following spring.

Sixteen years later—after Reynaldo followed her father in death—like her mother before her, Melatha returned to her people, the only safe place she knew. Miserable within the confines of the reservation, Isi soon ran away. She didn't see her prodigal son again until his twenty-first birthday.

"If I scratch out my letters, will you feed me, too?"

Melatha whirled from the stove. "Isi. You caught me dreaming again."

He kissed her cheek. "Pleasant dreams, I hope." He pointed at Jose. "I see you've found another eager student."

She smiled tightly. "More eager to eat than to learn. But this way we both gain satisfaction."

"Where did you get that old slate?"

"Rosita's mother gave it to me." She held up a box. "Plenty of chalk, too. It's turned into a blessing."

He nodded at Jose, so intent on his letters his face almost touched the board. "More a blessing for him than for you, though he doesn't know it yet. Chihowa Ushi must be pleased."

Melatha's heart glowed in her chest. She loved to hear Isi speak their native tongue.

She stopped stirring the eggs and studied him. Since Isi knew she loved to hear it, he must be up to no good. She determined to ferret out the details of his plan before he ensnared her.

He sat at the table and she set his eggs in front of him. "What does the day hold for you, son?"

Before he could answer, Jose rose from the floor, wriggling with excitement. "I've finished, Mama Melatha. H through Q, just as you asked."

She studied the scrawl of letters on the slate. "Muy bueno, Jose. These are beautiful letters."

"Sí. May I eat now?"

She pulled out a chair for him. "Yes, you may eat your fill."

The boy scrambled into the chair and snatched up his fork.

Melatha wagged her finger. "Uh, uh, uh, Jose. What comes first?"

Blushing, he lowered his lips to his folded hands.

Isi smiled at her over his head.

After what must have been the shortest prayer the Father ever received, Jose snatched up his fork and went to work on his plate.

Shaking her head, Melatha sat down across from her son and smiled. "You were saying?"

Isi's grin became a troubled frown. "I'm not sure what this day will bring. Likely more work than I can wring out of daylight as usual." He sighed. "I can't count on much help from Cuddy today."

She lifted her head. "Oh?"

Isi shoveled in another bite, waiting until he swallowed to speak. "I doubt his bed will turn him loose today. I'm sure he's nursing a weak stomach and a pounding head."

"Oh, Isi. You mean he—?" She stopped abruptly and glanced at the boy.

Isi nodded.

Her heart squeezed in protest of the news.

"So," he began casually, "after spending more time with them, what do you think of our guests?"

The trap was set. Here was the bait. Wisdom demanded she tread lightly. "I like the one called Bertha. Her spirit is free. She's not bound by the opinions of others."

He nodded thoughtfully. "And the rest?"

"What about them?"

He looked up. "There are four guests in the house, Mother. You only like Bertha?"

"I don't have much to go on, do I? Mr. and Mrs. Dane seem nice enough."

He pushed back his eggs. "So you like Bertha, and the Danes seem nice. . ."

"Yes."

"And that's it?"

"I suppose so."

Color crept up his cheeks. "Let me get this straight. You like Bertha. The Danes seem nice. But you can't find one thing to say about—"

A harsh rap on the door rattled the hinges, cutting him off and bringing Melatha to her feet. "All right, all right! I'm coming!"

Isi shrugged. "Perhaps I was wrong. That's likely Cuddy now."

"Or Jose's mother," she suggested over her shoulder as she crossed the room.

Isi feigned shock. "With that heavy-handed knock? If so, let's pray she's in a cheerful mood."

Melatha laughed and opened the door.

One of Isi's men, pacing and stamping his feet, stood at the end of the porch.

Melatha looked back at Isi. "It's Little Pete."

Isi pushed back his chair and joined Pete outside. He returned shoving the fingers of both hands through his hair the way he did when he was tense.

She gripped his arm. "What's wrong, son?"

He met her gaze and his eyes flashed fear. "Pete said I'm not to report into work today. Rawson's orders."

Melatha released her disbelief in a single word. "What?"

"He said the old man wants to see me. Right now. In the barn."

"Oh, Isi. Do you know what this is about?"

His face drawn in grim lines, he nodded. "I'm afraid so." With no further explanation, he pushed through the screen and jumped off the porch. As he crossed the yard, he pulled back and squared his shoulders, ready to take what was coming to him, whatever unthinkable thing it might be.

Melatha's thoughts returning to snares and traps, she wondered who had set one for her son. Tears clouding her eyes, she bowed her head to pray.

❧

The morning sun had yet to light the cool interior of the barn. Diego ducked inside and waited for his eyes to adjust.

Mr. Rawson, still unaware of his presence, slouched against Faron's stall, both arms atop the door, resting his forehead on his hands. He looked like a man with an unpleasant task ahead of him. Diego cleared his throat, and the big man straightened. "There you are."

Diego approached him. "I came as soon as you called." Bracing the heel of his boot against the bottom board of the stall, he looked the horse over. "He doing all right this morning?"

Mr. Rawson reached to stroke Faron's nose. "In body, yes. I'm not so sure about his spirit. He hates this loathsome stall."

The horse crowded closer to Diego and nickered box.

Mr. Rawson chuckled. "Faithless animal. For all my devotion to him, he loves you more."

Smiling, Diego scratched between the horse's ears. "It's not me he loves, sir. Rather the carrots I keep in my pocket." He patted the velvety nose. "You're out of luck today, amigo. We're fresh out."

Mr. Rawson appeared thoughtful. "Faron. That means pharaoh in Spanish?"

Diego nodded.

"Suits him, doesn't it?" He released a heavy sigh. "You suppose I'll ever be able to ride him?"

Diego gave a confident nod. "I'm sure of it, sir. He just needs a little more time learning to trust you." He attempted to swallow, but his throat was too dry. "Sir, Pete said you wanted to speak to me."

"I do." Usually by now, Mr. Rawson would be facing Diego, searching for the bottom of his pupils while he said what was on his mind. Instead, he seemed to avoid meeting Diego's eyes.

"He told me not to show up for work today. Said the order came from you."

"That's right."

Why wouldn't the man turn around? Why wouldn't he say the words and get it over with?

You're fired, Diego.

Turn in your lariat.

Pack your things.

Take your mother from the little house she loves and hit the trail.

What could be so hard about it? He should open his mouth and have it done.

"Cuddy will be taking your place today."

"Sir?"

"Cuddy." A hard edge crept into Mr. Rawson's voice. "I plan to work his tail off. Give him a taste of what your workday feels like. Let him see how a real man runs his business, with sweat and grit. Then maybe he'll lose his taste for booze." He frowned a warning. "Don't let him talk you into lifting a finger to help. I want that boy to learn something today."

Weight shifted off Diego's shoulders. "And tomorrow?"

"Humph." Mr. Rawson finally turned. "You don't get off that easy. It's back to business as usual tomorrow. Any longer at the helm of the Twisted-R and Cuddy would run it asunder." His gaze flitted past Diego's face while he worried his bottom lip with his teeth. "I want to thank you for last night."

Guilt stung Diego's insides. "Thank me?"

"For getting that dunderhead out of sight before more people noticed the state of him."

Diego lifted his brows. "I don't deserve your gratitude, sir. I have to confess that wasn't my motive."

Mr. Rawson waved him off. "Oh shoot, I know. You did it for Cuddy, though I fear he doesn't merit such loyalty. Still"—his eyes met Diego's at last—"like always, you wound up helping me in the bargain." Resting his hand on Diego's arm, he smiled. "I want to express my appreciation for your faithfulness. After God and your mother, you've always put the ranch and me first. You're a tireless, selfless boy, Diego, one I'd be honored to call my own. I'm proud of you, son."

Diego wrestled with his emotions so he could speak. Dropping his gaze, he rustled a mound of straw with the toe of his boot. "Thank you, sir. I'm not certain I'm worthy, but thank you."

They stood in silence, communicating their feelings with smiling eyes until Diego broke the stillness. "If you'll pardon my boldness, sir, Cuddy longs to hear such words from you."

Mr. Rawson stared. "Cuddy? Nonsense. He couldn't care less what I think."

Desperation shot boldness through Diego's veins. "That's where you're wrong. I've watched him try to please you. I've watched him fail and seen what it does to him. If you would just try to see—"

Mr. Rawson's hand shot up. "Hold on there. Don't you lecture me." His face blotched like the skin of a cactus pear, and he shook his finger in Diego's face. "Don't mistake my fondness for you as a license to butt into my business."

Though his eyes still bored into Diego's, something snuffed the furious fire. He sighed and relaxed his shoulders, and the purple hue faded from his cheeks. "You may have watched some things all right. I just don't think you've seen."

Diego longed to ask what he meant but didn't dare risk angering him further.

Mr. Rawson returned his attention to the horse. "Don't you think I want to be proud of my only son? I tried for years to turn Cuddy into the man he should be, longed to teach him everything I knew, but he wanted no part of my lessons. . .or me. His interests lie elsewhere, namely at the bottom of a bottle when he's not perfecting the art of chasing skirts."

"Forgive me, sir, but Cuddy has many other interests. He's always talking about politics and travel, and he studies a lot on what's going on in the world."

Mr. Rawson snorted. "What does any of that have to do with raising cattle?" He fiddled with Faron's mane, smoothing and combing it with his fingers. Faron edged closer, grunting his approval.

Diego joined them by the gate, lifting Faron's brush from its hook on the wall. They ministered together in silence, both men tending the horse they loved.

Mr. Rawson glanced over. "Want to know something funny?"

Diego smiled. "What's that?"

"The truth is you have Cuddy's stubbornness to thank for the turn your life has taken."

Diego's brows met in the middle. "How so?"

"When you showed up at the ranch, fresh and green as a spring shoot, I saw great potential there. So I took you under my wing, groomed you into what I longed to see Cuddy become, partly because I wanted him to see how his life could turn out if he'd let me help him, what great things we could accomplish together."

Diego scowled. "You used me?"

Mr. Rawson looked startled. "Used you? Yes, I suppose I did in a way." He latched onto Diego's forearm. "But along the way I grew to love you, came to respect the kind of man you are. I caught myself wishing we were blood relations. Then I noticed the way Greta looks at you, and I thought my wish might be fulfilled through my grandchildren."

He raised one busy brow. "There's a spark of expectation in my old heart yet." He nudged Diego with his shoulder. "Well, come on. . .do I still have reason to hope?"

Diego's smile wilted. He lowered his gaze and said nothing.

When he raised tortured eyes, Mr. Rawson nodded. "I feared as much. It's Emily Dane, isn't it? That girl could turn any man's head."

"Sir, I—"

The man took a ragged breath. "Don't say a word. It's not your fault, son." The chewing on his cheek intensified, and he blinked away sudden brightness from his eyes. "I guess that's it, then. I had hoped to die with some assurance the Twisted-R was in capable hands. Instead, I'll die disappointed." He turned on his heel and left the barn with sagging shoulders.

Diego followed and stood watching his back. He opened his mouth to call out, prepared to assure Mr. Rawson he'd marry Greta, give him grandchildren, tend the ranch the rest of his days. He longed to tell the man whatever it took to remove the hopelessness from his eyes, but the words wouldn't crowd past the lump in Diego's throat.

Feeling eyes on the back of his head, he spun.

Emmy stared at him in shocked silence.

Cuddy's vacant eyes were fixed on the ground. He seemed smaller, as if the pain etched on his face had caused him to shrivel. His trembling hand groped for a fistful of hair and gripped until the knuckles turned white.

Diego took a step toward him. "Cuddy?"

Cuddy whirled away from them and disappeared behind the barn.

Tears sprang to Emmy's eyes. Without a word, she tore out after him.

CHAPTER 16

Head drooping, Cuddy sat on the sun-dried bank of the Nueces with his arms resting on his knees, his hands dangling from his wrists like dead fish.

Emmy had found him in the same posture outside his room, only this time the pain shining from his eyes wasn't self-inflicted. She eased onto the ground beside him.

A ragged release of air was the only acknowledgment he gave that he noticed her there.

Miserable for him, she reached for his hand, but he shrugged her away. She decided not to push, but not to leave either.

They sat together, Emmy watching the wind rippling across the water, Cuddy staring at the ground between his knees.

She jumped when he snatched something from his shirt pocket and sailed it across the river. It hit the far bank then tumbled down the slope and into the water with a splash. Emmy caught the glint of sunlight on metal just before the flask settled to the murky depths.

She touched his arm. "Bravo, Cuddy. Now you're thinking, and that was the smartest decision yet. You don't need that foul stuff, and you know it. You're much better off without it."

His head still sagged, but the corners of his mouth tipped slightly. "It was empty."

She withdrew her hand. "Oh."

Glancing at her at last, the hint of a smile bloomed to an outright grin. "You're something else, you know that?"

She squeezed his fingers. "You are, too, Cuddy. I just hope you know it."

He sneered. "You and I know exactly what I am, honey. A fatal disappointment. You heard it straight from the one who decides such things, the great John Rawson."

Emmy leaned against his shoulder. Her next words spilled unplanned from her mouth. "It's not your father's right to decide such things, Cuddy. We're judged by God and no other." Shocked by her own words, she sat quietly, waiting for him to respond.

He didn't tense beside her, or laugh with scorn, or seem offended in any way. Instead he continued pulling up bright green blades of grass and tossing them into the water. "If that's the case, my goose is cooked." He sighed. "I'm told God knows more about me than my father does."

Emmy sat up and looked him over. Cuddy appeared to feel as worthless as she had felt before God showed up and changed everything in her life. Since the day she blundered into the sheltering arms of grace, she hadn't feared Papa's opinion so much. The only thing left was living with the pain of his rejection.

She tried to picture hearing Papa use the term "disappointment" to describe her. He could rant and rave, shake his head, glare at her with scorn, but until he actually said the word aloud, she could pretend he didn't consider her a failure.

Cuddy twisted his head to peer at her. "Why so quiet? Have I depressed you?"

"No. Just trying to imagine how you feel."

"I could describe it to you, but you'd be shocked at the language."

She laughed. "Oh, Cuddy! What am I to do with you?"

Mischief danced in his eyes. "You could kiss me."

She swatted his arm. "I believe praying for you would serve you best."

He seemed surprised. "You really believe all that God stuff, don't you?"

Scooting around to face him, she pinned him with her eyes. "I didn't used to. I found the whole thing a frightful bother. I watched people herd through the door of the church like sheep because it was expected of them, not because they found anything valuable on the other side. Most of them came out the same way they went in, miserable through and through. The man singing "Amazing Grace" the loudest kept a girl named Grace on the side. It left a bitter taste in my mouth, and the things of God seemed hardly worth my time."

Cuddy slapped his leg. "I never figured you for a cynic! So what changed?"

She bit her bottom lip. "Me."

He tucked his cheek between his teeth and seemed to ponder her answer, until finally, as though he found it too simple, he shook his head. "No, I mean what changed *you*."

"God changed me, but not until I let Him. Once I allowed Him close to me, I saw the truth of who He is." She grasped Cuddy's hands. "You see, the same things bother God about the church. He wants my devotion, not merely my attendance. Does that make sense?"

Cuddy gazed at her, unflinching. "Well, I'll be. Forgive me for saying this, but you're not the sort of girl I expected to be saying such things."

She laughed. "I wasn't for many years. Now, knowing Him is the dearest thing in my life."

His eyes widened in amazement. "Girl, you're lit up like a candle. You're pretty serious about this God of yours."

She cocked her head. "Why does that surprise you? Papa said your parents are Christians. And your best friend—"

He yanked a weed and snapped it in half. "No, sweetie. Diego's not a Christian. He's more like a saint."

~~~

Diego bit back a curse, shocked it had entered his mind. He'd left everything—work that Cuddy had been ordered to do—and searched the whole ranch, exhausting the last ounce of his energy praying for Cuddy's safekeeping and Emmy's comfort. Only to find them whispering together, their heads close and bobbing like a pair of silly lovebirds.

He had feared finding Cuddy wearing a noose, poised to kick the chair from under his legs. To find him cooing with Emmy instead was an insult. To hear their laughter stretched the boundaries of Diego's understanding. Madder than he'd been in his life, he gritted his teeth and rode toward them.

Watching Emmy snuggle with Cuddy, a sweet smile on her face, went a long way toward helping Diego understand the man's rapid recovery. Having a woman like her so near would comfort a dying man.

For her his anger blazed. She had deliberately strung him along with her dimples and sultry voice, her teasing laughter and meaningful glances, until he came to believe there was something between them. The glow of adoration on her face as she leaned close to Cuddy told Diego just what he needed to know. She'd have no more trouble from Diego Marcelo.

Engrossed in each other's company, they didn't notice Diego until he was practically on top of them. Emmy saw him first and nudged Cuddy. Something flashed across her face when she saw him riding toward her, a tenderness that started in the softness of her mouth then spread and settled in her eyes, somehow different from her earlier expression.

He jerked his gaze from hers and pronounced himself a desperate fool. He had read too much into something that was obviously his imagination.

Cuddy stood and helped Emmy to her feet. With his hand at her back, they walked to meet him. Cuddy's jaw hardened. "If he sent you after me, I won't go."

Diego dismounted. "Your father doesn't know you overheard."

Cuddy angled his face from sight, but not before Diego glimpsed the raw pain that twisted his features. A vein bulged in his neck, and a scarlet flush crept up from his collar. The man was fighting tears.

Diego's affection for Cuddy rose to the surface, displacing his ire. "I'm glad to see you're all right."

Cuddy leaned against the horse, fiddling with the saddle. "Oh, you know me. . .indestructible."

Still watching Diego's face, Emmy patted Cuddy on the shoulder. "I'll leave you to talk."

Cuddy latched onto her arm. "Remember to be careful."

Emmy nodded. "Snakes. And scorpions." She smiled. "How could I forget?"

She strolled to the water's edge, just out of earshot.

Diego placed a hand on Cuddy's arm. "It wasn't as bad as it sounded. Your father spoke out of pain."

Cuddy lifted flashing eyes. "Pain?" He spat on the ground. "You must be joking."

"He feels rejected by you. If you'd listened to his reason, you'd understand."

Visibly trembling, Cuddy gripped the saddle horn. "I listened plenty good. He said I'm the biggest disappointment in his life and he'll take that to the grave. What's there to understand about that? John Rawson doesn't feel rejection. He gives it. Defend him all you like, I'll never see things any other way."

Diego ran his fingers through his hair. "I'm telling you, Cuddy, you'd feel differently if you'd listened to everything he said."

"I wasn't invited to hear all he said, brother, but I noticed you were." He lifted his chin. "Come to think of it, I did hear something I won't soon forget."

Diego ducked his head and asked what he already knew. "What was that?"

"You're prepared to toss my little sister aside because you've set your sights on Emmy."

"I didn't—"

Cuddy held up his hand. "You didn't have to say it aloud. The old man's disappointment said it for you."

"So Emmy. . .did she. . .?"

"You already have my father, Diego. Now you want my girl?" He swelled his chest and took a step closer. "I love you like a brother, amigo, but you stay away from Emily or you'll answer to me. Understood?"

Diego swallowed against his suddenly tight collar. "You're my best friend, Cuddy, but threatening me is uncalled for." He brushed the blustering burro aside and swung into the saddle. "And dangerous." He laid his spurs to the horse's flank, needing to get as far from them as possible. Away from Cuddy before he had to hurt him. Away from Emmy before she caused him more pain.

She called out to him as he rode over the rise.

He didn't look back.

CHAPTER 17

Magda eyed the mountain of supplies Bertha had piled on the counter of McCaleb's Mercantile Store. Since John Rawson had decided they would travel to Catarina by wagon after all, they had room to carry more supplies. He never should've said such a thing to Bertha. After twiddling and touching every item for sale, she bought three times the amount John suggested they needed for the trip.

Once her business was settled, Bertha was ready to leave, so the wait made her fidgety. John finished his conversation with the clerk of the impressively large store then led the way outside. After enduring a half hour of Bertha twitching and sighing, Magda was relieved to step onto the sun-drenched porch.

John had mentioned at breakfast that they'd been his guests for a full week but hadn't yet been to town. As soon as they laid aside their forks, he loaded Magda, Willem, Bertha, and Kate into his wagon and proceeded to usher them through Carrizo Springs, giving the grand tour.

Holding the door of the mercantile, John smiled at each of them as they filed out. "Have I mentioned the name of our newspaper? It's called *The Javelin*. After the animal."

He pointed inside the store. "Got its start right in there, owned and edited by J. L. McCaleb. That little paper saved our town during the drought of '86 and '87. A gentleman sent McCaleb an ad stating he'd pay good money for javelina hides." He chuckled. "Well, there was no shortage of javelinas around these parts. McCaleb made a deal with a fellow in San Antonio who traded cash and groceries for hides. It's the only way these people survived."

"That's quite a story, John," Willem said.

John gazed across a nearby field, his mind clearly in the past. "The drought lasted so long that the cattle overgrazed the natural grassland. It never returned to what it was before. Thousands of cattle died of starvation. It almost meant the end of ranching in these parts. Ranchers took to burning the stickers from prickly pear to feed their stock." He shook his head. "A hard time indeed for Dimmit County."

In a brighter mood, John gripped his chin. "Now then, I've shown you the churches and the school." He turned to help Kate onto the wagon then offered his hand to Bertha. "Next we'll see the courthouse, an imposing structure built in '85. The new bank sits across from it, established just last year."

Bertha groaned. "If it's all the same to you, John, I'm up for missing some of that."

Magda gasped. "Bertha Maye Bloom! The very idea. . ."

She scowled right back. "My feet hurt. I told you I didn't want to wear these shoes."

Kate Rawson covered her mouth with her gloved hands and had herself a good laugh. When she recovered, she twisted on the seat to smile at them. "That's all right, dears. I'm a little tired myself." She patted her husband's shoulder. "This man is as proud of Carrizo Springs as he is our children. If I don't stop him occasionally, he talks my ear off."

John glanced back, looking sheepish. "Sorry, folks. I get carried away sometimes."

Furious, Magda buried her elbow in Bertha's side.

Pouting, Bertha scooted as far as her little body could fit into the corner of the seat.

Beaming at Bertha, John cleared his throat. "I see you're a woman of action. How about we dispense with all this nonsense and start making plans for our cattle drive? I say we leave first thing in the morning."

Bertha shot forward and pounded him on the back. "Now you're talking straight, John. Put the whip to that horse's behind and let's see how fast we can get to the house. We've got some packing to do."

⤳⟋

With a creature as proud as Faron, Diego had to let the horse think breaking him was his idea. Every small accomplishment, each tiny step forward had gained Diego progress.

First, the reins of braided horsehair draped gently on Faron's neck. Then the snaffle bit, which he took to surprisingly well, considering it took a week for him to accept a blanket resting on his back. When he tolerated the saddle, tears stung Diego's eyes. That fateful day Faron allowed him to mount, Diego had cried unashamedly.

He thought he'd burst waiting for the right moment to show John Rawson, and now the wait was over. Today marked the fifth ride. Usually skittish when Diego entered the barn, Faron's head had bobbed over the front of the stall, nickering his impatience. He stood trembling with anticipation while Diego hitched up his saddle, and Diego's boot hardly touched the stirrups before Faron trotted from the barn. The time had come to reveal his big surprise.

"Well, well."

Diego pulled on the reins and shifted his weight to look behind him.

Cuddy lounged next to the barn door with crossed arms. Not a word had passed between them for the last four days, not since Cuddy's threat beside the Nueces.

It didn't surprise Diego how simple it was to avoid him. Seeking out the hardest work on the ranch made it easy to bypass Cuddy Rawson.

He'd avoided Emmy, too. Much harder to do since she appeared at every turn. At first, she responded to his aloofness with flashing, angry eyes. The expression in their shaded blue depths soon changed to sadness and confusion.

"You have something to say, Rawson?"

One eyebrow raised, Cuddy's gaze wandered over Faron from hoof to mane and finally settled on Diego. "I didn't think anyone could tame that devil."

"It wasn't easy."

Cuddy laughed bitterly. "What won't you do to garner that old man's favor?"

Diego closed his eyes to steady his temper. "What won't you do to

127

hurt him?" he asked without a backward glance. Taking up the slack in the reins, he steeled himself and tapped Faron's sides with his heels.

Blood surged through Diego's veins as the horse leaped into a run. The wind whistled in his ears as they flew down the long drive in front of the house. Faron jumped the gate, hardly breaking his stride, and hit the road with lightning flashing from his hooves.

No wonder no fence could hold him. Faron needed to run, lived to stretch his body to its limits with the earth flying past beneath him. For weeks, no matter how tired, no matter how hungry, Diego had spent his free time working with Faron. The thrill of this ride proved to be worth every second.

He spotted a cloud of dust ahead and followed it with his eyes. Faron cut the distance between them so fast, Diego hardly blinked before he recognized it to be the Rawsons' rig. A thrill shot through him. He wished somehow to be in the saddle surprising Mr. Rawson, yet at the same time be in the wagon watching his face light up when he figured it out.

Diego decided to breeze right by him then circle back to get his reaction. As Faron passed in a blur, John Rawson let out a howl. Diego's grin was so wide he collected sand on his teeth. He slowed and turned the horse.

Mr. Rawson stood in the two-seater watching, though dancing in the two-seater seemed closer to the facts. As Diego approached, he shouted again, so loudly the horse jumped.

Diego steadied Faron and reined him in beside the cluster of astonished faces.

"Whooeeee! Son, my old eyes must be deceiving me. What's that thing you're riding?"

Diego's cheeks had found their limits. "Only the fastest beast in South Texas, sir."

Mr. Rawson clambered to the ground, his eyes aglow with excitement. "Can I ride him?"

Diego swung down. "There's only one way to find out."

Wringing her hands, Mrs. Rawson scooted to the driver's seat. "Oh, John, no."

He raised one beefy hand. "Now, Kate. . ." Running his fingers along Faron's glistening neck, he crooned to him. "Easy boy. That's it, now."

She stood up. "John Rawson, you promised you wouldn't let that animal hurt anyone."

"And I aim to keep my promise."

Mr. Dane leaned out of the rig. "Maybe she's right, John."

With eyes only for the horse now, John didn't seem to hear his friend's suggestion. He put his boot in the stirrup, and Mrs. Rawson squealed and stamped her foot. "I won't see you do this."

He swung into the saddle. "Then close your eyes."

She had time to gasp and he was gone, barreling down the road toward the house as if borne on angels' wings. As horse and rider dashed around a curve and disappeared, one more gleeful shout rang out.

Mrs. Rawson sat heavily on the seat. "Oh, Diego. What have you done?"

Wincing, he came alongside her and peered into her dismal face. "It was bound to happen, ma'am. Your husband was determined to ride that horse. Wouldn't you rather it be after I calmed him down some?"

She reached to pat his hand. "I know you're right, but I've dreaded this day."

Diego chuckled. "He'll be fine. He's an expert horseman."

She squeezed his fingers. "I know that, too. They're likely in the barn by now, Faron getting a rubdown while John congratulates himself on your accomplishment." She smiled and squirmed into her place. "The least you can do is drive me home."

Diego climbed aboard and untied the reins. "It won't be possible to get you there quite as fast as Mr. Rawson, but I'll get you there in one piece."

She gave him a look from under her lashes. "Very good, assuming John made it home in one piece."

Mrs. Bloom leaned in between them. "He's in one piece or hundreds. As fast as that horse was moving, there wouldn't be nothing left to sweep into a dustpan."

"Bertha!" Mrs. Dane bawled at her.

"Well. . ."

❧

Emmy slammed down her hairbrush and slumped on the bed. "It's not right. Why can't I go with you?"

Mama shot her a warning look. "Keep your voice down. I've told you why." She took Emmy's wrist and pulled her up. "I've also told you not to loll about on this bed, haven't I?"

Emmy had to admit the Redwork quilt was lovely. Blocks of embroidered flowers, animals, and children were set against a white background, each square outlined in red and white sashing. The quilter, evidently a young Katherine Colbeck, had stitched the initials K. C. and the year 1878 inside a wreath in the last square a few years before she became Kate Rawson.

Mama smoothed the rumpled spread and shook her head. "I don't know why Kate has all the beds spruced up like this. I'm not sure I'd want such lovely bedcovers for everyday. Makes you scared to move in here."

Emmy groaned. "Stick to the point, please. You know Papa's notion is ridiculous. I have to stay behind because of bandits that may never appear? Mama, listen to me. I will not stay without one of you here with me. I hardly know these people."

Mama shot her a dubious glance. "Don't twist the facts to suit you. You seem to know Cuddy well enough to add a few gray strands to your papa's head." She stood up from straightening the spread and frowned. "Don't think he hasn't mentioned his concerns about you two to Kate Rawson. If not for her offer to stay behind and chaperone, you'd have your papa in your lap until I got back."

Emmy bristled. "He spoke to her?" Burning with shame, she spun away from her mama and gripped the edge of the dresser. "How humiliating! What did he say?"

"I wasn't privy to the conversation." She held up her finger. "But I know this. . .you have Cuddy to blame. He shouldn't have opposed your papa like he did. So if you're entertaining thoughts about Cuddy, forget them. Papa would never give his blessing."

Emmy pushed off the dresser. "For pity's sake, Mama. Cuddy's just a friend."

Mama looked doubtful. "Friend or suitor, Willem will never accept Cuddy now."

Squealing her frustration, Emmy swept from the room. She'd done nothing all day but listen to plans she wouldn't be part of and helped everyone pack to leave her behind. She had to get out of the house or bust.

Mama jerked open the door and stuck her head out. "Where are you going?"

"No farther than the veranda, so don't call out the dogs."

"Emily!"

Emmy flounced down the stairs and out the back door, feeling like a spoiled child but too angry to care. She stared at the cloudless blue sky butting into the distant line of trees along the banks of the river, her thoughts as murky as the muddy bottom.

Mama and Papa didn't want her spending time with Cuddy. The others, including Cuddy, seemed to like it just fine. Emmy felt a bond of kinship with the troubled young man, even held affection for the tenderhearted, quick-to-smile rascal. But no matter how charming Cuddy Rawson might be, in matters of the heart, Emmy's interests lay elsewhere.

The heat of the midday sun on her bare head reminded her of two things. One, she'd left her hair unpinned, and two, it was August in what had to be the hottest place in the world.

Ducking into the shade of the covered patio, she perched on the wall of her haven to pout. Self-conscious, she gathered her thick mane over one shoulder and began to wind it into a braid.

"Leave it loose, Emmy."

She spun. "Diego! I didn't see you there."

He closed the distance between them and reached for her hair, wonder in his voice. "These curls are like twisted bands of sunshine."

Trembling inside, she let him twirl a blond ringlet around his finger. "Where have you been?"

He sobered and released her hair.

Horrified at her boldness, she tried to fix her blunder. Brightening her mood, she smiled. "It's been days since we've had a chance to talk. I guess you've been busy with the ranch." She ducked her head. "Unless. . ."

Diego touched her shoulder. "Unless?"

She lifted her eyes to his. "Have I offended you in some way?"

He turned aside and buried his fingers in his hair. "Emmy. . ." His jaw muscles worked and his gaze lost focus. "I owe you an apology. I've been blaming you for something that's not your fault. You can't help how you feel."

Jumping to her feet, she grasped his hands. "Exactly! I'm so glad you said that. I was just thinking the same—"

He withdrew from her touch. "Then you'll forgive me if I continue to keep my distance. It will make things easier."

She flashed him a startled look. "Pardon?"

Cuddy breezed around the corner of the house whistling a tune Emmy didn't recognize. Strolling lazily toward his father's rig with a packed crate in his hands, his head came up as if he'd sensed their presence. He paused and stared. The sight of him irked Emmy. His deliberate gaze bore the arrogance of a man who felt entitled to look.

Diego took a step away from her and bowed. "I'll be going. I've caused you enough trouble."

Cuddy lifted the crate over the tailgate then turned with his hands on his hips. "Thought the old man sent you to Carrizo for supplies."

Ignoring him, Diego strolled off the brick patio and crossed the yard.

Their confusing conversation concerned Emmy more than the fact that he'd left. Well, almost. She watched Diego's broad shoulders until he disappeared inside the barn.

"Afternoon, sweetheart."

The sultry voice in her ear lifted Emmy from the ground. She clutched her heart. "You shouldn't sneak up on folks like that."

Laughter rumbled in Cuddy's chest. "I didn't exactly sneak, now did I?" His attention shifted. "Well now, look at this. I sure like these pretty ringlets falling around your face." He reached to touch her hair, but she slapped his hand. He chuckled and rubbed the red spot. "Feisty today, are we?"

She nodded at the crate. "I see you're loading the wagon. Does that mean you're riding along to Catarina?"

"On a trip with my father?" He snorted. "No thank you. He roped me into helping them pack, that's all." A hopeful glint flickered in his eyes. "And you?"

Sorry she'd brought it up, Emmy frowned and shook her head.

Cozying up three steps too close, he leaned to whisper. "No one around to meddle in our business? Such an obliging arrangement. I'll have to remember to thank your father."

"Don't make me slap you again, Cuddy Rawson." She pushed

him away. "And wipe that silly leer off your face. It doesn't become you. Besides, are you so foolish to believe Papa would leave me alone in this house with you?"

He cringed. "He's staying behind?"

"No, not him."

"Your mother?"

She arched one brow. "No."

Cuddy scratched his head. "There's no one left but Rosita, and she goes home nights."

"You forgot your own mother."

He lifted a disbelieving eyebrow. "You're mistaken. Mother told me herself she was going."

"That was before Papa decided the trip might be too dangerous. Your mother offered to stay in his place."

Cuddy let his head fall back. "That's bad news. Mother considers chaperoning young ladies an art form." He touched her chin. "So that's what has you wrapped tighter than a cinch strap."

She pressed her lips together and let him assume what he wished.

He dashed his hat against his legs. "The whole thing is absurd. Children need a wet nurse. When will they consider us grown?"

Emmy leaned against a post with a sigh of resignation. "When we're married, I suppose."

Cuddy tucked his hat on his head and bent so close the brim touched her face. "Was that a proposal, Miss Dane?"

"Oh, stop!"

"It's very forward, considering we just met, but I promise to think about it."

She laughed. "Yes, for all of ten seconds. Somehow you don't seem the marrying kind."

Edging closer, he nudged the hat brim out of his way. "I think you may have misjudged me, Emily Dane." His worldly blue eyes closed in.

Emmy turned her face aside so abruptly he narrowly missed kissing the post. "I don't think so. Somehow I'm certain I called it right."

With a grunt from Cuddy and the hollow sound of a fist in his back, someone too short for Emmy to see over his shoulder latched onto him from behind and pulled him off her. Panting from the effort it took to toss Cuddy aside, Aunt Bertha glared.

Emmy gasped and held up one hand. "Aunt Bert, please don't look at me that way. This is not what you think."

"It never is, darlin'." She tipped her head at Cuddy. "I ain't too sure what I'm interrupting here, but this scalawag's mama is calling for him. I reckon she has more hauling she needs him to do." She wagged her finger in Cuddy's face. "You'd best get to it, before I call Willem and let him sort this out."

Cuddy tipped his hat. "There's no call for that, ma'am. I'm going." He winked at Emmy and hustled toward the house.

As he trotted past, Emmy caught sight of Diego's mama standing just outside the veranda, a pan of dried corn on her hip. She watched Emmy with ancient, knowing eyes—eyes that judged her and found her guilty. The little woman had seen everything and understood nothing.

Emmy's heart sank.

Melatha averted her gaze, hitched up the pan of bright yellow grain, and went her way.

Emmy longed to call out, to deny and explain, but what could she say that made a lick of sense? Besides, she still had to deal with Aunt Bertha.

"What am I supposed to do now, little girl? You've landed me in a right sore spot. If I tell your papa what I just saw, he won't go with me on this trip. Worse, he's liable to make your mama stay behind." She peered up at Emmy. "I'm just selfish enough to want to avoid such a thing because I don't know enough about what I'm doing. I need the both of them with me when I buy my cattle." She curled her first finger under her chin. "On the other hand, if I don't tell them and something happens to you while we're gone, I'll never forgive myself." She widened her eyes. "And neither would they."

Emmy gripped her shoulder. "There's no need to tell them, Aunt Bert."

The wise green eyes softened. "I expected that answer since it saves your hide. Now give me a good enough reason to believe you."

Emmy met her steady gaze. "I've done nothing wrong. I shouldn't be held responsible for Cuddy Rawson's actions."

One of Aunt Bertha's piercing eyes narrowed while she pondered

Emmy's words. Emmy held her ground without flinching until Aunt Bertha exhaled and nodded. "Child, you've been a handful all your life, except here lately. There've been considerable changes over the past year, and I want you to know that I've noticed."

Blushing at the praise, Emmy smiled. "Thank you, Aunt Bert."

"Thank yourself, because it's also the reason I'll be keeping what I saw to myself."

Emmy kissed her cheek. "In that case, God deserves the credit. Last year I would've been easy prey for the kind of attention Cuddy offers." She bent to wrap her arms around Aunt Bertha's narrow shoulders. "You won't be sorry you trusted me."

Aunt Bert thrust out her chin. "Make sure I'm not. I've never kept anything from your mama before. It ain't setting well with me."

Sliding one arm around her, Emmy walked her toward the back door. "In that case, why not tell her once you're on the road. She'll know you'd never leave me behind unless you had reason to believe in me."

Aunt Bertha squeezed Emmy's waist. "Sugar, I just might do that." She lowered her voice to a whisper. "If it's all the same to you, we might not mention anything to your papa for a while yet."

Emmy nudged her and grinned. "I have a better idea. How about never?"

Still laughing, they entered the house and parted company at the foot of the stairs.

Relieved to find she had her room to herself, Emmy glanced longingly at the comfortable quilt then perched obediently on the delicate stool in front of the dressing table. Her mind was a muddle of too strict parents, too forward friends, and too distant suitors.

Why did Cuddy seem so endearing one minute and so intolerable the next? And Diego? Seldom at a loss when it came to reading men, Emmy had yet to understand a single word he'd spoken to her in the shade of the covered porch. Part of the reason had to do with the dizzying effect of his finger twirling her hair, his hand so near her face she smelled his shaving cream.

"Blast it!" Bored silly with obedience to unreasonable requests, she flounced to the bed and fell backward, reaching her hands to her sides to gather the quilt about her. "After all," she demanded of the empty room, "what else are bedcovers for?" Wrapped in its comforting folds, she felt like a disgruntled enchilada, the savory dish Rosita had served the night before.

Rolling onto her side, she allowed anger like she'd not felt in months to churn inside. Who did Diego Marcelo imagine himself to be? How dare he announce his intention to keep his distance! He said it would make things easier. Easier for whom?

She tossed to the other side. "We'll just see about that, you arrogant, confusing man. I'll decide how much distance to put between us, thank you. When I'm done with you, you'll not want much, I assure you."

Emmy had tried to be good and found it a loathsome bother. Look where it had gotten her—one man who assumed her meekness made her easy, another who thought he could set her aside. Well, no more! Changing a man's mind came second nature to Emmy, and that was exactly what she intended to do.

Throwing the cover aside, she bolted upright on the side of the bed. Her image in the oval mirror across the room grinned at her like a long-lost friend. Her smile widened. One thing was certain, Katherine Rawson had best sharpen her chaperoning skills. If the twinkle in the eyes of the girl staring out from the mirror could be trusted, the old Emily Dane had returned.

CHAPTER 18

Melatha rolled off her cot onto her knees to thank God for another day. She praised Him for the cross of Christ. She blessed Him for blessing her with plenty, including the generous bounty of her garden, watered by the abundance of artesian wells that gave Carrizo the richest farmland in the South. She reminded Him to bless the Rawsons for providing her with a comfortable place to lay her head at night and a well-stocked kitchen to cook for her son. She'd hardly begun laying her petitions about Isi before the throne, requests concerning White Hair in particular, when the door creaked open behind her.

Melatha instinctively jerked her gaze to the crack at the side of the shade. Still pitch dark. Spinning to her feet, nearly tripping on her cotton nightdress, she crossed the room and hoisted the frying pan over her head before the intruder stepped over the threshold.

"You move with less stealth these days, Mother. I easily tracked you from the bed to the stove."

Weak in the knees, she lowered the heavy cast iron to the floor. "Isi! I nearly opened your skull with the skillet."

The scratch of a match preceded the glow of her lantern, lighting the room and chasing her fear to the shadows. Isi's familiar grin wavered above the flame, warped by the flickering light. "The skillet? Now that part I didn't track."

She lifted the pan to the stove and dusted her hands. "A mistake for which you almost paid dearly."

He laughed. "Do you always greet visitors with a crack on the head?"

Her brows crowded together. "No one enters my jacal so long before the sun does. Even you wait until the smell of bacon lures you. Why is this morning different?"

Head low, he shuffled to her and pulled her close. "I'm sorry I frightened you. Mr. Rawson and his guests are leaving soon for Catarina. He asked me to help see them off. I had hoped for an early breakfast this morning, that's all."

Pushing against him, Melatha gazed up. She'd already seen through his flimsy, bungled speech. "Breakfast? That's all?"

He nodded, but his eyes faltered.

She decided not to press. As sure as the sunrise, he'd open up before he left her table. She had only to wait for the chance to pull it out of him with the nimble, practiced fingers of a mother. Hopefully his present distress had nothing to do with the scheming Emily Dane.

"They're leaving Emmy behind. Did you know that?"

Her hope waned. She shrugged past him and bent to gather wood for the stove. "Do you mean Emily?"

He lifted her bag of coffee and spooned two large scoops into the pot. "Yes, Emily. She asked me to call her Emmy. It's the name her friends use."

I'm sure they do. "I would think she has many friends."

Isi paused. He stared at the side of her head while she mixed her corn cakes. Whatever words swirled in his mind, he bit them back and thankfully chose to tread the road to peace. She'd have to be more careful.

"As I was saying, they plan to leave her on the ranch until they return. Why do you suppose they'd do such a thing?"

It made little sense to Melatha. She'd never trust a daughter like Emily. "How do you know this?"

He twisted his mouth as if he tasted sour milk. "Cuddy boasted of it to Little Pete. I suppose he's led the men to believe he'll benefit from it somehow. Those animals jested and leered"—his lips tightened against his teeth—"until I shut them up."

Melatha pushed a dollop of churned butter off the edge of a spoon with her finger. It landed in the warming pan with a sizzle, so she gave the batter a final stir and ladled a generous spoonful on top of the foaming butter. Knowing she would cross a line with him, she spoke her heart. "At times fetid winds stir up truth."

He calmly finished filling the coffeepot with water, but his unruffled manner was deceptive. When he faced her, his eyes were flashing. "Why don't you like her?"

She tried to look innocent. "I never said I didn't. I only—"

He held up his hand. "Don't. You've made your feelings clear since the day she arrived. It's not like you, Mother. You taught me that it's God's business to judge. Yet, you've judged Emmy. What is it about this one girl that makes you lay aside your beliefs?"

Melatha wanted to shake him, to rail in his face until he opened his eyes. She bit her tongue instead. "I don't mean to judge, but I've already told you what I see in her."

He ran his fingers through his hair. "You said she has a restless spirit. For that you despise her? How many times have you said the same about me?"

Tendrils of desperation wound about her like the smoke rising off the corn cakes. Her temper as hot as the skillet, she shoved the pan to the back of the stove. The stench of burnt corn assailed her nostrils and stung her eyes, providing an excuse for her tears. "I'm trying to protect you, Isi."

He strode to the door and jerked it open.

She wondered if he believed it was to rid the room from smoke when she knew he intended to leave.

"Save your worries for something else. I don't need your protection from Emmy. I intend to stay far away from her."

The tears in his eyes wrenched her mother's heart because she couldn't tell if the smoke or something else had caused them. "What do you mean, son?"

"I mean I'd prance bare-bottomed through a field of cactus to steer clear of Emily Dane. The girl's eyes burn my flesh, Mother. I'm careful to avoid her touch for fear it will set me ablaze."

Melatha's heart dove. Things were worse than she imagined.

She started toward Isi, but he spun on his heel and bolted out the door.

❦

Diego bounded off his mother's porch and trotted in the opposite direction he needed to go. Not ready to wrestle with what might be waiting for him up at the main house, he rounded the weathered bunkhouse instead.

Hidden from the prying eyes of the casa mayor and his mother's jacal, he sagged against the rough boards of the narrow wall that faced the river and slid to the ground with a ragged sigh. Massaging his throbbing temples with his fingertips, Diego tried to sort out his confusing thoughts.

He had wasted the last eight years of his life running from himself, and he was exhausted. Denying his Choctaw blood, he had traveled the country, seeking a different link to his past. He'd hoped to locate someone who knew his father and gain information that would connect him to his Spanish relations.

If he'd found them during those early troubled years, he'd be basking by the sea on the southern coast of Spain instead of toiling on the bank of the Nueces. He'd be cavorting among almond trees instead of dust and cactus, dancing the flamenco and eating the *paella* on which his father had cut his teeth.

Diego's desire to find his paternal roots had all but consumed him. He'd tried to follow God's will when he reunited with his mother and brought her south. Though his love for her had never waned, the fire within him to be someone besides Little Deer still blazed, despite how hard he prayed.

The last few days with Emmy had stoked a new flame within. She made him whole again, more complete than he'd felt since his father died. Yet his mother, whose instincts he'd always trusted, considered Emmy too spirited. Cuddy saw her as a prize to conquer, perhaps a way to gain revenge.

Whatever his reasons, Cuddy wanted her, and she preferred him. The finality and hopelessness of these undeniable facts weighed down Diego's shoulders.

"I thought I saw you duck back here."

Suppressing a moan at the latest evidence of the recent turn of his luck, Diego's head jerked up. "Greta."

Her expression bounced from confusion to pleasure then made the rounds again. "What are you doing sitting here all alone?" She tilted her head to the side. "Are you all right?"

He pushed to his feet, digging deep for a smile. "Of course."

He waved his hand distractedly. "I come here sometimes to—" He suddenly felt ridiculous.

She pressed her hand to her forehead. "Say no more. I've intruded on your privacy and interrupted your thoughts. Forgive me." She turned to go.

He should've let her. Instead, he put out his hand. "Greta, wait."

She looked over her shoulder. "Yes?"

"Stay a minute, please."

"Are you sure?"

Her hopeful smile shamed him. He hadn't treated her well lately. "I'm certain. Come here."

She cast a guilty look toward the house. "I suppose it'll be all right. For a minute or two." She surprised him by lowering herself to the dewy grass and spreading her skirt beneath her.

To keep from embarrassing her, he sat, too, as if he intended all along for her to sit on the damp ground.

Letting her gaze wander the expanse of the yard, Greta toyed with the cotton sash at her waist. He'd never seen her so ill at ease, so unsure of herself, and hoped he wasn't the cause. Her delicate white throat bobbed above her lace collar. He couldn't tell if she was about to speak or swallow.

She did both. Gulping hard, she smiled at him. "It's a nice spot. Do you come here often?"

Diego bit back a grin. The underside of the bunkhouse smelled of musty dirt; the sparse island of grass they'd settled on was the only solid groundcover in a sea of sand, pebbles, and stubble; and the wind lifted the sharp stench of manure from the southeast pasture, blowing it under their noses. Nice was hardly the word he'd use. "I slip back here occasionally. It's quiet at least. No one bothers me."

She ducked her head. "Most of the time, anyway?"

He gave a throaty laugh and nodded. "Yes, most of the time." He felt her watching him so he quirked one brow in her direction.

Her cheeks reddened and she covered her face, but her laughter pealed, sounding relaxed and unforced again. "I've missed spending time with you, Diego. You make me feel good inside."

A playful smirk on his face, he leaned closer. "I do?"

She tittered and shifted her body, not away from him as she'd always done before but so near he smelled rosewater in her hair.

He touched the tip of her nose. "Suppose I say you make me feel good inside, too?"

It was true. He felt alive, every cell of his body glowing. He didn't want to be alone today. If he wanted to be with Greta, who would it hurt? Cuddy obviously didn't mind. Mr. Rawson would be overjoyed. His mother had hinted her approval. And Emmy? He doubted she would notice.

Greta gazed at him with hazy eyes that went to slits, and then she let her head fall back, an open invitation to kiss her.

He pressed the side of his mouth against her face. "You're so lovely."

She turned and he felt the softness of her lips against his cheek. "Oh, Diego."

He moved his head in small deliberate circles, nuzzling to find her mouth. "And so sweet."

She drew in sharply when he kissed her.

"Lovely, sweet Emmy," he whispered.

He thought the strangled gasp came from Greta until Cuddy spoke. "I see you found him, little sister."

Emmy stood beside him, staring at Diego with wounded eyes. Whirling, she pushed past Cuddy and disappeared.

Greta buried her clenched fists in Diego's chest and shoved him away then stood to her feet. Tears flowing, she gathered her skirts and dashed around the opposite side of the bunkhouse.

Leering, Cuddy leaned against the corner and crossed his arms. "I believe I may have misjudged you, Diego. I see you've been sweet on Greta all along."

Understanding slowly settled. Cuddy hadn't heard him call his sister the wrong name, so maybe Emmy hadn't either.

Cuddy squatted to eye level, squinting at Diego. "Unless you're trying to string them both along at the same time?"

"No! I—"

Cuddy laughed and swatted the air. "Just joking, friend," he boomed, grinning wider. "I know Saint Diego could never do such a thing. That's more my style."

Awash with guilt, Diego lowered his head.

"Hey, it's all right, amigo. I don't mind you courting my sister. I always figured you might." Brandishing one finger, he scowled. "Not that I approve of any more slip-ups like what I just witnessed. If you want to kiss Greta like that, you need to put a ring on her finger first."

He stood and sauntered over to take his sister's place on the ground. "So all that nonsense with Emmy. . .the stuff you told the old man. . .you were just confused?"

Diego opened his mouth to deny it, but Cuddy's upraised hand didn't give him the chance. "I understand completely. Emily Dane would confuse a celibate monk." He grinned then sobered. "I wish you'd come and set me straight, that's all. I haven't liked being on the outs with you. It feels unnatural."

"Cuddy, listen—"

"I hate that we stumbled onto you and embarrassed the women. Emmy's face was brick red when she spun out of here." He sobered. "And poor Greta was in tears."

Curious, Diego frowned. "Why did you two come back here?"

"Looking for you. Melatha said you came this way."

"Why were you looking for me?"

Cuddy cursed and struggled to his feet. "For the old man! He's blasting smoke from his ears by now. He sent us to find Greta, who he sent to find you a half hour ago."

Bouncing his palm off his forehead, Diego leaped up, too. "I forgot. He asked me to be present to make sure their departure went smoothly."

Cuddy nodded. "Yep, he figured you forgot. He wasn't in the best of moods about it either. If he saw Greta come back crying. . ."

They shared a look.

Cuddy grimaced. "He'll be looking for someone to blame it on. We'd best hightail it to the house."

Heart pounding, Diego wheeled around the front of the bunkhouse on Cuddy's heels, running to face the latest mess he'd made.

Thankfully, the wagon still sat in front of the house, fully loaded and tied down. Willem Dane sat stiffly in the driver's seat with his wife perched beside a fidgety Mrs. Bloom in back. Staring toward the house, he shook his head. "Magda, where's Emily? You'd think she'd want to see us off."

"I told you she's not feeling well. A headache, I think. She's resting upstairs."

Diego winced.

"Besides," Mrs. Dane continued, "she bid her farewells this morning. I do believe she can't stand to watch us go."

He snorted and Mrs. Dane leaned to squeeze his shoulder. "Try to be more understanding, Willem. Your daughter's upset."

Mr. Rawson stood on the front porch talking to his wife, one hand patting the side of her face. He tenderly kissed her then strode down the steps to the rig. Spotting Cuddy and Diego, his face blanched. By the time they reached him, his cheeks had mottled to various shades of red.

"Where the devil have you been?" He directed the question at Diego.

"I'm sorry, sir. There's no excuse. I should've been here like you asked."

His boss glowered. "You got that right. I needed you."

Diego cringed. This was more than bad luck. His life was falling apart. "If it's not too late, sir, I'm at your disposal. What can I do to help?"

Something over Diego's shoulder caught Mr. Rawson's eye. "It was too late an hour ago. Little Pete tended your business for you." He tilted his chin. "And here they come now."

Unprepared for what he would see, Diego looked behind him. His heart surged and he spun around. "Faron, sir?"

Mr. Rawson pushed past him. "Yes, Faron."

His heartbeat racing now, Diego ran after him. "Why is he saddled?" He knew his tone was harsh, demanding, but he couldn't help himself.

"I'm going to ride him, that's why."

Faron stood proudly pawing the ground and snorting his displeasure with the delay. Ready to run, he strained at the reins.

Muscles rippled in Little Pete's arms and back as he tried to hold him, and relief flooded his face when Mr. Rawson took over. "He is one spirited animal, this horse," Pete said, laughing and shaking his head.

"That's how I like them, Pete," Mr. Rawson boomed.

Pete grinned. "Sí, señor." Looking guilty, he stepped aside when Diego approached. Aside from feeding and brushing, Diego had instructed the men never to handle Faron.

"Mr. Rawson, wait. I don't understand. You're not taking him to Catarina?"

"No, son." He swung into the saddle and tapped the horse with his heels. "Weren't you listening? I'm riding him to Catarina."

Speechless for the second time in one morning, Diego stared after them.

Mr. Rawson turned Faron a few yards out and impaled Diego with a glare. "See to it you take running this place a little more seriously while I'm gone. Understood?"

Diego found his voice. "Sir, Faron's not ready for what you're asking of him."

Mr. Rawson defiantly raised his chin. "Well, I believe he is. What say you leave my animal to me and just tend my ranch like I asked?"

Diego's shoulders slumped. "Yes, sir."

Before riding away, Mr. Rawson pinned him with one more scowl. "When I get back, I intend to find out who made my little girl cry. You'd best hope it wasn't you."

He nudged Faron and trotted over to the wagon. Bolting into the lead, he signaled over his head for Mr. Dane to follow. The wagon rolled away from the house and down the drive, creaking under the weight of the supplies. The way Faron cantered and hopped, desire blazed within him to cut loose and run.

Sighing, Diego wondered how long Mr. Rawson could hold back the horse's fire. The thought stirred a memory of something his mother had said to him. Was it only days ago?

"Your future will appear in a whirlwind of smoke and rise to meet you in flames. . . ."

A flash of movement above his head drew his attention to the upstairs windows. At the same time the drape fluttered shut in Greta's room, the shutter snapped closed in Emmy's. It seemed the future his mother predicted had arrived. A whirlwind of guilt for what he'd done to Greta swept through him, while searing flames of desire for Emmy drove him from the yard.

CHAPTER 19

A piercing wail split the air, jolting Emmy upright and raising the hair on her arms. She first thought she'd heard the bellow of a wounded animal—perhaps one of the coyotes that howled the first night on the ranch—until the cry came again, eerily human and unquestionably from the bedroom below. Greta's room.

Emmy knelt on all fours and pressed her ear to the floor. Just as she thought, Greta's mournful sobs rattled the floorboards, rocking Emmy back on her heels. She hugged herself, aching inside for Greta. Naturally, the girl would be upset. Diego had kissed her but whispered Emmy's name against her lips.

This fact hadn't penetrated Emmy's understanding until she'd run halfway back to the house. When awareness dawned, it stopped her cold. Ready to retrace her steps and demand an explanation of Diego, she'd made her way to her room instead, her head reeling. After pondering the enormity of the situation, she'd decided Diego calling her name was a good thing, but Greta's pain doused the torch of joy the realization had kindled.

Still crouched in front of the vanity, she lifted her eyes to the looking glass, her tears blurring the image. What had she been thinking to believe the old Emmy was back? That Emmy would be spinning about the room, defiantly wrapped in the Redwork quilt, dancing a victory waltz on Greta's head. She'd be plotting her next move, finagling the best angle to use to her advantage in order to drive a wedge between Diego and Greta. She certainly wouldn't be kneeling in front of a mirror watching her heart breaking for her rival. If she ever doubted the change God had wrought in her life, she didn't now. The old Emmy wasn't back.

She was dead.

❧

"No more foolish women!" Diego shouted to the empty barn. His decision bounced among the overhead rafters, the echoing agreement a confirmation.

"Tend my ranch," Mr. Rawson had growled.

The order was exactly the medicine Diego needed in a double dose. Spine-busting labor was the only thing he'd ever known. He'd focus on hard work and horses now, the two things that had been his salvation.

The thought of horses reminded him of Faron, and his stomach pitched, though not with the queasy lurch that came after the word salvation reminded him of his neglect of the Savior.

"Foolish mothers, too?"

His back stiffened. "Foolish mothers top the list." Brushing past her, he hoisted the wide broom from the hook and went at Faron's stall as if he could sweep away his troubles along with the muck. Sulking, he pushed the debris from the rear of the enclosure toward the middle, intent on ignoring his mother until she left. He realized his plan was doomed when she latched onto the handle from behind.

"I won't leave your side until you hear me out."

Past experience had taught Diego she meant what she said. His mouth a thin line, he eased the handle from her hands and propped it against the wall. Crossing his arms, he leaned beside it. "Very well. I'm listening."

She peered up at him and shook her head. "No, son. You're not listening yet."

He frowned. "Yes, I am."

She cautiously touched his arm. "Not with your heart, Isi."

Shrugging away from her hand, Diego rolled his head against the rough adobe wall. "My patience is short just now, Mother. It's been a trying day."

She quirked her top lip. "A sad thing to hear, considering the early hour."

"Sad?" A harsh laugh rose inside his gut and blurted from his mouth. "You can't imagine how sad."

He didn't notice her move, yet suddenly she stood next to him. "What happened, Isi?"

Diego released a wavering breath. How could he tell her? *What happened, Mother? The son you're so proud of took advantage of a dear, trusting friend. He kissed her while pretending she was someone else.*

He opened his mouth two times before the words spilled out. "I shamed Greta Rawson, Mother. Shamed Greta, her family, and myself." He set his jaw in a grim line. "After you warned me not to."

Fear snuffed the compassion in her eyes. "What are you telling me, son?" She gripped his arms with her long fingers, surprising him with her strength. "How have you shamed her?"

"I hurt her." The pitch of his voice rose, sounding to his ears like the whine of a woman. "I made her cry." He ducked past his mother and out of the stall. Sitting down hard on a ragged bale of hay, he rested his forehead in his hand. "I may never forget the look in her eyes."

His mother scurried to him and knelt at his knees. "You're too harsh with yourself, son. Not preferring Greta, not choosing her, hasn't shamed her. It's kinder to tell her now so she won't harbor false hope."

He shuddered, shaking off her unmerited faith in his nobility. "I kissed her."

She picked up his hand. "It's natural you would want to kiss Greta. She's a very pretty girl." Was it hope he heard in her voice?

Lifting his eyes, he met hers head on. "I kissed her in a way I had no right to. . ." The weight of his shame dropped his head again. "And then called her by another woman's name."

Stewing in her silence, he waited. When nothing came, he looked to see why.

She had fallen on her behind in the dirt, lines of defeat etched on her face. She stared at the ground with hollow eyes, and the hopelessness in them added sorrow to his shame.

"I'm sorry, Mother."

She faced him. "John Rawson will hear of it."

"He already knows, at least in part."

She nodded thoughtfully. "What will happen now?" Her voice broke at the end, twisting flaming arrows in his heart.

"You won't be hurt by this, I promise. I'll plead on bended knee for Mr. Rawson to let you stay on in your jacal until I find you another home." He reached for her hands resting on her knees. "A real house this time, not a mud-brick hut."

Jerking her fingers free, she shot forward and grasped his chin. "For a mud hut you think I grieve?" She shook his face. "My son has scattered his principles to the wind, yet a one-room shack is my concern?"

Desperation crowded Diego's throat. He'd never seen her so angry. "Don't worry. I'll make it right."

"You foolish boy, don't you see it yet? There's no way to make this right. Mr. Rawson won't let you marry Greta after you disgraced her—"

"I don't want to marry Greta."

"And he will never allow you to bring a wife to this ranch to flaunt in his daughter's face." She pushed off the ground and paced in front of him, her doe-hide shoes soundless on the earthen floor. "If John Rawson doesn't fire you, though I suspect he will, you must leave the Twisted-R or face a lonely, childless life."

Diego stared dumbly.

She stopped so fast she kicked up dirt and spun to point her finger. "And for what? In case that girl has robbed you of the ability to think for yourself, let me explain what this means. You lose everything. Your job, your home, your reputation, the last four years of your life. . .White Hair took it all, just as I feared from the moment I first saw her."

She sank to her knees and covered her face with her hands. "Oh, Isi! Why didn't I see the truth? My vision was not a good omen as I thought." She raised her tear-streaked face. "Instead it foretold your doom."

CHAPTER 20

Magda relaxed once John Rawson got Faron settled into a lively walk and reined in beside the wagon. The big horse seemed eager to run clear to Catarina, so John had struggled for some time to calm him. Faron's high spirits didn't seem to faze John in the least, and in fact served to energize and cheer him considerably.

Bertha squirmed beside her on the seat. "Ain't we nearly there?"

John swiveled his head to look at Bertha. "Tired of traveling already?"

He shared a wink and a smile with Magda. She jabbed Bertha with her elbow. "This whole thing was your idea. Don't start in complaining."

Bertha rocked from side to side. "This seat is rough on a body, Magda. Something you'd understand if you weren't packing twin sofa cushions on your bottom."

Magda nudged her harder.

John chuckled merrily. "We've gone less than two miles, I'm afraid. That leaves about eighteen miles of bumpy road ahead."

Bertha groaned.

He pointed with his chin. "Dig up under the bench there and you'll find a folded blanket. Tuck it under you and it might help some."

Straddling her legs and bending between them until she nearly toppled, Bertha rummaged, surfacing with a horsehair blanket.

She held up her prize and grinned. "Why, thank you." Leaning forward, she poked and prodded the folded cloth beneath her in a most unladylike fashion until she'd rooted out a comfortable spot. Still beaming, Bertha looked overhead. "At least we don't have that unmerciful sun beating down. Sure was smart of you, John, to rig this special buggy."

She referred to the fringed surrey top John had fastened to a long-bedded farm wagon. In front of the large cargo area, he'd placed a buckboard seat. The sturdy, dependable vehicle provided extra room for passengers and shade with a clear, unobstructed view—important features in the rugged terrain of South Texas.

"Look here, John. A rider."

John jerked his head around to follow Willem's finger.

Magda's stomach tightened when he tensed and straightened in the saddle. She leaned to tug on Willem's sleeve. "Is he friendly?"

Willem snorted and raised his brows at John. "That's a woman for you. I'm supposed to know from a quarter mile away if that strange man is friendly." He twisted to look at her. "Even if he had the information penciled on his forehead, he's still too far out to read."

John joined in with the laughter, but not so merrily this time. "The rule of thumb in these parts is to assume they're unfriendly until they prove themselves otherwise." He motioned at the rifle propped against the rail. "I'd hold that ready if I were you."

Willem's frivolity dried as fast as the August dew. He hoisted the Marlin .44-40 and chambered a shell, resting it in plain sight on his knee. Just in time, since the rider had come within shouting distance.

"Mornin'," the stranger called as he approached. "No call for alarm, folks. I mean you no harm."

"Friendly," Bertha whispered.

"Not so fast," Magda whispered back. "Let's give him a minute more."

John nudged his hat up and studied him. "Where you headed, mister?"

"Out to the Twisted-R Ranch."

Magda opened her mouth to comment on the coincidence, but John motioned behind his back to be still. Relieved that John stopped her before she blurted what he didn't want known, she watched to see what he had up his sleeve.

John spit then wiped his mouth. "Is that so?"

"Yes, sir." The young man took off his hat and wiped his brow with his sleeve. "I think it's up this road a few miles."

John casually stroked Faron's neck. "What business do you have out at the Twisted-R, son?"

Magda watched the stranger's face. If he were the troublesome type, John's meddlesome question ought to rile him some.

"I aim to see a friend there. Ranch foreman by the name of Diego Marcelo."

John pushed back his hat. "Diego, eh?"

The boy grinned. "*El Toro*, we call him. Bullheaded at times, but a real nice fellow. He's been keen on showing me the ranch, so I thought I'd ride out and see the place. I hear it's an impressive spread."

"Is that a fact?" John said casually.

"Oh, yes, sir." More than happy to provide details, he leaned forward in the saddle. "I understand the owner's a prince of a man. To hear Diego tell it, John Rawson's been like a father to him."

A mischievous glint in his eye, John cocked his head. "Well, ain't that something? This Rawson sounds like a mighty fine man."

Magda struggled to keep a straight face.

Bertha ducked behind Willem with both hands over her mouth.

"Yes, sir. I hear the old man runs the tightest, cleanest ranch in Dimmit County."

John studied him for a few minutes before he spoke. "Where are you coming from?"

"We have a place out Catarina way. My father's a breeder. Maybe you've heard of him? Buck Campbell?"

No longer laughing, Bertha perked up, bobbing left and right, trying to see around the horse.

John asked the question Magda knew Bertha was busting to ask. "Hasn't your father been selling off some of his stock?"

The boy's grin stretched wider. "We sure have."

"Which Campbell are you, Les or Joe?"

He sat higher in the saddle. "I'm Joe. Les is my older brother." If he beamed any brighter, he'd outshine the sun. "Well I'll be hanged!

You folks heard about us way out here?"

"I've heard mention," John said. "As a matter of fact, we were just heading out to your place to take a look at what you have to offer."

Joe's smile died on his lips. He couldn't have looked more uncomfortable if his boots were on backward. "Well, shoot. I'm glad we bumped into each other, then. I can save you a wasted trip." He tucked his hat on his head, straightening it with both hands. "We ain't got no more animals for sale. Got carried away and about thinned ourselves out of business." He looked like it pained him to deliver the bad news.

John looked a mite pained himself. "That's too bad, Joe. I think we might've worked a deal."

The four of them slumped in defeat, as deflated as a flattened frog.

Bertha sighed from the depths of her belly. "I guess that's it, then."

Willem leaned to pat her hand. "I'm sorry, Bertha. But don't give up yet, we'll find you something."

Joe Campbell cleared his throat. "Sir?"

Willem glanced up. "Yes, son?"

"If you didn't specifically want to buy from us then maybe I can still help you out."

Hope flickered in Bertha's eyes. "You know where I can buy some cattle, boy?" Squinting, she pointed one finger. "Nothing ordinary, now. I'm looking for the best beef stock South Texas has to offer."

Joe tipped his hat. "Well, that'd be ours, ma'am. But if you want to settle for second best, I've heard there's a breeder down in Eagle Pass who's selling out."

Interest flickered on John's face. "Everything?"

"Down to the last horn and hoof. I suspect you could get a right fair price for an excellent herd."

His brows hovering in the vicinity of his hairline, John looked at each of them in turn. "What do you think, folks? Want to make a run for Eagle Pass?"

"Yes!" Bertha crowed.

Willem held up his hand. "Not so fast, Bertha. It's not a light decision. This is a dangerous region to travel, and unless I'm mistaken, it's much farther than we'd planned to go."

John nodded. "Willem's right. It's forty miles from Carrizo

Springs to Eagle Pass. Since we've come a couple of miles in the wrong direction that adds four more to the journey. I know of an old Indian trail a little west of here that will shave that off, but it might be rough going."

Bertha scooted to the edge of her seat. "I say we do it."

Magda drew back and stared. "What are you going on about? Weren't you the one complaining after only two miles on the road?"

She wiggled her behind. "This makeshift cushion took care of that. Come on, Magda. . .Willem. Let's go see Eagle Pass."

Willem sat quietly for a minute then peered at John. "How long do you think it would take?"

Rubbing his chin, John stared across the grassy plain that seemed to stretch on forever. "It won't always be like what you see here. Some parts of the ride will be harder than others and the heat won't help. The horses can make fifteen to twenty miles a day if we stop for rests and keep them well watered."

Alarmed, Magda sat forward. "That means we may be sleeping outside for two nights?"

John shook his head. "Not necessarily. I know a rancher who'll put us up tonight. He lives a little better than halfway, so if we push a bit, we can impose on his hospitality late tonight and make it to Eagle Pass by bedtime the next." His eyes grew intent. "That's if we leave now, so I'd suggest we make up our minds."

Bertha stood up in the wagon. "What are we waiting for? We got nothing but money and time."

John grimaced and glanced at Joe Campbell, who pretended not to notice. "I wouldn't make a habit of bragging on the money part," he whispered. "We'll be a target for every thief from here to the Rio Grande."

Straightening, he rode closer to Joe. "How do I find this man you speak of?"

"When you get into town, cross the bridge north of Fort Duncan. That's Van Buren Street. Go straight ahead to Main and take a left turn to Washington." Joe glanced at the women and a flush crept over his face. "You'll find the Piedra Parada Saloon on the corner. Go in and ask for Raul."

John balked. "The Piedra Parada? That's the rowdiest place in town."

"Yes, sir. I reckon I'd leave your womenfolk outside."

"You can count on that. You said to ask for Raul?"

"That's right. Look for a big man. He's a bouncer. Tell him Buck Campbell sent you." The blush deepened. "Buck's my pa. Raul wouldn't know my name. Tell him what you're looking for. He'll take it from there."

John stuck out his hand. "Much obliged, Joe."

The boy shook John's hand. "You're welcome, Mr.—" A curious look swept his face. "What'd you say your name was again?"

John picked up the reins. "I didn't."

"Sir?"

Twisting in the saddle, John jabbed behind them with his thumb. "You'll find the Twisted-R down this road a piece. You can't miss it." He smiled. "It's the tightest, cleanest ranch in Dimmit County."

Waving Willem on, John rode out ahead, leaving young Joe scratching his head.

Magda stared after him with a grin on her face. "After you knew you could trust him, why didn't you tell him who you were?"

John trotted Faron up beside her. "I figured once he'd said such nice things there was no reason he should learn the truth about me."

She laughed. "Imagine his surprise the next time he rides out to the ranch and Diego introduces him to John Rawson."

Willem interrupted their fun. "Where are we headed, John? I noticed we've taken a westerly turn. Why aren't we headed back the way we came?"

"Because of the shortcut I mentioned." He pointed. "The trailhead is right up this way."

Bertha gave Magda an impish glance. "You should be ashamed of yourself."

Magda touched her chest. "Me? What for?"

"For making fun of me in the mercantile store. Turns out the good Lord had a plan for me buying all those extra goods. He used me to watch out for us." She nudged Magda with her shoulder. "Now then, ain't you?"

"Ain't I what?"

"Ashamed."

"Maybe." Magda offered a petulant lift of one shoulder. "I'll decide once I see how much food you packed in those bundles."

Bertha cackled, drawing the amused attention of the men.

Magda waved. "Don't mind her. She's addlepated."

They rode toward an area of thick brush that seemed the end of the line.

Jumping off Faron, John tied him up then walked along the tangle of bushes and vines until he came to the densest part. Reaching carefully into the center of a laid-over tree, he caught hold of the thicker branches and pushed. It opened the way into a less brushy area that was hidden just seconds before. "Pull by me, Willem. Then you can help me bring Faron."

The two-horse team was reluctant at first, but with a bit of coaxing, they rushed past the overgrowth into a clearing. Willem climbed down and ran to take John's place, leaning his weight into the tree. John leaped on Faron and trotted him through with no trouble.

Ten feet away, the clearing narrowed into the trail John had promised, weaving through the heavy vegetation in front of them like the road to the Promised Land—with thorns.

Dismounting, John took a bucket from the wagon's rear boot. He pulled a plug from the bottom of a wooden drum and water streamed into the pail. Placing it on the ground for Faron, he glanced over his shoulder. "Help me water the horses, Willem. We'll rest them a few minutes since we're about to drive them hard."

He nodded at the team. "Be sure to watch them for any signs of stress. We'll aim to cool them down at regular intervals, but I think they'll be all right."

After they'd tended the animals, they ate a quick bite themselves then struck out. The scenery varied little, so they found other ways to entertain themselves along the way, playing silly games with words and matching wits.

As the temperature rose, the amusements lost most of their charm. The morning had dawned cloudy, making the day feel deceptively cool. Now the clouds had burned off, and beads of moisture persisted on Magda's top lip no matter how many times she swiped it away. As for Bertha, she had loosed her garments to a point that bordered on indecent.

The trip became a blur of blazing heat, sticky clothes, and the monotonous creak of wagon wheels. When it seemed they'd steeped in their juices long past done, the sun fell into the western sky and disappeared behind the trees. Birds swooped down with a flutter of wings to roost among the branches. Coyotes yipped and howled in the distance. Miraculously, Willem dozed, his head bobbing like his spine had worked loose.

Ahead of them, John reined in Faron and raised his hand.

Magda poked Willem in the ribs. "Wake up. He wants us to stop."

Willem fumbled for the leads and drew the horses to a halt. Coming alongside them, John took off his hat and wiped his forehead with a folded white hankie he took from his breast pocket. "I know how tired you are, folks. Believe it or not, I think we're almost there."

Willem yawned. "This soon? With all the stops, I expected to be riding all night."

John nodded. "So did I." He looked at the night sky. "This trail saved our hides. It ran farther than I expected, and it's cleared better than I might've hoped for. I'd say it bought us a couple of hours." He wedged his hat on his head and jutted his chin. "I can see the end of this thing, and once we come out, it's only a mile or so to my friend's ranch."

Magda sighed. "John, that's the best news I've heard all day."

Bertha stood up and stretched. "You reckon they'll let us take a bath? I'd settle for a washtub and cold water."

Magda pulled Bertha down so she could see John. "I'd trade the bath for something hot to eat."

Willem groaned and held his stomach. "I'll second that motion, dear."

John laughed. "They're good people. It's not the first time I've shown up unannounced, but day or night, they've treated me like a king." He dashed a large insect from his boot with the handle of his whip. "Don't worry. You can count on a table spread with food."

Willem picked up the reins. "What are we sitting around talking for then? Lead on."

CHAPTER 21

Melatha had misplaced God.

In a fit of worry, that gnawing state of unrest the Holy Bible warned against, she had stored Him carefully out of sight. In her pantry perhaps, or an apron pocket. Somewhere handy, so she might easily find Him when she decided to trust again.

That time had come, only now she couldn't locate her Creator. He didn't show up in that black hour before dawn when she'd awakened, crying out to Him on Isi's behalf. She couldn't rouse Him when she slipped from the bed to her knees weeping bitter tears. She didn't feel Him in her heart, no matter how feverishly she prayed.

She felt abandoned, as unloved as a motherless child. Starved for reassurance, she leaped to her feet and lit the lamp. Clutching her blanket around her, she swept her father's Bible from the shelf and huddled at the table, desperately flipping through the pages until she found the passage she sought. She read the scripture aloud, allowing the cooling waters of God's promise to quench her thirst for Him.

" 'For I am persuaded, that neither death, nor life, nor angels, nor principalities, nor powers, nor things present, nor things to come, nor height, nor depth, nor any other creature, shall be able to separate us from the love of God, which is in Christ Jesus our Lord.' "

Instantly He was there, wrapping His love around her as surely as the quilt about her shoulders. Of course, He'd been there all along, if the words she'd read held any truth. She had only to let go of her fear and let Him in. "Chihowa Palami, forgive me for doubting You. Help me to understand what has taken hold of Isi. Show me Your hand at work in his life."

A shaft of light fell on the page in front of her, startling her until she realized it was only a sunbeam. Pulling aside the shade, she winced at the brightly lit morning. The hour was late. She'd been so engrossed in her troubles she hadn't prepared breakfast. With a sudden jolt to her heart, she realized Isi had never shown up to eat.

Melatha stood so fast the quilt caught the edge of the chair, sending it crashing to the floor. Her heart in her throat, she scurried outside to the porch. Shading her eyes, she gazed over the property, searching the horizon. She peered toward the pasture, eager for any sign of Isi or his horse. She ran to the side rail and gazed toward the main house, hoping she'd see him loping across the yard or leaned against a tree talking to Cuddy.

The door to the bunkhouse creaked open, sending her flying down the steps, but only Little Pete slipped out, nodding and tipping his hat.

Embarrassed, she looked down at her flowing white gown, wondering if Pete thought she'd lost her mind. So be it, she felt she had. More so every minute that passed. Turning on her heel, she hurried inside to get dressed. She wouldn't find Isi while gazing barefoot from her porch.

As she dashed toward the basket where clean clothes were stored, a breeze from the open window lifted and fluttered the pages of the Bible, still open on the table. She slowed long enough to close the precious book and return it to the shelf. Another scripture blazed across her mind as her hand left the cracked leather binding.

"A bruised reed shall he not break, and the smoking flax shall he not quench. . ."

She'd learned the meaning of the beautiful words while crouched at her mother's knees. "It's a message of trust," Mother had whispered. "A promise that Chihowa Ushi will never crush the weak or quench our smallest hope."

Her head reeling, Melatha sank onto the side of her cot. Rushing out to scour the ranch for Isi would only prove she still dared to believe she had Almighty God tucked away in her pocket. The Ancient of Days didn't need assistance from the likes of Melatha

Rhona Marcelo, insignificant before Him in her finest hour, which this day was not.

Gritting her teeth against the flood of fear and doubt, she dressed herself with trembling hands then poured out two cups of dried beans. Spreading them over the table, she pushed aside pebbles, clods of dirt, and bits of chaff then pulled the rest into her pot. She would add pork fat and spices, boil them tender and savory, and bake corncakes in time for lunch.

She glanced at her father's Bible and nodded. When God brought Isi to her door seeking food and comfort, she'd be ready to provide him with both.

⌒◦∾

His stomach growling in protest, Diego led his horse to the next section of fence in need of repair—miles from the big house and still heading in the opposite direction from his mother's kitchen. He needed time to think more than he needed food, and time alone with God more than he needed to breathe. Besides, he wasn't eager to bear the scrutiny of his mother's searching eyes.

He hadn't seen her since the day before when she'd run from the barn, fleeing her disappointment in him. If only he could so easily escape himself.

How had he let so dreadful a thing happen? His feelings for Emmy started from the first day when she'd stolen glances at him on the trail. Embarrassment at ruining his hat had warred with obvious admiration as she gazed from beneath her lashes. In the days that followed, the seed of interest in her had pushed to the surface with very little prodding, exploding into a tangled vine around his heart. Despite his mother's warnings, he hadn't considered his great affection for her a bad thing. Until now.

He had hurt nearly every person in his life, and just as his mother said, the spell Emmy Dane had spun around him was the cause.

The mare he'd ridden to the pasture snorted and bobbed her head. Kneeling with a fistful of wire, Diego looked up to see what had her attention. Groaning, he threw down his pliers. One would think the Twisted-R Ranch would be plenty big enough for a man to escape his troubles. He'd forfeited breakfast to make good his escape, yet one of his most pressing problems rode toward him with a ridiculous smile on his face.

"Ho, there, Diego!"

Reluctant, Diego stood and raised his hand in greeting.

Cuddy closed the distance between them and slid off his horse. "Try telling someone where you'll be, amigo. I've been on parts of this ranch I've never seen before looking for you."

Diego snorted. "I hope you mended fences while you were there."

Cuddy laughed halfheartedly and gave him a jab in the arm. "No foolin', make sure we know where you're going next time. What if you hurt yourself or stumble onto a rattler? We wouldn't know where to find you."

"If a rattler struck me it wouldn't matter. You'd have plenty of time to find my lifeless body."

Cuddy grinned. "Not in this heat, brother. You'd swell up and pop. Then I'd be left to mop up the mess." He wrapped his arm around Diego's neck and walked him back to the post, giving him a good shake before turning him loose. "I sure am glad things are back to normal between us." He colored slightly and bent to pick up the pliers. "I really missed being on solid ground with you." He handed the tool to Diego and kneeled to help him hold the wire. "Truth be told, that's the reason I came to find you."

Diego tensed. He knew there had to be a reason as soon as he saw Cuddy riding toward him. He, too, had enjoyed the warmth of restored friendship, no matter how brief. Sensing it was over, he braced himself and breathed a silent prayer.

Cuddy's gaze darted to his face. "See, I want us to stay on solid ground. I also want you to know I don't hold it against you that things went sour with Greta, only. . ."

Diego's head came up.

Cuddy lifted his brows and nodded. "Mother told me. She said Greta doesn't ever want to see you again, but she didn't tell me why." He screwed up his face as if he tasted something bad. "Diego, I need to know what happened between you two." He paused. "You didn't do anything to hurt my sister, did you? If I thought you took advantage of her, I'd—"

Diego shot to his feet. "I took advantage, but not in the way you mean."

Cuddy stood with his hands clenched at his sides. "So she's still pure?"

"What! Yes, of course." He buried his hands in his hair and whirled away from Cuddy. "I can't believe you had to ask."

Cuddy released his breath in a *whoosh*. "I'm sorry I had to, and I want to believe you. But my sister has cried a river since yesterday, and she hasn't left her room. Can't you tell me why things took such a bad turn?"

Diego gathered his courage and faced him. "I'm not going to lie to you, Cuddy. I hurt Greta."

Cuddy's eyes bored into his, bright with unshed tears. "How? I need to know."

"I kissed her."

"I saw that much."

"Likely the first kiss she's ever had."

Cuddy nodded. "I think I can guarantee that."

Diego drew a shaky breath. "Only I wasn't thinking of Greta when I kissed her."

Tilting his head to the side, Cuddy's eyes narrowed to accusing slits. "And you were thinking of. . ." He held up his hand. "No, wait. Let me guess. You kissed my little sister while pretending she was my girl."

Diego held Cuddy's gaze, refusing to take the coward's way out. "I'd say that about covers it."

Cuddy frowned. "I don't understand. How could Greta know what you were thinking?"

Diego's stomach flipped. Beginning to reconsider the coward's way, he gritted his teeth and spit out the truth. "I called out Emmy's name."

Dangerous fury swirled in Cuddy's eyes, softening to pain in one blink of his lashes. His jaw tightened. "You did that to Greta? For a woman you hardly know?"

Frustration jangled Diego's nerves. "Listen to yourself, won't you? If I hardly know her, the same applies to you. Yet you just called her your girl."

Cuddy looked stunned.

Vindicated, Diego nodded. "Right. You see my point now. She slithers out of nowhere and coils up in your head. A man doesn't stand a chance until he gets wise to her ways." He placed his hands on Cuddy's shoulders. "But I'm wiser now. I don't know how I'll manage to fix the mess I made with Greta. I may not get the chance when your father gets wind of what I've done, but you can bet I'll do whatever it takes to set things right."

At the mention of his father, fear blanched Cuddy's face. He dropped to a squat, staring at the ground. "He'll run you off. I know he will."

Watching him curiously, Diego sank to the ground beside him. "I hope not. I pray not, but if he does, that won't affect our friendship, will it?"

Cuddy lifted his gaze to stare across the pasture, countless emotions jerking the muscles in his face. "If you leave, the old man will do what he's always wanted. He'll put me in charge." He swung tortured eyes to Diego. "I can't run this ranch, brother."

Diego patted his back. "Sure you can."

He gave his head a forceful shake. "Even if I tried my best, my best would never be good enough for the old man. I'd be compared to you every minute."

Knowing it was futile to deny a truth they'd both heard Mr. Rawson admit, Diego decided the kindest thing would be to change the subject. "Don't borrow trouble, amigo. Let's hope for a better outcome, shall we? I have no wish to leave the Twisted-R." He stood to his feet and Cuddy followed.

Squinting, Cuddy hunched his shoulders and thrust out his jaw. "I just have one more question. Is Emily still inside your head?"

Diego swallowed. "I'd like to tell you no, but I can't. Not yet anyway."

Cuddy nodded thoughtfully. "Where does that leave Greta?"

Patting Cuddy's boyish cheeks, Diego gave him the honest answer. "When I figure that out, you'll be the fourth to know."

"The fourth?"

He smiled. "After me, Greta, and my mother." His mood serious again, he gripped Cuddy's arm. "One thing I can promise you. God willing, I plan to stay as far from Emmy Dane as I possibly can."

CHAPTER 22

Magda's fingers picked at the edge of her hem. The unease in her stomach grew as the sun settled lower in the sky, and no amount of chatter from Bertha could quench it. The open road to Eagle Pass seemed treacherous compared to the secluded Indian trail, and Magda felt vulnerable and exposed to danger.

As night approached, John peered into every shadowy clump of bushes and jumped to attention at the slightest rustle or snap. So far, instead of skulking bandits lying in wait, every sound had proved to be the harmless stirring of animals on the prowl.

John's unease grew contagious. Poor frazzled Willem whipped around to look each time John did, his bulging eyes darting from his friend to the trail. Bertha abandoned her folded blanket and slipped to the edge of her seat, her eyes watchful, and the muscles in Magda's tensed legs began to tremble from the strain. The relaxed fellowship they'd shared around the table the night before and again at breakfast had dimmed to a pleasant memory.

Bertha seemed to read her mind as usual. "John, your friends sure were nice folks. They took us in and treated us like family." She paused. "Better than that, more like kings and queens, just like you said."

John answered without taking his attention from the road. "You'll find most folks in this region just as hospitable. They're a kindhearted, generous people." He smiled over his shoulder. "It's one of the reasons I rooted my family here."

Bertha's brows gathered like storm clouds. "Then why are you as jumpy as a cat?"

"Good question, Bertha. There are many fine citizens in Eagle Pass. Unfortunately, opportunists and thieves roam the streets as well. Saloons and gambling halls make life hard. Decent folks are fighting back and have recently cleaned up a lot of the garbage, but they have a ways to go before I'll breathe easy within ten miles of the place." He chuckled. "And we're considerably closer than that right now. Those lights you see up ahead mark the outskirts of town."

Magda moaned. "Bad element or not, that's blessed good news. Right now I'd welcome the sight of a gambling hall if it offered an empty bed."

John shot her a sympathetic glance. "An empty bed may be farther away than you think, Magda. We're not there yet, and we still have to find suitable lodging."

"That part will be easy," Bertha chimed in, reaching to pat her bag under the seat. "We'll stay at the best hotel money can buy."

"That's exactly what we won't do," John said. "Flaunting your wealth in Eagle Pass would be an act of suicide." He shook his head. "No, we'll book a room in the cleanest low-cost establishment we can find." He pointed at her. "You need to keep that satchel close to your body with the latch shut."

Magda took Bertha's chin and pulled her face around. "The same goes for your mouth."

Bertha slapped away her hand. "There's no call to take that tone."

"This is serious, Bertha. Your foolishness could get us killed in our sleep."

Arms crossed over her chest, she pouted. "I heard the man. Give me credit for having a thimbleful of sense."

Scooting closer to her on the seat, Magda wrapped her in a hug. "I'm dreadful sorry, honey. This trip has me on edge, that's all."

Bertha reached around Magda's waist and gave her an answering squeeze. "Aw, that's all right, sugar. I'm a bit jumpy myself."

Willem groaned. "John, you may need a drink to wash down all the confection those two tend to slosh about."

"*Buenas noches*, amigos."

The deep, unfamiliar voice nearly jolted Magda over the side, not to mention free of her bloomers. The only thing that held her on the seat and in her drawers was Bertha, whose grip around her middle tightened severely.

John pulled his pistol, the click of the hammer loud in the sudden stillness. At the same time, Willem yanked back on the reins and held up the lantern.

A short, swarthy man wearing a straw sombrero stood by the edge of the road. If he noticed that John cocked the gun, he pretended he hadn't. "Good evening, friends," he repeated in English. "If you please. . .I won't mind a little sip of that drink I heard you speak of."

John eased Faron closer, the horse balking at the stranger's scent. "Stepping out of the shadows can get a man killed, mister. Are you alone over there?"

The question roused Willem. He hurriedly lifted the rifle and scanned the darkness.

"Sí, alone." The man smiled and held his hands out to his sides. "Only me. . .Marcos." He took off his hat and held it over his chest. "I no mean to frighten you, señor."

John steadied the gun on Marcos's chest. "What are you doing hiding out here in the bushes?"

"Oh, no, señor. Not hiding. Merely walking along the road, that's all."

"Where are you headed?"

He gestured to the glow of lights in the distance. "I think to the same place you are going, no? Into town?" He raised his chin to the east. "My sister, she lives over that way about one mile. I go for visit three days ago, and now I go home." His smile broadened. "To Eagle Pass."

The way John's eyes flickered from Marcos to the thick brush on the roadside said he didn't quite trust the man. "Well, don't let us keep you, Marcos. I think we'll sit here for a spell and rest the horses." He waved with his gun. "Go ahead, be on your way."

Marcos leaned his head to one side. "Please, señor, allow me walk alongside you into town. There is safety in the company of friends. Do you agree?"

Eyes wary, John studied the little man.

Marcos laughed. "Still you don't believe me? I have more to fear of you." He offered his empty hands. "You see? I am alone and unarmed."

John looked over at Willem. "What do you think?"

Looking none too sure, Willem shrugged.

Marcos seized the advantage. "I will help you in return," he promised eagerly. "Whatever business brings you to Eagle Pass, I can help." He looked at them as if sizing them up. "You come for to buy coal?"

John shook his head.

"No? Business at the courthouse, then. Fort Duncan, perhaps."

Bertha released her hold on Magda and sat up. "We're looking for a man named Raul."

Marcos turned with startled eyes then began to laugh. "A man named Raul? There's one on every street corner, señora."

John laughed, too. "This one works in the Piedra Parada Saloon."

Grinning, he held up his finger. "Sí, sí, Raul. I know of him. One of Father Darius's boys."

Bertha leaned to see past Willem. "Can you help us find him?"

"It's no that easy. Raul no longer works at the saloon." At their obvious disappointment, he hurriedly amended his words. "But I can take you to Father Darius. He will help you to find Raul."

John dipped his head. "You just bought yourself an escort into town."

Grinning, Marcos rubbed his hands together. "Bueno. We can talk about that drink now?"

"I'm afraid there is no drink." John's eyes twinkled. "Unless you're thirsty for water."

Marcus pointed to Willem. "But, he said—"

"No drink."

The man gripped his head. "Ah, señor! Please, tell me you jest."

The men laughed heartily while Bertha leaned close to Magda to whisper. "It's a dirty shame he wasted his finagling skills for nothing." She cackled so loudly she turned everyone's head. "All that work with no payoff," she continued, her breath warm in Magda's ear.

"Bertha, behave yourself."

They rode for a spell before Willem's curiosity got the best of him. He cleared his throat, and Marcos glanced up at him. "You said this Raul was one of Father Darius's boys. That's got me baffled. How can a priest have a son?"

Marcos chuckled. "Raul is no son birthed to Father Darius, just as Father Darius is no priest of the church." He wagged his head. "Father Darius has many sons of the spirit. He runs a mission for wayward souls near the ferry crossing on the Rio Grande."

Willem opened his mouth to ask another question, but John's excited voice drowned him out. "Up ahead are the lights of Fort Duncan. Welcome to Eagle Pass, folks."

~⚬~

One thing was certain. Hiding in her room, no matter how charming the furnishings or comfortable the bed, had grown to be an irksome bother for Emmy. She yearned for her mother's counsel—even Aunt Bert's slapdash advice. However, she didn't look forward to Papa's reaction to the stink swirling around the rafters of the Rawson home, the whole sorry mess centered on her.

Neither Papa nor anyone else could blame her for what had happened. She'd done nothing to cause Cuddy's and Diego's sparring over her, snarling and snapping like hounds on a pork chop, and could do nothing to prevent it. Diego's indiscretion landed squarely on his own shoulders. In her opinion, any discomfort he felt over what he'd done to Greta wasn't harsh enough.

It troubled Emmy that Mrs. Rawson hadn't come to speak to her directly and had only sent Rosita to tap on her door after lunchtime the day before. When Emmy said she wasn't hungry, Rosita turned away with a grim look on her face. After that, no one had bothered.

Greta still hadn't left her room. In the afternoon, Emmy overheard Mrs. Rawson tell Rosita she would take her evening meal at her daughter's side. Driven by hunger, Emmy dared to slip downstairs where an oddly subdued Rosita had served her a meager late supper. After she ate, she begrudgingly returned to the room, having nowhere else to go.

A muffled rattle sounded from the balcony, like the disjointed clatter of a hailstorm back home. Considering the sweltering heat had diminished very little at sunset, she could likely discount hail as the cause. Frowning at the patio door, she jumped when a shower of pebbles hit the glass and rained down onto the porch.

Diego! It had to be him. Anyone else would simply knock on the bedroom door.

She checked her appearance in the mirror, pinching her cheeks and patting a stray curl into place. Yes, Diego's behavior had proved disappointing. It didn't mean she wouldn't be thrilled to see him.

She tucked her fingers inside the corners of her square neckline and tugged. The simple white dress, cut to a flattering V in back with a large circular buckle at her waist, might be the latest fashion, but it covered less of her skin than she liked. She twirled once in front of the vanity, noting how small the flowing fabric and cinched belt made her waist appear. Satisfied, she opened the door and stepped out onto the balcony.

Trying not to seem eager, she walked casually to the rail and peered into the yard below. Seeing nothing, her heart sank. She'd taken too long with her primping. Diego must have given up and gone his way. She turned to slip back inside her room.

"Emily!"

The hoarse whisper jolted her heart. Fighting a grin that would give away her pleasure, she pressed into the rail. "I'm here."

"I see that," he hissed.

Losing the battle with her smile, she scoured the ground. "Where? I can't see you."

Cuddy stepped into the light. "Here. Right under your pretty nose."

Emmy wilted with disappointment. "What on earth? Why are you sneaking around under my window?"

His exaggerated leer made him look like a simpleton. "I thought you might come out and play."

Laughing louder than she meant to, especially considering her room lay directly over Greta's, she covered her mouth. "I can't, foolish boy."

"Why not?"

"You know why. It's not proper."

"Since when did Emily Dane give two hoots about proper?" He cocked his head at her. "Come down. I'm harmless. I promise."

"In that case, march inside and request permission from your mother."

He widened his eyes.

She laughed. "Ah, ha! Just as I thought."

The mention of his mother reminded Emmy of the way Mrs. Rawson had ignored her and her needs. The woman hadn't cared if she ate, much less chaperoned her properly. Offended, Emmy rashly changed her mind. Cuddy was right, proper be hanged. "Stay where you are. I'll be right there."

"Now you're talking, sugar."

Gliding silently down the stairs, careful to make not a sound, guilt niggled the edges of Emmy's resolve. The swirling stink already raised would seem a trifle against the resulting stench of getting caught sneaking out of the house. Certain she'd taken leave of her senses, Emmy peeked once more toward the kitchen and lower hallway before slipping out the back door.

Growling in her ear, Cuddy caught her around the waist and twirled her away from the house. He caught her wrist and ran, pulling her along behind him. Their laughter stifled to giggles until they reached the barn. Once they stumbled inside, they howled like demented coyotes. Cuddy's horse stood waiting, already saddled.

Emmy curled a hand on her waist. "You're pretty sure of yourself, Cuthbert Rawson."

He grinned over his shoulder then reached for the reins. "Why do you say that?" He scowled. "And don't call me Cuthbert."

She waved him off. "Never mind. You're hopeless."

Cuddy mounted the horse then freed the stirrup for her. He offered his hand, pausing to hold her suspended at his side. His face inches away, he peered into her eyes. "Get ready for the ride of your life, darlin'."

Emmy stiffened. Too late, she caught the pungent odor of alcohol on his breath.

Without waiting for her answer, he pulled her up behind him. "Hang on," he cried and thundered past the wide double doors of the barn into the dark, moonless night.

CHAPTER 23

The little man in the wide sombrero had gone from walking alongside the wagon to sitting tall beside Willem in the front seat. Following Marcos's directions, they skirted Fort Duncan without alerting the attention of the posted sentinels, then crossed the bridge on Van Buren Street and turned left on Garrison. True to his word, he had many connections in Eagle Pass, considering every person they passed greeted him by name.

At a Y in the road, so near the river Magda smelled the fusty odor of mud, they veered to the left, passing a large, poorly lit building on the corner.

After one more block, they took a right turn on Rian Street, and Marcos led them around to the back of a seedy warehouse.

Willem set the brake on the rig.

John tied Faron to a dilapidated post and addressed Marcos. "Now what?"

"Please to follow me, señor." Aiming a nod and a mumbled greeting at a group of men gathered around a fire pit, Marcos questioned one of them in Spanish.

The tall, slender man smiled and hooked his thumb toward the building.

Marcos opened the door to a scene Magda would not soon forget. The inside of the warehouse was a large open space, except for a small office tucked in one corner. Cots took up most of the room, and where there were no cots, ragged quilts and bedspreads covered the floor. Stretched out on the makeshift beds were men both young and old, some huddled beneath worn blankets, some propped against pillows to read, others clustered together talking quietly. Nearby, a young boy sat cross-legged on a cot, spooning beans into his mouth, though how he managed to eat surrounded by the putrid smell of urine and unwashed bodies was more than Magda could fathom.

She controlled her roiling stomach and her emotions until she glanced at Bertha's face. Tears flowed unchecked down her friend's cheeks and her nose streamed. Magda slid an arm around her waist. "I know, sugar," she whispered. "I know."

Bertha wiped her nose on her sleeve. "This is dreadful, Magda."

She nodded. "Yes, it is. But, honey"—she wiped the tears from Bertha's eyes with her thumbs—"don't let them see you crying. Let's leave them some dignity."

A ruckus arose in the corner. Three men were seated around a table playing cards and one of them was shouting. The largest of the lot, an overweight, ruddy-cheeked bloke in a dirty white shirt and slacks held up by suspenders, scowled at a handsome young man of Latin descent. "You heard me, you dimwitted *naco*. Do I need to spell the words for you?"

Across the table, a slightly built, gray-haired man lifted his head, a serene expression of patience on his face. "Your tone is unnecessary, Mr. Malone. I'm certain Señor Ortiz doesn't mean to seem obtuse."

"But, Father, I've explained three times. I reckon he cain't understand no English. That or he plain ain't listening."

In a show of frustration, the young man threw down his cards. "I am trying to listen, Father. Most of his speech does not sound like English to me."

Ruddy-cheeks pointed at him. "There, you see? He's downright ignorant."

The distinguished gentleman they called Father studied Malone in silence until he squirmed, and then he lifted one eyebrow. "Mr. Malone, how much Spanish can you speak, sir?"

"Who me? I cain't speak a whit." He snorted. "Don't care to neither."

"I see." He pointed to the young fellow. "So, here we have a man accused of being unrefined and lacking social graces." He peered into

172

Mr. Malone's eyes. "This is the meaning of a naco, correct?"

"But, Father Darius. . ." Mr. Malone's gaze darted around the room, but he found no support among the silent, hollowed-eyed witnesses.

"Yet Mr. Ortiz has undertaken to learn English as well as his native Spanish." He redirected his finger at Mr. Malone. "And here we have one who speaks only his native tongue—having mastered it none too well, I might add."

Father Darius placed his arm around Señor Ortiz's thin shoulders. "He has attempted to learn to communicate with you, Mr. Malone. I would say that makes him a leader, not an ignorant naco. Wouldn't you agree?"

Mr. Malone hung his head. "I reckon so."

Father Darius patted him on the back. "I suggest you apply the golden rule to your dealings with Señor Ortiz from now on. How does that sound?"

He mumbled his agreement and glanced at Mr. Ortiz.

The young man offered his hand and they shook heartily.

Marcos saw his chance and moved in. "Father Darius?"

His attention still on the reconciling men, Father Darius lifted joyful eyes. "Yes?" He stood to his feet. "Why, hello, Marcos. I see you've brought me more customers." He glanced around and sighed. "We'll have to squeeze to make a bit more room, but I suppose we can take them in."

He nodded at Willem and John then smiled gently at Bertha and Magda. "I'm very sorry. I have no accommodations to offer women." His outstretched arm took in the crowded room. "I'm afraid this is no place for the fairer sex. There's absolutely no privacy. You'd be most uncomfortable here." He held up his finger. "But I can suggest the perfect alternative for you."

Marcos shook his head vigorously. "No, Father. They need only to talk to you. They're searching for Raul."

Concern lined his gentle face. "Is the boy in trouble?"

John smiled. "None that we know of." He held out his hand. "John Rawson of the Twisted-R Ranch in Carrizo Springs." He indicated Willem, Bertha, and Magda, introducing them in turn. "These fine people are guests on my ranch."

Father Darius colored slightly. "Of course. I'm very sorry. I have a simple mind, I'm afraid. I see everyone I meet as homeless waifs." He bowed at the waist. "Forgive my unfortunate assumption, ladies."

Magda offered her hand. "No apology necessary, Father."

He grinned. "Call me Darius, please. I'm not a priest and hardly deserving of the title. Father is a moniker the men pinned on me years ago when I took in a few orphan boys, and it stuck." He addressed John again. "You say you're looking for Raul?"

John nodded. "We were told he has information on some livestock for sale. Mrs. Bloom, here, is looking to buy several head of prime cattle to take home with her to Humble."

Father Darius's head shot up, his gaze fixed on Bertha. "Did he say Humble?"

Bertha smiled. "That's right."

"Texas?"

"Is there another one?"

He blinked. "And your name is Bloom?"

Perplexed by the questions, Bertha furrowed her brow. "That's what the man said, ain't it?"

He studied her, his eyes gone to narrow slits. "You wouldn't be kin to a fellow named Thaddeus Bloom, now would you?"

Bertha tensed and her mouth went slack. "As a matter of fact, I would." She stepped closer and tilted her face up to his. "What's your full name, mister?"

Beaming, he stuck out his hand. "Darius Q. Thedford at your service, ma'am."

"Cuddy, stop!" Emmy shouted louder, but the rushing wind and pounding of the horse's hooves drowned out her voice. She clung to Cuddy's back with all of her strength, praying the ride would end soon.

Relief flooded her middle with warmth when she recognized the slope to the river. Certainly Cuddy would let her down when they reached the water's edge.

The warm glow turned to icy fingers of fear when he turned the big mare and thundered along the bank, urging the horse to go faster than Emmy had ever ridden in her life.

She prayed either the horse or Cuddy knew where they were

going, because the overcast night was so murky, she could see nothing. Feeling the horse lift from the ground, she tightened her grip around Cuddy's waist, closed her eyes, and screamed.

His hoarse laughter floated on the breeze as they cleared the low fence and hurtled into a black veil.

When she thought he'd never stop, he did. Still laughing, he reined the panting mare to a halt. "Give me your hand," he said, groping behind him.

She pushed him away. "Why?"

"So I can help you down."

"I don't want down. Where are we, Cuddy? It's as dim as pitch out here."

He chuckled. "Ain't that nice?"

"No, it's not nice. Take me back this instant."

He groaned. "Come on, honey. Don't be like that. We have to give this horse a little rest first. Besides, I just want to talk for a while."

She let go of him and crossed her arms, though he couldn't see her. "I don't think so, Cuddy."

He sighed. "You're going to force me to embarrass myself, aren't you?"

Her interest piqued, she waited for him to explain.

He didn't.

"How might I do that?"

His shoulders rose and fell with a deep, shuddering breath. "It's just that. . .talking to you about our fathers makes me feel better. I mean. . .knowing there's someone who understands means the world to me."

Emmy dangled between hugging him and inviting him to peddle his wares elsewhere. The wild ride he'd just subjected her to swung the vote. "I don't believe you."

His silence made her fear she'd angered him. When he spoke, the weight of resignation pulled his voice to a whisper. "I can't say I blame you." He nudged the horse around.

Emmy's heart lurched. "Wait, Cuddy." She felt for his hand. "I'm being silly. Help me dismount."

He lowered her to the ground and she stood surrounded by night sounds and little else, wrapped in a soft cocoon of darkness. She shivered, willing Cuddy to hurry and join her. When he did, his arm went around her and she relaxed into him.

"Where are we?"

"A place I come when I need to be alone." He led her a few feet from the horse and spread a blanket on the ground. "It's a nice spot. I wish there was more light so you could see."

"So do I." She groped the ground before she sat. "What about snakes and scorpions?"

He squeezed her shoulders. "Stay close to me. I won't let them get you."

Bumping his arm, Emmy giggled. "Who will protect me from you?"

His answering laughter sounded more like the old Cuddy. "I won't hurt you. I only want to spend a little time with you."

A warning tensed her stomach. "Yes, to talk. That's what you said."

"To talk. Of course."

Now that her eyes weren't clenched tight with dread, they began to adjust to the meager light. Cuddy's dim outline blocked out the night sky. "Has something else happened? With your father, I mean?"

He ducked his head. "Not yet, but it's bound to. As sure as we're sitting here, it will happen when Father gets home. I see no way around it."

The alarm laced through his words clenched Emmy's fists. She shivered again, this time with foreboding. "What, Cuddy? What do you think will happen?"

Illogically, considering the gloomy turn of their conversation, the clouds overhead parted, allowing the starry sky to rain light across the open field.

Emmy could see Cuddy clearly now, trace the etched lines in his forehead, read the fear in his eyes.

"When my father returns from Catarina, Diego will be leaving the Twisted-R."

Stunned, Emmy stared at him. "For good?"

"Hauled to the gate by the scruff of his neck, if I know my father—which means I'll never get off this accursed ranch."

She gripped his arm. "I don't understand. Why would your father ask Diego to leave?"

He grunted. "Like I said, there won't be any asking." He speared her with a glance. "Diego committed the unpardonable. He hurt Greta." Bitterness tainted his laugh. "No one hurts John Rawson's family, especially his baby girl, without paying a mighty high price."

She squirmed. "So you heard?"

He shook his head. "Diego told me. I wasn't sure you heard until now."

Emmy stared. "He told you?"

"He tells me everything." He reached inside his jacket and drew out a small container, fumbling with the lid. "When Diego's gone, that just leaves me, the old man's favorite project." He turned up the flask and took a long drink then wiped his mouth on his sleeve. "Not to mention his biggest failure."

Emmy seized the bottle from his hand and held it up. "Where did this come from? I thought you threw it away."

"I had a spare."

He reached for it, but she snatched it away. "You're not getting this back."

He shrugged, his teeth flashing white against his shadowy face. "That's all right. It's empty."

She shook it but heard no sloshing sound. "Oh, Cuddy. How much have you had?"

"Not enough, evidently. I'm still conscious." His head drooped between his knees. "Aw, Emily. What will I do if Diego leaves? He's been my right arm. With him gone, it won't take long for the old man to figure out I don't know a thing about running the ranch."

There was no doubting his anguish. Once again, sympathy crowded her heart, and she touched his arm. "Why don't you talk to your father? Tell him the truth about how you feel?"

He snorted. "Talk to my father? Now that's a laugh." He lifted his head and stared thoughtfully. "Maybe I could plead my case to Mother. Have her soften him up for me."

Emmy lifted one shoulder. "Forgive me, but I'm not sure that's a good idea. Compassion is hardly her strongest trait."

His gaze shifted to Emmy. "What makes you say that? Kate Rawson is the model of compassion."

Emmy balked. "Not toward me. Papa entrusted her with my welfare, but she hasn't bothered to see to my needs for two days." She stuck out her lip. "I've nearly starved."

"But Rosita has." His eyes were troubled. "Hasn't she?"

"Only once, but she never came again."

He groaned and balled his fists at his temples. "Mother has no idea. She'd have a stroke if she knew."

Emmy swatted away his words. "That can't be so. How could she not know?"

"Her mind is preoccupied with Greta, so she put Rosita in charge of you. I heard her myself."

The bewildering words were a muddle in her mind. She might have discounted them except for the memory of Rosita's sullen face at her door.

"Then Rosita hasn't fulfilled her charge." She cocked an eyebrow at Cuddy. "Why would she do that?"

He spun on the blanket to face her, nearly toppling into her lap. "That's an easy answer. There's a rift between Diego and me that wasn't there before. She blames you."

His speech beginning to slur, he picked up her hands. "I'm sorry, Emmy. I should've checked on you myself. I knew Rosita was angry, but I never expected her to go this far." He squeezed her fingers. "Don't worry. I intend to speak to her."

Emmy squeezed back. "Please don't. We've had enough trouble in your house. Besides"—she made a face—"Rosita might poison my frijoles."

Laughing too loudly, he swayed toward her. "You're awfully cute. Did you know that?" He seemed to grow ten more hands, all busy grasping her arms, shoulders, and neck while he pulled himself closer. "Just plain cute," he drawled. "That's what you are."

"Stop it, now." Emmy strained to pull away. "You're too rough. Let me go, please."

"Sweet, too, ain't you? As sweet as a newborn calf."

The incredible strength in his hands shot fear to Emmy's heart and swelled her throat. "No, Cuddy. Please, don't!"

As he pressed her to the ground, his greedy mouth sought hers. "Sweetest little thing I ever—"

A sharp intake of air and a howl finished his sentence. With a roar, Diego ripped Cuddy's body free of Emmy, one hand buried in his hair, the other clutching the nape of his neck. Tossing him aside like a straw-filled scarecrow, Diego stood over him with balled fists, his chest heaving.

Obviously dazed, and frightened out of his wits, Cuddy cowered with his fingers splayed over his face. "What did you do that for?"

Diego started for him again and Cuddy crawled backward over the rocky ground like a crawfish. "Wait!" he cried. "I wasn't going to hurt her. I was just fooling around. I swear."

Still panting wildly, Diego stalked to Emmy and jerked her up by the arm. Before she could protest, he herded her to his horse and urged her into the saddle then climbed in behind her.

As they passed Cuddy, still on the ground, Diego stopped and spoke for the first time. "What's happened to you? I didn't think you capable of something like this. Don't you think it's time to lay off the booze?"

Eyes blazing, Cuddy leaped to his feet. "Blast you, Diego. You don't know a thing about me, including my intentions. What are you doing here anyway? Do you spy on me all the time now?"

"I have more important things to occupy my time. Little Pete saw the two of you ride out of the barn. He knew you'd been drinking."

"Why don't you mind your own business, brother?" He nodded at Emmy. "Though my guess is that's exactly what you think you're doing."

Cuddy grabbed hold of the reins and peered up at her. "Forgive me, Emily. I swear I meant you no harm. I only wanted to kiss you."

Before she could answer, Diego spurred the horse and bolted away.

The trip home was as frantic and fast as her last ride. The difference was in how it made her feel. Instead of fearful and desperately clinging, she rode cradled by Diego's body, his arms around her waist, the warmth of his chest at her back, his breath in her hair.

The madness and the sweetness of the moment made her cry, the tears barely touching her cheeks before the wind whisked them away. Her heart swelled in gratitude to Diego, her champion, her hero.

They ducked into the barn where Little Pete waited, his dark eyes pools of concern. Rushing to them, he held the horse while Diego helped her down. "You all right, miss?"

Embarrassed, she ducked her head. "I'm fine, thank you."

"That's all, Pete," Diego barked.

Pete nodded and hustled out the door.

Her emotions swelling in rolling waves of joy, Emmy turned and lifted grateful eyes. "Diego, I—"

His hand shot up. "Save your explanation for someone who cares. Close your mouth and get inside the house."

CHAPTER 24

Father Darius pulled out chairs for Bertha and Magda in the little boxed-in room that served as his office. Willem stood against the wall. Bertha sat at the edge of her seat, and Darius knelt before her, holding her hands. She gazed at him in wonder, disbelief and joy taking turns as well.

"It's really you? The same Darius Thedford that gave Thad the deed to our land so many years ago?"

He nodded. "None other."

She squeezed his fingers. "I've been looking for you for over a year now. Sent word across the country, but no news ever came back. It seemed like you fell off the face of the earth."

Darius smiled, his gesture taking in his shabby surroundings. "I guess you could say in a way I did."

"I wouldn't say it," Magda said, patting him on the shoulder. "You're doing a wonderful service to the Lord in this place."

"Thank you, Mrs. Dane." His attention returned to Bertha. "You say you've been looking for me, dear?"

"Yes," she whispered softly. "I have something I need to give you." She wiped her eyes on her sleeve. "I didn't understand the urge to see it done until now. At first, I thought I was meant to do it for my Thad."

Darius's eyes lit up. "How is young Thad?" Drawing back, he laughed at himself. "Oh, my, I suppose he's hardly the impetuous lad

I met on his way to college." Amazement clouding his eyes, he gazed at Bertha, making the connection. "Thad must be pushing fifty years old by now."

Magda slipped her arm around Bertha's trembling shoulders. "Father, Thad's been gone for more than six years. Bertha's a widow now."

"Oh no," he said, the word so filled with sorrow it came out a moan. "Bertha, I'm real sorry to hear that."

Her gaze losing focus, Bertha gripped Magda's hand. "Six years. It don't seem possible, does it?"

Darius patted her hand. "He was such a fine lad, too. How did it happen?"

Wrenching herself from the past, Bertha lifted tearful eyes. "River swallowed him. The water came up so fast it swept him away in plain sight of several witnesses. Thad was a right good swimmer, but he never stood a chance against a flash flood on the San Jacinto."

Darius cleared his throat. "The ways of our God are a source of unfathomable mystery, Bertha. My life took a new direction after I met your husband, and he was the reason. I was nothing more than a drifter, making a living by fleecing innocent victims. Then Thad came along, and I caught a glimpse of genuine goodness. Of course, he took none of the credit. Gave it all to God, and didn't mind telling me so. I decided then and there I needed the God I saw reflected in that boy's eyes."

Bertha clasped her hands and wiggled on the seat. "You got Him, too. I see Him right there in your eyes."

Darius swallowed hard and ducked his head. "I often lamented the fact that I lost contact with Thad and planned many times to travel to Humble and find him, to tell him what he'd done for me. Somehow that trip never took place, and now I've lost the chance forever."

A look of sweet peace softened Bertha's features. "Not forever, Father. My Thad awaits us both in heaven. Then you'll have forever to say what you need to say. I'm sure he'll have a thing or two to tell you as well. He was always mighty beholden to you for giving him that deed."

She paused, smiling a little. "There is one thing Thad always wondered. If you don't mind, can you clear it up for me now? I reckon he's on pins and needles up in heaven, waiting for me to ask you."

Father Darius grinned. "Ask me anything."

"Well"—she wiggled on the seat—"Thad always figured you won that deed in a poker game. Is that how you came to have it?"

He scratched his head, amusement tugging at his lips. "I suppose the boy would think that, considering we met over a hand of cards." He lifted his chin. "You know, I kind of like the idea that he saw it that way and never learned the truth. A poker game sounds far more interesting than the truth."

She scooted forward. "What is the truth?"

"Actually, an uncle up north willed it to his sister's son. Before my uncle's death, this same boy got on his bad side, so he blotted out his name and left it to me instead. I was on my way to see it when I ran into Thad."

"You never once saw Humble, Texas?"

He grunted and shook his head. "Never did. I gave that property to Thad before I ever set eyes on it." He looked up and smiled. "But you know something, Mrs. Bloom? Somehow I knew I was supposed to do it, and I never had a single moment's regret."

Bertha clutched both of his arms and gave him a shake. "Just like I'll never have a single moment's regret for what I'm about to do." She blinked away tears. "Especially now that I see the reason for God insisting that I find you."

She reached inside her blouse and then paused. "Turn your head, Father, if you don't mind. Willem, that goes for you, too." Winking at Magda, she reached deep inside the bodice of her dress. "You can look now. And stick out your hand."

Darius did as he was told, and she placed a folded document in his outstretched palm. "My dear, what's this?"

Satisfied, she folded her arms across her chest. "Just the rights to half the profits from one of the largest producing oil wells in the state of Texas."

❧

Emmy's jaw fell open and she stared at Diego with rounded eyes. "What did you say?" Her words came out low and breathless, intended to warn him he'd best not have said what she thought.

Unflinching, Diego folded his arms across his chest and met her glare. "I said close your mouth and get inside. I mean it, Emmy. Go to the house right now, and whatever you do, don't let those good people catch you sneaking back in from your sordid rendezvous."

Her head reeled. The warmth of gratitude turned to flames of fury. She stomped her foot. "How dare you!"

Diego took a step closer. "Let me tell you how I dare." One by one, he held up fingers, counting off his reasons. "I've broken my mother's heart. The only father I've ever known has lost faith in me. Half the time Cuddy acts like he hates me, and Greta, who's been like a sister to me, is locked in her room, refusing to see me." He leaned threateningly, his eyes menacing in a stormy face. "So I'm asking. . .haven't you done enough damage?"

Incredulous, Emmy gaped at him. "And you think even one of those things is my fault?" She held up a few fingers of her own. "First off, I have nothing to do with your mother. How could I? She won't spare a civil word in my direction. Second, for all I know, Cuddy may have a reason to hate you." She wound up for the kicker. "As for John Rawson, didn't he lose faith in you about the time you were sneaking behind the bunkhouse to kiss your *little sister?*"

She spun on her heels and left him floundering.

He caught up with her outside the barn, his fingers rough on her arm. "Your last point is more your fault than mine," he panted. "Because I wasn't kissing Greta." His eyes still blazed but not with anger. Longing, desperation, and shame all vied for fury's place. "I may have held Greta, Emmy, but I was kissing you."

Her heart breaking, Emmy wrapped him in her arms. He jerked her close and tangled his hands in her hair. Guiding her face beneath his, his lips hovered inches from hers. . .until he roughly pushed her aside.

Hugging his head, he whirled away from her. "What am I doing?" Fuming again, he latched onto her shoulders. "For that matter, what are you doing?" He pointed behind him. "Not ten minutes ago, you were wallowing on the ground with Cuddy. For all I know, you'd rather I hadn't showed up." He shoved past her. "Do us both a favor, Emmy. Stay out of my way."

Too crushed to cry out to him, too angry to deny his accusation, Emmy stared after him until he disappeared in the darkness.

She'd been accused of many hurtful deeds in her life, most of them quite justified. Never in her twenty-one years had a person accused her so unjustly, and it stung. Despite one reckless dalliance with her best friend's fiancé, no one had ever questioned Emmy's virtue except that black-hearted rascal. She found it hard to accept that a person she held in the highest regard had done the same.

Her spirits as flat as a fritter, she started for the house, ready to leave South Texas for good.

As she neared the back entrance, Cuddy rode into the yard. Ducking behind the patio wall, she watched his horse trot into the barn. He was the last person she wanted to see, especially tonight. Tomorrow would be soon enough to decide how to deal with Cuddy Rawson.

A couple of things were certain after the wild night she'd had. One, she wouldn't be accepting any more invitations from Cuddy, and two, the time had come to quit sneaking out of the house. The imprudent practice had never brought her anything but trouble.

Praying no one had slipped down and locked her out of the house, Emmy tried the knob, sighing with relief when it turned and the door opened. Knowing the spiteful Rosita would delight in telling on her, Emmy kept her eyes on the kitchen as she tiptoed to the stairs.

When she shut the door of her room, she closed her eyes and leaned against it.

"Who were you with, Emily?"

Emmy's eyes flew open. Her hand jerked to her hammering heart and her knees gave out. Sliding to the floor, she stared at the hollow-eyed girl sitting on her bed in a dingy cotton nightgown, her hair a matted, stringy mess. "Greta!"

Greta lifted her hand toward Emmy. "Oh, don't worry. I won't tell. Are you all right?"

Her chest heaving, Emmy took inventory before she answered. "I believe so. Give me a minute and I'll tell you for sure."

"I'm sorry. I didn't mean to startle you."

"Startle? I think my heart may burst."

Greta pushed off the bed and scurried to sit on the floor beside her. "Forgive me, but I must have an answer. Were you with Cuddy or Diego?"

Emmy stared at the pale, drawn face and cringed. How could she tell the poor girl the truth—that she'd been with both? She opted for half of the truth. "Cuddy asked me to go for a ride."

The lines eased from Greta's forehead and a bit of color returned to her cheeks. "Cuddy?" She released a long breath. "I heard Diego's voice near the barn, so I thought. . ." She looked up and shrugged. "Never mind what I thought."

Picking at the sleeve of her gown, she squirmed until she mustered her courage. "May I ask another question?"

The memory of heartrending sobs echoing through the floorboards touched a tender spot in Emmy's heart. "Of course, Greta. Anything."

Her icy blue eyes lifted to Emmy's, sending a chill down her back. "Do you know. . ." She faltered. "I mean, did you hear. . ."

The only thing to do was tell the truth. Emmy nodded grimly then watched Greta try to accept it.

"Did Cuddy hear, too?"

"No." She hated to crush the flicker of hope. "But he knows. Diego told him."

She moaned. "Why does Diego tell him everything?"

Emmy picked up her hands. "So it's only you, me, Diego, Cuddy, and your mother. Five people. No one else need ever know."

Her chin shot up, her eyes as wide as saucers. "Who told Mother?"

"Well, sweetie, I assumed you had."

"No! I'd never tell her. She'd only run to Father, and then he'd make Diego leave." A wistful sigh escaped her lips. "I don't want that." She squeezed Emmy's fingers. "Not ever."

"Of course you don't."

"Leave Cuddy to me. I can handle him. As for Mother, I told her I threw myself at Diego, and he let me down easy. She thinks I'm upset because I humiliated myself."

Emmy tried to make sense of it all. "Then why does she think I've hidden away in my room?"

"She's convinced you're pouting because your parents left you behind. I've told her no different." Her eyes darkened. "In fact, that's why I'm here, Emily. If my father asks Diego what happened to make me cry, Diego will tell him the truth. I know he will." Her fingers dug painfully into Emmy's hands. "We have to keep that from happening. Please say you'll help."

"But what can I do?"

The girl scooted until their knees bumped. "Talk to Diego. Tell him I'll never tell anyone what happened. We can go on like we were before. I just don't want him to leave."

Newfound respect for Greta swelled Emmy's chest, along with fresh hurt for the heartbroken girl and herself. There was no way to tell her that Diego had just ordered Emmy to stay out of his path. "What makes you think he'll listen to me?"

It was the wrong thing to say. Emmy knew as soon as she'd uttered the words.

Her eyes losing focus, Greta retreated into the memory that had brought her such pain. "He'll listen to you," she whispered. "I could tell by the passion in his kiss."

CHAPTER 25

Magda walked to the window of the Maverick Hotel and peered across the street. Other than the post office, she spotted a few businesses and shops, but to her dismay, there was no restaurant or café in sight.

Bertha stood by the bed, rummaging in her money satchel. Though she probably had enough cash in the bag to buy the hotel, it had seemed more reasonable to book two rooms instead of three, so Willem had taken the extra cot in John's room and Bertha slept on the divan across from Magda's bed.

Magda pulled her gaze from the window. "This is a nice-sized town, ain't it, Bertha?"

"Too big to suit me. I prefer wide-open spaces." She looked up. "Was that your belly I heard growling?"

Magda rubbed her middle. "This rowdy thing woke me up pitching a fit about our meager supper. I hope the hotel offers a decent breakfast."

By the time they'd hauled poor Darius off his backside the night before, where he'd landed in a heap when Bertha delivered her news, the hour was too late to find a meal. A jubilant Father Darius had offered them each a can of beans, which sounded right good by that time. But as hungry as she was, Magda agreed with the others that she'd never take food meant for those wretched homeless souls.

They'd settled for the remaining hardtack and venison jerky then found their hotel and turned in for the night. But not before Darius wrote out how to find Raul, who, thanks to Darius and the mission, had left behind his life of sin and returned like the prodigal to his father's home.

Bertha closed the satchel, hopped on the bed, and leaned against the wall, her arms crossed behind her head. "I expect the men are hungry, too. I'm right surprised we ain't heard from them by now. I thought John wanted to get an early start."

"He did. I heard him say so. I'm sure they'll be stirring soon." Magda sat beside Bertha on the bed, bunching pillows behind her back. "Meanwhile, tell me how long you've been keeping your plan to find Darius Thedford a secret." She leaned her head to gaze at Bertha. "And why withhold it? I thought we shared most everything, but this is the second time in a week I've learned you kept something from me."

Bertha's eyes held steady. "There was never a second I wasn't going to tell you about Emmy and that rascal Cuddy Rawson. I made the decision to trust her word, and I think I made a right one. As for my plan to find Darius, I never decided not to tell you. Before long, it became a thing too precious to talk about." She swatted at Magda, her eyes blurred with tears. "Oh, you know what I mean."

Magda smiled. "Of course I do. But I have one more question. How long have you been hauling that deed around in your bodice?"

Bertha frowned and scratched her side. "Long enough to cause an itchy rash. But what was I supposed to do? I don't carry a reticule."

"How did you know you'd need it?"

"I knew as sure as anything I had the call from God to find Darius and give him his share of the well. I reckon it was the same call Darius felt to give the land to Thad in the first place." She twisted around. "Don't you think so, Magda?"

Magda opened her mouth to remind Bertha that the judgments of God were unsearchable and His ways past finding out, but the scripture no sooner formed in her mind than a boisterous knock came at the door. She hefted herself toward the corner of the bed. "That's the fellows now."

Bertha, considerably spryer than Magda and closer to the door, vaulted off the bed like a springtail. Hustling to the door, she opened it wide. "It's about time you two turned loose of the sheets. Let's get this venture started."

John's booming laughter shook the hall. "We peeled back those sheets hours ago, little Bertha. Willem and I have been up since dawn, and we bring you good news."

Not waiting for Bertha to ask, Willem leaned in the door grinning. "We found Raul. Joe Campbell was right. Raul knows a man who's selling his stock."

John took up the story. "We've seen your cattle, Bertha. Some of the finest polled Herefords I've ever laid eyes on."

Bertha seemed caught between a smile and a frown. "You went without me?"

Willem's brows met in the middle. "I ducked in this morning, but all I heard were snores and snorts."

"Don't worry," John said. "No deals were struck on your behalf. We told the man you'd make the final decision. He's waiting for us to bring you back."

"The best part is you don't have to drive them to Carrizo. You can ship them out right here in Eagle Pass."

Bertha's countenance fell. "That's not good news, Willem. I was looking forward to a cattle drive."

Grinning, John patted her shoulder. "Well, you're in luck. I told him we'd cut out the thirty head you wanted from the best he had to offer, and they could save a few for me. You'll be helping me drive around twenty of those beauties back to Carrizo Springs."

She broke into a jig, circling the room with her hands on her hips. "Let's go, then. What are we waiting for?"

John held up both hands. "Hold on there. I hope we're waiting for breakfast. After all the excitement, Willem and I are starved."

Magda stretched her arm overhead. "I'll second that motion. My grub-catcher's on empty."

Never one to set much stock in food, Bertha frowned. "I'll wait if I have to for the sake of the men. But Magda, I don't plan to schedule my day around your meals. Try to shovel in enough to last awhile."

Turning at the door, John pointed at the bulging satchel. "You might want to bring that thing, Bertha. It'll finally come in handy. The next part of this trip is about to get expensive."

Bertha cocked her head and glared at him, her expression too solemn to be serious. "Hold up there, John. When I told Magda to eat her fill, I never intended to finance it."

Magda gasped. "He means the cattle!"

"Oh." A wide grin on her face, Bertha gathered the bag under her arm. "Well, that's different."

⁂

Melatha scraped Isi's eggs into a bowl and wrapped the container in a dishcloth. She stacked his tortillas and bacon in a separate dish and covered them with a plate. Setting the whole sodden mess on the back of the stove, she closed the damper to cool the fire. If he didn't show up soon, her eager students would gladly share his breakfast as they had done the day before. And Melatha would struggle to hide her tears while she watched them eat the food she'd prepared for her son.

She hadn't spent a day apart from Isi since he'd come back into her life. Their spirits had bonded and their time together had been sweet. The brooding young man who'd abandoned his roots still lurked beneath the surface, but Isi always had a quick smile and teasing tone for Melatha—at least until White Hair came along.

Melatha allowed the emotion she harbored for the girl to surface. She toyed with it, weighing it against the hatred she felt for the one who took her father's life. Despite the years and the prayers to Chihowa Palami asking His help to forgive the man, the scale still tipped in favor of her father's murderer, but only by a feather.

The spirit of her father had risen to eternal rest, leaving an empty husk where once had been a lively, determined man. Emily hadn't thrust a knife in Isi's heart or cut his fingers from his hands for paltry trinkets, but she'd left him as cut off from Melatha as her father's stiffened body had been when she'd found him.

Some new thing had happened between the girl and Isi. Melatha watched him leave the bunkhouse before dawn that morning and knew. His body slumped in the circle of lantern light, his shoulders still bent beneath shame for what he'd done to Greta. But in the angry cluster of lines above his brows and the rolling motion of his jaw, Melatha saw frustration. And fury. Only one person had the power over Isi to exact such raw emotion.

Footsteps on the porch, not heavy enough to be his, roused her from her spiteful place. Her stomach churning from her bitter musings, she reached for Isi's unclaimed plate of food. "Come in, Jose. I have a nice breakfast for you again this morning." Irritated with the dawdling boy, Melatha crossed the room and swung open the door.

White Hair's head jerked up, dread dancing in her eyes.

Melatha stared, her jaw slack. Then the only words she found to say tumbled from her mouth. "What do you want?"

White Hair stood as straight as a pine trunk, the fear gone from her eyes. "I've come to ask for your help."

Melatha's arching brows pulled at her deep-set lids. "What did you say?"

"Isi must not confess to John Rawson. I need your help to convince him."

Melatha cringed. She'd called him Isi. Deliberately. Most likely to gain favor. "What business is it of yours? Or mine, for that matter?"

"I'm here on Greta's behalf. She asked me to talk to him."

Melatha folded her arms. "Greta? I don't believe you."

"It's true. Greta loves Isi. She asked me to help save his job."

"Then you should be speaking to my son, not me. I hold no sway over him."

The girl flinched at last. "He won't listen to me because he believes me to be someone I'm not."

Melatha's mouth parted and she drew a steadying breath. "Why should I help you?"

The blue eyes narrowed but she held Melatha's gaze. "Because I'm not who you believe me to be either." She paused. "And because—" Her chin went up and her chest swelled.

Defiance? Melatha didn't think so.

"Because your son loves me." White Hair stood taller, her shoulders back, not in defiance but pride, reveling in the knowledge of Isi's love.

Melatha's grandfather once told her to serve her enemies her best wines and savory breads. *"And thereby keep their minds too muddled to outsmart you and their bellies too full to chase you."* She pushed open the screen door. "Come inside. I have breakfast."

CHAPTER 26

In all the years Magda had known Bertha Maye Bloom, she'd never seen her so excited. Ready to trade her seat on the wagon for a pair of jeans, a rope, and a cattle horse, she had every intention of riding along to help herd her cattle to the Galveston, Harrisburg, & San Antonio Railroad depot.

It took some fancy talking by John to convince her to let him hire a handful of experienced drovers instead. He finally got her settled down when he explained that the men, two of them seasoned vaqueros, the other a little green according to John, were too proud to work under the direction of a woman.

Magda didn't know if John had told Bertha the truth or just outsmarted her. Either way, she sat tall in the rig beside Magda, a huge smile on her face as John and the three hired men drove her cattle into the stockyard to be loaded onto the train.

Bertha let out a whoop when the last cherry red set of stocky legs and white switch scrambled up the ramp and into the stock car. John had helped her hire a livestock handler to accompany the Herefords all the way to Humble where Willem had arranged for their delivery to Bertha's waiting pasture. And now, just as John had predicted, Bertha's satchel sagged a bit instead of straining at the seams.

She rubbed her hands together. "Most of them had no horns at all, Magda. Did you notice?"

Bertha's mood had rubbed off on Magda to the point where her

192

cheeks ached from smiling. "I sure did, sugar. Ain't that something?"

Willem sat forward on the front seat and unwound the reins from the post. "That's what polled means—having no horns."

"Well, I like it," Bertha said. "And they have the prettiest white faces I ever saw. I can't wait to get home and start taking care of them."

Willem smiled back at her. "You'll be in Humble before you know it. All we have left to do is get John and his cattle back to Carrizo Springs then we can head north, if you gals are ready."

Magda stretched. "I'm sure ready. The Rawsons are attentive hosts, but I'm anxious to get that long, boring ride behind me."

John rode up on Faron, accompanied by the three drovers. "Willem, I'll be riding with Juan, Carl, and Benito to round up my herd. There's no reason for you folks to make that trek out to the ranch again."

He jerked his head toward town. "Why not kill some time shopping and seeing the sights? We'll meet up on the trail south of Fort Duncan in a couple of hours."

Willem saluted. "We'll be there, John."

John started to ride away then turned to shout over his shoulder. "Oh, and Willem. . .don't forget to buy feed for the stock." He shrugged. "Wouldn't hurt to buy a few extra rations, too. I fear it'll take a mite longer to return to Carrizo than it took us to get here. The livestock are sure to slow us down."

As they pulled out of the stockyard, Bertha tugged on Willem's sleeve. "You reckon we have time to say good-bye to Darius?"

He squirmed. "I don't know about that, Bertha. The mission is clear on the opposite end of town."

Magda cleared her throat.

"Then we'd have to drive from there to Fort Duncan," he said. "That's an extra half hour."

Magda cleared her throat louder.

Willem sighed and his shoulders drooped. "Of course, Bertha. I'll drop you and Magda at the mission while I tend to the supplies." He turned to aim a pointed glance at Magda. "But be ready when I pull up. We'll be cutting it close on time."

Bertha dropped the satchel on the seat beside him. "There are a few bundles of bills left in the bottom of this thing. Take it and use all you need."

He nodded and placed the bag at his feet. They pulled out of the G.H. & S.A. depot then turned off Quarry Street to Main, craning their necks as they passed the impressive Maverick County courthouse. It reminded Magda of a Spanish fortress. Or perhaps a royal palace.

There were so many shops along Main Street, Magda began to wish she'd kept her interfering nose out of Willem and Bertha's conversation. If Bertha didn't have her heart set on returning to the mission, Magda saw ample stalls and shops where a girl could spend a few dollars and an interesting couple of hours.

She repented of the selfish thought when they made the turn toward the Rian Street Mission and Bertha's face lit up like a harvest moon. Father Darius, well turned-out in far nicer clothes than the night before, met them on the street. "Dear Bertha, I'm overjoyed to see you again. I expected you'd be headed back to Carrizo by now."

Bertha climbed down from the rig and he kissed her hand. Blushing, and obviously too overcome with embarrassment to speak, she looked over her shoulder, her eyes begging Magda for rescue.

Magda followed her to the ground and waved Willem on his way. "My, but you're right duded-up today, Father."

This time he blushed. "Please, Mrs. Dane, call me Darius. I suppose I'm used to it from the men, but it doesn't sound quite right coming from a beautiful woman."

"I'll call you Darius if you'll call me Magda."

Still latched onto Bertha's hands, he smiled. "Magda it shall be. I'm glad you ladies caught me. Another minute and I'd be gone for the day."

"Are we keeping you from something?"

"Nothing too pressing. I'm off on a fishing expedition."

Bertha found her voice. "Fishing?" She looked him over. "Pardon me for saying, but that don't look the proper getup for wetting a hook."

"Ah, I can see how my attire might cause you confusion." He leaned closer to her face. "But you see, little Bertha, I'm casting for souls. A man can wear most anything in those perilous waters." He stood tall and preened. "In this case, the flashier the better. I aim to attract attention."

Magda smoothed his lapel. "You'll attract plenty dressed like that." The story came to her mind about the dandy who plied his bait on a green young boy bound for college, snaring Thad and reeling him into a poker game before he knew the hook had set. Magda smiled at the realization that Darius still used the same bag of tricks, only now the winning pot was redemption. She patted his shoulder. "So where are you trolling today?"

He shoved back his hat. "Actually, I was on my way to the Piedra Parada Saloon."

Bertha shot him a skeptical look. "A saloon?"

He gave her a tender smile and waved his arm behind him. "You think these men come to me?" He shook his head. "No, Bertha, I have to go out and find them where they are, whether a saloon, an alley, or a ditch."

Admiration shone from her eyes. "Just like Jesus did."

His smile said he liked her comparison. "I suppose you're right. And just like the men in Jesus' time—the deaf mute, the blind beggar, the leper—most men don't realize their real need until they see Jesus." He beamed. "That's my job. I make sure they see Him."

He offered his arm to Bertha. "Let me take you inside. My little office may be stuffy, but at least it provides shade."

Bertha took his arm and allowed him to usher her up the walk.

Behind them, Magda couldn't help but notice the change in her friend. Bertha held her shoulders back and her chin high. Her galloping gait had disappeared, replaced by delicate steps and an easy sway.

Astonished, Magda did a quick calculation on her fingers. Darius would only be a handful of years older than Bertha, six or eight at the most. Instead of a distinguished older man, Bertha must see him as an attractive and eligible suitor. The way Darius gazed at Bertha and hung on her every word, he had begun to think of himself in the same light. Suppressing a giggle, Magda followed them inside the mission.

The time before Willem arrived to collect them passed in a flash. Magda had little chance to contribute to the conversation, considering Bertha had no further need of rescue. She and Darius seemed lost in each other's company. Gazing tenderly across the corner of the desk, they reminisced about Thad, shared how he had affected their lives, and discussed the loneliness they'd endured over the years.

By the time the wagon pulled up loaded with supplies for the road, Darius held so tightly to Bertha's hands, Magda feared he'd never turn her loose. "It's time to go, sugar," Magda said softly, breaking the spell between them.

Bertha lowered her head and sighed. "I suppose it is." She met Darius's probing eyes. "We've got a long way to go before we see home again."

Darius scooted to the edge of his chair. "Bertha, forgive me for being forward, but our current situation demands it." His Adam's apple rose and fell. "Do you think . . .well. . .that Thad would mind if I saw you again?"

She flushed with pleasure. "Of course you'll see me again. We're partners in an oil well."

Darius shook his head, his face so lit from within that he glowed. "I'm not suggesting a business relationship, dear. I'd like to spend time with you on a more personal level."

Reminding Magda of a fresh young girl, Bertha flirted with her eyes. "I wouldn't mind that a bit, and I don't think Thad would either." She ducked her head. "Except we live so far apart. It's not like we can visit often."

Willem appeared at the door of the mission, his eyes searching the dimness. Spotting Magda, he waved impatiently.

"There's Willem, Bertha. Are you ready?"

Darius stood. "Magda, can you possibly give us a moment alone?"

"Of course, Father." She winced. "I mean Darius." Saying a hasty good-bye, she scurried out to her scowling husband.

"What's taking her so long? We're late now."

She took his arm and led him back to the rig. "Bertha's waited years for this moment, dear. We can give her a few more minutes."

Ignoring his puzzled frown, she rummaged through the crate of supplies he'd bought. "I hope there's something good in here. I'm hungry."

He reached beneath the seat and produced a short-sided box filled with wrapped sandwiches. "I figured you might be by now."

Clutching his face with both hands, she kissed him. "What on earth would I do without you?"

Blushing bright red, he spit and sputtered. Wagging his finger toward the warehouse, he changed the subject. "We're losing the time I thought to gain by eating on the road. What is she doing in there?"

Magda had already crawled onto the front seat and peeled back the paper on a fat turkey sandwich. She shrugged her shoulders and smiled, her cheeks too stuffed to answer.

Grumbling under his breath, Willem busied himself securing the load until the door opened and Bertha and Darius emerged.

With eyes only for Bertha, Darius bid them safe travel and stepped away from the rig as Willem pulled onto the street.

Each time Magda looked, Bertha still hung over the seat waving. When they turned the corner, she settled back and sighed. "The Lord is sure good at plotting and scheming, Magda. Here I thought God had me giving away something of value, and all the time He was intent on giving a priceless gift to me."

Willem nudged his hat aside and scratched behind his ear. "Can someone please tell me what's going on?"

Magda patted his hand. "I'll explain later, dear. For now, see how fast you can get us home."

John waited for them on the outskirts of the city, in a field a few miles past Fort Duncan. They were a remarkable sight from a distance, John and the men circling a sea of lowing red and white cattle.

"Jumping Jackstraws!" Willem exclaimed. "That's more than twenty head, or I need spectacles."

Bertha leaned between them. "There's nothing wrong with your eyes, Willem. John's done bought off the rest of that man's herd."

John waved at them then blew a sharp blast around two fingers and raised his arm high, signaling the drovers to start the restless animals moving. Cutting around the outer fringes, he spurred his horse into a gallop and rode up to meet them, his smile as wide as the horizon.

Whipping off his Stetson, he motioned behind him. "I got to picking the animals I wanted and couldn't stop." He dried his forehead and replaced the hat. "Got carried away, I think."

Bertha squirmed to John's side of the rig. "How many you got there, John?"

He shot her a sheepish grin. "Oh, fifty, sixty. I lost count after a while."

Bertha stood up to see them better. "Whoopee! That makes this a real cattle drive."

John laughed. "Well, close, little Bertha." He ran his hand along Faron's sleek neck. "I could've saved myself a few dollars back there. That rancher took quite a shine to this fellow. I think he might've made an even trade."

Willem jerked his chin at Faron. "I see who wound up with him, though."

John chuckled low in his throat. "Yep, I've taken a liking to the old man myself."

The distant shouts of the drovers turned John's attention back to the herd. Noting how fast they widened the distance lightened Magda's anxious heart. At that pace, they'd all be home the next day in time for supper.

John swiveled his head to speak to Willem. "A word of warning. With the larger herd, I felt the need to hire an extra hand."

Willem nodded. "I thought I saw four horsemen in the soup."

"Trouble is, in my haste, I let Carl, the young one, talk me into taking on his older brother. Fellow by the name of Wayne."

Willem squinted. "And?"

"Let's just say he bears watching."

"Not the fresh-faced innocent like his brother?"

John snorted. "Not even close. I'm glad I didn't bring along my daughter." He pinned Magda and Bertha with a look, his brow furrowed. "You ladies steer well clear of him, you hear? And if he does one thing to make you feel uncomfortable, just say the word. I'll send him packing."

Magda nodded solemnly. "You won't have to tell us twice, John."

He picked up his reins. "If you folks are ready, we'd better go. Looks like we have about four or five hours of good daylight left. We'll need every bit of that time to make it to the spot where we set up camp for the night."

Willem untied the leads from the post. "Head out. We're right behind you."

"Wait!" Bertha cried. Her head disappeared under the seat until she bounced up holding her prize. "Can't get started without this," she crowed, wadding the blanket beneath her and wiggling until she had it right. Satisfied, she waved them on.

As they rumbled across hard-crusted ruts at the mouth of the trail, so deep the wagon tossed them like water in a hot skillet, Bertha

CHAPTER 27

Emmy strolled into the dining room and sat across the table from Cuddy.

Greta, who had followed her down the stairs, pulled out a chair opposite her startled mother.

"What a thoroughly pleasant surprise!" Mrs. Rawson said, a rosy flush tinting her pale cheeks. "I'm happy to see you both feeling better."

Rosita couldn't say the same about Emmy. She dropped the dish in her hand on the table with a hollow thud and a wobble, startling Mrs. Rawson.

Emmy boldly met Cuddy's shamefaced glance. "Greta and I felt it might be time things got back to normal around here. I believe we've both missed the fellowship." She shot Rosita a winsome smile. "Not to mention the bountiful spread." Rosita flounced away and Emmy prayed she wasn't in the kitchen poisoning her food.

Mrs. Rawson passed Emmy the breadbasket. "I'm so glad, dear. I hated that we were missing so much of your visit." She filled two tall glasses with lemonade and handed one to Greta. "And you're looking much better, too, darling. I'm so happy you decided to join us."

Cuddy and Greta exchanged quick glances. Cuddy's impudent grin and cocky sneer had gone, replaced by the sympathetic smile of a doting brother. Watching him, Emmy could hardly believe he was the same man who'd made such bold advances. Of course, sitting in the well-lit dining room with his mother in attendance must feel very different than riding alone with Emmy in the dark, his belly filled with liquor.

A swish of the swinging doors, and Rosita returned with the main course.

Mrs. Rawson filled heaping platefuls and passed them around the table. "Has anyone seen Diego this evening?"

Four sets of hands stilled and fours pairs of eyes lifted to her face. Watching her in silence, they waited.

Distracted, she quietly returned the ladle to the serving dish. "I'd like for him to come up to the house. I have something important I wish to discuss with him."

Rosita wiped her hands on her apron and scurried toward the kitchen. "I will go and send him word."

Greta scooted to the edge of her chair. "Mother?" Her trembling voice held disbelief. And fear.

Shaking herself free of her thoughts, Mrs. Rawson patted her daughter's hand. "Oh, Greta. Nothing so dire." She smiled sweetly. "I'm growing a tad concerned about the length of your father's visit to the Campbells', that's all."

Dread clutched Emmy's middle. She laid aside her napkin and smoothed her skirt. "You think there's a problem?"

Mrs. Rawson clutched the silky bow on her chest. "Forgive me, Emily. Here I go, causing you concern with my silly musings. I'm only thinking aloud, dear."

Emmy swallowed, but not Kate Rawson's explanation. The unease on the woman's face contradicted her words. "But you think they've been gone too long, don't you?"

Cuddy snorted and picked up his fork. The understanding brother gone, his expression more resembled the Cuddy Emmy knew. "I wouldn't waste a lot of worry, folks. They're having a high old time, so they're not ready to come back to this pretentious graveyard."

Mrs. Rawson flashed him a sharp look. "Cuddy! Mind your manners, please."

"Sorry, Mother." He lifted one shoulder and shoved in a huge bite of food. "I know Father, that's all," he said with bulging cheeks. "He's too busy to think about any of us here. His mind is occupied by playing the highfalutin ranchero for the Danes."

"Some bread, brother?" Her own cheeks turning pink, Greta tossed the roll at Cuddy's plate. It tumbled through his spicy *mole poblano* and landed in his lap.

He retrieved the mess with two fingers, a storm building on his face darker than the chocolaty sauce. "You did that on purpose."

Greta patted the corner of her mouth with her napkin. "Mother asked you to mind your manners, Cuthbert. I was merely trying to distract you from your disobedient display."

His movements slow and exaggerated, Cuddy dragged the soggy bread through his plate and held it up. "Allow me to return the favor."

Greta narrowed her eyes. "You wouldn't dare."

With a wicked grin, he tossed the roll across the table. It slid down Greta's chest, leaving a brown trail, then flipped off her bosom and landed in her waiting hands.

"Cuthbert Rawson!" his mother cried.

Greta reached for her plate, but Cuddy was quicker, upending his food in her lap.

Greta screamed and stood to her feet just as Diego cleared his throat behind them. He stood in the arched doorway, his hat in his hands. "You asked to see me, Mrs. Rawson?"

Kate Rawson couldn't speak. Her gaze hopped from Diego to the dark greasy stain on Greta's dress then to Cuddy, casually licking sauce from his fingers.

Cuddy jutted his chin at Diego. "Hungry, brother?"

Greta's face and the skin of her chest, the part not covered in savory sauce, turned a frightening shade of red. Gathering the soiled area of her skirt as best she could, she bolted from the table, managing to ball herself tight enough to shrink past Diego without touching him.

Just as embarrassed, Emmy wanted to gather her skirts and brush past him, too.

Mrs. Rawson turned her rage on Cuddy. "I'd like you to leave as well, son." Her low, even voice contradicted her flashing eyes.

From beneath her lashes, Emmy watched Cuddy push up from the table, in no hurry to obey. "I'd like to be part of this conversation, Mother."

"Well, you won't be. Good night."

203

He stood with his hands clenched at his sides. Sighing dramatically, he tried once more. "Greta started the whole thing—"

She whirled on him. "Do you see your sister at my table?"

They remained silent until Emmy could stand it no longer. She stole a glance at each of them.

Cuddy stared straight ahead, gnawing the inside of his cheek.

Mrs. Rawson gripped the tablecloth on each side of her plate, her knuckles like white cypress knots. "I feel taken advantage of, Cuddy. None of this would've happened if your father was home."

He looked at her with dispassionate eyes.

"John would be so disappointed in you."

Cuddy gave the chair behind him a vicious kick. It crashed into the wall, sending a picture frame sliding to the floor.

Rosita, her eyes wild with fright, peered through a crack in the kitchen door. In her distress, she laid aside her dislike for Emmy and questioned her with raised brows.

Emmy drew up her shoulders.

Barreling around the table, Cuddy roared by Diego, slamming into him with his shoulder as he passed.

In the stillness that followed, Emmy felt an urge to crawl beneath the table. She felt Diego's presence by the door as strongly as if he were sitting in her lap.

Thankfully, Mrs. Rawson broke the silence. She heaved a labored sigh and released her death grip on the lace cloth. "I'm appalled at my children's conduct. I hope you won't think this is usual mealtime behavior."

Emmy looked up to see whom she had addressed.

Diego didn't wait to figure it out. "I can come back later, Mrs. Rawson."

She lifted her hand. "No. Sit down, please." She gave a shaky laugh. "If you can find a clean chair."

The door burst open and Rosita charged out, all busy hands and dishcloths. She stacked the dirty plates and the charger filled with food on the sideboard then expertly peeled away the splattered tablecloth.

Passing on the empty chair next to Emmy, Diego waited until Rosita dragged Greta's soiled chair away from the table and slid a clean one in its place, the legs scraping loudly across the wooden floor.

Her voice deceptively calm, Mrs. Rawson bid Rosita forward. "Dish a serving of mole for Diego."

He raised his hand. "No thank you. I'm having supper with my mother."

"Very well, if you're sure."

"Yes, ma'am."

She made a feeble gesture toward the door. "I apologize for my children. I can't say why they behaved so atrociously."

He smiled. "You don't have to apologize to me."

Mrs. Rawson was silent for so long Emmy's gaze swung back to her. Studying her hands, the usually eloquent woman seemed to be fishing for words. She lifted troubled eyes to Diego. "Don't you think John should've been home by now?"

He cut his eyes to Emmy. She laid both palms on the table and lifted her chin. "I believe this concerns me, too. My parents are with him."

Diego lifted his brows at Mrs. Rawson.

"She's right, son. Besides, we're merely discussing at this point."

He nodded. "What would you have me to do?"

She picked up the napkin in her lap and twisted it as she stared at Mr. Rawson's empty chair. "I'm not sure we should do anything just yet. I don't want to fret prematurely. John detests when I fuss." She gazed at Diego with searching eyes. "What do you think we should do?"

His face unreadable, Diego fingered the rim of his water glass. "I decided if they weren't here by morning, I'd ride out and take a look."

She reached across the table and clutched his hands. "You're that concerned? I knew something wasn't right. I just knew it."

He opened his mouth to speak, but she drowned him out. "When will I learn to trust my instincts? I should've sent you last night."

"That might've been premature fretting, ma'am. Tomorrow's soon enough." He gathered her trembling fingers in both of his big hands. "Please don't work yourself up, Mrs. Rawson. I'm sure they're socializing or seeing the sights. Relax and get a good night's sleep. I plan to be on the road before dawn. By this time tomorrow, we'll all be pulling past the front gate."

She gave him a firm nod. "Good. Then I'll show that man of mine what it means to fuss."

Diego laughed low in his throat and squeezed her fingers.

Emmy had heard enough. "I'm going with you. What time do we leave?"

They turned together and stared at her.

Diego started to shake his head, but she held up her hand. "I mean it. I'm going."

He looked baffled. "Why? There's no reason."

She felt her eyes bulge. "No reason?" She pointed behind her toward the tall curtained windows. "Those are my parents out there with banditos and bloodsuckers!"

Mrs. Rawson pushed away from the table and came around to where Emmy sat. Wrapping her arms around her shoulders, she gave her a tight hug. "I've upset you with my foolishness. Trust me on this, Emily. Diego is a very capable young man. He'll find your parents for you." She raised her face to Diego. "And my husband for me. Won't you, dear?"

Diego stood. He put on his hat, then jerked it off again and held it to his chest. "Yes, ma'am. I'll find them and bring them home."

Mrs. Rawson straightened. "That's all, dear. I won't keep you from your supper. If Melatha's food is ruined, you may blame it on me."

He started for the door. "I'm sure it's fine. Good night, Mrs. Rawson."

"Good night, son."

He ducked his head at Emmy but didn't call her name.

She gave an answering nod, and then he was gone.

Mrs. Rawson patted her arm. "Do you need anything else before you go up to your room?"

"No, ma'am. Thank you."

"Then I hope you'll excuse me. I'm suddenly very tired."

Her heart in her throat, Emmy caught Mrs. Rawson's hand before she pulled away. The poor dear's heaviness had little to do with fatigue.

Giving Emmy's fingers one last squeeze, Mrs. Rawson glided from the room with a swish of her skirts.

Rosita entered from the kitchen.

Emmy stood and pushed in her chair. She risked a chance. "Good night, Rosita."

The tall, slender woman smiled and nodded. "El *muerto* y el *arrimado a los tres días apesta.*"

Having no idea what Rosita said but pleased with her gracious manner, Emmy tilted her head and returned her smile warmly. "Very well. Thank you, and I'll see you in the morning."

She heard Cuddy laughing before she made it to the stairs. Staring at him perched on a step midway up, she put her hands on her hips. "What are you doing sitting there? And what's so funny?"

He cocked his head. "I'm sitting here because I had as much right to hear that little discussion as you did." He grinned. "I'm laughing because Rosita just told you that corpses and annoying guests stink by the third day." He chuckled merrily. "And you thanked her."

She put her hand to her forehead. "Oh, my. I'm firmly on her bad side, and I don't know how to change it."

Cuddy's smile vanished. "Am I firmly on your bad side, Emmy?"

Her heart flipped. She knew she should be furious with him, but he reminded her too much of herself before that fateful day when she allowed God to come in and change her. She raised her eyes to his pleading gaze. "I only wish you'd stop being so naughty. You really upset your mother tonight. And Greta." She gave him a penetrating look. "You're not going to tell Greta's secret, are you?"

He looked surprised. "Over a skirmish with mole poblano? Of course not. Besides, it wouldn't be in my best interest, now would it?" He patted the step beside him. "Come sit with me."

She caught hold of the banister and pulled herself even with him. Before she sat, she aimed a warning finger. "Have you been drinking?"

He held up his hand. "On my honor, I'm as parched as a crusty cow patty."

She laughed and eased down beside him. "Oh, Cuddy, you're incorrigible."

He smiled and took her hand. "So you forgive me for my stupidity? I swear I only wanted a kiss. I didn't mean to scare you."

She stared at her feet, trying to work up her nerve. When she felt she could speak the truth, she confronted him. "But you did scare me, Cuddy. I know it would never have happened if you'd been sober. This tells me you simply must stop drinking."

Sneering, he drew back. "Don't tell me you've banded with the abstinence club?"

"I'm sorry, but they're right. It's obvious alcohol alters your judgment. I can't help but wonder what might've happened had Diego not come along."

He stiffened. "You don't need Diego to defend your honor from me."

"I did last night."

He shook his head. "You only thought you did. Which is my fault, and I accept the blame." A brooding shadow crossed his face. "Diego's another matter. He should know me better."

Emmy jumped at the sound of a door closing somewhere in the house.

"Don't worry," Cuddy said. "That's just Rosita leaving for the night." He rubbed his hands down the front of his trousers, not the first time since his food fight given their stained condition. "I suppose I'd better get cleaned up then find a place in the bunkhouse to lay my head. Sounds like I have an early start ahead of me."

"An early start?" She studied his profile. "Cuddy, you're not thinking of going with Diego?"

He met her gaze. "Not thinking—my mind's made up." Determination burned in his eyes. "Diego doesn't know it yet, but I'm going."

Her heart skipped. "Then you're worried, too?"

He shrugged. "Call it insurance. I have to keep my old man alive until I prove myself to him." His boyish features hardened with determination. "He's planning to go to his grave disappointed in me, but I'm not giving him the satisfaction."

❧

Melatha's heart soared with joy at the familiar sound of Isi's boots hitting the porch. She whispered her thanks over folded hands and turned at the counter, ready to greet him. Certain her fervor reminded God of the parable of the persistent widow in Luke's Gospel, she also repented for wearying Him.

Isi stood on the threshold, his hat in his hands, as if hesitant to press on without an invitation.

His contrite manner pierced her heart. She smiled sweetly and motioned him in. "Good evening, son. Are you hungry?"

He ducked his chin, but his eyes burned into hers. "You wouldn't happen to have a pot of mole poblano, would you? I've developed a sudden urge for some."

Already turning to lift the lid on her kettle, she paused. "Mole? No mole, son. Only—" She was hesitant to admit what she had to offer him instead—pounded corn boiled with beans, a traditional food of the Choctaw.

He dropped his hat on the hook and approached the table. "Is that Tafula I smell? Even better."

Sighing with relief, she ladled a large bowlful and set it in front of him. Isi blew on a bite then took a taste from the end of the spoon. He nodded vigorously. "Very good, as usual."

Melatha's joyful heart swelling like the breast of a dove, she grinned at him. "You say the same every time. I find myself starting to doubt you."

Her chest deflated in a rush of shame when he halted mid-bite and laid down the spoon. She hurried to him, enveloping him with her arms from behind. "Stop it now, Isi. I will never really doubt you." She gave him a shake. "You know this."

He reached back to wrap his arm around her neck, drawing her closer. "I'm so sorry, Mother. I promise not to disappoint you ever again."

She laughed against his ear. "An impossible promise to keep. A mother's expectations are unreasonable." She swung around to kneel at his feet. "You will disappoint me many times if you're to live your own life." Her brown eyes bored into his. "It doesn't mean I won't worry, but I have to allow you to make your own mistakes, whatever the cost. I see this truth now."

His brows crowding together, Isi took hold of her arms. "Wait a second while I catch my balance."

"Your balance?"

"Yes, Mother." His eyes darted to the floor. "It seems the ground has shifted beneath my feet. Did I just hear Melatha Marcelo telling her son to live his own life? What happened to bring about this change?"

She lowered her gaze. "The old teacher is still teachable, I suppose."

He placed his big hand on her head then let it slide until he held her cheek. "You show me such respect after I've ruined both our lives?"

She pressed his palm to her face and shook her head. "But you haven't ruined our lives."

His eyes bulged. "When John Rawson finds out—"

She patted his roughened hand and stood to her feet. "He cannot find out, which brings me to the one mistake I can't allow you to make." She slipped into the chair opposite him and passed him his spoon. "Eat your supper, son, while I tell you about a very important visitor I had today."

CHAPTER 28

Magda awoke groggy and stiff. Her joints were sore and her patience at its limits. She groped for Willem's face to pinch his nose, determined to stifle his infernal snoring.

Her searching hand came up empty. Startled, she turned over in her bedroll.

Willem sat on a log near the campfire talking to John and Bertha. The real culprits responsible for the relentless bellows and moans that had invaded her sleep meandered nearby grazing.

Magda had marveled at how fast Benito, the lead vaquero, had constructed several lean-tos of forked sticks, ridgepoles, and cowhides. As long as Willem stretched out next to her, she'd slept beneath their shelter warm and comfortable. Only after he'd slipped away did the chill of the bare ground seep into her bones.

She wondered how Bertha had managed, sleeping in her bedding alone, and suspected it was the reason her bony friend huddled near the campfire with a cup of coffee in her hand.

Benito and Juan, the *segundo*, which meant second-in-command according to John, appeared from the rear of the wagon bearing an iron skillet and other supplies to make breakfast. John and Willem scooted aside to make a place for them near the fire.

"You cook, too?" John asked. "I didn't know that was a part of our bargain."

"Sí, señor," the slightly weathered Juan said, smiling. "For many years, I ran the chuck wagon for un rancho *grande*." He smiled toward Willem. "A very big ranch."

John gave him a broad smile. "Fine, fine. You'll be an asset to this trip." He frowned toward Benito. "Where are the other two fellows?"

Carl cut around behind them. "I'm here, Mr. Rawson." He squatted on the ground near the coffeepot and poured himself a cup. "Wayne will be along directly." He grinned. "His covers don't want to turn him loose this morning."

Accepting a refill from the boy, John frowned. "That won't do if we hope to get this livestock moving. I need you two to prowl the herd before we take them down to the river."

Benito stood and trotted out of sight, presumably to roust Wayne.

Bertha, her timing unfortunate as usual, peered around Willem to where Magda rested her head on her propped arm, listening to the conversation. "Speaking of turning loose of your covers, when do you plan to haul yourself up?"

Groaning when all eyes turned her way, Magda sank lower in the bedroll.

"There's fresh coffee here, sugar. And this nice Juan has camp bread and eggs in the skillet."

As nonchalantly as possible with six pairs of eyes glued to her, Magda unraveled herself from the lean-to and ambled to the fire. Beaming up at her, Bertha moved over and patted a spot on the log. "Morning, sunshine. It's been right tough going without you to light our way."

Magda nudged her. "I'm happy to see you in such good spirits. I think."

A bedraggled Wayne staggered toward them. His puffy eyes, slack mouth, and rumpled hair made him look as if he'd tied on a drunk the night before. He attempted to squat next to his brother, but lost his balance and fell on his backside instead. Rubbing crusted matter from his bloodshot eyes, he elbowed Carl and pointed at the pot. "I hope you saved me plenty of that muddy water. I need it something fierce this morning."

Benito signaled to Carl, who stood reluctantly. "Let Wayne find his own coffee. You and I will ride the herd then take them to drink."

Carl's face pulled into a frown. "But I ain't had me no breakfast yet."

Already headed for his horse, Benito didn't bother to answer. Wayne chuckled. "Don't worry, Carl. I'll eat yours for you."

Juan glanced up from his task. "There will be plenty, young man. You may eat when you return."

Carl stomped away like a pouting boy.

John, his jaw working, regarded Wayne. "If you want meals from now on, I expect you to show up groomed and on time. If not, you can find your way back to Eagle Pass. Understood?"

Sullen at first, Wayne put on a false brightness and saluted John, a guarded challenge in his eyes. "Yes, sir, boss." Snickering, he grabbed the plate Juan was handing to Bertha and sat back to dig in.

Bertha and Magda shared a look of disgust.

Maybe for the first time in her life, Magda was relieved to see a meal end. As delicious as the unexpected breakfast turned out to be, Wayne's presence spoiled her appetite. She didn't relax until they'd broken up camp and were on their way, with the coarse Wayne riding out in front of the herd and far away from the wagon.

"He's no good," Bertha announced beside her, reading her mind.

"We can't say John didn't warn us." She patted Bertha's hand. "Don't worry. The men can handle him. Soon we'll be well shed of him."

Bertha didn't look convinced. "I wish John *would* send him back to Eagle Pass. He's trouble. I can smell it."

Magda laughed. "Maybe you caught the scent of his unwashed body. My gut says he's not one for practicing good hygiene."

Bertha whipped her head around. "No fooling, Magda. I'm having one of my feelings."

"Oh, Bertha. . ."

"Don't make fun. I told you they're from God."

Magda crossed her arms. "All right, then. What would God have you to do about Wayne?"

Bertha shrugged. "We didn't get that far."

~⚬~

The sun hadn't yet risen high enough to be seen, just enough to lighten the eastern sky to a watery gray. A pale, fading moon hung low over the horizon, and a few of the brightest stars were still visible.

Despite the lack of piercing rays, sweat already pooled on Diego's top lip, meaning the day would be a scorcher.

He spotted the rider tailing him before he'd gone a quarter mile from the house. Little Pete had no reason to be following him so slyly, nor did any other man on the Twisted-R spread—except for Cuddy.

Making a mental note to teach him the art of stealthy tracking, Diego turned his horse and ambled toward him.

Cuddy must have realized Diego spotted him because he picked up his pace and met him halfway.

Diego circled and fell in beside him. "Good morning. Going my way?"

Cuddy crossed his hands over the saddle horn and grunted. "I see it's true you have eyes in the back of your head. Has anyone ever slipped up on you?"

"Greta." Wishing he hadn't brought her up, Diego cut his eyes to the ground. Would it ever seem natural to speak of her again? "Twice, in fact."

"Makes sense. She has years of practice from spying on me."

Diego had to smile. "You'll never catch me off guard, that's for sure. You track like a marauding grizzly." He lifted one brow. "I don't have to ask why you're here, do I?"

Cuddy raised one shoulder. "Who knows? I'm not even sure myself."

The day dawned at last, and they stared toward the sunrise in silence. Diego released the breath he'd held and looked at Cuddy, one side of his freckled face bathed in yellow light. "I wanted to talk to you about this trip before I ever spoke with your mother, but—"

"But you thought it might be bad form considering you so recently pummeled my head?" Cuddy leaned in the saddle to stress his point. "Over something I didn't do." His guarded eyes lifted. "Remember when we talked about Greta's purity, and you said you didn't believe I had to ask?"

Diego nodded grimly. "I do. I also remember you saying you wanted to believe me. That you wanted to, Cuddy—not that you did." He jerked his chin as if Emmy stood there. "How can you compare what you did to Emmy with what happened between me and Greta? From what I saw, it wasn't exactly the same."

Cuddy dashed his quirt on his leg, startling the horses. "How could you see anything? It was pitch black."

"I didn't need to see to know Emmy wanted it to stop," he

sputtered, faltering for words. "Cuddy. . .I heard her begging you."

If Diego had slapped his face, Cuddy couldn't have looked more startled. He pulled back on the reins, the shock in his eyes fading to dazed remembrance. "She did beg me. I remember now." He closed his eyes. "That's what Emily tried to tell me last night. That I scared her."

Diego stopped his horse, too, sympathy for his troubled friend welling inside. "I know you didn't mean to frighten her. You'd had too much to drink."

Cuddy gnawed his bottom lip. "That's not a good excuse, is it? Not if I hurt someone as wonderful as Emily." He nudged his horse to move again and they picked their way across the plain in brooding silence.

Cuddy seemed deep in thought, and Diego prayed he might come to the right conclusions about his life.

They'd gone quite a way before Cuddy spoke again. "What time did we leave the ranch?"

"Around six thirty."

"What time is it now?"

Diego studied the sky. "I'd say pushing eight thirty. At this clip, we'll be at the Campbells' before lunchtime." He glanced at Cuddy. "That means they'll clear a place at the table."

Cuddy grinned. "I wouldn't mind skipping lunch and going straight for Mrs. Campbell's sweet pecan bread."

Diego groaned. "Considering we have miles yet to go, it's outright cruelty to mention that bread so soon." He rubbed his stomach. "Especially since I left too early for breakfast."

"And Melatha let you get away with that? Better check your pockets. She's sure to have corn cakes stuffed inside."

"That may be wishful thinking on your part," Diego teased, but he patted them just in case.

Grateful they'd lightened the mood, Diego kept the conversation going with a joke he'd heard in the bunkhouse and telling a prank he'd played on Little Pete.

Just when he felt easy with Cuddy again, the simpleton opened his mouth. "Are you planning to tell the old man about Greta?"

Diego's shoulders drooped. Squinting in protest of the topic, he glanced at Cuddy. "I've had a curious parade of people ask me not to tell, with Greta at the top of the list. I'm still trying to decide what's right."

Cuddy pushed back his hat, eagerness to drive home his point evident in the deep lines of his brow. "I'll march in that parade, friend. I say don't tell." His anxious eyes studied Diego. "You said you were trying to make up your mind about Greta. If she turns out to be your choice, you don't want to rile the old man."

Diego shifted in the saddle. Time to tell the truth. "I made up my mind about Greta, Cuddy. If I marry your sister, it'll be for all the wrong reasons. And for all the wrong people."

Cuddy's eyes lowered to the high grass between them. "That's a shame. I always hoped you'd wind up a legitimate member of the family."

Diego stared wordlessly at Cuddy, the question he wanted to ask stuck in his throat.

Cuddy smiled and looked away. "I know what you're thinking. I guess I'm part *loco* to want you hanging about when my father prefers you to me. Shoot, to hear him talk, you're more his son than I'll ever be." He shrugged. "But I'm used to having you around, brother. In fact. . ." He chuckled. "I think you'll get a kick out of this. My hope that you'd marry my sister is the main reason I've tried so hard to steer you clear of Emily."

Diego gawked at him. "Are you saying you don't really care for Emily?"

"Care for her?" Cuddy wrinkled his face. "Sure, I care. I'm just not in love with her." He tilted his head. "Don't get me wrong, she's a real looker, but Emily's turned out to be a friend. A good friend and I don't want to mess it up." He winked. "Not that I wouldn't kiss her if she gave me the chance."

Finding not a speck of humor in Cuddy's last sentence, Diego shook his head to clear his muddled mind. Unsure what to do with the information, he fingered the rawhide riata notched in the groove at the base of his saddle horn while his heartbeat settled down.

Sobered, Cuddy cleared his throat. "The thing is, she won't be giving me that chance because. . . Actually, amigo, I'm fairly certain the only one Emily Dane wants to kiss is you."

Diego's head snapped around so fast his neck cracked. "Me?"

Cuddy nodded.

"But you must be mistaken."

Finding it impossible to think straight, Diego opened his mouth to ask more questions, but Cuddy's gaze flickered and he waved a greeting. "Eyes front. We got company."

Diego glanced up, relieved to see that friendly faces had gotten the jump on them and not strangers. Lester and Joe Campbell rode toward them at an easy canter.

Lester raised his hand to the sky as they approached. "Diego! Cuddy Rawson! What brings you out this way?"

Diego and Cuddy closed the distance between them, reining in a few feet from the beaming brothers. Relieved to see them smiling, Diego knew it foretold good news about Mr. Rawson and his guests. "We've come to bust up the party," he said, already dreading the exasperated look on his boss's face. He'd have to dream up a good excuse for butting into his good time and hauling him back to his waiting wife. "Where are you two headed?"

"Actually, we were on our way to the Twisted-R," Lester said. "Little brother here's been riding me real hard to drop everything and go see the ranch. We thought today was a good day." He chuckled and scratched his head. "Don't tell me you're headed for our place. That'd be a downright silly coincidence."

The slight crowding of Joe's eyebrows to the center of his forehead was Diego's first clue that things were not as they seemed. "Did you mention a party?" He looked offended. "If there's a party, someone left us off the guest list."

Diego smiled, trying to ignore the tension building in his stomach. "Not an official party, Joe. I'm referring to whatever shenanigans have kept Mr. Rawson and his guests at your place for the last few days."

The furrows in Joe's forehead deepened, matched by those in Lester's. Joe shook his head. "Ain't nobody staying at our house."

Cuddy sat forward in his saddle.

Diego swallowed against the growing knot in his throat. "When did they leave?"

Confusion clouded Lester's eyes. "There's been some sort of misunderstanding, friend. We haven't seen them."

Joe tilted his head. "I told my pa you thought your boss would stop by, but he never showed. We figured it for a mix-up."

Cuddy fired Diego a panicked look.

Diego's every muscle tingled with an urgency to spur his horse and ride. But where? Where did one look for a vanished wagon filled with people?

Joe leaned to peer at him. "You all right? You've gone pale around the mouth."

Understanding dawned on Lester's face. He nodded at Cuddy. "Sorry, old boy. Is there anything we can do?"

Out of fear and concern for Cuddy, Diego lashed out. "You can stop planning a funeral. We'll find them. . .alive and well."

Lester ducked his head. "Sure thing, Diego. Of course you will."

Ashamed of his outburst, Diego released a long breath. "I'm sorry, Les. Just keep your eyes peeled, won't you? If you run into Mr. Rawson, tell him the folks at the house are getting worried."

With no time or patience left to dawdle, Diego wheeled away from them and headed back the way they'd come.

Cuddy was fast on his heels and soon caught up. "Where are you going?" he cried. "We have to look for them!"

"It would take us days to cover any ground. We have to organize a search party, starting with the men on the ranch. But first we need to borrow fresh horses from Señor Boteo."

"What?" Cuddy vigorously shook his head. "There's no time for that."

Diego set his jaw. "It'll save time in the long run. At the pace I intend to keep, these two will drop from under us in this heat." In no mood to argue, he ignored Cuddy's sputtering and pointed his horse due south.

Settling into the idea, Cuddy stared toward the Boteos' modest house, corrals, and outbuildings in the distance. "Knowing my father, he could be anywhere, couldn't he? It would never occur to him that his actions might be irresponsible or cause Mother to worry."

"Anything's possible."

Cuddy watched him closely. "But you don't believe it, do you?"

Trying to comfort Cuddy with the intensity of his resolve, Diego leveled him with a determined look. "We're going to find them, Cuddy. The hard part will be explaining to your mother and Emmy why we haven't already."

CHAPTER 29

About the time Magda figured her stomach would collapse, John whistled the signal to Benito to turn the herd toward the river. Willem followed until John rode close to the wagon, fatigue lining his face. "Pull up into that clearing by the bank, Willem. We'll take a little break. I know I could sure use a rest."

Willem obliged, reining the team and setting the brake.

Magda studied John's chiseled features. "You all right, John? You look a mite peaked."

"I'll be fine, Magda." He swiped his arm across his chin. "But I shouldn't be driving you folks so hard in this heat. I figured if we pushed a couple of hours past noon, we could rest during the hottest part of the day."

Willem fumbled for his pocket watch. "It's two o'clock on the dot."

John smiled weakly. "Stay up under the shade of the surrey, ladies, until we call you for lunch. There's nothing for you to do. Juan's setting up now to cook." His gaze jumped to Willem. "Unless they'd like you to walk them down to the river for a splash of cool water on their faces."

Bertha squirmed on the seat. "That sounds more like it. I've got a pressing need to climb down from here for a while."

"Take that with you," John said, nodding at the Marlin.

Willem hoisted the loaded rifle. "Will do."

Juan looked up and waved as they passed the spot where he'd dug a pit and started a fire.

Bertha glanced back at Magda. "Feels strange not to be the one in charge of vittles. Makes me feel guilty." She chuckled. "But just a mite."

They followed what appeared to be an ancient trail leading down to the river. Passing between walls of bushes on each side, they dodged overgrown branches and grasping vines until the path opened out onto an overhanging shelf. Willem held each of their hands and eased them onto the sun-crusted ledge that butted up to the lapping water about two feet down.

Squealing, Bertha kicked off her shoes. "Turn away, Willem. I'm going in to wade."

"You be careful, Bertha," Willem said anxiously. "Don't slide down or step in a hole."

Laughing like a youngster, she stomped in. "Come on, Magda. It's warm on top but cool on the bottom."

The cool part was all Magda needed to hear. She held onto Willem for balance and pulled off her shoes. Clutching roots protruding from the bank near a fallen tree, she held them to steady herself while she lowered her bare feet one at a time. Laughing when mud oozed between her toes, she called to Willem. "Roll up your britches and join us, dear. It's very refreshing."

Her husband stood staring downriver to where the vaqueros watered the herd. The cattle drank at the river's edge, their heads bowed together. Their contented moos echoed across the water like old men clearing their throats. Willem shaded his eyes. "Where's that Wayne fellow? I haven't seen him since we stopped."

Bertha raised her leg and kicked, the top of her foot scooping a shower into the air to rain down onto the surface. "Maybe we got lucky and he hit the road."

Magda lifted her hands as a shield. "Stop that splashing, Bert. You're worse than a kid."

"Leave me be. I'm making sure no snake crawls up your dress."

"You can stop fretting about that. With all your ruckus, no clever snake is within miles of here."

Bertha froze and dropped her hem. Her eyes wide, she nodded behind Willem. "You're right. Just sorry, no 'count, sneaky snakes."

Magda whirled in time to see Wayne's leering face retreat into the brush. Releasing her own skirt, her feet made loud ploinking sounds as she high-stepped to the bank. "Willem!"

He spun, alarm in his eyes. "What's wrong?"

She pointed, her finger shaking. "That nasty Wayne. Skulking in the bushes to get a peek."

Willem wasted no time heading for the steep rise.

"Don't hurt yourself, dear. He's already gone."

"Get out of the water," he shouted over his shoulder, the only sign that he'd heard her at all.

Magda rushed to obey, her anxious eyes trained on Willem's back as he struggled to make the high step to the area above. "Be careful with that rifle, now!"

The top of his ears blazed red, and his panting desperation to be about the chase frightened her. Mentioning the gun flashed terrible possibilities across her mind. "Just catch him and let John handle this," she called as he fought his way up the incline.

He managed to get one leg atop the short cliff then leaned forward to haul the other foot up. As he pushed to his feet with the gun still in his hand, the dirt at the edge crumbled, and he lost his balance. Frantically pumping his arms was not enough to hold him up—especially when the gun went off. He sailed backward, seeming to hover briefly in midair before he landed headfirst on the trunk of the dead tree.

Magda's cry and the sound of gunfire roused the men downriver. With shouts and waving hats, they thundered into the water and raced toward them. By the time they reached Willem, Magda hovered over him, patting his cheeks.

Tossing modesty aside, she lifted her hem to bathe his face with the cool water, her tears preventing her from seeing him clearly. "Open your eyes, dear. Willem, please. Open your eyes."

John crowded up next to her. "Move aside, Magda. Let me have a look at him." He slid his hands beneath Willem's head to lift him gently from the trunk then paused, his eyes going to Magda's face.

She tensed and her stomach sank. "What is it, John?"

John raised his hand to have a look.

Magda's eyes jerked to the blood oozing between his fingers and dripping onto the ground. Her own screams impossibly loud in her ears, she stumbled backward into darkness.

Emmy slammed her fist against the table. "I'm coming with you, Diego. Don't try to talk me out of it this time."

They hovered around the dining table, a sobbing Greta with her head in her stricken mother's lap, Cuddy behind them with his hands on Mrs. Rawson's shoulders, and Diego standing behind Mr. Rawson's chair, gripping the ladder back with white knuckles. "I'm sorry, Emmy. I can't let you go."

She stood, shaking. "Let me? You can't stop me."

Mrs. Rawson lifted her head. "Tell me again what Mr. Boteo said."

Diego swept past Emmy as if she wasn't there. "He said Santos, his grandson, saw your husband's wagon headed southwest, away from Catarina and Carrizo Springs."

She stared with hollow eyes and her head swung side to side. "It makes no sense. There's nothing in that direction but the river." She glanced up at Diego. "Could they have been going after water?"

Cuddy patted her shoulder. "The river is miles out of the way, and the brush is too thick in that region to cross easily."

She wrung her hands. "Then why? Why would John drive a wagon filled with special guests to the middle of nowhere and disappear?"

Looking less than sure of his confident words, Cuddy smoothed her hair. "Don't fret, Mother. We'll find them if we have to turn over every blade of grass from here to Mexico."

Emmy took Diego's arm and turned him. "We're wasting time. It'll be dark soon."

He flexed his jaw. "Get it through your head, Emmy. You're staying here."

Fury made her dizzy. She stared boldly into his flashing, determined eyes. "For your information, I'm not in the habit of taking orders, and I don't intend to take any from you." She lifted her chin and sniffed. "The truth is I don't need your permission. Mrs. Rawson will help me."

She pulled out a chair across from Cuddy's mother and perched on the edge. "Ma'am, I'm very good on a horse, and I can find the business end of a gun. I'm a decent shot, and I know how to defend myself." She reached for Mrs. Rawson's hands. "This is not even the first manhunt I've been on. Why, back home—"

Diego pulled her chair around and leaned on the arms, so close to her face she felt the warmth of his breath. "It's a ridiculous notion. Who will watch out for you?"

"I can take care of myself."

He shook his head. "A woman will only slow us down." Letting go of her chair, he walked away a few paces, dismissing her.

Emmy stalked to him, pointing behind her at Greta and Mrs. Rawson. "I'm not like—" Catching herself before she said something hurtful, she dropped her arm and amended her words. "I'm not the weak, fragile female you make me out to be. I'm different, Diego. You should know that by now."

He gripped her shoulders hard, grit in his brown eyes. "Yes, you're different. I can't deny it if I try. But you're not a man, Emmy. What makes you think you can keep up with a man's business?"

"I can answer that." The quiet voice behind them spun Diego. Melatha stood under the arched doorway, her arms crossed over her chest. "Emmy can keep up because she has your same spirit, Isi."

She nodded at Mrs. Rawson. "Forgive me for coming unannounced, Kate. I just heard."

Mrs. Rawson held out her arms. "Oh, Melatha! I'm so frightened."

Melatha swept across the room, two thick braids dangling from the back of her head. She gathered Mrs. Rawson and pressed her cheek against her forehead, speaking low in a language very different from Spanish. Emmy realized she was praying in her native Choctaw.

Cuddy left his mother to Melatha's care and started for the door. "Come on, Emily. I'll show you what to pack."

Relief flooded Emmy's limbs. Smiling warmly, she took his arm. "Thank you, Cuddy."

He winked. "Greta will sort out our rations while we get things ready in the barn. There's no telling how many days we'll—"

"Hold up there." Diego took her other arm as she passed, stopping her in her tracks. "Nothing's been decided yet."

Mrs. Rawson interrupted from where she sat. "Let her go, Diego. It's her right to choose."

Confusion and rage battled in his eyes. He frowned at each sullen face. "So I'm outnumbered here?"

Their silence gave him the answer.

"Very well, Miss Dane. You'll have your way, I see." His threatening glare scared her more than she dared to let him see. "Just remember. . .I won't allow you to slow us down a single second from finding Mr. Rawson and your family. When you get into trouble—and you will—I won't lift a finger to save you. Not even from banditos and bloodsuckers."

~~~

Magda scrambled away from Bertha's grasping hands and pulled herself upright. Hastily spread and bunched beneath her, the blanket that had cushioned Bertha's behind for miles now cushioned her from the rocks and stubble. She looked around, noting the wagon and the campfire, heard the lowing cattle in the distance. She blinked up at her friend. "What's going on, Bertha? How'd I get here?"

Bertha pointed. "Those poor men carried you. It wasn't easy getting you up that ledge, I can tell you that much."

The terrible memory came in a rush. Magda's jaw dropped as a scream welled in her throat.

Bertha clamped a hand that smelled of mud across her mouth. Her eyes brimming with tears, she wagged her head back and forth. "It's all right. Willem's alive, Magda. He's hurt, but he's alive."

Magda struggled to her feet, looking around in a panic. "Where is he? I have to see for myself."

Bertha led her to the wagon.

The men had shoved aside boxes and crates to make room for Willem's squat body in the bed. He lay so pale and still, it took Magda's breath.

She clutched Bertha's hand. "Are you sure he's alive?"

Bertha nodded. "John said so."

"Is he. . ."

"Gunshot? No. We found the nub of a broke-off limb covered in blood. It poked the back of his head when he fell on that tree."

Magda drew in a ragged breath. "But that's even worse."

"Worse than taking a bullet in the brain? Not by a long shot, if you'll pardon the pun. John said he likely has a concussion, though, since he won't wake up."

Magda moved around closer to Willem's ghostly white face. "You mean he hasn't regained consciousness one time?"

Bertha shook her head.

Growing more concerned by the second, Magda raised up to scour the area. "Where is John?" she asked frantically. "Why aren't we rushing Willem to a doctor?"

"John jumped on that fast horse of his and said he'd fetch a doctor to tend Willem right where he lays."

Magda stared. "A doctor from where? We're miles from Eagle Pass."

"He said we passed a little community called El Indio a few miles back. He thinks there may be a doctor there."

"And if there's not?" Alarm made Magda's voice shrill.

"Don't borrow trouble, sugar. John won't let us down."

"Señora?"

Juan's gentle voice startled Magda so badly she jumped. Staring at his dark, weathered face, the realization struck. John had left Magda and Bertha alone with four strange men, Benito, Juan, Carl, and the terrible Wayne, with Willem as lifeless as a turnip.

"You should eat, ma'am," Juan continued, his eyes aglow with compassion. "Keep your strength up for your husband."

She raised her hand. "Food's the last thing I want just now, thank you. I should be doing something to help him."

Bertha gave her a gentle shake. "There's nothing you can do, sugar. John and the men made sure he's comfortable. He'll call out for you when he wakes up." She took hold of Magda's arm. "Come sit down and eat a bite."

Clinging to the rail, Magda dug in her heels. "No. I'm staying right here until John gets back with the doctor."

Juan motioned for Benito and Carl. The three of them cleared more space in the wagon then helped Magda climb in beside Willem. Only after she'd settled against the backboard clinging to his fingers did she accept a tortilla filled with shredded meat from Juan. The first bite tasted like dirt and refused to go down, so she handed the food off to Bertha when Juan wasn't looking.

Wayne was nowhere in sight. His brother Carl leaned against the tailgate, staring at the ground and idly chewing the end of a stick.

Bertha, who had crawled up to sit at Magda's feet, watched him with wide eyes. "Say, where'd that brother of yours run off to?"

Carl drew up his shoulders. "Can't say. I was just wondering the same. He was here when we stopped, but I ain't seen him since."

He grinned, flashing a mouth full of yellow teeth. "Wayne's like that, you know." He made a sweeping motion with his hand. "Disappears with the wind and then blows right back." Laughing, he ambled to where Benito and Juan sat on the ground in front of the fire.

Bertha made a face. "I'd just as soon the wind had carried him off for good, at least until John gets back."

Magda set her mouth grimly. "Not me. I hope he blows back just long enough for me to claw his eyes out."

Bertha patted her hand. "I'll hold him for you, honey."

CHAPTER 30

Diego stared in wonder at the number of riders clustered on the road in front of the house. Word had spread throughout the county, thanks to Rosita and Little Pete. Friends and neighbors had gathered for the last hour, eager to do anything to help the kind and generous Mr. Rawson. Even Joe and Les Campbell showed up to offer their time.

Diego tightened the horsehair girth and tied his leather quirt to the saddle. Luckily, these were tasks he could easily perform in his sleep, since his willful eyes were busy tracking Emmy's every move.

The soft clingy dresses and skin-revealing necklines were gone, along with the strappy suede shoes with little square heels. She wore men's clothing, complete with Cuddy's shirt, baggy slacks, and cowhide chaps buttoned behind her legs. Someone had even furnished her with a wide-brimmed straw hat. Only her boots were made for a woman, most likely lent by Greta.

Cuddy hovered like a bee on honey, helping Emmy with her rigging and double-checking her gear. Afterward, he mounted up and rode alongside her toward the entrance to the ranch.

Remembering the feckless boy's declaration that he'd kiss her if she'd let him, Diego slapped shut the flap on his saddlebag with more force than called for. Whirling, he nearly ran over his mother.

She gazed up at him with knowing eyes. "It's not like you to pout, son."

He brushed past her to gather his reins. "You're mistaken, Mother. I don't have time to pout."

She caught his arm before he swung onto the horse. "There's nothing between them, Isi."

Astonished, he met her probing eyes. "Your talent for reading minds has spread to Emmy and Cuddy now?"

She shrugged. "Emmy's too much woman. She won't wait for Cuddy to mature."

He gave her a piercing look. "You champion her now? Exactly what did that girl say to you?"

"Matters between women are best left to women."

He blew air from between his teeth and swung into the saddle. "On that point you won't get an argument from me. Still. . .Emmy managed to change your heart in one visit?"

His mother tilted her face, using one hand to shade her eyes from the afternoon sun. "She's a very persuasive girl."

He held up his finger. "Ah, there, you see? Careful, Mother. I'm not sure her powers of persuasion are from God." He reined the horse away from her.

"That remains to be seen," she called out behind him, "and this is Emmy's chance to prove it."

Laying to rest the idea that his mother could no longer surprise him, he stored away the confusing conversation for later. The time had come to turn his thoughts to the pressing matter at hand.

Anxious riders surrounded him outside the gate, all trying to speak at the same time. He held up his hand and whistled, and they stilled. "One at a time, please." He pointed to Little Pete.

"Sí, Diego." Pete sat taller in the saddle. "Where do we search? Around Catarina?"

"Well, Pete," Diego said, dreading the faithful hand's reaction, "you won't be searching anywhere. I need a man I can rely on to stay behind with the women."

Pete's countenance fell. "Sí, if you think it's best."

Diego's gaze took in the crowd. "As for the rest of you, I thought we'd split up. They were seen heading southwest, but the truth is, they could be anywhere. One group of riders will sweep in a wide circle around Catarina to the right, another to the left. The largest group will spread out in a line straight up the middle. We should all wind up near the road to San Antonio."

"And if we don't find them?" one of the men called out.

"We'll widen the circle."

He whistled again to quiet the murmuring reaction. "Let me make one thing clear, I'm not coming back without Mr. Rawson and his guests. Any of you who can't say the same, please stay home. I can't have you pulling out later, leaving your group short of men."

Another round of discussion followed, this time interspersed with nodding heads and vows of commitment.

Since Señor Boteo knew the area, Diego appointed him to head the Rio Grande search. He put Lester and Joe in charge of the opposite half of the circle. Diego and the rest would form the middle line.

Displaying the order and quickness of those accustomed to making fast decisions, the men and horses divided to Diego's specifications with the grace of a Spanish dance. Not waiting to be assigned, Emmy trotted her horse next to Diego's, her jaw set and her gaze fixed straight ahead.

Diego couldn't contain a stab of satisfaction when the seasoned ranchers and vaqueros stared at Emmy with disbelieving eyes. Forcing himself to contain his anger when their eyes lingered a bit too long, he thrust his arm out in front. "All right! Let's ride!"

∽≈↝

Melatha watched the cloud of dust on the road until it dwindled to a faint puff on the horizon. Her thoughts turned to prayer for the men. *"How excellent is thy lovingkindness, O God! Therefore the children of men put their trust under the shadow of thy wings."*

A sense of foreboding had settled on her the minute Isi rode out of sight. She told herself the sinister slide of cold hands up her back had to do with her fear for John Rawson and grief for his dear wife. Yet watching Isi lead the solemn band of men toward the road to Catarina was the hardest thing she'd ever done.

An urge to cut and run welled inside her, though from what, Melatha did not know. She whispered a prayer for her son instead. "Keep him safe, Chihowa Palami. As the apple of Your eye, hide Isi beneath the shadow of Your wings."

She pulled her gaze from the empty road and hurried toward the house. The kitchen would be in chaos, so Rosita and the girls would need her. When the searchers returned, whether celebrating around a wagon heralding the prodigals' return, or—she shuddered—mourning behind a wagon in service as a funeral bier, they would be hot, tired, and hungry. There was no way of knowing if they had hours or days to prepare.

Melatha pictured Kate Rawson's drawn mouth and tortured eyes. She prayed for her sake the wait would end soon.

∼≪≫∼

Emmy followed Diego and Cuddy off the road into an area thick with briars, brambles, and mesquite trees, more afraid than she'd ever been in her life. At the beginning of the last few torturous hours, she had tried to search apart from them, to prove herself to Diego, until an encounter between a rattlesnake and a startled horse left an experienced horseman hugging a cactus.

The boots Emmy wore were so big her toes slid forward with each step of the horse, causing pain so intense she feared finding her feet covered in blisters. The heat was atrocious, even with the sun dipping closer to the earth. Her hair hung in dripping strands beneath the hat, but taking it off meant having her head baked.

Now the same sun that seemed determined to bake her alive looked ready to bail out on her. Her heart crowded into her throat as the last bright orange sliver dropped into a deep pocket on the far horizon, and the vivid watercolor landscape became a child's charcoal sketch on gray paper. Even a cluster of yellow green fireflies bobbing and dancing in the brush failed to cheer her.

No matter how awful things were, she knew the nighttime would be worse. She also knew no matter how frightening the darkness, she'd never be sorry she came. To be stuck on the ranch harboring dreadful thoughts of her parents' predicament would be hard to bear alone, and Emmy had never felt so alone in her life.

Letting her guard down briefly, she explored the murky cauldron of fear that seethed inside—a mistake considering Mama's smiling face swam into view, blinding her.

"You all right over there?"

Diego's voice startled her but soothed her, too. More grateful for his presence than she'd ever let on, she hurriedly wiped her eyes. "Oh, yes. I'm fine." Even to her ears, she didn't sound fine. Her stuffy, nasal tone gave away her tears.

Diego's horse cut in closer. "We'll find them, Emmy."

She shuddered, startling herself. "I. . .I know we will. But no matter how I arrange the facts, it doesn't make sense." She sought the comfort of his brown eyes. "If you have a theory to share that ends with a positive outcome, I'd be grateful to hear."

He glanced away quickly then back. "I'd love to say something to comfort you, but I'm afraid I'm struggling with the same questions. The explanation I cling to is Cuddy's—that Mr. Rawson is somewhere 'playing the highfalutin ranchero' for your parents, having too much fun to spare a thought for home."

She let his words sink in before she spoke. "Then where are they? They were headed to the Campbells'. Why didn't they make it?"

Staring into the distance, he blew out his breath. "If we had those answers, we'd be home in our beds tonight."

His words brought another involuntary shudder.

Diego shot her an anxious look. "That's the second time you've done that. Are you feeling all right? You can't be cold."

"I'm the furthest thing from cold." She gave him a tight smile. "To be honest, I haven't looked forward to nightfall." Her smile turned sheepish. "It's a lot easier to be brave in the light."

Amusement flashed in his eyes. To his credit, he squelched it. "Don't fear the darkness, Emmy. My mother taught me to see the lessons God intended when He created night and day."

Emmy raised her brows. "Lessons?"

He nodded. "Nighttime represents the fall of man and how God mourned when sin separated Him from His children. Daytime points to His forgiveness and our restoration."

She stared, amazed by the simple truth. "I've never heard that before."

He smiled. "There's more. The Choctaw believe that man can read the salvation story in the earth's four seasons."

Mesmerized, she studied his face. "The seasons?"

He held up one finger, citing Melatha. "Summer represents the time when Jesus walked the earth with man. Fall signals the death of summer and the death of Christ. Leaves begin to die and hang from their branches, drenched in gold and crimson. Fall represents the beauty of a blood-drenched King on a cross."

The breath caught in her throat. "Diego, that's incredible."

"Winter is the tomb," he said, his eyes closed. "A time when hope seems lost. Sap stops flowing. Plants and leaves decay. Animals stumble into hibernation as dens become graves. Creation is in mourning and mimics His death." He opened his eyes. "Spring is a portrait of hope. Green buds, rainbow flowers, daisy yellow chicks, and lily white lambs tumble off God's palette in a celebration of new life. The least subtle season, spring flaunts our risen Savior and begs us to see." He smiled. "And there you have it."

"That was the most beautiful thing that I've ever heard," she breathed.

"It's a fair translation. Better in the original Choctaw." He shrugged. "I've heard it so many times, it loses its charm. . .until I see it again through the eyes of someone else." He smiled sweetly and nodded at her. "Like now. You're glowing."

It felt good to laugh. "A reflection of my heart, Diego. Thank you for sharing that with me. It brought me great comfort and took my mind off things for a while."

He grinned. "My pleasure."

Cuddy had slipped up beside Emmy. "What are we sharing, and where's my part?" he demanded with his usual charm.

Leaning past Emmy to see him, Diego snorted. "Nothing I haven't offered you a dozen times before."

"He was reciting his mother's lessons for me," Emmy said. "About the seasons."

Cuddy rolled his eyes. "Oh, yes. Winter is death and all of that drivel. Aren't you two depressed enough?"

Diego shared a glance with Emmy. "We were feeling better until you came along."

Cuddy flashed a grin. "Nonsense. I bring light and joy wherever I go."

Diego groaned and waved his hat at an approaching rider. The man trotted the rest of the way and pulled up alongside them. "We'd better decide where we want to rest and water the horses. About another hour is all I'd want to push them."

Diego glanced at Emmy. By the skeptical look on his face, he was thinking an hour was all she could take, too. He turned to the man. "We're almost to Buck Campbell's place. Spread the word that we'll pull in there."

EMMY'S EQUAL

Exhausted, Magda dozed, waking up each time her head lolled to the side. She awoke for good to find the surrounding brush alive with the sounds of approaching nightfall. Filled with dread, she willed with all her might for John to ride out of the shadows on Faron, a doctor close on his heels.

Straining to see Willem's features in the last faint traces of light, she scooted around to lay her head on his chest. His torso rose and fell too fast and his heart beat in time with the crickets. She'd been trickling water into his mouth in small amounts so he wouldn't choke, and she thought he might have swallowed some.

Lifting her head, she peered into the crowding darkness. Benito and Juan lurked nearby speaking Spanish in hushed voices. Her eyes on them seemed to make up their minds, and they sprang into action, scurrying to set up camp for the night. Carl hopped from one to the other, trying to keep up with the orders they barked.

Beside her, Bertha swatted a swarm of mosquitoes from her face. "We need to pull our beds closer to the fire tonight. Might help to keep these infernal pests away."

Frustration threatened to smother Magda. "Stop it, all of you!"

Bertha stilled. The men paused mid-stride and gaped at her.

"Stop making camp. We won't be spending the night here." Tears stung her eyes. "John Rawson will ride up any minute with that doctor. Then we'll be taking my husband home."

Benito bowed. "Sí, Señora Dane." Shoving his hands in his pockets, he shrugged at Juan and sat down in front of the fire.

Bertha nodded at the men. "We'll wait just a while longer, if you fellers don't mind." Patting Magda's leg to soften her determined words, she added, "If he's not here soon, we'll have no choice but to go to bed. I suspect there's a long day ahead for all of us."

CHAPTER 31

Diego rode toward the Campbell ranch glowing with pride, thinking about the eternal lessons he had just shared with Emmy. For the first time he understood that his mother's people were his Christian ancestors, those men and women whose decisions to follow Jesus Christ were the reason Diego knew Him. The proud swell in his chest turned to shame as he realized they were the same ancestors he had fought so hard to deny.

The lights of the Campbells' two-story, plastered-stone house beckoned in the distance. Standing against the dusky sky, it was a welcome sight. Diego was happy to see the end of the driveway, but no happier than his backside and the horse he sat. In some ways, Mr. Boteo's Spanish mare had it better than Diego. She'd only made the trek to Catarina once that day.

Buck Campbell stepped onto the porch as they arrived. Squinting and twiddling his bushy moustache, he surveyed the large group of men as if trying to put a name to every face. His gaze came to rest on Diego. "Any luck?"

Diego dismounted, glad to be on the ground. "No, sir. Not yet."

The man ducked to scan the riders again. "My boys with you?"

"No, sir. They're with a party of searchers somewhere north of here. We've come in hopes of taking advantage of your hospitality for a bit. I've got some tired men and thirsty horses."

Mr. Campbell nodded. "Fine, fine. You get those animals tended then come to the house. The missus will be waiting with coffee and something hot to eat."

He turned to go, but Diego held up his hand. "That coffee sounds good, but there's no need to put Mrs. Campbell to any trouble. Most of the men have trail rations."

He gave a curt wave. "Nonsense. A man can't beat the brush all night on trail rations."

"Sir, I've got better than twenty men out here."

He chuckled. "That's when a slew of daughters comes in handy. Won't take them girls no time to fix your men something." He pointed a warning finger. "So come back up to the house. You hear?"

Diego grinned. "Will do."

He started to go inside again, but Diego cleared his throat. "Mr. Campbell?"

"Yes?"

Diego walked to Emmy's horse and helped her down. "Would it be too much trouble if Miss Dane here freshens up inside?"

Under less trying circumstances, Mr. Campbell's bug-eyed stare would be amusing. "That is a female! I was thinking she was the prettiest fellow I ever did see." He laughed wildly. "Sure, she'll clean up inside." He offered his arm to Emmy. "I won't have no little gal splashing off in a watering trough."

Feeling more protective than he had the right, Diego handed her off to Buck Campbell. His restless men meandering behind him, Diego stayed rooted to the spot until Emmy disappeared through the door.

Cuddy sailed his hat over his horse, hitting Diego in the chest and almost startling him out of his chaps. "Peel your eyes off Emily and help me get these horses watered."

He frowned at Cuddy. "Sí, amigo. I'm coming." He took the reins of the big mare and started for the barn, deliberately tromping on Cuddy's hat as he went.

By the time the last horse had cooled then drunk its fill, Mr. Campbell's womenfolk had a table pulled out to the veranda and covered with food. Exhausted, dusty men settled wherever they could, whether the steps, the edge of the porch, or the ground. They ate quietly. Most, like Diego and probably Cuddy, were disturbed by the fact they'd found nothing.

The back door opened and Emmy stepped out, her eyes wide and searching. Spotting Diego and Cuddy, she lit up then pressed past the table to join them on the porch, limping and wincing with every step. Diego sat up straighter. "What happened to your feet?"

She eased herself carefully to the porch and swung her legs to the ground. "Greta's boots are too big for me. They've rubbed blisters."

Without waiting for permission, he pulled her foot across his knees. "That won't do, Emmy. You'll wind up with an infection." He pulled on the heel and the boot slid right off. "No wonder. Knitted stockings. Look how thin they are." He craned his neck behind him until he caught Mrs. Campbell's attention. "Could we trouble you for a pair of thick woven socks?" He glanced at the size of her foot. "Make that two pair."

Emmy struggled to pull her leg down. "Diego, please."

"No arguments. This will make all the difference."

She sat quietly while he carefully peeled the silky material away from the balls of her feet. He flinched at the angry red skin, but only the side of her big toe had a small watery bump. "It's not as bad as it could be. We caught it in time."

Mrs. Campbell dangled the socks across his shoulder, one pair red, the other a faded blue. "These do?"

"Oh, yes, ma'am. And I'll make sure these are returned," Diego said, gently slipping them on Emmy's feet.

"Washed," Emmy added, but Mrs. Campbell had already rushed inside for more clean plates.

After Diego felt satisfied with the fit of her boots, he brought her a plate piled high with bacon, eggs, and flapjacks, evidently the fastest meal the ladies could prepare with such short notice.

Emmy dug in like she'd not seen food in days.

Cuddy leaned against the corner post with his arms crossed, silently watching. If Diego happened to glance at him, he'd wiggle his brows or widen his eyes.

Diego was ready to thrash him when one of the younger Campbell girls approached Emmy and shyly held out her hand. "Some ladies from the church have organized a prayer circle for your folks in the parlor. Mama said you might care to join them."

Tears sprang to Emmy's eyes. She took the small hand in hers, and with a backward sniff at Diego, disappeared inside the house.

He spun on Cuddy. "What's all the foolishness with those faces? If you have something to say, come out and say it."

Cuddy held up both hands. "Don't mind me. I'm just doing a little speculating, that's all."

"About?"

"Just noticing you being extra accommodating to Miss Emily. Makes me think you might step between her and a goat sucker after all."

Diego blew out a breath in disgust. "Aren't you ever serious about anything, Cuddy?" He pointed past the outbuildings. "That's your father somewhere out there. Don't you care?"

Cuddy leaped up and stood over him ashen-faced, his hands balled into fists. "You know I care! And don't you act like you care more." His eyes rimmed with red and a haze of tears blurred his eyes.

Ashamed, Diego gripped his clenched fist. "I'm sorry, Cuddy. I had no right."

Resembling one of Mother's young students, Cuddy snuffled and wiped his nose on his sleeve. "Just because I don't wear my feelings in plain sight don't mean they ain't there."

"I know, amigo." He stood and gave Cuddy a hearty pat on the back. "I hope you'll forgive me. It's been a long day."

Mr. Campbell left his station on the porch where he'd been sitting all evening and took a seat on the top step. "So Mr. Rawson was on his way here, you say? Several days ago?"

Diego spit out the stalk of grass he'd been chewing and nodded. "Yes, sir. I told him you had some cattle for sale."

He stuck out his bottom lip and angled his head at Cuddy. "You Rawsons looking to expand your stock?"

The poised son of a South Texas rancher again, Cuddy lifted his chin. "Nah, we're happy with what we have."

"Mr. Rawson's inquiries would've been on behalf of a guest to the Twisted-R," Diego provided. "A wealthy woman from Humble, a little town north of Houston."

Mr. Campbell nodded. "I've been through Humble once." He rubbed his chin. "What do you make of them never arriving, Diego? Beats all I ever did see."

"That it does, sir. But we'll find them. You can bet on it."

"I know you will, son." He glanced toward the barn. "Tell your men to mind their tackle. We have a problem with blue rats around here. They'll gnaw your stuff to bits by morning if they find it on the ground."

Diego nodded. "Yes, sir. I'll tell them."

They talked a bit longer, and Diego tried to answer his questions the best he could, but the horses were rested and the men were getting too settled.

A clutch of solemn-faced women filed out the back door, and Diego stood to face the scattered men on the porch. "Like it or not, gents, the time has come. Let's wind things up here and get back on the trail."

His gaze darted over to the ladies. Mrs. Campbell noticed and hooked her thumb toward the house. "The poor dear is stretched across the bed in the guestroom fast asleep. Still crying, she was. I spread a blanket over her."

Diego nodded and made a quick decision. "You mind if I leave her where she is for now?"

Hands clasped in front of her apron, Mrs. Campbell solemnly nodded. "I think it would be a shame to wake her."

Cuddy sighed. "I don't know, Diego. Emily wants to look for her folks, and I don't blame her."

Diego placed a hand on his shoulder. "I don't either, but she'll sleep until we get back. If we have her parents with us, she'll be happy. If we don't, she can spit and spew while she helps us search some more, but at least she'll be rested."

Cuddy nodded. "You have a point." He grinned. "I mean besides the one on your head."

Diego slapped him on the back, probably too hard. "Come on, then. Let's go find your father."

❧

Magda was ten years old again, running along the windswept bank of Big Cypress Bayou. Her matted curls streamed behind her head as she dodged crawdad mounds and cypress knees.

Bertha gave chase, her head tossed back and her mouth wide with laughter. As they ran, the mists rising from the bayou darkened, enclosing them in thick, black froth.

Two figures appeared—Thad, Bertha's long-departed husband, and Willem, smiling sweetly. A brilliant beam swirled from them in a rush, penetrating the haze and stabbing Magda's eyes. She frantically tossed her head to get free of the piercing light.

Bertha shook her shoulder. "Wake up, sugar. With all that thrashing about, you must be having a dream."

Magda sat up in the wagon and squinted against the sun's rays. "Gracious! What time is it?"

"I don't know. Well past dawn, that's for sure. We must've slept like the dead."

Magda's gaze shot to Willem and her heart plunged. "Oh, Bertha. I think Willem might be."

"Might be what?"

"Dead."

Bertha's head swung around. "Why do you say a thing like that?"

"Because I saw him in my dream, standing beside Thad in a mist."

Bertha moved faster than Magda thought possible and pressed her ear to Willem's chest. After a moment, she raised her head. "Nope. Still ticking."

Running her trembling hand over his hair, a lump formed in Magda's throat. "He's still out, though. I don't think he could sleep this long and be all right. Do you?" She wrung her hands. "Where in the devil could John be with that doctor?"

Bertha lifted one hand. "Hush a minute." Looking scared, she pushed to her knees, listening carefully. "Magda, why's it so quiet?" Standing, she spun in a circle. "Where on earth are the men?"

Magda held one hand over her heart. "What do you mean where are they? Stop that. You're scaring me."

Bertha shaded her eyes and stared toward the cattle, grazing much farther away than they'd been the day before. "I'm afraid it may be time to get scared." Her face as pale as Willem's, she blinked down at Magda. "There's not a soul here but us, sugar. We're all alone."

CHAPTER 32

M iss Emily?"

Emmy whirled toward the sound, nearly falling off the bed in her haste. Fully dressed and tangled in covers from the waist down, she lay in a strange bed in a strange room staring at a lovely young woman she'd never met.

Her heartbeat swelled in her chest until it frightened her. "Where am I?"

A little brown-haired girl with big eyes peeked from behind the young woman's skirt. "We're the Campbells, ma'am. Don't you remember?"

The picture of a small hand tucked in hers flashed through Emmy's mind. The prayer circle. The search party. Mama and Papa.

Struggling against the covers, she swung her legs to the floor. Her stormy gaze flashed to the square of light around the window shade. "They left me?"

"You were sleeping," the little one announced.

"Hush, Racheal. Let her get her bearings." The older girl approached cautiously. "I'm Margaret. The oldest. Please, call me Megan. I hope you slept well"—her sweeping hand took in Emmy's boots and clothes—"despite all that."

Staring dully, Emmy brushed unruly strands of hair from her eyes, but static from the blue blanket teased them into the air in wriggling strands. "I can't believe Diego left me." She lifted her eyes.

"Did he say anything?"

Megan pointed at the bed. "May I sit?"

Emmy nodded and slid to the side.

"Diego felt there was no reason to wake you. He said if you were that exhausted you needed to rest."

Little Racheal jumped when Emmy slapped the side of the bed. "He had no right. It should've been my decision to make."

The door creaked open and four more sets of curious eyes peered from the hall. Megan stamped her foot. "Stop all that sneaking about and say good morning to Emily."

The girls filed in like obedient stair-steps, each a bit taller than the next. With their hands behind their backs, they curtsied one at a time in the order of their height. In other circumstances, Emmy would've been charmed.

The tallest came forward. "Morning, ma'am. I'm Samantha. They call me Sami."

"And I'm Lauren," the next one said. "Named after my uncle Laurence. I fetched you for the prayer circle. Remember?"

They were all blond, but the girl standing next to last had hair as white as Emmy's. "My name is Emily." Her cherry red mouth parted in a self-conscious smile. "Same as you." She picked up the last tyke in line, a curly-topped angel. "This here's Layla. She's four."

A bedraggled Mrs. Campbell appeared in the doorway, one hand holding a stack of folded clothes, the other over her heart. "Heavens! I see you've all disobeyed me. I asked you not to make pests of yourselves." She smiled gently at Emmy. "You must be hungry. You've slept right though breakfast, but I've kept a plate warming for you."

Emmy fought through her bitter disappointment to find her manners. "Thank you, ma'am. I suppose I am."

"I've got clean clothes here for you. Megan's about your size." She laughed. "Wouldn't have been last summer, but she hit a growing spurt." She pointed at Emmy's feet. "And two pair of fresh socks."

"Oh, I couldn't impose."

"It's no trouble at all. We're glad to help."

Waving her apron like a matador, Mrs. Campbell swept her brood of girls from the room. "All right now, let's go and leave our guest some privacy." She turned at the entrance. "I'm sorry they descended upon you before you'd barely opened your eyes. They meant no harm, just curious."

Emmy nodded. "Of course."

"Take your time, dear," she said before easing the door shut.

Alone with her thoughts, Emmy mulled over how Diego could possibly have betrayed her trust. After the way he'd so tenderly ministered to her the night before, she thought he'd accepted her need to be part of the search.

She struggled to free herself from the pesky cover that wound around her lower body. Jerking the last persistent corner from under her bottom, she dashed it to the floor.

A pan of warm water and a clean towel awaited her on the dressing table, so she freshened up the best she could without a way to clean her teeth or brush her knotted hair. Rinsing the former and combing her fingers through the latter, she made a note to herself to pack her toiletries the next time she dashed off on a search party.

Her eyes flickered away from her image in the mirror. The flippant thought shamed her. Too much was at stake to find humor in any part of the situation.

She changed clothes then washed her tender feet before pulling on the socks and dreaded boots. With a heavy heart, she headed down to the Campbells' kitchen, but not before folding the blue blanket and placing it on the end of the bed.

It wasn't hard to find her way. The chatter of little girls led her into an open, cheery room lined with bright yellow shelves. Mrs. Campbell hovered over a pan of dishes—washing while Megan, the oldest, dried. Fair-haired Emily, who shared Emmy's name, plied a broom on the kitchen floor. Lauren on the left and Sami on the right, if she remembered them correctly, bent over lessons at the table. Racheal and Layla sat on the floor scribbling pictures on a sheet of paper.

Emmy cleared her throat. "Good morning."

All eyes in the room swung her way. Little Racheal's forehead creased. "We already said that."

"Hush!" her mother said, pulling out an empty chair for Emmy. "I know these eggs have turned to rubber. I'll fix you fresh if you'd like."

Emmy waved her hand. "No, ma'am. These are fine."

Seven pairs of eyes followed the track of her fork to her mouth. Her cheeks warming, she pressed her napkin to her lips and swallowed.

Mrs. Campbell drew in a sharp breath, breaking the trance. "All right, ladies. Back to your own business. Let Miss Emily eat in peace."

They quickly obeyed, Megan to her dishcloth, Emily to her broom, Layla to her drawing, and the middle two returned to their studies. Only pot-bellied Racheal stood clinging to the side of the table, staring at Emmy with wide brown eyes.

Emmy tore off a bite of bacon and tucked it into the child's mouth. She blinked, her long lashes sweeping close to her cheeks, and then she beamed like a ray of sunshine and opened for more. Together, they had the plate nearly clean when Emmy heard the unmistakable sound of approaching riders.

She stood so fast she had to reach and steady Racheal before running to the window. Her heart crowding her throat, she whirled. "It's them. It's Diego."

The girls scrambled to their feet, all talking at once. Mrs. Campbell spun from the counter. "Do they have your parents?"

Anticipation coursed through Emmy's body, and her hand clutched her throat. "Oh, Mrs. Campbell. I don't know." Weaving past the inquisitive little girls, she burst out onto the porch, hope so strong in her heart she felt faint.

Followed by Cuddy and the Campbell brothers, Diego rode into the yard and came to a stop near the porch. One look at his drawn, dejected face as he dismounted gave Emmy her answer before she asked. Her parents were still lost.

❧

Diego lowered his eyes. He couldn't bear Emmy's air of lost hope. For the last ten miles of grueling, spirit-busting trail, he'd prayed to stumble onto Mr. Rawson and her parents so he could return rejoicing instead of bearing bad news. One look at her told him he'd be spared speaking the words aloud.

Head down, she ran to him. He opened his arms, ready to comfort her, but she rammed him instead, her fists pounding his chest. "Why did you leave me? I could've done something."

Diego pressed her closer. "No, honey. You couldn't succeed where eighty men failed."

She pushed away from him. "Where is everyone? Where are the rest?"

He tensed and swallowed hard. "I sent them home."

She gaped at him. "How could you do that? We haven't found them yet."

Catching hold of her wrists, he lowered her to the porch and sat beside her. "They were spent, Emmy. We've covered miles of the roughest country in South Texas. I had to send them home before I lost most of them."

He put his arm around her shoulders. "But I won't give up, I promise." He lifted his chin at Cuddy. "Neither will Cuddy. We plan to sleep for a couple of hours then head back out."

"I'm going with you."

He pulled her close and smoothed her hair. "We'll talk about it."

Mrs. Campbell stood on the threshold holding back the screen door. Lester crossed the yard and glanced up at her. "Where's Pa?"

"He's been at it all morning, covering for you boys." She waved her dishcloth. "Don't worry about that now. Tend all these horses, then eat something and go to bed. You can take over his chores this afternoon."

Diego took off his hat and peered up at Mrs. Campbell. "We're grateful for their help. I hope it hasn't caused too much trouble."

She smiled down at him. "What are neighbors for? We're glad to—" Her gazed jumped from Diego to something behind him. "Look." She pointed. "There comes a rider."

Cuddy jumped on the porch and shaded his eyes. "Coming fast, too."

Diego joined him. "Can you see who it is?"

"No, but I know that horse. It's Little Pete."

Emmy flew to her feet. "Little Pete? You don't suppose he has good news?"

Diego glanced at her. The tone of her voice was hopeful, but her unease and the way she asked the question said she was afraid to get her hopes up too high. Diego tried not to add fuel to the fire. "Relax, honey. It could be about anything. Something's always going wrong on a ranch."

Cuddy leaped down. "Whatever it is, we're about to find out."

The three of them hurried to meet Little Pete as he drove the frothing horse into the yard. Cuddy reached him first. "What's wrong, Pete? Has something happened?"

Looking past Cuddy, his eyes full moons, Little Pete sought Diego's face. "Señor! He's come home!"

Joy surged in Diego's chest. "Mr. Rawson? He's home?"

Emmy squeezed between them and clutched the front of Pete's shirt. "And my parents, too?"

Shock registered on Little Pete's face. "No, no, Señorita Dane." He pushed her aside and stalked to Diego. "Not Mr. Rawson, señor!" His hysterical voice was shrill. "Faron! Faron's come home without a rider."

White-faced, Cuddy jerked his gaze to Diego.

Emmy spun, desperately clinging to Diego's shirt before she crumpled. Grief-stricken, Diego picked her up and carried her limp body to the house.

CHAPTER 33

Terrified, Magda clung to Willem's lifeless hand. Her eyes darting at every sound, she prayed for John to ride up on Faron telling her everything would be fine. She prayed for Benito, Juan, even Carl to saunter out of the brush. Tightening into a ball in the rear of the wagon, she prayed for God at least to bring Bertha back from where she'd gone.

More than half an hour had passed since she'd announced she was going to scout out their situation. No matter how hard Magda begged, the spunky little woman had wriggled to the end of the wagon bed and dropped off the end. "Stay here," she'd ordered, as if Magda had anywhere to go. "I've got to try and sort this out."

Magda tried to busy herself with caring for Willem, wiping his face and trickling more water into his mouth, but she grew more frightened with each passing second. Shuddering, she imagined the dried-up shells of men scattered somewhere nearby, drained of every drop of blood by a sharp-fanged beast.

If Bertha had fallen into the clutches of whatever was picking them off, she and Willem were next. Glancing around, she scoured the wagon for a weapon, but all she had at her disposal were Bertha's crates from the mercantile.

She broke into the two nearest boxes and groaned. No matter how imaginative Magda was, she couldn't devise a way of using child-sized bloomers or hardtack to fend off a carnivorous animal thirsty for her life's blood.

The third box held more promise. She took a quick count of the contents, wondering how long she could hold off a bloodsucker with twenty cans of beans.

"This ain't no time for filling your gut."

Nearly swallowing her tongue, Magda drew back and threw.

Bertha ducked and the can sailed over her head, bouncing off the trunk of an oak tree with a dull thud. She peeked over the wagon bed with astonished eyes. "Did you just throw a can of beans at me?"

Limp, Magda fell against the backboard. "I reckon I did."

"What possessed you?"

"Something with fangs, I think."

Bertha stood up straight. "What?"

"Never mind. What did you find out?"

"I found out we're alone, all right. There's no trace of those men." She pointed. "Except for their things. Juan even left his cooking pots behind." She shook her head. "Why would they go with only the clothes on their backs and leave two women to fend for themselves?"

Magda heaved a sigh. "For themselves and a whole herd of cattle."

Bertha pursed her lips. "Well, that's another thing. There ain't near the cattle there was last night. The herd's smaller by half."

Magda rose to her knees and crawled to where Bertha stood, wincing at the stiffness that had set in from sitting so long beside Willem. "Would you like to tell me how six grown men and half a herd could simply vanish?" She shook her head. "It don't happen, Bertha. What's going on here?"

"Six?" Bertha counted on her fingers. "How do you cipher six men?"

"First, that no 'count Wayne—"

"Wayne ran off."

"Then John and the doctor—"

"It's wishful thinking to assume there's a doctor. I don't think John made it that far."

"Now Benito, Juan, and Carl. That makes six." Tears sprang to Magda's eyes. "Whether five or six, half the herd or one, they're gone. Missing under very peculiar circumstances." She lowered her voice to a whisper. "And we're next."

Bertha furrowed her brow. "Don't start making something spooky out of this. There's got to be a simple explanation."

Magda slid her legs off the wagon to dangle them from the side.

"I wish you'd explain it then, because I'm downright scared." She glanced over her shoulder. "Not so much for myself. It's Willem. He's lying there so helpless."

She wiped her eyes with the palms of her hands. "That man has taken care of me for twenty-two years. When he needs me the most, I'm not sure I can return the favor."

"Why couldn't you?"

Magda flapped her hands in frustration. "I don't even know what we're up against."

Crossing her arms, Bertha stared in concentration. "First off, them cows ain't missing under peculiar circumstances."

Magda squinted at her. "So you believe some ran away and the others stayed?"

Bertha snorted. "I think they was escorted away. Those men stole them."

"Why half the herd?"

Bertha raised her chin. "The best half, them with no horns."

Magda placed her hands on her hips. "I'll never believe Benito and that nice Juan are capable of such a thing. Don't you remember how kind their eyes were and how they looked after us on the trail?"

Bertha scratched her head. "I'll agree they didn't seem to have any potential for mischief. And poor simple Carl couldn't pull this off without written instructions." Her eyes narrowed. "But that brother of his sure could."

Magda lifted her finger. "True, but he'd have to convince Benito and Juan to go along. He wasn't around long enough. And don't forget John. What happened to him?" She looked at Willem again. "John would never leave his friend in this condition."

Walking thoughtfully to the thrown can, Bertha picked it up and examined it through squinted eyes. "We're spinning in the wind with all this jaw flapping. We're only sure of one thing at this point—we have to find help for Willem." She tossed the can at Magda. "Climb down out of there and fix us something to eat. I'll be hitching up the horses."

Magda scrambled to the ground, hope surging in her chest. "You really think we can find help, Bertha?"

"I reckon we'd better."

"But where do we go? For that matter, where are we now?"

Bertha wadded her fists on her hips and stared in the direction they'd come. "John's had us following the river since Eagle Pass. I'd say we've come better than twenty miles." She looked over her shoulder. "Which means we're halfway to Carrizo Springs." She made a quarter turn and pointed. "All we have to do is head due east. We're bound to hit that Indian trail eventually. From there we know the way home."

Excitement and fear built twin fires in Magda's gut. "But that's a long, hard ride. What if Willem can't make it, Bertha? And what if we get lost?"

Bertha swiveled at the waist to glare at her. "What if we sit right here and wait for the three of us to die?"

Magda swallowed. "Wouldn't it be smarter to find this El Indio place John told us about? He said it was only a few miles back."

"Good idea, sugar." Bertha held her arm out, swiveling it as she spoke. "Is it that way, close to the river? Maybe more northeast? What about right down the middle?" She shook her head. "Unless John drew you a map you haven't told me about, I say we stick to what we know." She ducked her head at Willem. "We know there's a doctor in Carrizo Springs."

Magda glanced at the remaining cattle on the distant plain. "What about the herd?"

"We leave them here. We're not drovers, and there's enough to worry about with Willem. John can round them up later." She waved at the supplies. "Forget cooking. Just rustle up something we can eat on the way."

Magda's ears buzzed as if a cricket sing-along swelled inside her head. "I don't know, Bertha. I'm still not sure."

Bertha tromped to where she stood. "Merciful heavens! All this hand wringing and second-guessing ain't your style. What's got into you?" Her stormy gaze flew to Willem again. "We need to make a decision and get on the road. We're wasting precious time."

Sobs welled inside of Magda. She released them in a piteous moan. "I'm sorry, Bertha. And grateful. I've always been the strong one, but with Willem so bad off, I've wilted like hot greens."

Bertha hugged her around the middle. "What's really bothering you, sugar?"

The tears flowed harder. She wiped them from her cheeks before they dripped on Bertha's head. "I'm afraid to find a doctor. I don't think I'll like what he has to say."

Bertha leaned back and gave her a shake. "You're stronger than that, honey. And if not, I'll be with you."

Magda wiped her eyes. "You've been there for me already. I can never repay you."

"No need. You were there for me when I lost Thad." She released Magda, her jaw set. "Only we ain't losing Willem. I say we head toward Carrizo Springs as fast as we can."

Tilting her head, Magda gazed at her from narrowed eyes. "You're having one of your feelings, aren't you?"

Bertha nodded firmly. "Yep, a strong feeling, and one we'd best heed."

Smiling, Magda mimicked her nod. "Go hitch the horses, then. I'll get us ready to go."

❧

Emmy bolted upright on the Campbells' settee. Before her spinning head convinced her to squeeze her eyes shut again, she caught a glimpse of Diego's drawn face. Unless she was mistaken, Mrs. Campbell and her frightened girls flanked him. She shook her head to clear it and carefully opened her eyes.

Diego pressed closer. "Are you all right?"

She scooted to the edge of the cushion, forcing him to make room for her knees. "Tell me what it means, Diego," she pleaded, resting her forehead on her palms. "If Faron returned without Mr. Rawson, they're not coming home, are they?"

He grabbed her wrists and pulled her hands away. "It means no such thing."

Her head jerked up. "Then explain it."

His bluster wilted. "I can't, not yet. I'll know a lot more when I see Faron."

"What will that tell you?" she asked.

"If he's been wet or he's muddy, if he's scratched up from briars, then I'll have a better idea of where he's been." He averted his eyes. "The condition of the saddle or stirrups might tell me if he's been dragging a rider."

He latched onto her arms. "One thing I do know. We've been going about the search all wrong."

She sat up straighter. "What do you mean?"

"Remember what you asked me? If they were headed to the Campbells', why didn't they make it?"

She nodded.

"It's because they were no longer headed to the Campbells'. Little Pete said Faron came home along the road to Eagle Pass."

She blinked. "That's far away, isn't it?"

"About forty miles." His mouth tightened. "Forty miles in the opposite direction."

Her head reeled again. "They wouldn't go all the way to Eagle Pass without telling anyone. Would they?"

Joe Campbell stepped out of the kitchen with a plate of food in his hand. "Did somebody say Eagle Pass?"

Diego nodded.

The color drained from the boy's face. He sat on the arm of an easy chair and slid his plate onto the low table in front of him. Staring at the floor, he shook his head. "Naw, it couldn't be."

Concern lining her brow, Mrs. Campbell stepped closer. "What is it, son?"

He gazed up at her, his face a blank slate. "I think I saw Mr. Rawson on the road. In fact, I sent him and his friends to Eagle Pass."

"What?"

With so many voices shouting the word, Joe couldn't make up his mind who to answer. He settled on his mother. "I met some folks on their way here to buy stock. I told them we sold all we had then suggested a breeder in Eagle Pass."

"Joseph Campbell! Why didn't you speak up sooner?"

He cut frightened eyes to Diego. "The man never said he was Mr. Rawson, that's why. I told him I was headed for the Twisted-R Ranch, and he never said a word. If he was the owner, wouldn't he have said something?"

Laughing, Cuddy spoke up from the corner where he lounged against the wall. "I told you there wasn't anything wrong. They're living it up in Eagle Pass without a care in the world, just like I thought."

Emmy swung toward him. "Then what about Faron?"

He waved off her concern. "Faron got away from the old man and came home. Though my father would never admit it, that horse is too much for him."

Little Pete cleared his throat. "Um. . .Diego?"

251

Diego swiveled to see him better. "What is it, Pete?"

Pete tugged on his collar and swallowed. "Speaking of Faron, I forgot to tell you one thing."

Diego stood, his back rigid. "Go ahead."

"Señora Rawson? She's ordered him shot."

"And you're telling me now?"

"*Siento mucho*, señor. When the lady fainted, I—"

Diego whirled to Emmy. "Can you ride?"

She leaped to her feet. "Yes!"

He waved over his shoulder and ran for the door. "Let's go!"

Emmy rushed to follow the men outside, calling her thanks to Mrs. Campbell as she went.

Megan waved from the porch, but the five younger girls chased them from the yard, squealing and shouting their good-byes.

Emmy's gaze followed Diego riding just ahead. Concern for him stirred an ache inside worse than sore muscles or tender feet. His rich complexion appeared ashy with fatigue, and dark smudges around his eyes deepened the sockets. It amazed her how the news about Faron brought a surge of new life. His distress was more than the normal reaction for the welfare of a helpless animal. Diego had to love the big horse very much.

Dodging flying debris from the thundering hooves up ahead, Emmy prayed Faron wouldn't wind up the first tragic casualty in a string of potential losses.

❧

Cringing, Melatha tossed the pan of bread in the sink with a rattle and clang then closed the oven door and ran.

Kate Rawson had awakened. Her shrill voice on the back porch left no doubt of the fact. Still in her dressing gown and slippers, the hair on her head shot in every direction, not unlike a disgruntled badger.

Melatha eased closer, but not too close.

The woman brandished a long-barreled pistol in her hand. "I want it done, and done now!" she shrieked. "No more delays."

Poor Felipe squirmed, twisting his hat in his hands. "I have not the authority, señora." He looked over his shoulder, desperation widening his eyes. "I only cover for Pete. He will return soon."

She raised the gun, waving it for emphasis, sending Felipe ducking and spinning out of range. "What do you mean you have no authority? *I* am your authority, and I'm ordering you to shoot that horse." She stamped her foot. "This instant."

"But, señora. . ."

Slipping a few steps nearer, Melatha began to speak to her in a soothing voice. "Mrs. Rawson? Kate?"

She whirled. "Melatha, it won't work this time. You convinced me to lie down for a bit so I wouldn't be acting in haste. Well, I've done as you asked, and I'm more determined than ever. That demon should've been put down hours ago," she pressed her free hand to her trembling mouth, and her voice rose to a shrill wail, "when he trotted into this yard looking for feed after killing my John!"

Melatha reached around Kate's waist while gently lowering the arm holding the gun, all the while cooing comfort in her ear. Kate's shoulders went limp, and Melatha guided her toward the house.

At the door, the distraught woman lifted startled eyes and spun away. "I'm sorry," she whispered. "I can't allow him to live."

She bolted down the steps with the pistol, passing a cowering Felipe and sailing across the yard with the hem of her robe flapping behind her.

Melatha screamed for Felipe to get help then lit out after her. "Kate, please! Don't do this thing."

Not even glancing behind her, Kate disappeared inside the barn. Bounding toward the wide doorway, Melatha prayed for wings on her feet. She dashed inside and froze, holding her breath.

Kate stood before Faron's stall with the gun trained on him.

Dark as pitch in the shadowy barn, Faron held his nose high, the agitated toss of his head flashing pinpoints of light from his black mane. His ears were pinned back and his wide stare revealed the glowing whites of his eyes. In that moment, Faron looked the part of a devil.

Melatha inched forward. "Kate, don't. This act will haunt you all your days."

Kate cocked the hammer.

Faron reared.

Melatha covered her eyes and opened her mouth to scream.

Something tore past her in a *whoosh*. Startled, she opened her eyes.

Isi, his outstretched arms reaching for Kate Rawson, dove. A blast from the pistol rocked the barn.

CHAPTER 34

The wagon bumped along the uneven ground, tossing Willem's body like corkwood. Magda held his head, trying with little success to hold it steady. She bobbed to see Bertha between the slats of the rear seat. "This isn't going to work! We're going to kill him."

Bertha looked over her shoulder. "This is a rough patch, honey. We'll be past it soon." She turned to the front, but her voice carried to Magda. "I see a clear spot just ahead."

"Hurry and reach it then," Magda cried.

"If I hurry, you'll both be tossed out on your ears."

Fighting tears, Magda let her little finger slide to the back of Willem's head to probe around the wound for signs of infection. She felt no extra heat or excess swelling in the area and breathed a sigh of relief. She made a mental note to give him a bit of water when they stopped. If she tried it now, she'd likely drown him.

Magda studied his serene face and a smile tugged at her lips. Her husband's Scandinavian roots had sprouted a fine figure of a man in Willem Dane. Despite attempts to keep him shaded, the sun he staunchly avoided due to his pale complexion had found him in South Texas. It had reddened his cheeks to a rosy glow and masked the deathly white pallor of the day before. Dark lines beneath his eyes and a thin white ring around his blush-colored lips were the only signs of his current distress.

She leaned to kiss him gently on the mouth, and his lack of

response broke her heart.

"Magda," Bertha called. "That ain't no clearing ahead." She paused. "Honey, I think it's a road."

Rising to her knees, Magda strained to see past Bertha. "Are you sure? That would be an answer to prayer."

Bertha let out a whoop. "Get busy thanking God then, because it's a road."

"Where?"

"Just a few yards in front of us." She twisted on the seat. "But don't get your hopes up until we make sure it's going our way."

Magda held Willem's head, and despite Bertha's warning, clung to her hope until the uneven ground gave way to a smooth track for the wheels.

Bertha pulled back on the reins and set the brake.

Relieved to let go of Willem's head, Magda shook the cramps out of her arms and scooted off the end of the wagon.

They met in the middle of the dirt road that stretched for miles in both directions.

"Well?" Magda asked.

"It's headed east, all right." She peered up at the sun. "At least I think."

"You think? What kind of answer is that?"

Bertha swatted the air behind her and walked a few steps. "I ain't good at reading the sky, but, Magda, it must be."

Turning, she gazed in the other direction. "It has to be the road connecting El Indio with Carrizo Springs." She slapped her leg. "I'd bet my last dollar, which means we'll be within shouting distance of the Twisted-R before nightfall."

They stared at each other for a second while the information sank in. Bertha pulled up her skirt and danced an Irish jig on the hard-packed ground while Magda laughed and kept time with her hands.

Sobering, she caught Bertha's arm. "Stop that before you have a stroke. In this heat, it ain't safe."

Breathing hard, Bertha bent at the waist, panting. "Why didn't you say that sooner?" She looked up and grinned. "You might be too late."

Hustling to the rig, Magda reached over the side for the canteen and brought it to Bertha. "Have a sip of water before I give Willem some, and then we'd better get going."

Still clutching her side, Bertha twisted off the top then gave the canteen a little shake. "This sure feels light. Better hand me a full one."

Magda dug in the box where they kept the canteens, testing the weight of them and growing more upset with each one she lifted. "They're all light." She spun to stare at Bertha. "I think they're empty."

Bertha lowered her head and gave Magda a menacing look. "That can't be. I told you to fill them."

Magda waved her finger back and forth. "No, you didn't. You said *you* filled them."

Running to see for herself, Bertha buried her arms in the wooden box, tossing the empty containers like a crazed juggler. Turning, she gave Magda a scorching glance. "What sort of dim-witted stunt have we pulled?"

The enormity of the situation slammed Magda between the eyes. A mix-up had cost them six canteens of water. "Check the drums John brought for the horses."

Bertha shook her head and rattled the barrel. "Empty. I heard him say so. He planned to fill them before we left the river."

Magda's eyes darted to Willem. She raised her head and squinted at the blazing overhead sun. "Bertha, this is awful."

Reading the panic on her face, Bertha patted her arm. "Don't fret, now. We're bound to run across a creek or something." Glancing at the canteen still in her hand, she licked her dry lips and held it out to Magda. "Meanwhile, we save every drop for Willem."

Magda placed her hand on the life-giving gift. "But you're thirsty."

Bertha shoved it away. "For Willem."

❧

Diego raised himself to his elbows then sprang to his feet and leaned over Mrs. Rawson. "Are you all right, ma'am?" He glanced at Faron. The frantic horse paced his stall.

Mrs. Rawson huddled on the ground crying softly, ignoring him.

Cuddy knelt behind her, his hands on her shoulders. "I'll take it from here, Diego. See about Faron."

The horse's name triggered hysterical wails from the prone woman. She pushed off the ground and staggered from the barn with Cuddy and Diego's mother at her side.

Diego hurried to the stall. Faron still snorted and pawed but settled down some when Diego slipped inside and began to slide his hands over the horse's body. He explored every inch of the trembling stallion, checking his fingers often for any sign of blood.

Emmy stood at the door, gripping the top slat with white-knuckled fingers.

Little Pete stood beside her, his hands shoved deep inside his pockets. Watching Diego check Faron, Pete moaned and shifted from side to side. "It's my fault, Diego. If I'd told you sooner. . ."

Diego spared a tight smile for Pete then returned his attention to Faron. "Nonsense. It's no one's fault."

Greta, her eyes wide with fright, hurried inside the barn with Diego's mother on her heels. The women stared toward Faron.

"Is he all right?" Diego's mother asked.

Diego gazed at her in wonder. "There's not a mark on him."

"Thank God!"

He grinned. "I already have."

Greta reached for Emmy's hand. "I'm so glad, Diego."

Diego returned her warm smile. "So am I. For your mother's sake as much as Faron's." He gave Faron one last pat, signaling for Pete to take over his care, and stepped out of the stall. He walked to Greta and gave a slight bow. "I pray I didn't harm your mother."

Greta bit her bottom lip. "She's fine. Physically, at least." The wistful smile disappeared, replaced by despair. "Do you think my father's really dead?"

Emmy's arm went around her shoulders. "We refuse to think it. Cuddy says Faron got away from your father and came home, that's all. He's convinced our parents and my aunt Bertha are having a high old time in Eagle Pass."

"Do you believe him?"

Emmy gave her a gentle squeeze. "I choose to believe it for now. I suggest you do the same."

Helplessness welled in Greta's eyes. "So we're just going to sit here and wait for them to return?"

Diego shook his head. "No, Greta. In fact, I'll be heading out to search for them again as soon as I get a bath and a couple of hours' sleep." He stretched and glanced at his mother. "I wouldn't mind a bite of food."

She dipped her head and hurried for the door.

Diego smiled and nodded after her. "That means I'd better hurry. She'll expect me to arrive clean at her table, so if you'll excuse me."

Emmy latched onto his arm as he passed. "What time do we leave?"

Diego stiffened. He had dreaded the question. Facing her, determination sharpened his tone. "Not this time."

"Excuse me?"

"You're not coming this time."

Her searching gaze bored under his skin. "What are you saying? Of course I'm coming."

He tried to fill his voice with authority. "I'm taking Pete with me this time. We can make better time alone."

Emmy's fingers tightened on his arm. "Wait a minute. What about Cuddy?"

"Since Cuddy needs to stay behind and tend his mother, he'll be in charge of the ranch."

She released him, her eyes like burning coals. "Who are you to make these decisions for us? You have no right."

He drew in a breath to help calm his anger. It didn't work. "This country's too rough for you, Emmy. There's no place in South Texas for frills and piled-up hair."

She drew back and glared. "You don't waste words, do you?"

He wanted to shake her. "Don't you remember the condition you were in last night? You could hardly walk and fell asleep the first time you laid your head down."

She dropped her gaze.

"At the first hint of bad news, I had to carry you inside the house."

She flinched.

He wished he'd bitten his tongue before adding the last part, but he had to make her see.

She stood silent, offering no more resistance.

He nodded toward Little Pete. "Get some rest. We're pulling out in four hours. We'll be heading to El Indio then along the river to Eagle

Pass. They'd take that route if they were driving cattle. We'll circle back around to Carrizo from there. I think we'll know something by then." Striding from the barn, he stopped on the threshold. "And Pete. . ."

"Señor?"

"Have Faron saddled and ready."

"Sí, señor."

❧

Emmy stormed from the barn, raging fury stealing her peace, her good sense, her very breath. Seeking privacy, she circled the house and sat in the shade of the seldom-used front porch, gulping to breathe and struggling to compose herself.

Self-disappointment burned hotter than her anger toward Diego. There would be no more rash threats to borrow a horse and search for her parents alone. She was weak, a failing she couldn't deny after the last two days. Diego had merely shined a light on her limitations. But if he knew what she'd finally admitted to herself—that she couldn't find Mama and Papa without him—how could he so cruelly deny her?

The front door opened and Cuddy stepped out. "Mind a little company?"

Emmy gaped at him. "How did you know I was here?"

He hooked his thumb toward the house. "We have windows, and you were hard to miss. You shot past the parlor blowing enough steam to boil potatoes."

She grimaced. "I could still simmer a couple."

He chuckled. "What happened? If you don't mind my asking."

Emmy considered not telling him. Why make it easy for Diego? Let him gaze at Cuddy with steel in his jaw and explain how he'd made all his decisions for him.

Cuddy angled his head and peered at her. "Why am I certain this has something to do with Diego?"

Propping her elbows on her knees, she hid her face in her hands. "You're only half right." She peeked at him. "I'm just as mad at myself."

He reached for her hand. "No one should get mad at you." He grinned. "Not even you."

Swiveling toward him, she groaned. "You won't be in a joking mood when I tell you what's about to happen."

Suddenly serious, he squeezed her fingers. "Tell me."

"In four hours, Diego's headed for Eagle Pass to find our parents."

He nodded thoughtfully. "I didn't think he'd wait that long, but—"

"We're not invited."

He lifted his brows. "What?"

"Diego decided I can't handle the trail, and he thinks you're needed here."

Color flooded Cuddy's freckled cheeks. He closed his eyes, tightening his fingers around hers. "He decided that, did he?" He scowled. "That's our Diego. If you're ever short on opinions, he has one to spare."

He faced her and took her other hand. "How tired are you?"

She took a quick breath. "Me? I'm too wound up to be tired."

"How would you like to accompany me to Eagle Pass?"

"But Diego won't let—"

"You said Diego's leaving in four hours. I can be ready to go in three. How about you?"

She stared. "Really, Cuddy?"

He nodded, his eyes twinkling.

"What about the ranch?"

He waved off her concern. "Diego trained his men well. They can run the Twisted-R for a few days. Besides"—he sneered—"unlike Diego, I wouldn't care if the earth opened up and swallowed this place."

"And your mother? Shouldn't you be here with her? Diego said she needed you to take care of her."

"She has Greta." He glanced away. "Besides, the best thing I can do for her right now is find my father."

Emmy sighed, excited and afraid at the same time. "I don't know, Cuddy. Aren't you exhausted?"

He rolled his shoulders. "A little sore but not tired. I've perfected the art of sleeping in the saddle."

She laughed and gripped his hands. "Are you sure we should do this?"

He drew back and gave her a sideways look. "Oh, yes. Very sure. Are you in?"

She leaped to her feet, pulling him with her. Throwing her arms around his neck, she kissed his cheek. "Yes! Oh, Cuddy, this means so much to me."

He gave her one more squeeze then set her at arm's length. "Go get ready, then."

She gave him a jaunty salute. "Yes, sir."

"Emily?"

She turned.

"I'll meet you right here in three hours with the horses. I'll have Rosita pack our provisions, but don't forget to bring plenty of socks."

"Plenty of socks." She grinned. "Good thinking."

She threw open the door and hurried into the parlor.

Rosita, pretending to dust the low table in front of the window, shot her a frosty glare. She'd obviously seen everything—the laughter, the handholding, the kiss—and pinned her own interpretation to each detail.

So be it, let her think what she would. Emmy had grown tired of trying to sway the woman's opinion.

Lifting her chin and adding a little extra strut to her step, Emmy flounced from the room.

CHAPTER 35

Diego shot upright on his bunkhouse cot, his mind searching for the source of his heightened unease. Any rest the brief few hours of sleep afforded him slid away as the crushing burden of the last few days shifted onto his shoulders. Swinging his feet to the floor, he kneaded his face like a lump of dough, trying to rub out the need for sleep along with the memory of Emmy's disappointed eyes.

He'd made the decision not to take her while they were still in Catarina. Hopefully, one day she'd understand how hard it was for him to deny her, but he had to for her sake. Eagle Pass could be a rowdy town, and something told him the next ride held danger. Perhaps he might've used less force in delivering the message, but he'd yet to learn how to sway her determined heart.

One glance at the shade told him he'd slept too long. The jarring knowledge chasing the last bit of fog from his head, he hurriedly pulled on his boots. Where was Little Pete? He'd sent word by his mother that Pete was to awaken him at three thirty. If the shadowy corners of the bunkhouse meant anything, it was closer to five.

The door creaked open and Diego reached for his shirt, cross words of rebuke ready on his tongue.

Instead of Pete, his mother stood on the threshold. She smiled. "I was coming to wake you."

"Where's Pete?"

She ducked her head. "I never told Pete, Isi. I decided to rouse you myself."

Sliding one arm in his sleeve, he paused. "Why?"

Staring at the floor, she bit her bottom lip. "I wanted you to rest as long as possible."

Gritting his teeth, he shoved his other arm in the shirt. "Mother! This was too important for you to interfere."

She calmly approached to straighten his collar. "It's all right, son. While you slept, I had the men make every preparation for the trip. What they couldn't do, I tended to myself." She patted his shoulder. "Faron's waiting in the yard. All you have to do is get on him and ride."

Diego wilted in the warmth of her selfless love. He pulled her close for a hug. "Come here, meddling woman."

She hugged him back with a shuddering sigh. "I worry, Isi. You'll be careful?"

He patted the top of her head. "What need do I have to be careful? I know you've spent the last few hours praying for my safety."

She turned her face up and grinned. "This is true, so tread lightly. Try not to overturn a treaty between your mother and God."

He laughed. "I wouldn't dare."

Outside, his eyes lit on Rosita standing near Faron's head and the merry mood lifted. She had the fingers of one hand curled on her hip, and a cross scowl hardened her features. The other hand she used to drive home a point to Little Pete with waves and jabs to his chest.

As Diego approached, Little Pete swatted her finger away. "It's not my place," he growled in Spanish. "Tell him yourself. Diego needs to know."

"What do I need to know?"

Rosita jumped and squealed, holding her heart. "Diego! You startled me."

He placed his hand on her shoulder. "You have information for me?"

Guilty eyes told him she wasn't meant to tell. Her breathless words confirmed it. "Señor Cuddy counts on my silence. But I feel you should know." She lifted a haughty chin. "Besides, it's the fault of that girl. If not for the spell of the white-haired witch, Cuddy would never think to go against your decision."

Cold dread rushed to Diego's belly. "What decision?" Even as he asked, he knew. Cuddy would ride up behind him a few yards from the house with Emmy in tow and expect him to relent. Well, he wouldn't give in so easily this time. Cuddy could do what he blasted well pleased. Emmy would go straight back to the house.

Diego's mother slid her arm around Rosita. "Your opinion of Emily may be too harsh, Rosita. I feel responsible."

Rosita withdrew. "She's bewitched you, too?"

His mother laughed. "Not at all. Perhaps the only dark magic was my unforgiving attitude toward the girl. I should've taken the time to know Emily's heart before I judged her."

Diego smiled to himself. He'd have to congratulate Emmy on how skillfully she'd won over his mother.

Unconvinced, Rosita turned flashing eyes to Diego. "If her heart is pure, why did she offer herself to Cuddy in exchange for taking her to Eagle Pass?"

His stomach lurched and he felt turned to stone. "What are you saying?"

"It's true," she spat.

He caught Rosita's wrist and shook her.

Fear and pain registered in her eyes. "I watched her throw herself at Cuddy under the front portico, away from prying eyes. I saw everything from the window. The girl knew I caught them, but she felt no shame." She looked over her shoulder at his mother. "Melatha, I swear it happened. She pranced into the house like a jezebel, flaunting her dishonor in my face."

Struggling for a calming breath, Diego released her. "You are mistaken. I don't know what you saw, but you must have misunderstood."

Rubbing her wrist and shaking her head, Rosita stood in silent testimony of Emmy's betrayal.

With more calm than he felt inside, Diego slid his boot in the stirrup and swung onto Faron's back. Bobbing his head, the horse danced impatiently. "It doesn't matter. Whatever Emmy enticed Cuddy with, her efforts were wasted. She won't be riding with us to Eagle Pass."

Little Pete mounted his horse then cleared his throat. "You are correct, señor. She won't be riding with us because she and young Cuddy, they already left."

Diego's bulging eyes swung to Rosita. She solemnly nodded. "I packed their provisions myself, Diego. I watched them leave the gate."

"How long ago?"

She shrugged. "A long time. Hours."

With the barest nod to his mother, Diego spurred the eager horse into a run for the gate. Little Pete could catch up in El Indio.

❧

Melatha stood on the porch of her jacal, clutching the rail and peering past the big house to the east. Fear seeped into her bones as the blanket of black stretching along the horizon grew darker and wider, inching closer to her son with every tick of the clock.

Isi raced toward the storm on the back of a horse that may have killed John Rawson, his mind on nothing but protecting White Hair.

"She's bewitched you, too?" Rosita's question echoed in Melatha's mind, and she shivered.

Steeling her resolve, she fled to the only solid ground. "I have no trust in Emily Dane, Lord. I trust only what You've shown me of her heart."

From the moment Emily stepped across the threshold two days ago, God began to whisper in Melatha's ear. His assurance grew louder each time she saw the girl.

Emily spoke that day of Isi's love for her. Signs deeper than mere words could convey—her glowing eyes and trembling smile, the way she spoke his name—told Melatha she loved Isi, too.

These things alone did not sway Melatha or melt her stony heart. Only when Emily began to speak of the Father did the spiritual bond they shared come to light. The passion Melatha sensed while Emily spoke of Isi was but a flickering ember in comparison.

A brisk wind stirred the high grass and rattled the empty baskets in the corner. Melatha lifted her chin to the cool breeze and swallowed her fear. She determined to trust Chihowa Palami in all matters pertaining to Isi and White Hair, no matter how threatening the storm.

⤜⤛⤜

Emmy watched the churning wall of clouds on the horizon, more menacing by far than the patchy canopy overhead. They'd been grateful since they left the ranch for the overcast sky that blocked the sun, and the cool, brisk wind coming off the approaching storm caught Emmy's breath.

The closer the wall advanced, the more dangerous it appeared. A gust caught her whispered prayer for safety and carried it away, she hoped, toward heaven. She thanked God that for the last few miles, the angry swirl had seemed stagnant, a faraway puffed-up bully, blowing hard but harmless.

She turned her attention to Cuddy. Obviously deep in thought, he rode quietly, his gaze fixed somewhere in the distance.

"It's getting dark," Emmy said, and he jumped. She laughed. "I didn't mean to startle you."

He shrugged and grinned. "I'm afraid it'll be very gloomy tonight with the weather so foul. Makes it better on the horses, though. Cooler." He rolled his head to study the twilight sky. "New moon, too. If you don't like the dark, you'll be glad to see El Indio."

She shuddered, but he didn't seem to notice. Before long, he'd retreated into his thoughts again. Ducking her head, she peered closer. "You know what they say? A penny for your thoughts?"

He shot her a sideways glance. "There's not a thought in my head worth that much."

She gave him a mock frown. "I'm sorry, but I don't believe you."

He raised his brows. "Oh, it's true."

Emmy giggled, her lilting laugh out of place in the murky setting.

Cuddy crossed his hands over the saddle horn. "Since you asked, I'll tell you my thoughts. Free of charge."

She twisted to see him better. "All right. I never could pass up a bargain."

A flush crept up from his collar, visible even in the meager light. "I was wondering. . ." His gaze flickered to her face then down. "Well. . . I heard you praying back there."

It was her turn to blush. "Yes, I was."

As if determined to finish something he'd started, he met her

266

eyes. "Do you actually think someone heard you?"

At first, the strain in his voice made her think he was mocking her. After searching his face, she realized he desperately needed to know. "Yes, I do. In fact, I'm convinced."

He narrowed his eyes. "How?"

Cuddy's question brought the past flooding back, the emptiness Emmy had felt before the day she'd whispered a tortured prayer, asking herself the same question: Did someone hear?

The evidence that God Himself heard came later in startling bits and pieces. First, the calm that settled over her soul like a comforting quilt after that prayer, blocking out the darkness and filling the empty places. Where once her eyes in the mirror had darted, guilty and ashamed, now they gazed back at her, clear and unflinching, in a way they'd never done before. The day she awoke knowing God was there, so present she felt compelled to bid Him good morning, she knew her life had forever changed.

She related these proofs and more to Cuddy as they rode.

He listened quietly, thoughtfully chewing the inside of his cheek. When she finished, he whistled softly. "When we first met I said you weren't the sort of girl I expected to say such things."

She nodded, remembering.

"I was wrong."

His attempt to compliment her warmed her heart. "Thank you. It means a lot to hear you say so." She paused. "But Cuddy, I don't want you harboring the wrong idea. There is no particular 'sort' of person that prays to God." She smiled. "He takes all comers."

He clutched his chest and pretended to wince with pain. "Except someone like me."

She gave her head a vigorous shake. "Especially someone like you."

Cuddy threw back his head and laughed so hard he nearly fell out of the saddle.

Emmy watched him, amazed and a little frightened. "Stop it! Why are you howling? You'll attract a pack of coyotes."

Holding his middle, he pointed. "Didn't you hear yourself? You just confirmed that I'm a special case. I always thought I was such a mess that God would go out of his way to snag a trophy like me for His belt." He roared again. "Now you've confirmed it."

She fought a smile. "Oh, shush."

He wiped his eyes, controlling his snickers with effort. Gazing warmly at her, he smiled. "Seriously, I appreciate your honesty, and I think I'd like to know more."

She let her jaw drop dramatically then winked. "Why, Cuddy Rawson, I believe you're sincere. What do you want to know?"

His head jerked around and he held up his hand. "Shh! Wait a second." He leaned forward in the saddle and stared. "Unless my eyes are deceiving me, I see a campfire up ahead."

Emmy whirled to look and her heart skipped a beat. "Oh, Cuddy. Could it possibly be them?"

His teeth flashed in the dimness. "There's only one way to find out." He tapped his horse with his heels. "Let's ride."

<hr/>

The wind howled around the wagon, flapping the tarps tied over the crates and threatening to lift Magda's hat right off her head. She clung to it with her free hand while the brim battered her forehead. With her other hand, she held a cloth over Willem's mouth to try to keep out the swirling dust.

In one way, the coming rain would be a relief. Magda planned to open her mouth and turn her face to the sky. She'd never been thirstier in her life. It amazed her that Bertha, already parched when they discovered the empty canteens, hadn't asked for a drop to cool her tongue.

"It's coming a right rowdy blow," Bertha shouted.

Magda looked behind her. "You don't say? What are we going to do when it starts to rain?"

"I suppose we'll get mighty wet." Bertha seemed a fount of pointless information. She tipped her head and stared at the sky. "It's the lightning that's got me worried. Getting worse, too."

Her words struck fear in Magda. She hadn't even considered the lightning. "We need to find shelter, Bert."

"I know it's dark out, but have you forgot what this country looks like? There ain't no shelter. This here is wide-open plain." She cackled. "I suppose we could crawl under the wagon."

Tired of bawling back and forth like a cow and her weaning calf, Magda got up on all fours. "Have you forgot about Willem? What do you propose we do, drag him off this rig by his heels?"

It seemed foolish to her to ride along pretending there wasn't a monster chasing them. They needed to come up with a plan for weathering the storm. Before she could holler for Bert to pull over, Bertha hauled on the reins so hard Magda slammed forward and bumped her head. Falling on her bottom, she rubbed the swelling on her forehead. "For pity's sake! What'd you do that for?"

Bertha scrambled over the front seat, knelt on the rear, and leaned over the wooden slats.

Magda scooted closer and peered up at her. "What's wrong? You cracked my head and joggled Willem something fierce."

She slapped her hand over Magda's mouth. "Keep your voice down and listen." Letting go slowly, she pulled Magda's face to the left and angled it down the road. "What do you see?"

Magda gasped. "A light."

"Is it a light? Or a campfire?"

"What difference does it make? Either way, it means people. Help for Willem." Excitement welling inside, Magda shoved her toward the front. "What are you waiting for? Get up there and drive."

Bertha slumped on the seat. "Not so fast. Suppose it's bandits. . . or worse, Indians?"

"There are no more war parties in South Texas."

"How do you know?"

Magda was fairly sure of what she knew, just not positive. "We have to take the chance, don't we? We have no choice."

Thunder rolled from one side of the endless, dark sky to the other, followed by countless jagged streaks in the heavens. They both jumped at a louder crash that spiked a bolt of white light to the ground.

Magda shrank nearer to Willem. "How close was that? It's hard to tell out here."

"Too close," Bertha said, a quaver in her voice.

"What are we going to do, Bert?"

"I have a plan, but you won't like it."

Magda's stomach lurched. "If it gets Willem out of this weather, I'm game."

"That part's a gamble." A flash lit Bertha's profile as she stared up the road. "I have to get close enough to see who that is over yonder."

"How? They're sure to hear us. They'll likely even see us in this lightning if they haven't already."

Bertha's head turned. "Not if I go by myself. I can slip up on them."

"And leave me here alone?" She shivered. "With the storm and the coyotes? Not to mention the goat suckers?" She clutched Bertha's sleeve. "No. Come up with another plan."

Bertha pulled free. "There is no other plan. You want to find help for Willem, don't you?"

A sob threatened Magda's throat. "You know I do."

"All right, then. We either head for that light and we're safe, or we skirt around it and we're safe." Her voice slowly faded as she spoke. "The only way to choose the right path is for me to go look."

Fear clawed Magda's chest. She grasped the seatback and peered into the darkness. "Bertha Maye! Where did you go? You're already on the ground, aren't you?"

Bertha popped up at the side rail. "Keep your trap shut. They'll hear you."

"Please don't go."

"Stay here and be quiet." It was the second time Bertha had issued the order to stay, ridiculous considering Magda would be loath to leave the wagon if Gabriel appeared and blew his horn.

She didn't hear Bertha leave, but she knew the minute she was alone. A solid wall of darkness enveloped her, thick enough to slap her in the face each time a bolt of lightning waned.

She felt for the comforting warmth of Willem's chest, still faithfully rising and falling. Odd how he could be so lifeless yet at the same time full of life. Despite his helplessness, his nearness made her feel safe—until a rustling sound in the nearby brush tossed her heart at her throat.

The horses seemed suddenly restless, and she imagined them bolting in fear of whatever crouched in the bushes. Had Bertha set the brake? If so, would the rig topple, dragging them to their deaths?

Maybe the bandits up the road had already seen them. Perhaps they'd acted first and sent a murdering thief to slip up on them with a patch on his eye and a knife between his teeth. He would've already slit Bertha's throat and left her for dead. Now he shimmied through the tall grass, coming for her.

"It's them!" Bertha hissed at her side.

Magda screamed as thunder pealed overhead.

In the silence that followed, she felt downright silly. And mad. "What did you do that for?"

Standing at the rail, Bertha let out her breath in a rush. "I was about to ask you the same fool question. You'd better hope that thunder drowned out your caterwauling, or we're in big trouble."

Magda leaned over Willem. "Why? Who is it?"

"None other than our peeping Tom, nasty Wayne, and his brother, Carl."

"No!"

"I'm afraid so." She sniffed. "Here's the worst part, Magda. Benito and Juan are with them."

Magda gripped the rail. "Oh, Bertha. I can't believe it. They seemed so nice."

Bertha patted her hand. "They are nice. You were right about them all along. They're sitting back to back near the fire, trussed up in heavy rope. John's cattle are grazing in a nearby field."

Magda shot a worried glance down the road toward the campfire. "What are we going to do?"

"Nothing we can do for Benito and Juan just now. We're no match for those men. Besides, we've got to think of Willem." She sighed. "Looks like we're going around."

CHAPTER 36

Diego sailed along the road to El Indio, Faron's impressive strength, beauty, and speed churning beneath him. He allowed the horse to run for as long as he dared before pulling him up. Faron's swiftness and willingness had bought Diego a lot of time. He had the feeling the horse would cheerfully dash to his death if Diego required it of him.

Dismal, unwelcome thoughts simmered in Diego's head. In his zeal to save Faron, he'd never allowed himself to accept what Mrs. Rawson considered obvious. Had Faron thrown John Rawson? Trampled him to death? Was Mrs. Rawson a widow who deserved her vengeance? The possibility left Diego's insides roiling worse than the imminent storm.

A faint light flickered up ahead. Diego stood in the stirrups and tried to focus his eyes on the fiery blur. He first thought lightning had started a brush fire in the distance but soon realized it must be a campfire. His heartbeat quickened. It made no sense for Cuddy to pull off and camp halfway to El Indio, unless he sought shelter from the rain, or unless. . .

The other possibility shot warmth through his body. Could Mr. Rawson and Emmy's family have set up camp along the roadside?

Diego tapped Faron's sides to spur him to a trot. They didn't get far before a noisy commotion commenced behind him to the right. Faron sprang off his haunches, dancing away from the noise, but Diego held the edgy horse steady.

Something big trundled in a wide swath somewhere in the brush, angling toward the road.

Diego strained to see, but the shroud of darkness blotted out everything beyond a few feet. Deciding curiosity could be dangerous, he waited, his ears straining for more information.

A high-pitched caterwaul pierced the night, tensing every muscle in his body. "We've done it, Magda! We found the road."

"Halleluiah! I knew you could do it, Bert."

Grinning from east to west, Diego slapped his leg then leaned forward to whisper into the horse's twitching ears. "Well, what do you know, Faron? We didn't need to find them. They found us."

Filled with relief so fierce his chest was sure to burst, Diego spurred the horse and lit out after them. "Mr. Rawson! Sir! Wait up." They were nearly on top of the wagon when Faron swung to the side. Diego reined him in and circled back. "You folks can't imagine what a hullabaloo you've caused on the ranch." He chuckled. "Sir, your wife may be ready to see you hanged."

He squinted, trying to find Mr. Rawson's face, listening to hear his booming laughter.

A plump face materialized from the side of the wagon. "Diego!" Mrs. Dane cried. "Is it really you? We're so grateful to see you."

"We've had a terrible time of it, son," Mrs. Bloom added, her voice thick with unshed tears.

Fear tickled the edges of Diego's mind. He could see two shadowy figures in the wagon now. Two figures. Two voices.

"Mr. Rawson?"

"That's what we're trying to tell you," Mrs. Bloom said gently. "Willem is lying in back, and he's hurt real bad. As for John Rawson. . . he lit out on Faron two days ago to fetch a doctor for Willem and we haven't seen him since."

Diego's heart sank and he fought back tears. He'd cling to hope until there was proof, but the grisly facts were lining up against Mr. Rawson.

He pictured the man's poor wife holding a pistol on Faron, the hem of her dressing gown soiled by the barn floor, her hair an untidy mess. Shuddering at the feel of the horse under him, he dismounted and climbed aboard the rig. "What happened to your husband, Mrs. Dane?"

She sniffed loudly. "He fell. Landed on a broke-off tree limb that punctured the back of his head." Her voice broke. "It knocked him unconscious and he never woke up." A loud peal of thunder made Mrs. Dane jump and cry out.

Mrs. Bloom took up the story. "We waited at the camp all night for John and the doctor. When he didn't show, we figured we'd best head out and find help."

Diego's head reeled. "You two have been wandering alone, trying to make your way from Eagle Pass?"

"Not Eagle Pass. Willem got hurt along the river near El Indio."

"But you were coming from the direction of Eagle Pass."

"I reckon it looked that way to you." She felt for his head and turned it to look behind them. "Actually, we'd just driven around that."

The campsite.

He laughed. "You didn't have much to fear. I think I know who that is."

Bertha snorted. "We know exactly who it is, young feller. You may not fear them, but we sure do."

Diego narrowed his eyes. "But that's Cuddy and Emmy, isn't it?"

Fumbling in the darkness, Mrs. Dane scrambled to her feet. "What did you say? Why would you think that's my daughter?"

He turned from one to the other, trying to see enough of their faces to read them. "Because they were ahead of me, traveling this same road."

Their simultaneous gasps sent a chill down Diego's back. He stared toward the distant fire that once seemed cheerful and promising but now cast an ominous glow. "Maybe one of you had better tell me what's going on."

◦◦◦

Her eyes swollen from crying, Emmy strained against the rope that bound her hands. She glanced at Cuddy lying across from her and shuddered at his battered, bloody face. His incoherent babbling stirred fear in Emmy. She whispered his name, begging him to look at her, to say he was all right, but he didn't answer.

The cruel men had ambushed them as soon as they'd ridden into camp, pulling Cuddy shouting and kicking from his horse and hitting him over the head. Once Cuddy hit the ground, the beating continued, leaving him in a huddle, dazed and moaning. They'd tied him up and slammed him against a wagon wheel, leaving him for dead, and lashed Emmy to a musty-smelling trunk.

She glanced toward the fire. The wind whipped the flames in a crazy dance, and the occasional fat raindrop landed with a sizzle. Her gaze lifted to the two bronze-skinned men in front of the blaze. Their demeanor struck Emmy as peculiar, not because they were bound together, captives of the same evil men, but that they seemed to accept it with dignity and grace. One of them raised his head then tilted it, flashing Emmy a sympathetic smile.

The younger of the wicked men paced between the two sets of prisoners. "This is getting scary now, Wayne," he ranted. "I didn't say much when you hauled that cook and drover with us even after I asked you not to." He ran his hands through his hair. "And, yes, I can see how we might need them to get the cattle clear to Cotulla." He whirled and pointed at Emmy. "But this right here will get us hanged."

The man he called Wayne, the same one who'd kicked Cuddy when he was on the ground, sat on a stained bucket cleaning his finger-nails with a hunting knife. "Little brother, you worry too much." He spread his hands to take in their surroundings. "Do you see anyone around here for miles who might care?"

His vulgar laughter echoed through the camp. "That's the beauty of the wide-open spaces. The possibilities are wide open, too."

The worried one named Carl bent over at the waist, his arms out to his sides like a flustered goose. "We don't *need* them! Why bring extra heat on our heads?"

Wayne fixed a thoughtful gaze on Cuddy. "Unfortunately for him, I agree with you." The look he turned on Emmy held a greedy glint. "But that pretty little thing right there?" He sneered. "I reckon I could find a use for her."

Emmy cringed and dropped her gaze, stiffening her spine. He wouldn't see her cry.

Ferocious, howling gusts announced the storm's arrival. Carl came to life, chasing after flying clothing and tumbling boxes while Wayne laughed like a lunatic, nearly upsetting his bucket.

The lightning, splitting the sky in jagged bolts, scared Emmy almost as badly as Wayne did. Close by, the cattle increased their uneasy lowing. Emmy understood their frightened bellows. She wouldn't mind bellowing herself.

A few feet away, Cuddy had gone motionless. Emmy discreetly fought against her ropes, longing to be free so she could go to him, make sure he was all right, and huddle beside him until the storm passed.

"S'matter, little gal?"

Heart leaping, she jerked toward the voice in her ear. Wayne had slithered up to crouch at her side. She leaned away from his putrid breath and didn't answer, so he ran his filthy finger down her cheek. Cringing, she turned her head until her neck muscles strained.

Angered, he gripped her jaw and pressed his mouth to her ear. Lifting the knife, he swiveled the blade in front of her face. "You be nice to me and you'll come out of this in one piece. Keep thinking you're better'n me, and I'll make things very uncomfortable." He gave her face a harsh shake, his fingers biting into her flesh. "Be a good girl now and give me a sign that you understand."

She swallowed a cry of pain and tried to nod.

His cold laughter mocked her. "That's more like it, darlin'." He pressed against her, wrapping his arms around her waist to fumble with the ropes. A chill gripped her spine when his fetid breathing quickened. "I'm going to cut you loose for a little bit. How's that?"

Emmy's stomach lurched. "Why?"

"I thought you might like to take a little walk."

"Señor, please."

Wayne glanced back at the kind-faced man by the fire. "What do you want?" he growled.

"Don't hurt the lady, señor."

Wayne leaped up and struck with the speed of a striking rattler, his blow so brutal Emmy gasped and turned away. Concern quickly brought her eyes to the front again.

Bright red blood flowed from a gash on her defender's cheek. She first thought Wayne had slashed the helpless man with his knife, until he cleaned the butt of the knife on his shirt. "Maybe next time you'll mind your own business."

He spun around to Emmy with an air of nonchalance. "Now then, little lady. . .where were we?"

EMMY'S EQUAL

෫ඁ෨

Diego crawled backward to the end of the wagon and dropped to the ground. "He has no fever, Mrs. Dane. That's a good sign. But you'd best get him on to Carrizo Springs."

The women huddled together, their skirts flapping wildly in the wind. Mrs. Dane latched onto his arm. "What do you mean? Aren't you coming with us?"

"You'll be fine. Just stay on this road. It'll lead you straight into town."

"Where are you going? To look for Emmy?"

"Yes, ma'am." He nodded behind her. "Starting among your friends there."

Mrs. Dane clung so tightly, her fingers pinched Diego's flesh. "I'm going with you."

¡Ay! Where had he heard that before? He released a heavy sigh. "You can't, Mrs. Dane. I'll be down on my belly, crawling through the grass."

"I don't care. I'm going."

"Magda, don't be silly," Mrs. Bloom said, flapping her thin hands in Mrs. Dane's face. "You ain't laid flat of your belly in twenty years. Besides, there's too much of you to hide."

Mrs. Dane puffed like a porcupine and shook a stern finger at Mrs. Bloom. "You hush, Bertha. My baby might be back there."

"If she is, this young feller is just the one to save her. You'll only get in the way."

Diego breathed a prayer of thanksgiving for Mrs. Bloom. "Your friend's right, ma'am. Concentrate on getting your husband to a doctor."

"But—"

"If she's in that camp, which is highly unlikely, I'll get her for you." He flexed his jaw. "Don't doubt it for a minute."

The sound of hooves on the road behind them sent the women crowding against him in the darkness. He laughed softly. "I expect that's Little Pete. If so, you need to leave with him right away."

"No!" Mrs. Dane protested. "Not until I know about Emily."

He slid his arm around her shoulders. "Let me tend to Emmy. I give you my word I'll take care of her."

277

Little Pete signaled from the murky road.

Diego whistled back. "It's Pete."

"Oh, Bertha," Mrs. Dane moaned. She whirled into her friend's waiting arms. "I feel so torn."

Mrs. Bloom clucked her tongue. "Listen to me, sugar. Willem may die if we don't get help for him soon." She patted her back. "Besides, you know what Emmy would want you to do."

Pete drew alongside them. A long, jarring scratch produced a glow at the end of a match, with Pete's curious face etched in shadow behind it.

Diego sprang into action, batting the hand Pete held cupped around the flame. The match flew out of Pete's hand and Diego ground the embers into the sandy soil.

"¡Oye, Diego!" Pete yelled. "Are you loco?"

"Lower your voice, amigo. We've got company a little west of here, and I'm not ready to announce our presence."

Pete stared toward the firelight and lowered his voice. "Who are they?"

"Nobody you'd ask to supper," Mrs. Bloom hissed.

Placing his hand on the horse's neck, Diego tilted his face to Little Pete. "Mr. Dane has been injured. I want you to get him and the ladies to the ranch right away then ride into town for a doctor."

"Sí, Diego. Right away." Pete's voice softened with concern. "Very sorry, Señora Dane."

Diego helped Mrs. Dane climb up beside her husband. Without waiting for assistance, Mrs. Bloom scrambled into the driver's seat. "We're ready," she called.

Diego patted Little Pete's boot. "Try to hurry, but take it easy, huh? Her husband's badly hurt."

"Sí, sí. I will take good care of him," Pete said. He rode away a few feet and stopped. "Diego? Where is Mr. Rawson?"

A wind gust squalled behind Diego, billowing his shirt and raining sand on his back. "I'll try to answer that question when I come, Pete. Get those women home."

"Sí, señor."

Before another thing could keep him from Emmy, Diego fumbled Faron's leads free from a young mesquite tree and led him a little farther down the road. Obviously sensing the storm ahead, Faron resisted, bobbing his head and dragging his feet. Giving in, Diego left him secured behind a larger tree and hurried toward the campsite.

The lightning, now constant and intense, lit up the surroundings so often Diego wove among the scrub brush and cactus to prevent being spotted. He didn't stop until he came alongside the camp on the left and slid into the high grass a few yards away.

Crawling closer, he spotted the two men Bertha Bloom had seen tied together in front of the fire. With no protection from the storm, they watched the erupting sky with terror on their faces.

Thunder crashed directly overhead with a noise like the heavens had split. Diego ducked from the resulting explosion of light, the brightest he'd ever seen in his life, but not before the flash illuminated Cuddy tied to a wagon wheel. Instinctively, Diego came up on his knees then dropped again when a young man scurried past Cuddy and bailed into the covered wagon.

As Diego tried to decide what to do, the rumbling started again, this time moving the earth beneath him. Realizing the sound was bearing down on him, he glanced up in time to roll out of the path of a madly dashing cow.

Two more sailed past, running right through the middle of the camp, dodging the fire so they missed the two wild-eyed men.

A scream rang out, coming from the direction of the charging herd. Diego flew to his feet and ran. He roared for Emmy, but she couldn't have heard. The unending crash of thunder colliding with pounding hooves and frightened bellows was deafening.

The scene before him was the essence of a man's nightmares. An endless sea of red cattle charged his direction, appearing then disappearing as jagged spikes of light exploded around them. Bodies of downed cattle scattered the ground, tripping the others, creating a mad game of falling dominoes.

Emmy, her hair unpinned and her dress torn from one shoulder, darted in front of the driving wall of terror. Her mouth opened in another scream as she ran blindly into the path of certain death. Without a moment's hesitation, Diego hurtled toward her.

CHAPTER 37

Magda placed Emmy in God's keeping and let go of her fear. After all, she had enough on her plate for the moment. She groped for Willem's warm hand and squeezed, thrilled that she felt the tiniest response.

She decided that while she was yielding her loved ones to the Lord, she'd poke Willem in His hands as well. It seemed only God could save him, and she prayed He would. . .if the lightning prowling the sky behind them didn't get him first.

Little Pete slowed his horse even with them. "I don't believe we will outrun this storm, señoras, but we must try. It's very dangerous." He drew closer. "Forgive me, Mrs. Dane, but will it harm your husband to go faster?"

"We've taken him on bumpier rides," Bertha piped up. "Ain't we, Magda?"

"That doesn't mean it was good for him, Bertha," she called back.

Pete cleared his throat. "There's a cut-off up ahead that leads to my good friend's jacal. We can take shelter there."

Magda's throat tightened. "I suppose we have to risk it."

Pete spurred his horse. "Follow me. Don't worry, it's not far."

"Hang on to Willem," Bertha cried, her voice nearly lost in the wind.

Magda held Willem's head the way she had before, braced between her two hands. The rig took off so fast she felt it might rumble from

280

beneath her, especially since she couldn't hold on. Her bottom, already sore, took a pounding on the rough boards of the wagon bed. "I'll be black and blue," she shouted. If Bertha answered, she didn't hear.

The ride jostled her to the side, and she bumped her head hard on the rail. With no hands free to right herself, she lay draped behind Willem, helpless. Her head took another sharp rap every time they hit a bump, and there were too many to count.

A sob tore from her throat, carried away by strong gusts and crashing thunder. She felt alone in her suffering. While seeking God's protection for Willem and Emmy, she'd forgotten to lay herself on the altar as well.

"Are You even there?" she cried in anguish.

She craned to see the heavens past the surrey top. A bolt of lightning, so close she felt the hair rise on her head, was her only answer—until Willem's searching fingers found her face and patted her cheek.

❧

An inferno surged within Diego. He shot forward, tackling Emmy and knocking her clear seconds before the stampeding beasts would have trampled her. She screeched his name and clung to his neck. Scrambling to his feet, he pulled her ahead of the next set of hooves and rolled her beneath the wagon.

Emmy heaved with sobs. Something told Diego it had nothing to do with their narrow escape. Struggling to catch her breath, she twisted beneath him to stare over her shoulder. Her eyes were bulging pools of fear.

He smoothed her hair. "You're safe now, *mi querida*." The endearment slipped from his heart to his lips. "It's over now."

She fiercely shook her head. "He's still out there."

He pressed his finger to her lips and pointed above them, posing the question in his eyes.

She shook her head no.

"Who, Emmy?"

She shuddered. "Please be careful. He has a knife."

Diego's spine tingled. He hurriedly assessed the situation. One man above him in the wagon. One more skulking in the darkness with a blade. Cuddy, groggy and tied to a wheel beside him. Two unarmed men trussed up beside the fire.

He had a knife, too, but he needed to even the odds. Bending his knee, he slid the pistol from his boot and showed it to her.

She nodded.

He surveyed the area around them. The worst of the storm had blown over, leaving hardly a drop of rain behind. The wind was still up, but only weak gusts rustled the wagon cover. The campfire had died to embers and one of the two lanterns had gone out.

Diego remembered Little Pete and the women, directly in the path of the rushing cattle and perilous lightning. Wincing, he pushed the thought away. He could only manage one crisis at a time.

He patted Emmy's shoulder. "Don't move," he whispered. "I'll be back."

Careful to not bump or jostle the rig, he eased himself out on the unlighted side and crawled around to Cuddy.

Cuddy lifted dazed eyes that cleared when he saw Diego. "Real nice to see you, amigo."

Shushing him, Diego took his knife from the scabbard and cut him free. "Stay put unless I need you."

Cuddy started to argue, but Diego wiggled his finger in his face. "Stay put." He pointed under the wagon. "Keep an eye on Emmy."

Diego darted into the darkness again. He circled the camp on the other side and slipped up on the weary-looking captives. Startled, the eldest started to cry out, but Diego covered his mouth. The man nodded and Diego removed his hand.

Severing the ropes that held them, Diego handed the knife to the younger man, who stood slowly, likely stiff from sitting so long. Smiling, Diego lifted his pistol and nodded at the knife in the man's hand. Together they moved to stand behind the opening of the wagon.

"Come out," Diego shouted. "We have a surprise for you."

The flap flew back and the lanky boy made a run for it. The toe of the last boot to clear the canvas caught on the brake and he landed on his belly on the ground. He grunted as the air rushed out of him. Gasping like a landed trout, he rolled in the dirt at their feet.

Diego looked up and winked. "Well, that was easy."

His companion held out his hand. "Benito Guerra. Over there is my uncle, Juan. We are much indebted to you, señor."

Tipping his hat, Diego grinned. "It was nothing." Tapping the sprawling young man with his foot, he winked at Benito. "Nothing at all."

Catching his breath, the boy pushed to his feet.

Diego grasped him around the neck with his arm and held him steady. He began to wail like a branded calf. "Wayne! They got me!" He struggled against Diego. "Help me, Wayne!"

Cuddy limped up beside them. "I guess old Wayne ain't coming, partner. Looks like he bailed out on you." Cuddy's face was a mass of cuts and purple bruises, but at least he was talking.

Diego thrust out his chin. "They thrashed you good. Are you all right?"

Cuddy rubbed his jaw. "Maybe not as pretty, but I'm awake now."

"Señores!" Benito cried behind them. He stared at something outside the camp, his eyes glowing with terror. He pointed just as the acrid smell of smoke on the wind tickled Diego's nostrils. "Fire, señores!"

Diego jerked around to look. Sparked by lightning, a wall of flames spread across the distant plain. Driven by the wind, it whipped closer every second. He gripped the back of Cuddy's shirt. "We've got to get out of here."

He handed Cuddy the gun and trotted to where he'd left Emmy huddled. Reeling away, he whirled in a tight circle, his eyes searching every corner of the campsite. "Emmy!" he shouted, so loudly his throat hurt.

Cuddy ran up beside him. "What's wrong, brother?"

"It's Emmy." Molten fear layered the walls of Diego's gut. "She's gone."

∼✺∼

Little Pete's prediction had proven true. They hadn't outrun the storm. The wind blew so hard it felt as if the furious gusts racing along the plain lifted the wagon and hurtled it forward.

Magda cuddled on Willem's shoulder, delighting in the feel of his arm around her. He didn't have enough strength to tighten his hold, but he gave her frequent little pats, and each time her heart soared. She held his head steady with one hand on his cheek as they barreled along the road—she hoped to safety. She had just gotten her husband back and couldn't lose him now.

Fickle about its choice of targets, the lightning struck on every side without warning, splitting the air with sharp cracks. Anxious, Magda sat up to see how Bertha fared. Sitting on the driver's seat made her the highest point on the wagon and the most likely target, so Magda feared for her safety.

Small brush fires followed every strike, but the heavy sheet of rain coming behind them quenched the flames before they spread. Staring toward the approaching downpour, a ghastly sight caught Magda's eye. A quivering dark wall surged toward them, not unlike a bank of floodwater or a wave on Galveston Beach. She rubbed her eyes in disbelief, but the apparition remained, still rolling right for them.

Magda pulled up on the backboard and screamed for Bertha, but the whistling of the wind was too shrill. Terror weakening her limbs, she managed to push to her feet and crawl over.

On the other side, she promptly slid off the seat, scrambling and clutching at anything to stop her from sailing off onto the ground. Catching her balance at the last second, she hurled herself toward the front, screaming for Bertha.

Bertha turned her head halfway, her eyes wide with surprise.

Magda fell to her knees, still clinging to Bertha's seat. "Something's behind us!" she shouted.

"What did you say?"

"Something's chasing us. Something big!"

Bertha twisted to look. "I don't see anything."

"Keep looking."

The sky lit up briefly, long enough for them both to get a good look.

"The cattle!" Bertha cried.

Up ahead, Little Pete held up his arm before hurtling down a lane to the left.

Magda nudged Bertha's attention around to the front. "Go that way!"

A nervous glance to the rear revealed that the herd had just about caught up to them. Would they go around or blindly plow into the back, upsetting the speeding wagon? Cringing, she pictured them rolling, being crushed beneath the seat, Willem's helpless body flying out.

Dear Jesus, help us!

"Hang on!" Bertha screeched and jerked the reins to the left.

Magda's body slammed into the back of the seat she clung to, wrenching her wrists almost free of their sockets. Feeling herself losing her grip, they sailed in front of the thundering herd.

CHAPTER 38

Diego pointed beneath the wagon. "I left her right there, Cuddy. I told her to stay put." He glared, fingers of rage tickling his throat. "You were supposed to watch her."

"Don't worry, brother. We'll find her." Though he tried to sound calm, Cuddy's gaze darted around the campsite.

Sensing the fire, the horses tied nearby became restless, whinnying and pawing the ground. Diego's mind went to Faron and he groaned. He hoped the mesquite branch had held him. He'd need a fast horse to take Emmy out of danger once he found her.

Smoke swirled into camp, burning their eyes and causing their noses to stream. Juan approached from behind, a handkerchief over his mouth. "This is loco, señores. We must go!"

Diego squeezed Cuddy's shoulder. "Take these men to safety. I'll meet you at the ranch."

Cuddy shook his head, a determined glint in his eyes. "Forget it. I'm not leaving you."

"Do like I say, Cuddy."

He held up his hand. "Not today, amigo." The set of his jaw dared Diego to argue. "This is my fault. Besides, I care about her, too, don't forget."

Diego gave in with a pat to Cuddy's back. "Let's go, then. I'll head right. You go left."

Cuddy nodded.

Benito clutched his sleeve. "And me?"

Diego lifted his chin at Juan and Carl. "Get these men out of here. When you make it to town, hand Carl over to the authorities."

The seasoned vaquero turned a steely glare on Carl, cowering on the ground. "Sí, señor."

Cuddy bolted away from him and disappeared in the smoky mist.

Diego ran toward a cluster of brush along the fringes of the clearing and crouched, his eyes scanning the scrub for any sign of movement. Remembering Emmy's warning that Wayne had a knife, he wished he'd mentioned it to Cuddy. He could hear the witless boy crashing through the brush, shouting Emmy's name.

Diego made his way along the rim, keeping low and out of the smoke. The last time he'd checked the fire's progress, it had been close enough to seize his heart with fear, yet he found himself grateful for the light it provided.

He searched deep into the thorny branches of baby mesquite, as thick as corn pudding, and watched for rustling of the high grass in front. With the roar of the fire in his ears, urgency to find her overwhelmed him. In desperation, he shot to his feet and cried her name.

Emmy rose from the smoke, her body outlined from behind by a backdrop of fiery flames. The orange glow lit her flowing white curls and they danced with reflected light.

"You will find what you seek in the fire, Isi."

His mother's words burned in his heart brighter than the blazing field behind Emmy. He ran to meet her and pulled her close to the ground. "Honey, what were you thinking?" He wanted to shake her, but she looked already shaken.

Her eyes enormous, she lifted her chin to stare toward the camp. "I heard that boy calling Wayne. I couldn't bear to see him."

The dread in her quavering voice clenched Diego's stomach. He took in her bedraggled hair, her torn clothes, and her fear and felt a swirling agony so intense it left him dizzy. He wanted to charge the brush, guns blazing. Instead, he touched her cheek. "Stay low, sweetheart. I'll get you out of here."

She watched with a blank expression as he tore a length of cloth from her hem and covered her mouth. Clutching her wrist, he pulled her along the ground toward the campsite.

Diego called Cuddy's name, and he ran out of the smoke to help with Emmy. Benito and Juan had taken her horse and the horse that pulled the wagon, leaving only Cuddy's terrified gelding behind.

Diego nudged Cuddy's ribs. "Mount up."

"What about you two?"

"Just pray Faron's still where I left him."

Without waiting for an answer, he took Emmy's hand and ran. Following his own advice, he prayed to God with all his might that he'd find the stallion standing next to the mesquite. With the lightning, the stampede, and the fire, it seemed too big a miracle to expect.

Snatching the lantern that still burned, Cuddy rode alongside them until they neared the spot where Diego had tied the horse. His heart sank when the light from the brush fire revealed that Faron was gone.

"Now what?" Cuddy shouted.

Diego pulled Emmy toward Cuddy's horse. "Come on. I'll help you up."

She dug in her heels. "What about you?"

"Don't worry about me. Just get on the horse."

"No, Diego!"

He was about to pick her up and forcibly seat her behind Cuddy when he heard Faron's unmistakable whinny and whirled toward the sound. Faron stood ten feet away, pawing the ground.

Asking a prayer of forgiveness for doubting God's power, Diego slowly approached the big horse and took up the reins. Emmy ran to him and he helped her mount then jumped up behind her and gave Faron his head.

Driving the horses in a mad rush, they raced along in front of the fire. Diego heard the rain before the first fat drops landed on his back. Cuddy whooped beside him and Diego tossed his head back and laughed. A hundred yards past the pounding rain, Diego called to Cuddy and they stopped. Pulling Emmy off behind him, he held her trembling shoulders and stared at her face in the light from the waning fire. "Relax, honey. You're safe now."

She still peered past him with darting eyes, and rage seared his heart. He caressed her face, as gentle as he'd been with Faron. "Did those men hurt you, Emmy?"

Looking away from his searching gaze, she wrapped her arms around his neck. Quiet sobs shook her body. "I'm so glad to see you."

"I asked you a question. Did they hurt you?" He gently pushed her to arm's length. "Wayne hurt you, didn't he?"

Covering her face, she shook her head. "Not the way you mean, but he will, Diego. He swore it."

Relief flooded his chest. "I won't let him."

Quivering with fright, she jumped at the sound of distant thunder, her restless eyes straining at the dark. "You don't know what he's capable of. He's evil."

⁓⁓⁓

Diego took her arms and shook her. "Emmy, look at me. You have to know I'm prepared to defend you with my life."

Her gaze swung to him. Spoken with passion she'd never witnessed, the words rang in her head like the Rawsons' dinner gong. He'd said them once before, with less fervor, on the day they'd met. Gazing into the depths of his ardent brown eyes, she knew he spoke the truth.

Letting go of her fear, she relaxed against him. "Your life for my safety is not a trade I'm willing to make, but hearing it makes me feel better."

The drenching rain was over as fast as it had come, leaving sodden ground at their feet and Emmy's hair a streaming mass of soaking curls.

Breathless, Cuddy appeared with a blanket to wrap around her shoulders. Bending down, he relit the lantern and set it near her feet. "This might help chase away the ghosts, Emily, but you don't have to fret about Wayne. I found him when I was looking for you."

She tensed, and Diego gathered her to his chest. "Did he give you any trouble?"

Cuddy raised his brows. "Not a bit." He angled his head behind them. "Lightning got him. Along with about ten cows."

Trembling, Emmy covered her face. "Oh, no. Oh, Diego."

He held her while she cried, her thoughts racing. Despite all Wayne had done—and what he'd tried to do—no one deserved to die without a chance to make things right with God.

Diego tilted her dripping face. "I'm sorry all this happened,

Emmy, but there is good news."

She could think of only one thing Diego would consider good news in the aftermath of such tragedy. Afraid to hope, her breath caught. "You found my parents?"

Smiling, he nodded. She fell against him, relief swelling her chest.

Cuddy's shout echoed around them. "You found them?" He spun and slapped his leg. "I knew it! Where were they?"

Diego frowned. "Well, I—"

"I told you, didn't I?" Cuddy continued. "The old man can't pass up a good time." He laughed rowdily. "¡Ay! Will he ever be in trouble with Mother! Death might've been better than facing her wrath." He stood beaming foolishly at Diego.

Diego stared back with a drawn face.

Emmy nudged him. "Something's wrong, isn't it?"

Diego nodded.

She steeled herself. "Tell us."

Sadness filled his eyes. "We haven't found your father, Cuddy."

Cuddy sobered and sank to the ground beside them. "What do you mean you haven't found him?"

"He's still missing. No one knows where he is."

Diego turned from Cuddy's blanched face to Emmy. "And, honey . . .I'm afraid your father's been hurt."

A sick look on his face, Diego told them a sketchy story of what had happened. His careful attempt to be vague scared her worse than any details he might provide.

"Please, Diego. I need to go see my papa."

"Of course."

He turned to hold the stirrup for her, but Cuddy caught the back of his shirt. "Wait. You can't go. We haven't found my father yet."

Diego shook loose from his grip. "I haven't given up on finding him, and I won't. We'll take Emmy to the ranch then get right back on the road."

"No." Cuddy gave his head a determined shake. "Uh, uh. It's not going to be like that." He glanced at Emmy. "Sorry, sugar, but they found your old man. Mine's still out there somewhere, and I'm not going home without him."

"Cuddy"—Diego pled with his eyes—"use your head. I don't have to tell you how I feel about your father, but we don't even know where to look until we question the women."

"You just saw the women. You didn't ask them anything?"

"Mrs. Bloom said they last saw him two days ago along the river to El Indio. He took off to find a doctor for Mr. Dane. They didn't say if he was headed to Carrizo, El Indio, or back to Eagle Pass." He frowned. "And no, I didn't ask. About that time I had to come rescue you."

"All right." The betrayed look in Cuddy's eyes broke Diego's heart. "Do what you must, brother. If you care to find me, I'll be searching along the Rio Grande."

He spun on his heel, but Emmy grabbed his sleeve and pulled him back. She searched his face with compassionate eyes. "You need sleep, Cuddy. You could use a hot meal and a bath, but you've slept less than any of us." She touched his swollen cheek. "Unless you count the little nap you took, which means you're piling fatigue on top of injury." She shook her head. "I don't see how you're still upright. You won't do your father any good in this condition."

Diego dropped his hand on Cuddy's shoulder. "She's right, amigo. It wouldn't hurt to have the doctor take a look at you."

The wet grass snuffed the last of the flames at their backs as Diego draped his arm around Cuddy's neck and led him to his horse. "We'll leave the ranch first thing tomorrow morning, fresh, fed, and bandaged. I give you my word we won't stop looking until we find him."

❧

The wagon roared across the leading edge of the cattle, clearing the last wild-eyed Hereford by the width of a wispy hair.

Bertha let the horses run a little farther then pulled them to a stop in the middle of the lane as the danger rumbled past behind them.

Magda, soaking wet and huddled on bruised knees between the seats, hauled herself up and limped to peer in the bed. "Willem? Please be all right. I'm coming, dear."

Feeling a bit like an Olympic hurdler, she bailed over the backboard again and crouched beside her husband. Drowsiness gave his eyelids a swollen, heavy look, but he feebly reached for her hand. Though the rain had let up, Magda dug for a canvas bag and held it over his head to shield him.

Little Pete trotted up to them, his eyes wide with fear. "Very sorry, señoras. I did not hear them coming with your rig at my back. Is anyone hurt?"

Bertha twisted on the seat. "How's Willem?"

"He woke up. For a few minutes at least."

Bertha laughed gleefully. "Is that so?"

"Yes, but I think he's out again." Magda gently probed Willem's face. "At least he's alive."

"Pete, I don't reckon we're hurt any worse than we were," Bertha said. "But thanks for asking." She nodded in the direction the cattle had gone. "Will them critters be all right?"

He shrugged. "They'll run out of steam eventually."

Magda studied the sky. Once the front started moving, it had galloped through like a racehorse. The only flashes of light were sporadic bursts to the west. "One thing we can be grateful for, when they ran out of here they took the worst of the storm with them."

Pete lit a sputtering match, his face tight with concern in the flickering light. "If you want, I can take you to my friend now."

"No, thanks," Magda called out. "I want to get my husband to a doctor."

"I agree," Bertha said, her head bobbing. "As long as we don't meet up with them Herefords coming back the other way."

"Very well," Pete said, backing his horse. "Turn the rig around, and I'll take you to the ranch."

Bertha goaded the weary horses into a tight circle. Back on the lane, they headed for the road. As they plodded into the turn, a sharp whistle came from behind them.

Pete returned the signal then gave a low laugh. "It's Diego."

Magda rose up on her knees and put her hands around her mouth. "Emily Bertha Dane!"

Silence followed. Then a voice tight with emotion carried on the brisk wind. "Mama! Is that you?"

"It's me, baby!"

"Don't you move! I'm coming!"

CHAPTER 39

Emmy opened her eyes, expecting to find her legs bound by a blue blanket with six girls lined up at her bedside. Only she wasn't at the Campbells' ranch, or even in her cheery room in Humble with the yellow wallpaper and lace curtains. She was in a bedroom at the Rawsons' ranch beneath the lovely Redwork quilt, basking in the glow of the morning sun.

She stretched and turned over, wincing when the motion fired stinging needles of pain through her shoulder. Sitting up gingerly, she slid aside the delicate sleeve of her pink cotton nightshirt. Bile forced its way up her throat at the sight of four angry red scratches put there by Wayne's dirty fingernails.

The shuddering remembrance brought others just as grim. The dread on Cuddy's face when he'd broken the news of his father's disappearance to his mother; the horror in Mrs. Rawson's eyes before she collapsed in Cuddy's arms; poor Greta, forgetting herself in her grief and clinging to Diego; and Emmy's first look at the bloody wound on her bewildered papa's head.

A gentle knock roused her from her thoughts. Grateful, she slipped on her robe and opened the door.

Mama stood there, her face pale and marred by weary lines. Still, she gathered Emmy in her arms and kissed the top of her head. "Good morning, sugar. I hope I didn't wake you."

Emmy rested her head on Mama's ever-dependable shoulder. "I

293

was awake. How's Papa?"

Mama held her at arm's length. "Still sleeping. The doctor said he'll continue to drift in and out until the swelling goes down in his brain."

The words heightened the pain building in Emmy's chest. She pulled away to peer into her mother's face. "How long will it take?"

"That remains to be seen in this type of accident. The doctor called it a closed skull injury. All along, I thought the stick hurt his head, but that turned out to be a shallow puncture. Your papa damaged his brain by the fall."

"Will he be all right?"

Mama glanced away, and Emmy's heart pounded. "Not overnight. He'll need time to recover, and may have periods of forgetfulness." She brightened. "With plenty of love and care, we'll have him good as new in no time."

Emmy stiffened. Pushing past her mama, she stalked to the patio door.

"Emmy?" Mama said after a moment of silence.

She couldn't answer.

Determined footsteps approached from behind and her mama's arms enveloped her. "What is it, lamb?"

"I–" Emmy sniffed and wiped her streaming nose on her sleeve. "I want to help Papa heal," she sobbed, "but if love and care are what it takes then I can't."

Her mama took her shoulders and turned her around. "What do you mean, you can't? You love him, don't you?"

"Very much." The wall inside Emmy fell. The rush of emotion Mama's question roused stirred a mournful wail from her depths. "But he doesn't love me!"

Reaching blindly, Emmy wrapped her arms around her mama's neck and sobbed out years of pain and rejection. Mama held her, cooing quietly and rubbing her back. Spent, Emmy rested against her chest until the gulps and little catches in her breath subsided.

Leading her gently to the bed, Mama sat with her and picked up her hands. The familiar brown eyes studied her. "That's what you think? That he doesn't love you?"

Emmy glanced away. "I don't want to think it, but how could he deal so harshly with someone he loves?" She lifted an accusing gaze.

"He's never harsh with you. I wouldn't know Papa had a tender side if I hadn't watched the two of you together."

"Oh, honey, you've got it all wrong. He's tender with me because he doesn't have to share me."

Emmy blinked. "What?"

Incredibly, Mama was smiling. "It's not that he doesn't love you. Your papa's love for you knows no bounds. The truth is he's jealous of your relationship with Nash."

"Nash?" Emmy shook her head. "What does any of this have to do with Nash?"

Patience softening her voice, Mama wrapped her arm around Emmy and tried to explain. "Papa's job kept him on the road so much you had to grow up without him. It's only natural you'd turn to the man who's been a constant presence. You began to love Nash like a father, and your own finally took notice."

She lifted Emmy's chin. "He feels left out of your life. I'm afraid he's been taking that out on you."

Joy and the courage to hope soared in Emmy's chest. "Are you certain, Mama?"

She nodded gravely.

Not sure what to do with the information, Emmy stared at the floor. When she looked up, her mama's eyes were moist with tears. "This might be a good time to change the direction of your relationship. Loving care, the thing he needs to recover, might be the same medicine to heal your broken bond." She stood, pulling Emmy with her. "Give it time to sink in, sugar. Meanwhile, dress yourself and come downstairs. If I'm not mistaken, I caught the smell of fried ham wafting up from the kitchen. Rosita must have breakfast ready."

Emmy kissed her cheek. "I'll be along soon."

Mama started for the door, turning when Emmy called her. "Yes, sugar?"

"What about Cuddy and Diego?"

Worry returned to Mama's face. "They left before daybreak, honey. You might think to offer a little prayer on their behalf."

She grimaced. "I think I'd prefer to offer a big prayer."

Reaching for the doorknob, Mama paused again. "Your papa's asleep, but if you want to duck in for a minute, you can."

Emmy's hand fluttered to her throat. "Are you sure? I don't want to disturb him."

Mama sighed. "I wish he was alert enough to be disturbed. I'd gladly disturb him myself." She smiled. "Go on in and sit with him a spell. Might do you both some good."

Emmy dressed as fast as she could then slipped into the hall. Her heart hammered so hard at the door to Papa's room, she smiled at the thought it might awaken him. Gathering her courage, she turned the knob and stepped inside.

The soothing rays warming Emmy's corner room had yet to find Papa. His windows were southerly facing, so he lay quietly in the early-morning shadows beneath a jewel-toned quilt.

The rhythmic movements of his chest mimicked normal sleep instead of the deep, merciless slumber that held him the past few hours. She ventured closer, expecting any moment for Papa to sit up and demand an explanation for interrupting his rest.

A scrollwork chair with an inviting cushion sat beside the bed, recently vacated by Mama, no doubt. Emmy tiptoed over and took a seat.

Papa's expression was peaceful. Except for his lips, chapped a flaming red, and faint circles under his eyes, he didn't even appear injured. She watched his lashes flicker in sleep and suddenly longed to hear his voice, even if it held a critical edge.

Emmy didn't expect what happened next and didn't plan it. Almost of their own will, her fingers inched forward to brush his hand. Watching carefully for a reaction, she touched him again, a bit more boldly. He didn't respond. Feeling like a thief, she slipped her hand in his, caressing it with her thumb.

Sorrow welled so strongly it took her breath. Drawing air, she exhaled on a sob. Pressing her hand to her mouth to stifle the sound of her weeping, she sat on the side of the bed and laid her head on Papa's chest. The warmth of the stolen hug flooded her heart with bittersweet pain. Reaching to pat his cheek, she grieved for all the hugs he'd withheld from her.

It hurt even worse knowing the reason Papa had been so harsh. He'd punished her for needing him so badly she'd turned to Nash for comfort.

Sitting upright, Emmy wiped her eyes. She slid to her knees

still clutching Papa's hand and asked God to help her forgive him so she could offer the loving care he so desperately needed. Asking forgiveness for her own behavior, she promised God to honor Papa and show him love no matter how he acted toward her. She determined in her heart to help him recover from the terrible thing that had happened to him so they could begin anew.

Planting a soft kiss on the back of his hand, she tucked his arm inside the covers and pulled the quilt to his chin. With one last pat on his cheek, she left the room.

❧

Diego eased the mare he rode closer to the fire pit and glanced over his shoulder at Cuddy. "This is the spot where they camped. It's just as Mrs. Bloom described."

Cuddy nodded grimly. "Which means my father rode out from here toward El Indio." He smiled, hope shining from his eyes. "All we have to do is head that way. We're sure to find him somewhere along the trail."

Gritting his teeth, Diego forced himself to say the loathsome words. "Your father's been lost for nearly three days"—he winced at the look in Cuddy's eyes—"and it's August in South Texas." He shook his head. "I don't want to find him somewhere along the trail."

Anger replaced Cuddy's hopeful expression. "What then?"

Diego looked toward the mid-morning sun, already baking his skin. "If he hasn't found shelter, he's in trouble. We'll look along the trail but not just out in the open. If he's able to move, he's crawled into the brush by now. Otherwise—"

Cuddy's hand shot up. "I get the picture. We'll scour every inch of scrub between here and El Indio."

Chattering with excitement, Little Pete and Felipe rode into the clearing. Little Pete pointed over his shoulder with his quirt. "We found the rest of the Herefords, Diego. Downriver about a mile from here."

Diego laced his fingers to tighten his leather gloves. "It wasn't as easy as having them run halfway to Carrizo like the other herd, but I knew you'd find them."

Preening in front of Felipe, Pete's shoulders shot back. "Sí, señor. I told you I would."

Diego scowled, feigning anger. "I wouldn't boast until after you drive them into the corral. For all you know, they've been rustled into Mexico by now."

Pete's eyes widened. "No, señor! It's not possible."

"Sí, es muy posible. What are you waiting for?" Diego shooed them like naughty children. "Have your men round them up and take them home."

Grinning, Pete saluted. "Sí, Diego. We're going."

They rode off laughing, and Diego nodded toward the river. "Let's tend the horses. The sooner we start looking the better."

After they rested their mounts, they led them to the bank and encouraged them to drink. Diego cooled them by wetting rags and sponging along the underside of their necks and down their lower legs. The minute they dared, they set out on the fresher horses and headed for El Indio.

Dismounting often along the seldom-used track, they searched carefully along each side of the trail. By the time they made it to the sleepy little town, a two-hour trip that should've taken twenty minutes, they were hot, tired, and discouraged. Careful to appear friendly, they rode along the dusty main street, nodding their heads at the locals.

Diego lifted his chin toward a shabby adobe building with a low, flat roof. "Let's ask a few questions inside. Maybe someone has seen him."

Tying their horses to the rail, they stepped into the cool shadows of the tavern.

Sleepy-eyed men turned from the bar, regarding them with open curiosity.

Diego mumbled a greeting in Spanish and approached the bartender.

"Buenas *tardes*, señores," the balding man said. "What can I get for you?"

Diego pulled a folded bill from his pocket. "We're in the market for cool water and information, señor."

The man reached for the currency, but Diego flicked it backward, away from his grasping fingers. "We're looking for someone. A fellow out of Carrizo Springs. He rode in this direction three days ago and hasn't been heard from since."

The man's moustache twitched. "It would be a shame indeed if I knew something, considering you only hold payment for water in your hand."

Diego and Cuddy exchanged looks. Cuddy produced another bill, this one a slightly higher denomination. He held it up beside Diego's money. "What will this buy us?"

The bartender glanced toward his watching patrons. They swiveled on their barstools and pretended not to listen. He leaned close, his breath heavy with the scent of bourbon. "I can help you."

"Prove it," Cuddy demanded, a hard edge to his voice.

The man rubbed his chin. "This is a gringo you seek? Stout as a bull?"

Excitement surged through Diego, tightening the muscles in his limbs. He struggled to contain himself before he cost them every dollar they had. He shot a warning look at Cuddy then leaned casually on the bar. "Do you know where we might find him?"

A thick arm, so covered in hair it resembled a black bear's, reached between Cuddy and Diego and snatched the currency.

They whirled, ready to give chase.

Instead of running, the stocky thief stood his ground, popping the bills between his fingers to test them. He held up the money as if to say thanks and then shoved it into his pocket. "The gringo you're looking for is in my house. Follow me. I'll take you there."

❧

Melatha sat in a corner of Kate Rawson's room watching Greta comfort her mother. When Kate slept at last, under sedation by doctor's orders, Greta smoothed her brow and slid off the high bed. Melatha stood as she approached and gathered her into her arms. Greta wept quietly as Melatha rocked her.

She looked up, her lashes wet with tears, and searched Melatha's face. "My father's gone, isn't he?"

Melatha shook her head. "Don't give up on him."

Greta brushed a wilted curl from her forehead with a shaky hand. "I don't mean to, Melatha." Her wide blue eyes seemed to stare into eternity and see her father there. "I just have a bad feeling." She shook her head as if coming awake. "I only pray they find out something today." She glanced at her mother's restless form. "I'm not sure how much more uncertainty she can stand."

Melatha gazed out the window at the empty lane. "I'm certain they'll be home soon." She sighed. "They'll be hungry. Men always are, no matter what the circumstances. I'd better make sure there's plenty to feed them." She gave Greta one last pat then started for the door.

"Melatha?"

She turned. "Yes?"

Greta's lips quivered with suppressed emotion. "Thank you for being here for us. You know I've loved you from the beginning." Profound sadness drew a curtain over her features. "I even hoped we might one day be family."

Melatha crossed the room and held her. "Will you be all right, Greta?"

Her smile was tight. "Someday. I've asked Mother to send me to my grandparents in Ripponden to finish my education." She lifted her chin. "Of course, now we await news about my father that could change everything."

Melatha nodded. "Or change nothing."

❧

A humble jacal hunkered at the edge of El Indio, the door swinging loose on its hinges and the thatched roof needing repair, but a welcome sight nonetheless. Diego hastily tethered the horses, and then he and Cuddy followed the man inside.

A sheet had been nailed as a makeshift curtain across the door of the dining room. Diego swept it aside.

The owners of the house had shoved the table and chairs to one side of the tidy room and set up a cot against the far wall. When Diego's eyes adjusted to the absence of light, searing pain pierced his chest. He moved forward, but Cuddy rushed past him and threw himself to the floor beside the gaunt figure on the bed. "Father!"

Despite a noticeable weight loss and sunken cheeks, the bulk of John Rawson's big-boned frame took up all of the cot and more, and his feet dangled from the end. He reached a feeble hand to Cuddy's neck. "I've been waiting for you."

Tears flowed down Cuddy's cheeks. "Forgive me! I should've found you sooner."

Mr. Rawson was shaking his head. "No more regret, son."

Cuddy buried his face in his father's hand and wept.

"So this is Cuddy?" a pleasant voice said behind Diego. He moved aside to let the kind-faced woman slide past. "Awake or asleep, John's been calling that name since we found him."

"Where was he?" Diego asked softly.

"About a mile from town," said the furry-armed fellow from the tavern. "Me and my wife came across him yesterday on the way to the river. We'd never have seen him so far off the road, but he summoned the strength to cry out."

Diego winced. Mr. Rawson had survived alone in the brush for two days.

"He was in bad shape when we found him," the man said and added a sad cluck with his tongue. "Delirious."

The dark-eyed woman folded her arms over her ample chest. "I tell you, this man's will is stronger than most." She nodded at Cuddy. "His determination to speak to that boy kept him alive." She smiled toward Mr. Rawson. "Now God has answered his prayer. He can die in peace."

Cuddy's head jerked up. "Die? He's not going to die."

Mr. Rawson tried to speak, but dry coughs wracked his body. When he caught his breath, he reached for Cuddy's hand. "There's something I have to tell you, son."

The line of Cuddy's jaw hardened. "Hush, Father. Save your strength. We can talk later after we get you to a doctor."

Mr. Rawson shook his head. "I won't be seeing the Twisted-R again." His voice broke. "Or your mother."

Cuddy's face twisted in agony. "Don't say that."

Tears sprang to Mr. Rawson's weak eyes. "Cuddy, I—"

Cuddy shot to his knees, his body in a protective huddle over his father. "Go hire a wagon, Diego. And hurry! We have to take him home."

The woman moved to Cuddy's side and placed her hand on his shoulder. "Let him speak, boy. The chance to say what's on his mind has cost him dearly." She patted him. "Don't disappoint him now."

She walked past Diego, pulling her husband out the door.

Heartbroken, Diego reluctantly followed them to the kitchen. Bewildered, he sought the woman's eyes. "How are you so sure he won't live?"

"We have a doctor here in town. He gave him up for dead last night. We're surprised your friend has held on for so long."

"So he hit his head?"

She blinked. "His head?"

Diego nodded. "When his horse threw him."

She glanced at her husband then licked her lips. "I don't know what horse you mean, son. John was afoot."

The woman's husband poured a cup of stout-looking coffee and handed it to Diego. "We don't know anything about a horse, mister. It's John's heart that's broke, not his head."

Diego nearly dropped the cup. "His heart?"

The man nodded. "Poor fellow's got a bum thumper."

CHAPTER 40

"They are home!" Rosita's shrill voice rang through the house, echoing up the stairs to Emmy's room.

Emmy ducked to peer from the window, her searching eyes finding Diego. He rode his mare in the lead. Cuddy followed, driving a wagon through the gate.

A burst of golden light from the sunset lit them from behind like a giant halo. Praying the sunburst was a good sign and the wagon wasn't a bad omen, she tore open the door and ran, nearly colliding with Aunt Bertha and Mama sailing from their rooms.

Emmy led the way down the stairs and hurried for the door. Greta stood on the threshold staring straight ahead as if unable to move. Emmy smoothed a hand down her back, and Greta turned woodenly. "I'm so scared, Emily."

Lifting her chin, Emmy took hold of her hand. "Hang onto me. I won't leave you."

Rosita and Melatha stood on the porch. The rest of the women filed from the house to stand beside them, except for Mrs. Rawson still resting in her room.

Little Pete came running from the barn, the sight of the wagon breaking his stride. "God help us," he muttered then glanced nervously toward the women.

Diego stopped his mare and dismounted. Cuddy pulled the wagon in front of the house and set the brake. One look at their faces and Emmy knew.

Greta pulled away from her and ran. Searing pain on his face, Cuddy caught her before she reached the wagon bed and spun her around, yanking her to his chest. She collapsed against him in bitter tears.

Pete whirled away and ran for the barn.

Rosita, a look of horror on her face, shot past them into the house.

Melatha bounded the other direction, down the steps to help Cuddy with Greta.

An anguished wail pierced the air.

Cuddy's gaze flew to his mother's balcony. He handed Greta off to Melatha and took the steps in one leap. Pitiful cries rocked the front yard until Cuddy reached his mother and pulled her inside the house.

Diego stood rigidly beside his horse, apart from the scene. His haunted eyes held a lost look. A Rawson in heart, but not in blood or name, he grieved alone.

Emmy rushed off the porch calling his name.

In a daze, he walked into her arms.

She pressed his head to the hollow of her neck and smoothed his hair while he cried.

"Is there anything I can do to help?" Mama called to Melatha.

Melatha looked over her shoulder. "Yes, take Greta to her mother, please."

Mama hustled to Greta and led her into the house.

"Is there something I can do?" Aunt Bertha asked.

"Yes." Melatha pulled her gaze from the wagon bed. "You can help me prepare this poor man for burial."

⁶∕₂∕⌐

The big ranch house loomed around Magda as silent and somber as a tomb. Rosita and Melatha had prepared enough food for another pachanga, but no one seemed to have an appetite, even Magda, though her stomach growled beneath her belt.

They'd all slipped away to deal with John Rawson's death in their own fashion. Cuddy, Greta, and their mother had locked themselves in Mrs. Rawson's bedroom. Rosita and Melatha hovered somewhere in the house tending the family's needs. Emmy had disappeared, clinging to Diego's arm as they melted into the evening shadows.

Magda ventured into the dimly lit parlor to pay her last respects to John, but the sight of the big man in death disturbed her to the core. The memory of his booming voice and laughing eyes sent her scurrying to her room in tears. Knowing it could've been her husband didn't help. After checking on Willem, she tiptoed across the hall to Bertha's room.

Bertha let her in then crawled to the middle of the bed and propped her back against the wall. "It's never easy to look eternity in the face, is it? Especially when it's a man as alive as John was."

Magda kicked off her shoes and crawled up beside her. "He was a fine man. I feel for Kate. I don't see how she'll manage."

Bertha grew silent, staring down at her fingers she'd laced together in her lap. Deep furrows creased her brow.

Magda turned over and patted her arm. "What's wrong, sugar? Something's in your craw."

Bertha lifted her brows. "Is this my fault?"

Magda frowned and drew her head back. "Is what your fault?"

Bertha's thin hand fluttered through the air. "The whole thing—John's death, what happened to Willem. . ."

"Oh, Bertha. Of course not."

Bertha sat up, pleading the case against herself. "If I hadn't insisted on coming to South Texas, if I hadn't forced you all to find me some cattle, Willem wouldn't be lying across the hall with a hole in his head, and John would be sitting to supper with his family tonight."

Magda picked up her hand and squeezed. "You stop this instant. Willem could just as easily have fallen down the stairs at home. And John had a bad heart. This was coming with or without you."

She nodded thoughtfully and propped her head on her arms. "I do wish we'd paid closer attention and taken John to a doctor. He was feeling poorly that day, remember? Pale as paste and green around the gills."

Sadness filled Magda's chest. "I remember. But at the time, we all looked a little ragged from the heat." She let go a weary sigh. "I can't see any way to have avoided his death. I'm just grateful he was right with the Lord so we'll see him again one day." She glanced at

Bertha. "That fact alone will comfort Willem. I dread breaking the news to him."

Bertha's wide eyes darkened with pity. "I wouldn't be in a big hurry. There'll be plenty of time to tell him when he's stronger."

Magda touched her arm. "He will get stronger, won't he, Bertha?"

Bertha winked. "I reckon he's bound to once the good Lord tires of my voice. I've sent up more than my share of prayers on Willem's behalf." She gave Magda a weighty look. "I don't want to watch you grieve the way I did for Thad."

Magda shuddered. "That makes two of us. I hope I never see another soul experience loss the way you did."

They were silent, Magda picking at a thread on the sheet, Bertha leaning back on her arms staring at the ceiling.

After a bit she leaned to nudge Magda. "Besides, you need Willem. Otherwise you'll be going back to that big house in Humble all alone."

Magda studied her mischievous face. "What are you talking about?"

Bertha beamed like a preacher on Sunday. "Don't tell me you expect to leave this ranch with Emmy in tow?"

Shooting upright, Magda offered a scowl. "I certainly do. Why shouldn't I?"

Bertha shook her head. "Honey, you must be blind because I know you ain't stupid. The only way you'll get Emmy to Humble is to tuck Diego in her satchel—and he won't fit." She bent over and pinched Magda's cheeks. "Our Emmy's in love or my name ain't Bertha Bloom. I reckon you'd best start adjusting to the idea. Your daughter will be staying in South Texas."

❧

Tormented by his thoughts, Diego gazed toward the light in the parlor window, wondering how he'd ever imagined himself a part of the Rawson family. John Rawson had sought him out, encouraged him, and groomed him in the role of a son. Young, fatherless, and confused about his place in the world, Diego had lapped up the attention.

Ironic that Cuddy had felt such envy. In Mr. Rawson's final hour, he called for Cuddy, clung to Cuddy's hand as he drew his final breath. Diego hadn't even had a chance to say good-bye.

Even now, the family grieved together behind closed doors while

Diego watched from the outside.

The worst evidence of his true place in the Rawsons' lives—Cuddy's silence on the ride home.

Scooting closer on the low wall of the patio, Emmy touched his hand. "What can I do?"

He laced his fingers with hers. "You're doing it."

"Do you want to talk about it?"

Diego lowered his head and gave her a sideways glance. "There's not much to tell. We found him too late." He released a shuddering breath. "Actually, I think it was too late from the first day."

Emmy squeezed his hand. "I'm so sorry."

He nodded. "He only lasted a few minutes after we got to him." He raised his head. "He was hanging on just long enough to talk to Cuddy."

Surprise sparked in her eyes. "And?"

He shrugged. "It was a private conversation."

"And Cuddy didn't—"

He shook his head.

Emmy lifted her face to the sky. "I'm so glad they had the chance to talk. I pray Mr. Rawson said the right things." She faced him. "It will make all the difference in Cuddy's life."

Diego remained silent.

"It shows incredible strength, doesn't it?" she continued. "Living until he could talk to Cuddy. It's just the sort of thing a man like him would do." Emmy's chin shot up and she winced. "Diego, what's wrong?"

Realizing he'd tightened his fingers around her hand, he released her and covered his face. "I didn't get to tell him good-bye."

Emmy gave a soft gasp. "You didn't speak to him at all?"

He shook his head. "I wanted to."

"But he didn't ask for you." It wasn't a question. She had figured it out.

Unable to answer, he wagged his head again.

Her arms went around him. "Oh, Diego. I'm so sorry, but I know exactly why he didn't."

"So do I," he whispered. "I'm not his son."

She pushed off the wall and stooped at his feet. "Look at me." She pulled his hands from his face. "Look at me, please."

He lifted his gaze to her passionate eyes.

"John Rawson knew he was dying and out of chances to make things right—and he had to make them right for Cuddy's sake." She cupped his cheek. "Mr. Rawson didn't call for you, and I know that hurts, but he didn't call for his wife or Greta either. He called for Cuddy because he needed his son's forgiveness."

"She's right, amigo."

Cuddy bounded down the back steps and sat on the wall beside them. Draping his arm around Diego's neck, he gave him a little shake. "Forgive me for leaving you hanging, brother."

The nickname tightened Diego's gut.

Cuddy shook him harder. "Don't give me that look. We are brothers. I haven't been a very good one, but I plan to do better in the future." He smiled softly. "Starting with an explanation."

Diego stiffened. "You don't owe me anything."

"Shut up and listen."

Emmy stood. "I'll leave you two alone."

Cuddy caught her arm. "No, you won't. I have a feeling what I'm about to say has a lot to do with your future." He waved at the wall. "Sit down."

Emmy sat, a puzzled frown on her face.

Cuddy braced his hands on the rough stones. "To start off, Emmy's right. I figured I owed my father a pretty big apology, but he apologized to me instead." He drew a shaky breath. "He told me while he lay helpless under the stars listening to the coyotes howl and thinking about dying he realized he had wronged me by not accepting me for who I was. He said he was sorry for forcing the ranch down my throat and for trying to turn me into him." Cuddy stared across the shadowy yard, reliving the conversation. "He said his biggest regret was being so busy trying to change me he never took time to appreciate who I was."

Ashamed of the envious thoughts he'd harbored, Diego wanted to hang his head, but Cuddy twisted around to look at him. "Father said things to me today I never thought I'd hear come out of his mouth, and I'm so blasted grateful. Then he told me to take care of Mother and Greta." His eyes burned into Diego's. "But his last words were for you."

The breath caught in Diego's throat. "For me?"

"He told me to tell you he loves you." Tears swam in Cuddy's eyes. He wiped them away with his sleeve. "Then he kissed me good-bye, and he was gone."

Diego wrapped his arm around Cuddy's neck and pulled his head to his chest. They sat quietly, Diego praying for forgiveness. He had longed for Mr. Rawson to accept Cuddy then got jealous when he did. He had also doubted the most important man in his life.

Cuddy sat up and a smile tugged at the corners of his mouth. "There's one more thing. It looks like you're stuck with me for a while considering we're joint heirs."

Diego stared, struggling to understand. "What are you saying?"

He shrugged. "Father got the last laugh, it seems. He left half of this accursed ranch to me." Eyes twinkling, he raised his brows at Diego. "And the other half to you. We're business partners, brother."

Diego's head reeled. It was the most meaningful gesture of adoption Mr. Rawson could bestow. "I don't believe it."

Cuddy elbowed him. "You'd better start. Father changed his will before he left for Catarina." He shrugged and his eyes softened. "Before he died, he asked me if I minded. I told him what I'd already told you. I couldn't run this place without you." He ducked his head. "I suppose he'd been hiding symptoms. I expect it was the reason for all of his talk about leaving the ranch in capable hands. It seems he decided that should be you and me."

Still unable to grasp the truth, Diego pressed further. "What about your mother? And Greta?"

Cuddy glanced toward the house. "He left them well cared for. Besides, those two don't belong in South Texas. Especially now that Father's gone. Too many memories."

The news stunned Diego. He turned his gaze toward the house. "What will they do?"

"They're going back to England. Mother had already decided to send Greta to Ripponden for her education. Now she plans to join her." He placed his hand on Diego's back. "As for me, you won't mind if I do a bit of traveling before I settle down to cattle ranching?" He grinned. "I figure you can muddle along without me for a while."

Diego smiled. "I'll do my best. Where will you go?"

Staring in the direction of the road, Cuddy took a deep, cleansing breath. "There's a lot out there I've yet to lay eyes on. I've always wanted to do my part to curtail the violence along the Rio Grande. I might see if I can give the Texas Rangers a hand." His face brightened. "Of course, you know they just had that big earthquake in San Francisco. Who knows what a fellow could get into out there?" He cocked his head. "Then there's always the East Coast."

Emmy leaned to look past Diego. "I'm confused, Cuddy. This is all wonderful news, but what does any of it have to do with my future?"

Cuddy stood. "I think that's my cue to leave you two alone." He winked at Diego. "Do yourself a favor and enlighten the lady, amigo."

His head reeling, Diego watched his friend take long strides to the porch.

In sparse words and spare minutes, Cuddy had removed every obstacle standing between Diego and the woman he loved. Before Diego could look at Emmy again, he took a moment to accept it, to allow the truth to burrow deep inside his gut.

The gift God had granted him through John Rawson was a great deal more than part ownership in a South Texas ranch. It was something he didn't have before, a life worthy to offer Emmy so he could ask her to be his wife. And though the loss of the man would never be worth the inheritance, with Emmy at his side, Diego would honor John Rawson's wishes and do his best to run the ranch with capable hands.

She tugged at his sleeve. "Diego?"

He couldn't suppress his silly grin. He gave up trying and turned. "Yes?"

"What did Cuddy mean?"

He tilted his head and studied her guileless eyes. The rascal. Surely she knew, but she would make him say it.

"In his inimitable way, Cuddy was inferring that your future lies here on the Twisted-R Ranch with us." He picked up her hand. "With me."

She knew, all right. The twitch of her lips gave her away. She lowered her eyes to their tangled fingers. "And what do you think about that?"

Diego stood, pulling her to her feet and wrapping his arms around her waist. "My impatient nature yearns to stomp about and order it done. But a gentleman must leave the decision in the lady's hands."

Swirling her around so the lantern on the low wall would light their faces, he raised one brow. "Well, then? Has the lady reached a decision?"

Sadness darkened her features, snuffing the glow of her broad smile.

He tilted her head up to his. "Forgive me, Emmy. I don't mean to rush you. I'll wait. . .as long as it takes."

Her brows drew into a knot. "It's not that, Diego. I just. . .well, I was thinking about Papa. We're supposed to ask for his blessing."

Diego leaned back and released his breath in a rush. "Your father's blessing. Of course. And I will ask him, Emmy. Your papa will recover very soon. You must believe this. And when he does, I'll ask for his lovely daughter's hand."

Smiling down at her again, he kissed her softly on her pouting mouth. "And this is your final objection?"

She bit her bottom lip as if to corral her amusement. It didn't work. "Well, there is one more."

He blinked. "One more?"

She nodded. "You haven't really asked *me* yet."

Stunned, Diego stared at her. Shaking his head at his own incompetence, he guided her back to the wall and eased her down. Lowering himself to one knee, he took her by the hand. "Miss Dane? If you will allow me. . .I'd like to correct my blunder."

❧

Diego opened the door of the jacal and gazed inside. His mother glanced over her shoulder and then rose from her knees where she'd been praying. "Come in, son." She started for the stove. "I saved you some bean soup. It won't take a minute to warm."

He crossed the room and took her shoulders, guiding her toward the kitchen table. "It's not food I've come for."

Curiosity flickered on her face. "Oh?"

He sat down across from her. "I've come to tell you some news."

Smiling, she reached across the table for his hands. "What news do you have for me?"

He ducked his head and peered into her eyes. "Suppose I said you never have to leave the Twisted-R Ranch?"

Her brows crowded together. She opened her mouth to speak, but nothing came out.

He squeezed her fingers. "What if you could move to the big house, pick out the room of your choice? You wouldn't have to stand over a hot stove anymore because Rosita would cook our food. One day you'd bounce my children on your knee under the portico. You'd grow old and die right here on this land and be buried beside the river." He tilted his head thoughtfully. "Or would you prefer to be buried next to the onion fields behind the jacal?"

Scowling darkly, his mother pursed her lips. "Diego! Before you plant me with the onions, first explain what you're saying."

He drew back. She had called him Diego, the only time in his life she'd done so. "What did you say?"

"I said to tell me what you're babbling about."

"No, why did you call me Diego?"

Pain dimming her eyes, she released his hands and lifted her chin. "It's your name, isn't it?"

For the second time in one night, Diego's head spun. In one glaring second, he saw the truth. His mother's efforts to keep him proud of his Choctaw roots were really a refusal to allow him to be ashamed of her. Out of love for him, she was willing to give up that right.

He reached for her hands again, but she pulled them into her lap. "Don't change the subject. Tell me why I would go live inside the big house when I'd rather stay in my own home."

With his fingernail, he picked at a crack in the tabletop. "Suppose I told you the big house *is* your home?"

Her eyes opened wider than he'd ever seen them. "I would say you have some explaining to do."

Laughing, he told her about Mr. Rawson's generous gift, about Mrs. Rawson's decision to leave, and about Cuddy's travel plans. When he finished, she sat back in her chair looking shocked.

Disappointed, he watched her closely. "I thought you'd be happy."

She smiled. "I think I need time to accept something so wonderful."

"There's more."

"More than what you've already told me?" She covered her heart. "I'm not sure I can handle more."

"I've asked Emmy to be my wife."

This time she reached for his hands. "Oh, Diego! I'm so pleased. Emmy will make you so happy."

He stood, pulling her up with him. "If you want to make me happy, call me Isi."

She blinked up at him. "But I thought—"

He pulled her to his chest and kissed the top of her head. "This is no time for you to abandon our heritage. I'll need you to teach the Choctaw way to your grandchildren."

Choking on a sob, she wrapped her arms around his waist. "I love you, Isi."

He kissed her again. "I love you, too, Mother."

❧

They buried Mr. Rawson the next day in Cuddy's favorite place, beneath a live oak near the bank of the Nueces River. It was a solemn ceremony yet filled with the promise of hope for a believer's heart.

Emmy watched Cuddy's face as the preacher assured those present they would see their loved one again, as long as they put their trust in God's provision for making heaven.

When it was over, her mama, Aunt Bertha, Rosita, and Melatha huddled protectively around Mrs. Rawson and Greta, helping them into the wagon and signaling Little Pete to drive them to the house.

Cuddy hung back. Though his expression sagged with grief as he watched his mother and sister go, he didn't seem eager to leave the gravesite. When the wagon disappeared over the rise, he leaned his back against the oak tree and slid to the ground, staring toward the water.

Shifting her attention to Diego, Emmy squeezed his hand. "Are you all right?"

He pulled her into his arms. "I will be."

He held her for a moment then pushed her to arm's length. As if he'd read her mind, he nodded toward Cuddy. "Why don't you go talk to him?"

She nodded and kissed his cheek.

Cuddy glanced up as she approached but remained silent.

She dipped to the ground beside him and took his hand. "This is such a nice spot."

He nodded. "The Twisted-R was a part of my father. It's comforting to know he'll remain a part of this ranch forever." He glanced toward Diego and laughed. "Diego's the only person I've ever seen that loved South Texas better than my father. Diego calls this place God's country."

She smiled. "You don't agree with him, do you?"

He shrugged. "I just always wondered why God's country would have thorns and stickers on everything you touched. But I've been thinking about something my father told me."

Emmy tilted her head. "What's that?"

Cuddy's gaze swung to the scatter of new-growth mesquite and the steadily invading cactus. "He said with most of the grassland going to scrub, the trees and bushes grow thorns for protection. Otherwise, the cattle and deer would strip this part of the country down to nothing."

He sighed. "Thinking about it now, it reminds me of myself, considering I've always been a fairly sticky problem for my parents. I'm not making excuses, but I guess I act prickly for protection." He raised his brow. "Still, I'm not especially proud of the things I've done."

Emmy said a quick prayer for guidance. "But your father loved you anyway, didn't he? Prickly or not?"

Cuddy stared down at his hands. "Yes, he did."

"He not only asked you to forgive him, he forgave you, didn't he?"

Cuddy nodded. "From the moment I knelt beside him, he acted as though I'd never disappointed him."

She lifted his chin with her finger. "God's the same way, Cuddy."

Understanding dawned in his eyes. He grasped her wrist with the passion of a drowning man. "I want my face to glow like yours does when you talk about God. I want to be able to whisper a prayer in a storm and know He heard." His voice broke. "I want to see my father again."

Her heart swelling with gratitude toward God, Emmy gazed into Cuddy's earnest blue eyes. "It's yours for the taking, Cuddy. All you have to do is kneel by His side."

CHAPTER 41

Emmy opened the wide doors to the veranda and stared toward the fields, hoping to catch sight of Diego. Her heart skipped as he rode past the bunkhouse to the barn. Taking no time to go around, she rolled across the bed between her and the door and dashed for the stairs.

Grinning at the familiar scene of her papa sitting behind a newspaper, Emmy waved as she passed him. He lowered the paper and blew her a kiss.

Three months had passed while Papa recovered from his head injury. He grew stronger every day, and the only memory loss he suffered was of the accident itself, which was a blessing.

Emmy sat with him often while he needed her, reading a book or the headlines of *The Javelin*, but lately he'd been able to read them for himself. He seemed a different person toward her from the time his mind had cleared, and they laughed and talked with ease.

When Emmy wasn't with Papa, she spent her days riding fences with Diego, picking beans with Melatha, and learning to cook tortillas with Rosita.

The feisty cook had opened up her kitchen and her arms to Emmy. Her disapproving glances and disparaging remarks in Spanish had stopped without explanation. Diego felt his mother had a hand in Rosita's change of heart, and Emmy agreed.

Kate Rawson took Greta and left the Twisted-R two weeks after she buried her husband by the river. She apologized profusely for leaving her company behind, but Mama assured her she understood.

Eager to meet her grandson, Aunt Bert rode to Uvalde with the Rawsons to catch the train to Humble. She promised to return in time for the wedding, bringing Charity and the baby, Buddy, and Nash along with her. Before she left, she contacted her friend Darius in Eagle Pass. He came to see her off, promising to see her again very soon.

Cuddy postponed his trip to California the minute he got wind of the upcoming wedding. He said they'd have to start putting San Francisco back together without him, since Diego would need a best man.

Sailing out the back door, Emmy ran as fast as a lady should to the barn. Rounding the corner, she plowed into Diego coming from the other direction.

"Whoa!" he yelled, grabbing her around the waist and twirling her. Laughing, she clung to him a little tighter than necessary to maintain her balance. Eyes twinkling, he tilted her chin. "Where are you going in such a hurry?"

"To fetch you for lunch." She narrowed her eyes and affected a haughty stance. "Mole poblano. I made it myself."

He took her face in his hands and kissed her. "Aren't you becoming the perfect little rancher's wife?"

She touched the hollow in his chin. "Not yet. Making me a rancher's wife is your job."

He furrowed his brow in mock disapproval. "Brazen, aren't you?"

"I usually get what I set my cap for."

A fire in his eyes, he tugged her close. "So do I, Miss Dane. Next week won't come soon enough to suit me." He kissed the end of her nose. "Is Mama Dane still mad at me?"

Her mama had balked in the beginning when she learned Emmy planned to marry Diego and stay on the ranch when they left. She'd tried to convince them to wait a more respectable six months out of respect for Mr. Rawson.

Cuddy, unable to delay his plans that long, had intervened.

Emmy's lips pulled into a frown. "Mama would rather we waited. We're spoiling her plans for the wedding she's always dreamed for me." She caressed his cheek. "But I suspect your charm has won her over. She's actually getting excited about the party your mama and Rosita have planned."

"Pachanga," he corrected. "If you're going to live among the people of South Texas, you must learn to speak our language."

Emmy wrinkled her nose. "Sí, señor. A muy big wedding pachanga with our friends and family in attendance." She patted his shoulders. "Oh, Diego, I can hardly wait to see Charity and Nash." She gasped. "And little Thad! I'll finally see Charity's baby."

He tilted her chin. "And your father won't mind you being so eager to see Nash?"

Smiling softly, Emmy shook her head. "The old grumpy Papa might have. My kind and gentle Papa won't mind a bit. He accepts my love for Nash because he knows I love him, too." She stared dreamily over Diego's shoulder. "Speaking of little Thad. . .we'll have children of our own someday, won't we?"

Diego kissed her forehead. "As many as you wish."

She met his eyes. "Very well. I wish for six. All feisty little girls like the Campbells."

He shrank back. "All girls? I don't get one little vaquero to help me with chores?"

"A boy?" She scrunched up her face. "Well, maybe one."

He tapped her nose. "I'm not worried. After you hold Charity's son, you'll ask for six of each."

She feigned shock. "Six boys? Heaven forbid!"

Laughing, he took her hand and pulled her along with him. "Come, I want to tell you something." He reentered the barn and led her to Faron's stable.

The horse came toward them and tucked his head over the stall to nuzzle Diego's hand.

Diego gave Emmy a guarded look. "I've decided to turn him loose."

Emmy's jaw dropped and her gaze swung to the horse. "Turn him loose? I can't believe I'm hearing this."

He ran his hands down the sleek black neck. "I can't believe I'm saying it. But, I tried putting him in a fence again. He was gone by morning." He turned thoughtful eyes to her. "I won't keep him penned in this stall."

"Won't someone else get him?"

He laughed. "Even if they caught him, he'd escape again. Besides, he's smart. If he hadn't trusted me, he'd never have allowed me to catch him in the first place." He scratched Faron's nose. "You agree completely, don't you, amigo?" Pulling a wilted carrot from his pocket, he offered it to the snuffling horse then unlatched the stall door.

Emmy's eyes widened. "Now?"

Diego gave her a look of resignation. "Can you think of a reason to wait?"

She followed in amazement as Diego led Faron outside the barn and took off his lead.

The horse seemed reluctant at first, bumping Diego with his nose and nuzzling his pocket.

"No more carrots, my friend. Or saddles. You'll have to learn to live without them both."

As if Faron understood, he bobbed his head and whirled away, trotting down the drive with his tail lifted proudly before bolting into a run outside the gate.

Emmy reached for Diego's hand. "Do you think he'll ever come back?"

"If he does, it will be because he wants to, but don't expect it. There's plenty of space for him out there, and space is what he needs."

Emmy smiled up at him. "Like Cuddy."

Diego circled her waist with his arm. "Just like Cuddy. He spent his whole life trying to break free. His father turned him loose and he can't wait to run."

She wiggled her finger. "Mr. Rawson freed Cuddy's mind and heart. It took God to free his spirit. Cuddy won't need to run. He can fly."

Diego pulled the clip from her hair and buried his fingers in her curls. "I'm soaring pretty high myself these days."

She puckered her lips in thought. "Oh, really? Does this mean I need to give you plenty of space, too?"

Diego hooked his thumb toward his chest. "Me?" He grinned. "I won't kick against my stall, mi querida. I've spent my life finding out where I belong."

She raised questioning brows. "And have you?"

He nodded solemnly, the depths of his heart shining from his eyes. "You know our twelve children will be part Indian, don't you?"

She laughed heartily. "And part Spanish, Irish, German, Italian, Swedish. . .and goodness knows what else."

He lowered his gaze and busied his fingers with her collar. "Would you mind very much if we raised them to embrace the Choctaw way?" He glanced up shyly. "The way of faith and peace?"

Emmy took his face in her hands. "The way of faith and peace is found in every culture that honors God, Diego, but I'd be honored to have your mother help me raise our children. After all"—she kissed his chin—"look how well their father turned out."

MARCIA GRUVER

Marcia is a full-time writer who hails from Southeast Texas. Inordinately enamored by the past, she delights in writing historical fiction. Marcia's deep south-central roots lend a southern-comfortable style and touch of humor to her writing. Through her books, she hopes to leave behind a legacy of hope and faith to the coming generations.

When she's not plotting stories about God's grace, Marcia spends her time reading, playing video games, or taking long drives through the Texas hill country. She and her husband, Lee, have one daughter and four sons. Collectively, this motley crew has graced them with eleven grandchildren and one great-granddaughter—so far.